JONATHAN JANZ

CASTLE OF SORROWS

This is a **FLAME TREE PRESS** book

Text copyright © 2019 Jonathan Janz

FLAME TREE PRESS
6 Melbray Mews, London, SW6 3NS, UK
flametreepress.com

Distribution and warehouse:
Baker & Taylor Publisher Services (BTPS)
30 Amberwood Parkway, Ashland, OH 44805
btpubservices.com

Thanks to the Flame Tree Press team, including:
Taylor Bentley, Frances Bodiam, Federica Ciaravella, Don D'Auria, Chris Herbert, Matteo Middlemiss, Josie Mitchell, Mike Spender, Cat Taylor, Maria Tissot, Nick Wells, Gillian Whitaker.

The cover is created by Flame Tree Studio with thanks to Nik Keevil and Shutterstock.com. The font families used are Avenir and Bembo.

Flame Tree Press is an imprint of Flame Tree Publishing Ltd
flametreepublishing.com

A copy of the CIP data for this book is available from the British Library and the Library of Congress.

HB ISBN: 978-1-78758-250-7
PB ISBN: 978-1-78758-248-4
ebook ISBN: 978-1-78758-251-4
Also available in FLAME TREE AUDIO

Printed in the US at Bookmasters, Ashland, Ohio

JONATHAN JANZ

CASTLE OF SORROWS

FLAME TREE PRESS
London & New York

Juliet, the first eleven years of your life have flown by faster than I would have thought possible. And for eleven years you have brought me happiness, laughter, joy, and more love than I thought was possible. You're an amazing person, and I pray that others see in you all the wonderful things I see. This one's for you, my beautiful daughter.
I love you dearly.

And the gates of this chapel were shut,
And 'Thou shalt not' writ over the door;
So I turn'd to the Garden of Love
That so many sweet flowers bore;

And I saw it was filled with graves,
And tomb-stones where flowers should be;
And Priests in black gowns were walking their rounds,
And binding with briars my joys & desires.
William Blake
'The Garden of Love'

BEFORE

It all began with the music. Quinton Early sensed an alteration in his partner during their fourth day on the island. Nothing obvious, just a strange shadow about Agent Moss's face that had appeared when Early, stuck for a diversion from their investigation of this godforsaken place, had suggested they use the old-fashioned record player to spin some tunes.

The first album Early had selected had been a collection of Robert Blackwood's most famous music. The first song was "Forest of the Faun."

Caleb Moss's sunny expression – the guy was always cheerful, which was one of the reasons Quinton was glad Moss had been assigned with him to this investigation – had quickly been replaced by a saturnine look. As if an old memory were being dredged up in Moss's psyche.

"What's wrong, buddy?" Quinton asked.

"Turn that fucking thing off," Moss growled.

Quinton blinked at his partner. Moss had never spoken to him like that. *No one* ever spoke to Quinton like that. Quinton was six-five, for one thing, and for another he went two-hundred-and-fifty pounds, and not a bit of that weight was fat. Add to that Quinton's cold-blooded glare, and it wasn't any wonder folks treated him with respect.

But Moss had just spoken to him as though Quinton was his servant or something. Quinton felt a dangerous heat begin to build at the base of his neck.

"If you have a problem with the music," Quinton said, "you can move to another room."

Quinton remained facing the record player, showing he was into the music. And he was. "Forest of the Faun" was a peculiar, atonal piece, but it had a way of reaching into you and grabbing hold. Besides, Quinton reasoned, Caleb Moss wasn't a bad dude. Was in fact Quinton's favorite of all the guys he'd worked with over his ten years at the agency. He shot Moss a furtive glance to see if the man had taken him up on his offer to leave, but there Moss still stood, bending over, his hands squeezing the back of one of the couches positioned near the sixth floor studio's center. Moss's face was pinched in what Quinton first mistook for concentration, but soon realized was physical pain. Was his partner suffering from a headache? A migraine maybe? If he was – and Moss certainly did look like he was in a hell of a lot of pain – that would explain the disrespectful way he'd spoken to Quinton moments ago.

The ball of rage between Quinton's shoulders began to loosen. He reached out, twisted down the volume on the record player. "Hey, Caleb. You don't feel good, why don't you go downstairs, rest for a while? There's nothing we can do anyway with all this rain."

It was true too. They'd spent the first three days busting their asses trying to piece together just what the hell might've happened here two months ago, taking what the forensics team had given them, crosschecking that information with what little testimony they were able to squeeze out of Ben Shadeland and Claire Harden, two of the three survivors of the bloodbath that had taken place here. The third survivor, the little boy, had been completely ruled out for questioning by the higher-ups; Ben, the boy's father, didn't want his son Joshua interviewed, and so far the FBI had respected those wishes. If it had been Quinton's call, he would've talked to the kid anyway. As a father of two little girls, Quinton Early understood a father's protective urge as well as anybody, but this was a special situation. This had been the deaths of *ten people*, and these weren't just any run-of-the-mill lowlifes either. Among the victims were Stephen Blackwood, a perennial member of the *Forbes* 500; his son and heir Chris Blackwood, who'd supposedly incurred the ire of some very nasty gangsters; Lee Stanley, who just happened to be one of the hottest directors in the world, and who, on a more personal note, had made three of Quinton's favorite horror films; Eva Rosales, Stanley's gorgeous assistant; Ben Shadeland's ex-wife, Jenny, which to Quinton was damned suspicious; and Ryan Brady, a respected commercial pilot and the man who'd stolen Ben's wife away from him, and to Quinton that part was *really* damned suspicious.

Thinking of this massive toll, Quinton wrinkled his nose, glared down at the revolving turntable. The Shadelands' story was unquestionably bullshit, and a good deal too convenient: Ben Shadeland, rising movie composer, is up shit creek without a paddle. He's late on his deadline for the new Lee Stanley picture – a movie called *House of Skin* that Quinton couldn't wait to see – and he's losing his wife and son to a good-looking young stud who happens to fly airplanes. Everybody involved goes to the same island, where no one can witness anything should something unpleasant take place. Then Ben, his son, and the woman he just happens to now be engaged to, are the only survivors of whatever happens on that island.

Quinton's nostrils flared thinking about it. It was bullshit. All of it. Ben Shadeland's amnesia story was pure fantasy. And Claire's fantastic tale about Ryan Brady going postal and killing everyone?

The biggest, smelliest mound of bullshit he'd ever inhaled.

Moss was gesturing vaguely in Quinton's direction, his words too low to be intelligible. Quinton turned the record player down to near inaudibility and said, "What's the matter, pal?"

"*Coming...he's coming...he's...*"

Now what the hell was this?

Not bothering with the turntable any longer, Quinton hurried over to where Moss was now slumped over the couch back, his body shuddering as if in the grips of some sort of seizure.

For the first time, Quinton began to worry.

For one thing, there was no medical help on the island. Hell, there was no one *on* the island. There was only Quinton Early and Caleb Moss, and the nearest doctor was back on the mainland, eighty miles away in Petaluma. Shit, they might as well be on another planet. And forget calling anybody. Their cell phones might as well be paperweights here on the Sorrows. Their helicopter ride back to California wouldn't arrive for another three days. If something happened to one of them between now and then, they were on their own.

Caleb's convulsions worsened, the spasms first growing more pronounced, and soon becoming violent.

"Oh shit," Quinton muttered. He feverishly scanned his memory for what little first aid he knew...

Check the patient's airway. He grabbed hold of Moss's shoulders, made to flip the man over onto his back, but it was like trying to wrangle a bucking horse. Man, Quinton thought, this was even harder than corralling his two-year-old daughter when she didn't want a diaper change.

Moss's body twisted, writhed.

"Dammit, come *on*," Quinton breathed.

He finally got a good grasp on Moss's shoulders, and, careful not to let his partner's head crack against the floor, he eased Moss down as well as he could. Moss's feet drummed, his hands flopping about like he was doing some trendy new dance. One knee shot up, nailed Quinton in the ribs. A flailing wrist gave him a smart whap in the nose. Quinton's eyes began to water.

Quinton wrestled Moss's arms down, but his partner's body was like an enormous pressurized fire hose made intractable by the flow of water pulsing through it.

"Calm down, damn you!" Quinton yelled. From across the room, it seemed like the record player had been cranked up again, and now the music was anything but beautiful. Far from it, the song had become grating and unpleasant. And how the hell was Quinton supposed to check Moss's airway for obstructions when he couldn't even get close enough to the man's face to *see* his airway?

"I said," Quinton muttered, "calm...the hell...*down*."

Moss's hips lifted off the floor, bucking Quinton into the air like some inexperienced cowboy, the motion taking him so by surprise that he damn near smashed down on Moss before he could catch himself. His arms free, Moss resumed his weird, chaotic dance moves and promptly whipped Quinton across the mouth, busting Quinton's bottom lip wide open.

Jerking his head to the side and spitting out a stream of bright red blood, Quinton crawled grimly forward until he sat astraddle Moss's midsection. Then, hating himself for it but not knowing any other way to help his partner, he gripped the jagging arms and lifted them above Moss's head until they were pinned against the floor. For a crazy moment Moss reminded him of one of the Village People in that "YMCA" song; lying on the ground with his arms up, Moss looked like the A.

And speaking of music, what the hell was up with that record player? Quinton hadn't touched it since racing over here to help Moss, but now the thing was blaring as though Quinton had cranked it up full blast. And not only was the volume twice as loud as it had been earlier, now it was repeating the same song – "Forest of the Faun."

Quinton was no vinyl aficionado – he'd been born during the era of the cassette tape and had graduated to compact discs by his eighth birthday – but he'd never heard of a record player with a repeat track mode. And even if such a player existed, this machine looked old enough to have been made when his grandma was a little girl.

Bloody lips pressed together, Quinton wrapped one huge hand around both of Moss's wrists to bind them together. Then, pinning the man down with his superior weight, he reached toward Moss's mouth with his free hand.

Moss's teeth clicked and snapped, almost as if he were eager to eat some of Quinton's fingers. Moss's body writhed beneath him, the power surging beneath Quinton's big frame terrible in its vitality. What in God's name was wrong with Moss? The man had no irregular medical history, at least not that Quinton knew of. Was it something Moss had never told him about? Or a condition of which Moss had been previously unaware?

Whichever the case, this was bad. Really, really bad. Maybe even *dying* bad if Quinton didn't locate the source of the problem fast.

Terrified he'd lose his fingers but knowing Moss could choke on his own tongue if he didn't act, Quinton reached toward Moss's snapping jaws. He'd just about gotten hold of his partner's cleft chin when Moss's big brown eyes snapped wide, his body arching in a long, trembling convulsion. Despite Quinton's girth, he felt himself lifted two feet off the ground as Moss's hips rose.

Then both men landed with a bone-jarring thump.

It hurt Quinton's testicles something fierce, but despite the sickly ache issuing from his groin, he was transfixed by the sight of Moss's face.

Moss's eyes were wide open. They were glazed with a look of utmost terror.

Moss fainted.

★   ★   ★

Quinton managed to get him down to Moss's room on the third floor. A part of him, the part that bristled whenever his wife would waste their money on something frivolous, thought picking out suites on the lavish fifth floor was impractical and a little extravagant. The bedrooms on the third floor, he'd argued, were just as good, and they'd be located in the most central part of the castle.

But now he was grateful for Caleb Moss's affinity for the nicer things because it saved Quinton the trouble of lugging the guy down more flights of steps. Quinton was in great shape – he bench pressed more than anyone he knew in the Bureau. But controlled weight was one thing; dead lifting an over-two-hundred-pound man was another matter entirely. And by the time he deposited Moss on the immense four-poster bed, Quinton was sweating and huffing like a chronic asthmatic.

Quinton stood erect, mopped sweat off his brow and looked around to see if he could find anything to make Moss more comfortable. The guy seemed to be breathing evenly now, the convulsion having run its course. Quinton had received solid marks in every level of schooling he'd been through, but now he wished he'd paid more attention in high school health. He was pretty sure they'd covered this sort of thing. It seemed to him that Moss might be an epileptic. Couldn't that occur due to some sort of accident or fall? Yeah, he thought. It could be a brain lesion, and that could bring about a seizure. There were petit mal and grand mal seizures, and this one was without a doubt a grand fucking mal. In fact, if there existed an even greater classification – great grand mal or maybe grand slam mal – he was pretty sure Moss had achieved it.

Quinton wondered what else he could do. There was an untouched salad sitting on the nightstand. A fork lay next to the big bowl, which contained not only lettuce and cherry tomatoes, but sliced cucumbers, mandarin oranges, walnuts, spinach – all kinds of shit. He'd made fun of Moss for hauling all that fresh produce to the island, but now Moss's salad looked damned tasty. Maybe he'd eat it while he waited, tell Moss it was his fault for losing consciousness, and it was Quinton's payment for lugging his sorry ass down all those stairs.

Smiling, Quinton's gaze fastened on the bathroom door. Maybe he should get a cool washcloth, fold it a couple times and lay it across Moss's forehead, the way Quinton's own mother used to do when he was younger and feeling puny.

Yeah, Quinton thought, that would make Moss feel...

He stopped, half in, half out of the bathroom.

Music echoed through the walls.

No, Quinton thought, the hair on his neck standing up straight. The music wasn't *echoing* through the walls. It was *bleeding* through the walls. Why he should imagine it that way, he had no idea, but it was the only word that seemed to fit. The style was similar to "Forest of the Faun," but this tune was undeniably darker and tinged with a deeply sinister undercurrent. Augmenting this impression was the bizarre liquid quality of the notes, the manner in which the strings and woodwinds seemed to ooze out of the old stone surrounding him.

Quinton hurried back into the bedroom, his heart a thudding mallet.

The music was growing louder, the percussion deepening, so loud now it battered his eardrums. Quinton threw a helpless glance down at Moss, who seemed damnably serene. *How can he not hear that?* Quinton wondered. The music wasn't loud, it wasn't earsplitting, it was absolutely *thunderous*, the kind of sound that makes you jump in fright. Holy shit, he thought, if he didn't get the hell out of this castle soon, his eardrums would burst.

He took a tortured step toward the door, then paused and stared back at Moss. Caleb didn't seem bothered by the music, but what the hell did he know? He was recovering from whatever the hell had happened to him earlier. Or maybe he'd just hated "Forest of the Faun" that much and was now relaxing pleasantly because he liked this track more.

The music swelled, that peculiar underwater quality only increasing with the volume.

Hands clamped over his ears, Quinton decided he'd been humanitarian enough for one day. He'd lugged his damned partner down the stairs already; did he have to carry him down four more flights with that mind-destroying symphony hammering his ears?

Screw it, he thought and plunged through the doorway. A powerful wave of guilt swept over him as he moved farther and farther away from Moss's door, but the decision was made and he wasn't about to go back now.

He started down the stairs, his long, muscular legs moving with the speed and grace that had made him a football star at the University of Florida. Those were the days, he thought, rushing even faster now. It had sure beaten life in the FBI. In fact, he was tired of being gone from his wife and his kids so much, even if his wife did hold out on him way too often. Maybe if he got a job with regular hours and less travel, she'd be less inclined to have headaches and suffer through menstrual periods that went on for three weeks. He made it around another flight of spiral stairs, thinking if his wife really bled as much as she claimed, the woman needed to be checked for hemophilia.

Quinton made it out of the stairwell and into the great hall. The music seemed less severe in here, but his head still ached something fierce. Maybe some fresh air would alleviate the sick gonging in his brain.

He crossed the hall and headed toward the foyer thinking the source had been the sixth floor studio after all. Not the record player, alone, of course. That was impossible. But maybe the recently deceased Stephen Blackwood had footed the bill for some god almighty sound system to be installed, and the turntable had been attached by some wires he hadn't spotted. This didn't entirely satisfy Quinton, but it did ease his fear somewhat. He passed through the foyer and swung the front door open. The chill autumn breeze hit him right away, along with stinging beads of rain. Wincing, Quinton turned his back on the rain and immediately felt better.

Yes, Quinton thought, eyes closing languidly. This was a good deal better. He backpedaled slowly down the stone walkway and extended his arms, the bite of the raindrops almost pleasant now. There was nothing supernatural occurring on the Sorrows. The rumors he and Moss had heard were just that – spooky stories uttered and embellished by querulous forensics geeks who just wanted a little attention.

Quinton sighed. It was all perfectly explainable now. Moss had a seizure brought on by some undetected brain lesion. Despite Quinton's lack of medical background, he'd acquitted himself rather nicely. Maybe he'd even receive some sort of commendation.

As for the impossibly loud music, that was explainable too. Stephen Blackwood had long ago installed some sort of sound system, but because of time and lack of use – hell, how long had it been since this island had been inhabited on a regular basis? – the thing had malfunctioned, resulting in the explosion of sound Quinton experienced earlier.

The wind whipped up, the freshets of rain growing in intensity. He no longer minded, however, because everything was a-okay. He'd been silly to think of leaving the Bureau. The money was excellent, and his job was secure. As for his wife and her refusal to put out, he guessed he'd have to live with that. Maybe he'd buy a couple of books on how to thaw a frigid wife. Sensitivity training, something along those lines.

Quinton stopped walking. He remembered Caleb Moss, lying on the bed on the fifth floor. Out here the music was less offensive, but maybe upstairs it was still severe. If it was, that couldn't be good for Moss's hearing. Quinton had an abrupt, unwelcome vision of his partner's eardrums exploding like paintballs all over the white pillowcase. Shit, he couldn't believe he'd left him up there. Maybe if he hurried...

Something made Quinton stop and peer up at the castle.

A figure sat in Moss's window. It was Moss himself, Quinton realized a moment later. Of course it was Moss. The only reason he hadn't recognized him at first was because...

Well, because Moss was naked.

At least Quinton was pretty sure he was naked. His upper body and legs were certainly bare, and if he had any underwear on, it had to be the skimpy kind, not Fruit-of-the-Looms. Everything but the man's genitals were exposed; thankfully, those were obscured by the way the man sat in the window, just like some country boy lounging beside a stream. Only this wasn't some bubbling forest creek teeming with crawdads. This was the fifth story of a supposedly haunted castle, and damn near all of Caleb Moss was leaning out of the casement window with a carelessness that set Quinton's teeth on edge.

"What are you doing, partner?" Quinton called up, striving for a casual tone but failing miserably.

Caleb grinned beatifically. "I'm calling."

Quinton stepped backward to better see Moss's face, and as he did, one mystery was solved. Yep, the guy was buck naked. Quinton could see the man's flaccid member dangling over the windowsill like a pale and rather pathetic jalapeño pepper. Maybe if Quinton had a dick that small, he reasoned, his wife would want sex more often. She certainly couldn't claim he hurt her, which was an excuse she used often.

"What do you mean, you're 'calling'?" Quinton asked. "Who the hell you calling? The reception's for shit on this island."

"I'm calling him," Moss said, and in spite of the dopey grin stretching the man's face, Quinton noticed something that made his stomach ball into a hard knot.

There was blood dripping down Moss's legs.

"Hey, what the hell's happening up there?" Quinton said, no longer attempting to mask his nervousness. This was messed up, and messed up good. Quinton wanted off this damned island. Haunted or not, he'd had enough unusual shit for one lifetime.

Moss didn't answer this time, was seemingly too immersed in whatever he was doing to speak. Quinton strained to see what was happening up there in the window. The rain and wind were picking up, so Quinton had to squint to compete with the elements. Moss appeared to be checking his wristwatch, but that couldn't be right because Moss didn't wear a watch. Yet the man had his wrist turned – palm up – and appeared to be pushing buttons. Like he was timing a race or something. Only there was no race going on, and for that matter, there was no watch on Moss's wrist. Quinton could see how bare it was from here. He could also see how pink Moss's skin was because the contrast of the blood was…was…

Oh shit, Quinton thought. Blood was gushing from Moss's wrist.

Quinton's fist went to his mouth. He bit down on his knuckles hard enough to break the skin.

Moss had discovered the salad fork. Quinton had no idea whether Moss had sampled the salad or not, but he doubted very much either of them would have an appetite now. Moss had punctured the skin of his wrist and flayed it open in ragged flaps. The tines of the fork were digging inside the veins and sinew of the man's forearm, and blood was sluicing out of the wound. It looked like Moss was trying to commit suicide in the most gruesome way possible. He hadn't slit his wrists sideways the way novices did. He hadn't even made a vertical incision the way the serious ones did it. No, he'd decided to get in there and treat the insides of his forearm like a kid treated some cast-off electronic toy, severing nerves and arteries like a bunch of colorful plastic-coated wires, stretching them until they popped and then watching with a child's glee as they spurted blood.

Gagging, Quinton weaved toward the castle, not only to put a stop to Moss's self-mutilation, but to escape the sight of it. He knew he'd have to behold the gut-wrenching scene in moments – the man would need a tourniquet and serious medical attention afterward, the kind Quinton was woefully unprepared to provide – but if he could banish the image from his mind long enough, he might be able to make the journey back up the staircase without spewing his lunch all over the place. He ripped open the front door, sprinted through the foyer and the great hall.

Grimly, Quinton rushed up the stairs. If anybody was equipped to deal with a crisis, he told himself, he was. This was his partner, and for his partner he could stomach some blood and gore, couldn't he? Hell, hadn't Quinton always enjoyed scary movies?

Quinton made the fifth floor and dashed down its stone length. Something about the music was different now, but there was no time to consider that. He reached Moss's door, which still hung open.

Quinton experienced a fleeting terror of finding the window empty, his partner having already consummated his self-violence by leaping to his death. But Moss was where Quinton hoped he'd be. The guy's pimply ass was draped over the sill, his hairy crack staring at Quinton like a furry black caterpillar.

Quinton headed straight toward Moss. Sure, he could do it with finesse, talk the guy down like you saw on all those cop shows, but what was the point? If he fell out the window, he fell out. If Quinton waited any longer to make his move, Moss would bleed to death anyway.

Quinton got behind Moss, grabbed the man around the midsection, then ignoring the nudity and the dopey drugged-up grin, Quinton carried him over to the bed, stripped off his own shirt and wound it around the man's mutilated arm. Quinton tried not to look at it as he did, but he nevertheless got an eyeful of meaty gore, the savaged veins and pulpy tendons reminding him of roadkill after the buzzards have been at it. Jesus, what had compelled Moss to do this?

More to distract himself than to help Moss, Quinton asked, "You said you were calling him. Who the hell were you calling?"

"Gabriel," Moss said.

Quinton cinched the shirt tighter around the forearm, looked about for a belt or something to tie off the blood flow at Moss's elbow. "I don't know a Gabriel. Wasn't he an angel or something?"

"He's making the music."

Quinton scowled. "What are you talking about? The song's coming from that old Victrola. You heard it yourself."

Moss shook his head dreamily. "It's coming from the tower."

"Tower? You're crazy." Quinton ceased what he was doing though and listened. The sound did seem to be filtering in through the window.

He stepped over to the bloody sill and stared out at the single tower that rose like a spire about fifty yards from the castle. Son of a bitch, he thought. The music *was* coming from there. How had he not noticed it before? There was a barred window in the uppermost part of the tower, and it was through that window the music was drifting. It wasn't a full orchestra anymore either, was just a piano. But that piano was really working overtime, whoever was playing it somehow tinkling out the myriad notes and rhythms of the entire symphony. And it was clear as day too.

However, he'd sort of preferred the previous incarnation of the song to the one he was hearing now. Because the first version had come, unquestionably, from some sort of machine. But this version…this version was being performed by an incredibly talented but somehow *present* individual. And the thought of this – the thought that someone else was now on the island with him and his bleeding partner – filled Quinton with such a soul-shattering dread that he found he was unable to step away from the window no matter how hard he tried. What had Caleb said?

I'm calling him.

Quinton swallowed. Was the *him* in question the dude burning up that tower piano?

And more importantly, Quinton thought, why the hell was Moss calling him by mutilating himself? Just how did taking a salad fork to one's arm *call* someone? Who was it he was calling, a goddamned vampire?

Quinton tried to smile, but couldn't. Uh-uh. Because this wasn't funny at all. In fact, it was the furthest thing in the world from funny, it was—

"He's coming!" Moss called, and Quinton leapt several inches off the ground.

Whirling, one hand clamped to his chest, he snapped, "What the hell's wrong with you, Caleb? You trying to give a guy a coronary?"

Moss's eyes were open, on his face the vapid grin of a brainwashed zealot.

Quinton drew in a deep breath, blew it out slowly. He said, "Man, I don't know what's gotten into you, but I'm ready for the Caleb I know to pay a visit. This weirdo shit is scaring me half to death. Now let's get that bleeding stopped and talk this over like reasonable…"

Quinton's mouth went dry. He turned slowly toward the window. The music still played, but now there was another sound beneath it, an arrhythmic accompaniment that had nothing to do with the song. It was a thick, heavy, clopping sound, like gigantic cloven feet were treading on concrete. Frightened like he hadn't been since he was a very young child, Quinton listened.

The footsteps were coming from the tower. *Descending* the tower.

"There ain't nobody," Quinton whispered to himself. "There ain't nobody coming."

But there was somebody coming. Quinton knew it. He heard the hooves reach the base of the tower, pause. Then the door was swinging slowly open, a figure emerging.

The figure stared up at him. It was colossal, it was black and it had horns. *Holy shit,* Quinton thought. The beast made Quinton look like the little kid he once was, the one whose big brother terrified him with stories of Greek gods, of mothers that ate their children and of fathers that sacrificed their sons. There was a book his brother would read out of, a kids' version of all the old myths. The creature peering up at him, its huge white eyes fraught with hunger, looked just like the picture that had given Quinton the most nightmares, the one of the god Pan, the horned satyr who played the flute and had half-naked women swooning around him, the one whose lusty grin and mad eyes had pursued Quinton into nightmares so wretched he'd awaken gasping for air and pleading with his parents to let him sleep in their bed.

The beast began stalking toward Castle Blackwood.

Quinton sucked in a horrified breath, stumbled away from the window. He had to shut the bedroom door, had to bar the damned thing. He'd never be able to get downstairs in time to prevent the monster from entering the castle, but he could sure as shit get their door closed and throw every goddamned piece of furniture in the room in front of it. After that, who the hell knew? He only knew he had to keep that monster from getting in, from slaughtering him, from feasting on his...

Quinton froze.

I'm calling him.

Quinton threw a panicked glance at Moss, whose eyes were still open, who still wore that goofy grin, only the grin was no longer just goofy, it was downright rapturous. And though Quinton had mistaken that expression for vacant earlier on, there was nothing vacant about it at all. Just *eager*. Eager about what was on the way, and happy as a pig in shit that the summoning had been successful.

On legs he could no longer feel, Quinton tiptoed to the window. He eyed the spill of Moss's blood leaking over the sill, imagined the dark, viscid stuff oozing down the castle's pale façade.

I'm calling him.

Cold fingers of dread choking off his breath, Quinton took one last step toward the window and peered down. He saw the glistening rivulets of blood crawling down the castle.

Quinton looked below that.

And saw the monster scaling the castle wall.

PART ONE
THE GARDEN OF LOVE
CHAPTER ONE

Ben Shadeland was outside when the detective showed up. It was just after three o'clock, near the end of Joshua's nap. Baby Julia was also asleep, which gave Ben the rare opportunity to get some yard work done. The flagstone walkway they'd had put in that spring was already a riot of weeds, and since Ben didn't trust the herbicides, he had to yank them out by hand.

He stood and wiped his palms on his cargo shorts.

Coming across the yard Teddy Brooks smiled at him, his white teeth in startling contrast to his dark brown skin. "Big composer like you, I figured you'd hire out all your menial labor."

Brooks was five-eight or so, and he looked fit. Brooks had the body of a guy in his mid-thirties, but Ben put him at least a decade older than that.

Brooks nodded at the flagstone walk. "You do that yourself?"

"Why? Does it look like it?"

"You want me to be honest or save your feelings?"

"We had it done professionally."

Brooks's eyebrows went up. "No kiddin'?"

Ben surveyed the cracked mortar sourly. "I hoped it would look better than this."

"I kind of figured it was a weekend project. Maybe something you and your boy worked on together."

Ben mopped his forehead with his shirtfront. "Would've turned out better."

"Joshua asleep?"

"Uh-huh. Julia too."

"You seen the black Escalade lately?"

Ben felt his muscles freeze. "Have you?"

"I had, don't you think I would've told you about it?"

Ben stared at Teddy Brooks. Stared at him hard. "Would you have?"

Brooks reached into his dark brown slacks, produced a pack of Lucky Strikes and an engraved silver lighter. The cigarette smoking, Brooks had told him shortly after they'd met last fall, was a product of his failed marriage. The lighter had been a present to himself.

Ben moved away so his clothes wouldn't smell of smoke. He'd be holding Julia soon, wrestling with Joshua.

"I don't blame you for being paranoid," Brooks said. "Man goes through something like you did, he gets protective." Brooks blew out a hazy plume of smoke. "Watches his best friend lose his mind and turn violent. Sees his ex-wife die in a helicopter crash. His son gets taken away from him, and after he gets his boy back, the kidnapper shoots him in the belly."

"I told you who took Joshua."

Brooks chuckled out smoke. "Shit, Ben. You still stickin' to that mythological story? Expect me to believe some giant black goat man took your son?"

"It's the truth."

"I bet a psychoanalyst would have a field day with you. Like maybe you have some deep-seated fear of a black man stealing your pure white woman. An Othello complex or something." Brooks chuckled, favored him with a sidelong glance.

Ben resisted the urge to knock him on his ass.

But Brooks persisted. "You're causing all kinds of problems, you know that? My employer thinks I'm stealing her money. No matter how much time I spend talking to you, all I get is satyrs and apparitions and other shit straight out of *The Twilight Zone*. You gotta give me something concrete, Ben. Just to get her off my back."

Ben opened his mouth to say something, but Brooks told him to wait a minute and set off toward his car. Ben watched the small man's spry gait and remembered how fit Eddie Blaze had been before they'd ventured to the island, before they'd stayed in Castle Blackwood, Eddie striving to rid Ben of his writer's block because their deadline had been approaching. That prick of a director Lee Stanley – now that *dead* prick, Ben amended – railing at them to deliver the score for his horror film *House of Skin*, Eddie desperate to kickstart Ben's creative juices, juices that had dried up when Ben's ex-wife had left him for the handsome pilot named Ryan. Ryan who was also now dead. Like everyone but Ben and Claire and Joshua, everyone else murdered on that godforsaken island.

On the Sorrows.

Brooks was opening his passenger door and bending to retrieve something from the glove box, and as he did Ben thought of Chris Blackwood, son of the woman who was paying Teddy Brooks to find out what had happened on the island last summer. Chris Blackwood had been deep in debt to some very scary gangsters and had needed money, which was how Ben and Eddie and Claire and Eva had gotten to the island in the first place.

Brooks was making his way back toward Ben now, a manila envelope tucked between his elbow and his side. Brooks had a bottle of water in one hand and his diminishing cigarette in the other. Ben eyed the manila envelope and tried to convince himself the nightmare would be over soon.

Brooks caught the look on Ben's face. "Don't worry, hoss, this isn't a good news, bad news kind of thing."

"You haven't told me anything yet," Ben said, "except my sidewalk looks like a three-year-old did it."

Brooks tilted his head. "I thought he was four."

"You're slipping. Joshua doesn't turn four until Wednesday."

Brooks snapped his fingers. "That's right. July sixth."

"What's in the envelope?"

Brooks began the job of opening it. "The good news is that I haven't seen any of Marvin's thugs around here lately. And since you haven't either, I'm assuming they've lost interest in you."

Ben faced Brooks, unable to keep the excitement out of his voice. "You sure?"

"Course I'm not sure," Brooks said. "How could I be? But I've driven your road every day for the past month, and I haven't seen one hint of Marvin's men. Not a black Escalade, not any other of the vehicles those assholes drive. And since you haven't seen them either, the logical conclusion is that the assholes have turned their attention elsewhere."

"Toward Christina Blackwood?"

Brooks smiled ruefully. "Their attention's never wavered from Christina. Hell, Marvin Irvin's like the Eye of Sauron where Christina's concerned. He'd no more forget about her than he'd forget that damned cane he totes wherever he goes."

"He have some disability?"

"Yeah," Brooks said. "He enjoys torturing people."

Ben's mouth went dry.

"Anyhow," Brooks went on, "Marvin's men are always near Mrs. Blackwood's estate. Whenever she goes into Frisco, Malibu, anywhere, they're skulking in the background. Like a cloud of gnats."

"Why doesn't she just pay them off?"

Brooks gave him a look that suggested he was helplessly naïve. "The mob doesn't work like that. You don't sign a contract, agree to a set amount. One minute Chris Blackwood was in the hole nearly half a million, and the next thing he knew, that number doubled."

"I take it Marvin still wants his million."

"Million? Hell, Marvin's askin' for ten."

Ben barely caught that last bit because his attention had been diverted to the photographs Brooks had fished out of the manila envelope. There were three of them, glossy eight-by-tens that Brooks clutched like playing cards. The one in front was a handsome guy with a blond crew cut.

"This is Troy Castillo," Brooks said by way of explanation. "White guy, Hispanic name. He's one of the new feds assigned to your case."

Ben frowned. "My case?"

"Don't be coy now. You didn't think the authorities were just gonna walk away after you stonewalled the first pair they threw at you?"

Ben kicked at a thick weed. "I didn't stonewall anybody. If I'd told them the truth, they'd have had me committed."

Brooks laughed. "So you're tellin' me I should feel special. That right? Since I'm the only one you trusted with your goat-man tale?"

"I never should've told you."

Brooks flapped the eight-by-tens. "Well, you better come up with a better story, you're gonna try to outsmart these three. A guy I know from my days at the LAPD, he says the one named Morton *always* finishes the job."

"That supposed to scare me?"

"Why should it scare you? How much you benchin' these days?"

"I don't know."

"Estimate for me."

Ben shrugged. "Three-fifty, three-seventy-five?"

Brooks whistled. "You'll match up well with Castillo then." Brooks handed him the picture of the blond FBI agent. "He's a musclehead like yourself. Former collegiate wrestler. Hear he's got a short fuse."

Ben studied the square jaw, the no-nonsense expression. The photo looked to have been taken in a parking lot. "He military?"

"Uh-uh," Brooks said, waggling the second eight-by-ten. "But Morton was."

Ben accepted the second eight-by-ten, a mugshot that could have been lifted straight out of a high school yearbook. But this was no teenager staring at Ben. This man was sober-looking, conservative. He had short dark hair and sharp features. He was older than Castillo, perhaps Brooks's age.

"Sean Morton," Brooks explained. "He's head of their cadre. Cool, clinical. Very smart. He's been on Marvin now for several weeks. Now he's on you too."

"Why do you keep saying that?" Ben asked. "What do I have to do with the mob?"

"You were *there*, man. Chris Blackwood and his dad are both dead, along with a hell of a lot of other people. And since you're alive, everybody thinks you've got the answers."

"I gave you the answers," Ben said, "and look how you reacted."

Brooks laughed. "Sure you gave me answers. 'Once upon a time back in the 1800s, there was this composer who found a naked child in the woods...'"

Ben felt the anger melt out of him, in its place a resigned lethargy. "I've got to check on the kids."

"We're almost done," Brooks said. He handed Ben the last photograph, this one taken in what appeared to be the foyer of a large office building. "Jessica Gary. Goes by Jessie. She's a rising young star. First in her class, aced every exam she ever had. She'll be accompanying Morton and Castillo."

Ben examined the portrait more closely. The hair was a striking scarlet hue. She was gorgeous, which wouldn't help. Claire would probably hate her right away.

Brooks was beside him. "Hottie, right?"

Ben continued to study the photo. Jessie Gary had a dimple in her chin, but rather than making her look boyish, this only added an impish good humor to her otherwise solemn expression. Yes, Ben reflected. She was indeed attractive. He only hoped Claire would avoid picking a fight. Despite his wife's beauty and despite Ben's devotion to her, Claire was still ruled by an insecurity where Ben and other women were concerned. She often joked – not really joking at all – that Ben would someday leave her for a skinnier girl.

"So you see," Brooks said, "it would be wise of you to tell me what you know before these three professionals get ahold of you."

"And what, waterboard me?"

"That's not their style," Brooks said, returning the eight-by-tens to their folder. "But they will subpoena you. They will make you testify. And they'll indict you if you perjure yourself."

"I suppose that's why you're telling me this, right? Because you're worried about me? Worried my family won't be able to cope if I'm in prison?"

Brooks glanced up at him. "I wouldn't like to see that, no, you want the truth. But that's not why we're talking."

"How much?"

Teddy grinned. "You were supposed to let me spring it on you. You know, let me surprise you with it?"

Ben waited.

"Two hundred," Teddy said. "One each for Chris Blackwood and his dad."

"Two hundred thousand dollars," Ben said.

"Tell Christina what really happened and you'll get the money within a week."

Ben studied Brooks a moment. "You're not telling me everything."

"It's a simple transaction."

"You're holding something back. Why the urgency now? This

thing happened last summer, and all of a sudden Christina Blackwood is willing to pay me two hundred grand?"

Teddy held his gaze, but only for a moment. Then he patted his shirt pocket, began to draw out the pack of cigarettes again.

"No more of that," Ben said.

Brooks looked around the yard. "We're outside, man."

"It still stinks. It gets in my clothes, I go in and pick Julia up, her mouth and nose press right against the shoulder of my shirt, which smells like an ashtray."

Brooks rolled his eyes, but he let the pack slide back into his shirt pocket. "Sensitive," he muttered.

"What happened to your boss?"

Brooks brushed his shirt pocket absently, as if hoping Ben would change his mind about the smoking. Then, after a long moment's deliberation, he said, "Christina has three bodyguards. Or had. One of them disappeared a few days ago."

"Maybe he quit."

Brooks scuffed the toe of a loafer on the walk. "Tyler Funkhouser is the guy's name. He's always been a flake." Brooks shook his head. "Have no idea why Christina hired him. The two she's got are fine. But she hired Funkhouser a few months ago for extra security. He was a piss-poor bodyguard. Unobservant, totally unreliable. Funkhouser didn't show up for work a few days ago, and no one's been able to get ahold of him."

"You said he was a flake."

"He is."

"So why the concern now?"

Brooks looked askance at Ben as though he was feebleminded. "Christina Blackwood is worth billions, which makes her a target for a lot of people. Especially if a guy like Marvin feels she owes him restitution."

"Marvin threaten her?"

Brooks laughed. "Get this. Christmas Eve, Christina's out shopping. No idea why, her son and her husband are both dead. But one of Marvin's goons walks right up to her – guy by the name of Ray Rubio, big Italian guy – he stands beside her near a rack of dresses at Saks Fifth Avenue? Says he figured she wouldn't see him at her mansion so why don't they just talk here?"

Ben pictured Rubio, who in his mind looked like one of the henchmen in *The Godfather*. "What'd she say?"

"Didn't have time to say anything. Jorge stepped between them—"

"Who's Jorge?"

"Navarro. Excellent bodyguard. Jorge steps between them and tells Rubio he's gonna regret it if he doesn't leave Christina alone."

"What happened?"

"Rubio just says, 'Ten million. It'll be more if you don't pay up,' and leaves."

Ben thought it over. "And now the other bodyguard is missing?"

Brooks made a pained face. "I don't know we want to say 'missing' yet. Let's just say Christina's concerned about what it could mean if Funkhouser doesn't turn up soon."

Ben heard a muffled cry from the house. "That's Julia," he said, and moved away.

"So we got a deal?" Brooks called after him.

"I'm not going to lie for money," Ben said.

"You already lied for free, why not tell me the truth and get paid?"

CHAPTER TWO

Griffin Toomey knew he'd made a mistake when he snitched on the guy cheating at blackjack. Knew it was wrong to tell on a guy for no other reason than the guy had stolen his girl. The girl in question, of course, had been a hooker – all of Griffin's dates, it seemed, were with hookers – so Griffin supposed the guy hadn't actually stolen anything. But he was still incensed when the other guy – twenty years older and sporting a toupee that looked like an inexpertly skinned prairie dog – stole the leggy blonde.

Prairie Dog had sauntered up to the table and began beating the house. Within five minutes Griffin's stack of chips looked like some midget's stubby pecker. The fact that Prairie Dog was counting cards didn't even occur to Griffin until the crowd had swollen to maybe twenty people. Griffin was too busy eyeing the blonde's long pink fingernails as they settled on the sleeve of Prairie Dog's polyester sports jacket and then began to caress that sleeve. Soon she was leaning in close to him, whispering words of encouragement and once even giving his grizzled cheek a good-luck peck. The crowd soon became so boisterous that Griffin and the blonde with the endless brown legs became separated, which was just as well, Griffin figured, because that was what permitted him to concentrate on Prairie Dog's eyes as the dealer dealt.

Griffin made his way over to the red-vested security guard, a surly-looking guy who was watching the crowd celebrate around the blackjack table.

"What?" the surly guy had growled.

"That guy with the toupee," Griffin said.

"What about him?"

"He's counting cards."

The guard turned to Griffin, as if noticing him for the first time. Griffin thought the man would go over and collar Prairie Dog then. Instead, the guard crossed silently to a wall phone, punched a couple numbers, and said something into the receiver. He neither thanked Griffin nor gave him another glance.

Which was why Griffin was so shaken when the man he eventually learned to be Ray Rubio loomed up beside him later that evening at the hotel bar. Rubio and his round, masklike face, which was runneled with scars and the color of ravaged leather. Rubio saying, "You the bird who told on the cardsharper?"

Griffin had downed several shots by this time and had no idea what a cardsharper was. Nor did he have any idea why this scary man with the slicked-back hair was calling him a bird. But he heard himself saying yes, he was the bird who told on the cardsharper.

Rubio, his grip on Griffin's arm like an overinflated blood pressure band, practically carried him over to a dim but expansive corner table, where sat a short man and two scantily dressed women who made Griffin's leggy blonde look like a dog. At Rubio's appearance, both women rose and scooted hurriedly around the table to allow him ingress. Griffin scooted toward the short man and was pleasantly surprised to feel the bare arm of one of the scantily clad hotties settle against him. The hottie – this one had dark brown hair and so much cleavage her chest looked like a butt – was smiling broadly, but her eyes were on the short man. Griffin smiled happily back at her, took one more satisfied gander at her bulging boobs, then turned to the short man, who was staring at him.

Griffin felt his euphoria slip away.

"You're perceptive," the short man said.

As if to give lie to this sentiment, Griffin stared blankly back at the man, unable to formulate a coherent thought.

"He's drunk," Ray Rubio muttered.

"I can see that," the short man said without irritation. His charcoal-colored eyes swept Griffin appraisingly. "You noticed what my man on the floor didn't."

"He stole my girl," Griffin replied. Or at least had tried to reply. The words came out in a monosyllabic slur, like an old-fashioned cartoon character who'd become comically drunk. Only, Griffin realized, there was nothing comical about the short man's black eyes. Or about the way the supermodels at the table suddenly looked worried. *Mother of God*, Griffin had time to think. *Am I going to die?*

But the small man's intense expression gave way to an easy grin. The small man turned to another man, who at some point had sat down across the table from Griffin. "Hey, Nicky, what do you think of this guy?"

Nicky didn't even turn to look at Griffin. A toothpick poking out of his thin lips, Nicky said, "He looks like a baby eagle."

Griffin chuckled and hooked a thumb at Rubio. "He called me a bird earlier."

"Your hair is very fine," the small man commented. "Does it always stick up like that?"

"It's always been like this," Griffin said. "I try to make it lay down, but it always springs back up." Griffin patted his hair to demonstrate.

The one named Nicky was watching him now, one eyebrow raised. "He's a goddamned moron."

Griffin knew he should have been offended, but all at once he was mesmerized by Nicky's toothpick, the way it rolled from one corner of his mouth to the other.

"He's certainly inebriated," the small man allowed, "but he's not an idiot. I think our bird here notices far more than the average individual." The small man clapped a hand on the nape of Griffin's neck. The touch was not overly rough, but Griffin sensed immense strength in the man's stumpy fingers. He leaned close to Griffin's ear and said, "You're a perceptive young man. Aren't you?"

"Yes," Griffin said.

"What's your name, my young bird?"

Griffin told him.

"Toomey," Rubio said, chuckling. "Reminds me of cancer."

There was something unsettling about Rubio's laughter. The sound reminded Griffin of madness. Unconsciously, he scooted closer to the small man, whose arm was around his shoulders now.

The small man gave him an oddly paternal squeeze. "You wanna work for me, Birdman? I think you'd like working for me."

Griffin looked deep into those black, unblinking eyes and thought, *If I say no, he'll kill me. He'll kill me if I say no...*

...and he'll kill me if I puke, Griffin thought. So he kept scanning the room for things he could focus on rather than seeing what was happening to the man in the chair, the one named Tyler Funkhouser, the bodyguard of Christina Blackwood.

Griffin wished Marvin Irvin's living room were dimmer. But the canned lights in the steeply pitched ceiling were angling down to exactly where Funkhouser sat, the feet of the folding chair to which he was trussed crunching and crackling on the blue tarp. Funkhouser writhed in agony as Marvin let the glowing orange eye of his cane tip drift closer and closer to Funkhouser's bare chest. Marvin had already burned Tyler Funkhouser three times, once on the navel, once each on Funkhouser's shaved pectoral muscles.

"Please!" Funkhouser was screaming, and though Griffin wasn't looking at Funkhouser or Marvin – was in fact raptly examining the shag carpet between his feet – he could hear well enough the snuffling wetness of the man's voice. Even worse – far, far worse – he could smell the scorched bacon scent of the man's flesh. God, like the gamey odor of a cook's griddle after a long night of frying.

Griffin's stomach clenched.

A voice at his ear said, "You want your mommy?"

Griffin turned and looked into the pitiless face of Nicky Irvin, the boss's son.

With a feeling of dread, Griffin turned back to the gruesome tableau:

Funkhouser still tied to the chair, his bare shoulders heaving, his body rimed with sweat. Marvin Irvin favoring Funkhouser with a speculative look that carried with it a jolly good humor that Griffin found, under the circumstances, horribly inappropriate. Jim Bullington – the giant – looking on impassively from his position ten feet away. But no Rubio. Where the hell had Ray Rubio gone?

Griffin felt a hand press the middle of his back and compel him around the struggling bodyguard, no doubt to afford him a better view of the proceedings. This close everything looked even more hideous, the beating Bullington and Rubio had delivered showing in the lacerations covering Funkhouser's face. The worst was the bubbled swelling of the bodyguard's left eyelid, the skin there puffed up so taut it looked ready to explode like an overripe zit.

"Please don't," Funkhouser said. "Please don't do anything more to me. I've told you all the stuff I…" A gasping inhalation. "…all the stuff I know. Please—"

"You've told me stuff, sure," Marvin said. "But you haven't told me anything useful."

"Bullshit," Tyler Funkhouser said, then his one good eye opened wide in terror. "I'm sorry, Mr. Irvin, I didn't mean to disrespect you, but what I mean is—"

"—you don't know," Marvin finished for him. "Yeah, you said that already. Whether it's true or not remains to be seen."

Funkhouser's mouth fell open. "True or not? Course it's true! You think I'd go through all this for some rich bitch who couldn't care less whether I lived or died? Hell, I worked for her three months, you think she ever said more'n a few words to me?"

Nicky stepped between Funkhouser and Marvin. "You don't care about her, why not give us the code to the security system?"

Funkhouser sagged. "I already *told* you that. I told your old man I don't know it. *No one* knows it. No one but Jorge and Christina and the old farts in the security shack. You really wanna know something, whyn't you kidnap one of them?"

"You hear that, Nicky?" Marvin said. "The prick's willing to sacrifice some old men, but he's not willing to risk his own neck."

"I heard him," Nicky answered without taking his eyes off Funkhouser.

"You see, Nicky, this is why I take care of my own business." Marvin stepped up next to his son so that both men loomed over the trussed bodyguard. "Guy like this," Marvin said and unleashed a vicious right hook on Funkhouser, whose head whipped sideways with the blow, "he thinks once a man reaches a state of advanced years, he ain't good for much anymore. You hear him? 'Take one of them old farts, they don't matter.'"

"I didn't mean it that way," Funkhouser protested, but his voice was small and scared.

"Oh you meant it all right," Marvin said. "You meant it as sure as I'm sixty-one this August. And I'm gonna tell you something, you mewling little maggot..." Marvin got right up into the muscular bodyguard's grill, bent over and rested his hands on his knees. "I'm more a man at age sixty-one than you are at whatever the fuck you are." Marvin slashed down with a brutal left fist.

"Got it, boss," a voice said from the doorway.

Marvin sighed happily, stood erect. "Good." He glanced back at Ray Rubio, who clutched something at his side. Rubio watched the bodyguard with that dead stare of his. It was the way Rubio looked unless he was being cruel. When he was being cruel, his dead stare was replaced by a look of maniacal glee. The kind of look a mean six-year-old gets when vivisecting ants or plucking the wings off houseflies.

Marvin murmured, "Step aside, Nicky."

Nicky took a few steps backward, and in his place came Ray Rubio. The object dangling from Rubio's side was flat, comprised of white plastic, and had braces at each end so the flat part would be raised. Something in its center glinted.

"You know what this is?" Marvin asked.

Funkhouser was huffing quickly again, hyperventilation not far off. "It's for cutting vegetables, I think. My mom used to have one."

Marvin gave him an admiring nod. "Not bad for a primate." Marvin gestured toward the implement Rubio grasped. "Its proper name is a mandolin slicer, but you're correct, Tyler, it is for cutting vegetables."

Rubio stepped closer. Funkhouser started to whimper.

Marvin smiled. "But we're not going to slice vegetables with it today, are we, Ray?"

"No, sir," Rubio said, the dead stare giving way to that predatory glee.

"Oh man, you gotta stop this," Funkhouser said. "I told you all I know. I know it ain't much but—"

"Hold the slicer, Jim."

Jim Bullington strode forward expressionlessly, took the mandolin slicer and situated it firmly on the bodyguard's lap. Now that the slicer caught the full light from above, Griffin could see how sharp the diagonal blade was, how the surface wasn't quite level. He imagined someone sliding a cucumber over the white surface and how the blade would shear a thin slice neatly off.

Hot bile began to burn the back of Griffin's throat.

Rubio went around and untied Funkhouser's wrists, but as he did, Nicky grasped his left wrist so that it remained pinned uselessly against the chair. Straining, Rubio muscled the bodyguard's right hand up so that it hovered just over the mandolin slicer. Funkhouser's hand was balled into a trembling fist, but Rubio was more than powerful enough to move it into position.

"Aw shit," Tyler Funkhouser moaned. "Aw shit, don't do this. Don't do this to me."

"Stick out your fingers," Rubio grunted.

"I'm tellin' you I don't know any—"

"Have it your way," Rubio said and jerked Funkhouser's fist over the plastic board.

Griffin heard a nauseating *shnick* and then blood was pouring out of Funkhouser's knuckles, the tops of which had been sheared clean off by the sharp blade. Funkhouser let loose with a high, keening wail, his head thrown back, his back arching against the chair, the blood from his knuckles pattering over the blue tarp.

Rubio brayed laughter, glanced back at Marvin, whose face betrayed no emotion. "That got his attention, didn't it, boss!" Rubio said through his laughter. "Oh, oh, that hurt you, fella? That hurt your big bad hand?"

Funkhouser made the mistake of unflexing his fist. The moment he did Rubio slapped the open palm on the mandolin slicer and jerked it over the cutting board. This time a whole sheet of skin was peeled away from the bodyguard's hand. Sheaths of flesh from his palm, his fingers, even his fingerprints were sliced neatly off.

Funkhouser's feet drummed the floor, his screams nearly intolerable, and when Griffin caught sight of that pink-red hand with its pared epidermis and its network of blood streams dribbling down the man's forearm, he could control his gorge no longer. Griffin prescribed a half-turn and unleashed a flood of vomit on Marvin's white shag carpet.

"Moron," Nicky growled. "Look at what he did, Dad. Dumb shit doesn't have the sense to do it on the tarp."

But Marvin didn't sound mad at all. "It'll clean," he said. "This is all part of the bird's initiation."

Funkhouser was sobbing.

Rubio giggled. "Poor Toomey. He thinks this is bad, wait till we start in on the bastard's face."

Funkhouser wailed.

"We'll lop off that pretty nose of his," Rubio said. "Then we'll make sure he's circumcised good and proper."

And as Tyler Funkhouser continued to shriek and thrash in the chair, Griffin Toomey pitched forward, his consciousness mercifully abandoning him.

CHAPTER THREE

Claire Shadeland pushed her stepson on the swing and eyed her husband, who had on that distracted look he wore too often lately. Claire gave Joshua one more push on the swing and said, "Pump your legs a little, okay? Mommy's gonna talk to Daddy a minute."

She sat next to Ben on the wooden swing, where Julia slept on his shoulder. "You're scowling again," she said.

Ben's eyes tracked his son's arc. "Joshua's not ready to go that high yet."

"He's fine, honey. It's not like he's going to let go in midair."

"He could slip."

Claire let it pass. Ben continued to caress Julia's bare back. The temperature was in the upper eighties, which meant Ben would allow Julia to go without her onesie for a few minutes. Anything eighty-five or cooler and he insisted on wrapping their infant up like a mummy.

Claire cleared her throat. "Did you call your mom back yet?"

"I've been writing."

Claire knew that was a lie, but again she let it go. She'd heard him earlier, plinking out a few reluctant notes on their Steinway, but if that was writing, Claire figured they were in even worse shape than she'd thought. The score for *The Nightmare Girl* was due by September, but Ben had only composed a couple minor themes. He was too busy worrying, too busy monitoring his family's safety. Too busy brooding about how everything could fall apart.

Claire took a breath. "I think we should take her up on her offer."

For a long moment she was sure Ben wouldn't respond, but at length he muttered, "I'm not ready for that yet."

"It's just dinner, honey. An hour and a half. Two hours tops."

"We'll take Julia with us. She's portable."

"It's Joshua's birthday, honey. He's been asking about this for weeks now. Months. You're really too paranoid to leave her alone for a couple hours?"

Ben's gaze went stony. "It's not paranoia. Paranoia means there's nothing to worry about."

"There *isn't*," she said. "It's been a year since the island, and we've been totally safe. Joshua doesn't even talk about it anymore. Other than the nightmares—"

"'Other than the nightmares,' Claire? You say it like it's no big deal, like it's normal for a kid to wake up screaming bloody murder night after night." His voice had coarsened to nearly a growl. On his shoulder, baby Julia stirred.

"Please don't yell at me," Claire said.

"Then knock off the accusations."

"No one's accusing you—"

"The hell they're not. First Brooks, now you. I'm tired of everyone acting like I'm some kind of lunatic for wanting my family safe."

"Teddy Brooks was here?"

Ben made a sour face. "Yesterday, when you were taking a nap."

Claire searched his features for signs of recrimination, but found none. The truth was, she'd felt guilty for napping most of the afternoon yesterday, but her body had badly needed the rest.

Claire glanced at Joshua, whose swinging trajectory had slowed to nearly a halt. Now he was doing little more than bucking in the seat, like he was doing crunches. "What did Teddy say?" she asked.

"What does it matter?" Ben said and got up.

"Was it about the bookie?"

"He's not a bookie, he's a gangster. And according to Teddy, the gangster's men haven't been near the ranch for over a month."

Claire sat forward. "So it's safe to take Joshua out for his birthday."

"Why are you so intent on leaving her here? You act like Julia's a burden."

"I love her too, Ben. But she's colicky. Every time we take her out with us she screams through dinner."

"That's what babies do, Claire, they scream."

She stood, a hotness burning behind her ears. "Don't give me that. The whole 'You've never raised a child before, Claire, so you have no idea how they are'."

"Well, you *haven't*," Ben said. "So quit trying to pawn Julia off on my mom."

"Pawn her off?" Claire uttered a breathless little laugh. "How can you say that? Who was up with her all night last night while she screamed? Who—"

"*I* had her until two a.m."

Claire tapped her chest with an index finger. "And I had her until eight this morning, while you slept like a lamb."

Ben stepped nearer, teeth bared. "I never sleep well and you know it. I haven't since..."

Despite his tone, the torment she saw twisting his face took away some of her anger. "I know you don't sleep much. You know I understand."

He cupped Julia tighter against him, a desperate plea in his eyes. "*Do you*, Claire? Do you really? If you did, you'd know I can barely stand to be in different rooms than the kids, much less in different zip codes. You don't know what it was like to have your boy stolen from you by that—" He broke off, his muscled neck straining.

But Claire did know. She remembered the nightmarish moment as clearly as if it were unfolding before her right now...in the uppermost room of Castle Blackwood, the vast window-lined studio...stashing Joshua in a bench compartment, telling herself he'd be safe from the monster there, safe from Gabriel...then the lid swinging back, Joshua opening the lid...and a moment later the monster crashing through the window, seizing Joshua in its filthy black talons, and leaping through the window to land six stories below...the feeling of abject terror and dismal failure that drowned her as she watched Joshua being borne away...

Claire exhaled shuddering breath. "I saw it happen, Ben. I know how it feels."

"You didn't know Joshua then," Ben said, and when Claire made to interrupt, he overrode her. "And I know you love him now – I know you love him more than Jenny ever did – but you didn't love him then. Not yet. So you can't know how it was for me, how it was to know a monster took my boy." He shook his head, tears of rage pooling in his eyes. "Never again, Claire. By God, I'll never let it happen again."

Claire saw the steely determination in his eyes, and all at once she longed to slip her arms over his broad shoulders and hug him. She raised her arms to do just that, but something in her periphery drew her attention, and then she remembered Joshua, her adopted son dangling in the swing less than twenty feet away. He was watching her and Ben with trepidation.

"It's okay, honey," Claire said. "Mommy and Daddy aren't mad at each other." She couldn't believe Julia hadn't wakened yet. Why couldn't their baby sleep this well at night?

"Here," Ben said and handed Julia over. Claire cradled her and moved toward the house. Ben went to Joshua and said, "Bath time." Joshua groaned, but when she got to the deck and looked back, she saw Ben carrying him upside down toward the house, Joshua squealing with laughter.

★   ★   ★

That night Ben was on the phone with Nat Zimmerman, one of the producers of *The Nightmare Girl*, until well past ten. It galled Claire that she had to wait so long for Ben, not because she wanted to continue their argument and certainly not because of whom Ben was talking to – on the contrary, without Nat Zimmerman, things would be a hell of a lot tenser between them and the studio – but for the simple reason that Claire was horny. She reckoned it was the first time she'd been truly aroused since she'd given birth four months ago. She knew the forced celibacy bothered Ben – heck, it bothered *her* – but the combination of nursing Julia what felt like fifty times a day and what Claire suspected was a mild case of post-partum depression had pretty well derailed whatever sex drive she'd had while pregnant.

So she contented herself with re-reading *The Nightmare Girl* and waiting for her husband to come to bed.

As it had the first three times she'd read it, the novel drew her in immediately. She liked it even better than the last adapted novel they'd scored, a ghost story called *House of Skin*. The movie version of *House of Skin* had gone on to become the surprise hit of the winter season, partially due to the fact that its director, the infamous Lee Stanley, had died before it was released, but also because – if the critics were to be believed – of the haunting music by Ben and Claire Shadeland. The success of *House of Skin* and its score helped them secure the contract for *The Nightmare Girl* – itself one of the bestselling novels of last year

– but it also brought with it heightened expectations to which Claire was unaccustomed.

She'd gotten to a tense scene at a gas station when she heard the muffled footfalls of her husband returning from his call. Claire quickly returned the book to her nightstand drawer – having it constantly out in the open, she feared, might increase the pressure Ben felt to compose the music that was due in under six weeks – and pushed the blankets down to her waist. Propping herself on her elbows, she surveyed her breasts to make sure there was no milk leaking through her pink nightgown, then debated shoving the covers down farther. Nursing had enlarged her breasts a full cup size, but she'd also gained some weight in her hips. Lifting the covers and eyeing her thighs dubiously, she finally decided Ben would be too grateful for the prospect of intercourse to be turned off by her weight gain, and pushed the blankets all the way down to her knees.

A doorway creaked from down the hall.

Ben checking on Joshua.

Claire noticed her nightgown was long enough to cover the expensive lace underwear she'd selected for the festivities tonight. With a tremor of excitement, she drew up the pink gown to reveal a hint of the underwear beneath. She deliberated a moment longer before hiking up the gown another couple inches so that a pink V of lace would greet Ben as he opened the bedroom door.

She hoped he'd ravage her.

Footsteps approached.

Claire lay back, placed her hands behind her head so her breasts would jut up at him. They were enormous these days. Full of milk, yes, but enormous nonetheless. She was sure Ben would enjoy the view.

The footsteps continued past her door.

Arching an eyebrow, Claire sat up and listened. Ben had continued on to the nursery to check on Julia. Claire gritted her teeth. She had the video baby monitor right beside her, for goodness sakes; why must he also open Julia's door to confirm she was okay? What if he woke her up? Claire leaned over and pushed the button on top of the monitor. Her lips thinned. Not only had Ben gone to the nursery to check on Julia, he'd actually ventured inside to stand over her crib. Claire watched with apprehension as Ben reached out and caressed the soft down of Julia's pate. *Don't wake her up!* she wanted to shout. *It might be another month before we get another chance to have sex!*

But Julia did not stir.

After what seemed an age, Ben straightened and made his way out of the nursery. Claire smiled ruefully and shook her head. She was thankful Ben was such a devoted father, but sometimes she wanted to remind him that she had needs too.

Ben let himself in and eased shut their door. Claire assumed her prior position.

He'd taken three strides when he stopped and saw her lying there. "Nice outfit," he said.

"Like it?"

He grinned, sat next to her. "A lot."

She trailed a hand over the silky pink material. "Why don't you show me how much you like it?"

His eyebrows went up. "Really?"

She smiled languidly.

He reached down, let his fingertips caress her from throat to sternum. Tiny goosebumps rose at his touch. "That's two good pieces of news this evening," he said.

"Oh yeah?" she asked, her voice thick.

He nodded. "Nat's going to help us out tomorrow night."

She barely heard his remark, was too busy focusing on the delicious tingling between her legs. "Help us out how?"

"He and my mom are going to watch Julia for us," Ben answered.

"They're coming here?"

Ben's fingers had moved to her right breast. His index finger made little swirls on the fabric over her nipple, which responded by pressing painfully against his fingertip. In a faraway voice, he said, "You know how persuasive Nat is. He told me you were right about Joshua's birthday, that I need to stop being so protective."

"Wise," Claire said, closing her eyes.

"So he's gonna be here with Mom, make sure the house is safe while we're gone."

"Whatever makes you comfortable," Claire said, nestling into the mattress.

"Comfortable," Ben repeated and drew down the shoulder straps of the gown. Peeling off the cups sheathing her breasts, Ben leaned down and began kissing the white flesh, his lips skimming the bunched areolae.

"Careful," Claire said. "You do much more of that, you're gonna get sprayed."

Ben laughed softly. "Kinky."

Claire lowered her arms so Ben could slide the nightgown down her body. Then he kissed the inside of her calves, licked his way up her thighs, began to rub her through her panties. He drew aside her underwear, kissed her sex, but before he could get too involved, she cinched her fingers in his brown hair, compelled him up her body.

"Don't want me down there?" he asked as their lips came together.

"Not yet. I'm still self-conscious about that whole area."

"You sure?" he asked, kissing her. Their tongues came together, pushing, tasting.

"Mm-hm," she breathed into his open mouth. "Tonight I'll settle for the real thing." Her hands lowered to the front of his cargo shorts.

"You will, will you?" he asked, helping her get his shorts open.

"Uh-huh." She licked his lips, plunged her tongue inside his mouth. Then her hand was around him, squeezing. Ben moaned.

"Here," she said and guided him inside.

It didn't take him long, but it was enough for her to get there too, and when it was done, they lay there sated, the glow of the bedside lamp still bathing them in its amber warmth.

She had an arm thrown over his chest, the tip of her nose touching his big shoulder. He'd been very muscular when they met last summer, but a year of intense weightlifting and running had transformed him into a hulking physical specimen. His six-foot-four frame was so strong and sculpted that the baser part of her nature worried about women coming onto him, especially ones who wanted a piece of his growing fame.

Knock it off, she reminded herself. *He's faithful. That's all you need to know.*

"What are you thinking about?" she asked.

"Tell you the truth, I'd started to doze a bit."

"Sorry. I'm not used to you sleeping."

"Me either," he said. "I guess sex relaxes me."

She caressed his chest. "We should do it more often then."

"How about hourly?"

She smiled, kissed his shoulder. "So where are you taking us?"

"Somewhere close," he said, his voice tightening slightly.

She tried to keep it light. "Shouldn't we let Joshua choose? It's his birthday after all."

"He can choose next year. This year we're going somewhere nearby."

"But Nat's going to be—"

"I feel better with Nat being here, but it doesn't mean I'm comfortable."

Claire nodded. "Joshua will be thrilled. We can concentrate on him rather than his little sister's screaming."

Ben said nothing to that, and Claire didn't press it.

She figured if she did Ben might cancel.

★   ★   ★

Later that night, Ben finally sleeps. What's more, his dreams are not sweat-soaked nightmares that make him moan and whimper and wake up dry-mouthed with terror.

In his dream Ben is in the hospital room, and everything is exactly as it was the day Julia was born. Ben's dream-self waits until everyone is gone from their hospital room. Claire is sound asleep now, the adrenaline of the birth, the stress of labor, the joy and exultation over seeing baby Julia and nursing her for the first time, and the exhaustion of not having slept in over thirty hours having slammed down on Claire like an avalanche. Ben looks at his wife for a long moment, tears welling in his eyes. He doesn't know how she did it, but he is proud of her. So proud of her.

He lowers his eyes to his daughter.

When Ben and his ex-wife had Joshua, Ben had let the doctors and nurses call the shots, and when there had been a moment without white-coated people bustling around their room, Jenny had insisted on stashing little Joshua in the hospital nursery, where Ben was forced to stare at him through the glass partition.

Not this time.

Ben and Claire have an agreement that Julia is never to leave their room unless the doctors or nurses need to weigh her or perform some other measurement, and even in those situations Ben will be accompanying her. This isn't paranoia or micromanagement. This is love.

Ben stares down at the tiny body asleep in his arms and thinks, *I love you, Julia Grace Shadeland. I love you more than you will ever know. Not in a thousand lifetimes could you understand what I feel for you, nor will anyone who isn't in my heart understand how powerful this is. I will protect you and I will cherish you. I will change your diapers and I will stay up all night holding you against my chest. When you won't stop crying I will dance you around the room, and I will sing you country songs off key for hours until you feel better or are too sick of my voice to cry any longer.*

Julia's little forehead pinches briefly, the little pelt of black down shifting almost imperceptibly with the movement. At this moment Julia looks like Claire. That frown is the one Claire gets when she's misplaced something and is trying to remember where she left it. Ben cranes over Julia and kisses her hair. Though her scalp feels warm on his lips, he realizes they've forgotten to replace the pink cap that's supposed to cover her head. Claire had taken off the cap so she could nurse Julia, and the cap is right where she left it, lying beside her on the hospital bed. Ben briefly considers ignoring it, but then he remembers the doctor saying something about how the cap keeps the baby's body heat in, which Ben assumes is a good thing.

Gingerly, he scoots forward on the green vinyl recliner. He takes great care not to awaken her, but she stirs anyway, her curled fingers curling even more. Her balled fists and the somehow determined appearance of her closed lips remind him of a sports fan rooting on her favorite team. *I'll take you to the Cubs games with us*, he thinks. *Your mommy will want you to do all the girly stuff too, and that's fine, but you're gonna watch* Lord of the Rings *and play catch with me and wrestle with me just like your brother does. I'll shower you with clothes and jewelry and all that stuff if you want – I'll even learn about different kinds of makeup if you're into that – but you're sure as heck gonna know that Han Solo shot first.*

Carefully, Ben rises out of his recliner, careful to keep his arms level. Julia isn't moving now, her sleep gone deeper, so as he tiptoes over to Claire's bed he whispers, "I'm gonna teach you piano, I'm gonna read to you, I'm gonna push you on the swing for as long as you want..."

Halfway to the bed, the door opens and Ben freezes. It is an older nurse. Her teeth show apologetically and she mouths, *Sorry.* Ben smiles at her and beckons her over with a twitch of his head. When she gets to him she spots the pink hat, jerks her thumb at the chair to let Ben know he can sit back down, and then follows him over to the recliner. Once seated Ben starts to raise Julia's head a bit so the nurse can slide the cap over Julia's head, but the nurse gives a quick shake of the head, and then with a practiced pair of hands – the nails are cut short, Ben observes – proceeds to snug the cap over Julia's head. And she does it without waking Julia up.

When the cap is on, Ben resumes staring at his daughter, but then he notices the nurse is still bent over Julia too, a soft look in the nurse's otherwise stern face. The woman, he notices for the first time, has worry lines on her forehead and the ghosts of crow's feet around her brown eyes. The nurse's hair is curly and brown, but there are strands of white woven through.

"I lost mine," the nurse whispers.

Ben looks up at her face, only a couple feet away. He has no idea what to say.

"I have two boys," the nurse goes on. "Both grown now. They're starting families." She reaches out and with a thumb and forefinger gives Julia's hand a brief rub. "But my daughter died when she was sixteen. Crashed on the way to school with her boyfriend. He lived."

Ben looks down at Julia's sleeping face. He decides he can't wait for the nurse to go; he has to do this now. He raises Julia up a little and lowers his face to hers. He kisses his baby girl on the lips. She makes a little chipmunk sound, rustles in her sleep, and hides her bottom lip under her top one. She sighs.

Wordlessly, the nurse reaches out and places a hand on Ben's forearm. She squeezes it, but her eyes are on Julia. Then the hand goes away and so does the nurse, who exits as noiselessly as she entered.

Ben glances at his baby, tells her, "No dating until you're thirty. And then I get to screen every guy, make sure he's a good driver. And that he likes *Lord of the Rings*."

CHAPTER FOUR

"Would you get your ass out of the house?" Nat Zimmerman said. He was as tall as Ben, but he had a bony build, so when he pushed Ben toward the front door, Ben hardly budged.

Claire saw the look on Ben's face and thought, *Please don't back out now.*

Joshua was already waiting in the car. Through the glass front door she could see his expectant little face peering through the back window of the car. Even on the booster seat, his face didn't come up far enough for her to see his mouth, but his big, blue, worried eyes were enough to galvanize her into action.

She linked her arm with Ben's. Ben was explaining to Nat – rather redundantly, Claire judged – how often Julia needed to be fed and could he make sure he took the baby monitor with him if he and Ben's mother went to the kitchen together?

"Go to the kitchen together?" Nat asked. "I hardly think we need to use the buddy system."

Ben turned, nodded toward his mother, who stood with arms folded and a sympathetic smile on her lips.

Ben said, "I just mean if you should happen to both get a beer at the same time, something like that."

"Ben," Charlotte Shadeland said. "I haven't had a beer since your father and I were married."

Ben shrugged. "Or something else."

Claire gave his arm a firm tug. He glanced down at her, brow knitted.

"It's time to celebrate your son's birthday," she said.

He made a pained face. "I still don't see why we have to go out. We can bring the food here, let Julia watch him blow out the candles."

"Look out the window, Ben."

Reluctantly, Ben did.

From the back window of the car, Joshua's small, pale face peered at them. Ben seemed to deflate. "Okay," he said. "Let's go."

Nat held the door while Claire led Ben through. As she passed Nat, he winked at her, and as usual, she was struck by how handsome he was, how he looked every bit his sixty years, but somehow seemed twice as virile as a man half his age. The salt-and-pepper hair was trimmed neatly, the matching mustache reminding her a little of Sam Elliott. And also like Sam Elliott, Nat Zimmerman was tall and rangy, like a cowboy or an ex-baseball player.

Claire and Ben made their way down the walk.

"You think there's enough milk?" Ben asked her, throwing a glance back at the house.

"Honey, even if I died, I've pumped enough bottles for Julia to survive for the next six months."

Ben's face went tight. "That's not funny."

"Please don't ruin this."

He glanced down at her.

"Joshua needs this," she went on. "He hasn't had us to himself since the day Julia was born. He's a super kid, but even he has to get jealous sometimes, doesn't he?"

Ben ran a hand over his mouth and studied his shoes. "What if something goes wrong with the bottle warmer? Julia could burn her mouth."

"Your mom is almost as cautious as you are," Claire said. "Where do you think you get that from?"

Ben nodded.

"Nat's here in case anything happens—"

Ben looked up at her.

"—which it won't," she added quickly. "And your mom still has her nursing training. You couldn't ask for a safer environment."

"It'd be safer if I was here."

She stared at him until he met her eyes.

"Ben?" she said.

"What?"

"Put on your big boy pants."

★   ★   ★

Ben was wrong. They had a wonderful time at the seafood place Joshua chose. They went out afterward for ice cream and a walk, and they returned to the ranch road at around nine forty-five.

Joshua and Claire were debating whether Joshua would have to go straight to bed when they got home when Ben felt it for the first time, the whisper of unease. He told himself it was pointless paranoia, but as they threaded their way up the mountain road, the whisper grew in strength and clarity: *You made a mistake.*

Ben clenched the wheel harder. He flicked on his brights, though a lusterless orange twilight still lingered. He didn't like it, that tingling at the nape of his neck. It was like they were driving under a high-tension wire, some of the electricity transferring to them through the air.

Ben swallowed. Claire and Joshua hadn't noticed his disquiet yet. He supposed that was good. But their arguing had grown loud enough to distract him, and not in a good way. Not in a way that took his mind off Julia — in a way that made him yearn to shout at them, to demand they shut the hell up for one minute so he could get them home. And then Claire and Nat and his mom could make fun of him all they wanted. At this particular moment Ben cared about nothing else but his baby girl, his sweet little trusting Julia, who was

(*dead*)

probably lying on her tummy asleep, the way she often rested despite the fact that Ben worried about crib death, and what a stupid, senseless phrase that was. Why did there even have to be such a thing? Why couldn't babies just be safe until they got old enough to deserve the consequences of their actions? No baby deserved to have a rash, much less anything as serious as

(*murdered*)

NO! Ben's mind screamed. No murder, no injury, no anything, not even a blistered tongue from a too-hot bottle. Julia was going to be fine, she was going to be—

They rounded the last corner, and when Ben looked at the house and saw the glass front door, he knew nothing was ever going to be fine again.

CHAPTER FIVE

Ben brought the Camry to a halt and barely remembered to throw it into Park before climbing out.

"Ben?" Claire was saying, her voice stitched with fear. "Honey, what's the matter?"

Ben said nothing, only moved toward the house on legs he could no longer feel. He heard Claire's door open.

"*What's wrong, Ben?*" she called in a frightened voice.

Ben stopped and turned. "Get in the car, honey. Lock the doors."

"What is it?"

He attempted to swallow, but his efforts only produced a painful grinding sensation. "Now, Claire. Please," he said, and he watched her sink down to her seat.

Ben turned and faced the glass door, twenty feet away.

The glass door stippled with drops of blood.

Ben drifted nearer and as he did he saw with a sense of fatedness that the droplets had spattered the inside of the door. Ten feet away now he tilted his gaze downward, searching for the first glimpse of a body within the foyer. It would be Nat, he was sure. Nat would have answered the door because Nat was like Ben. He believed a man had certain duties no matter how outmoded or sexist modern society might deem such thinking.

Another couple strides and Ben was on the porch. He reached the door, peered down through the glass. No body on the tiled floor.

No body, but more blood. Smears of it. And something else.

Ben's heart thundered in his chest. Acid had climbed all the way up his throat, the insides of his mouth, yet the sensation was diminished by the flood of unreality that had inundated him. Even the steady drip, drip, drip from within the house was a sound scarcely heard, just the ghost of a sound really. Ben stepped into the house and felt the door ease shut behind him. The halls were dark, but there were plenty of lights on in the family room, and as a result the object on the wood floor was backlit, merely a shape.

Ben's whole body went limp when he realized what it was.

A human forearm. Severed at the elbow.

There was hair tufted along its length, a gold ring with an onyx stone on one finger. Nat Zimmerman wasn't married anymore, but he still wore a gold ring with an onyx stone in it. Ben stared down at the forearm stupidly. The quiver gripped him again, a voice in his head

(*Julia*)

demanding he continue forward, where another grisly surprise awaited him. A trail of blood led away from Nat's severed arm, and the walls of the hallway leading to the family room were festooned with roller coasters of red liquid, the splash and spray of Nat's severed stump decorating the wallpaper like a ghoulish exhibit of modern art.

Ben pictured the scene: Nat first demanding whoever had done this to leave the ranch and then struggling fruitlessly to fend off his attacker. Ben stepped into the family room and all coherent thought scattered in a single blast of horror.

The entire room was bathed in carnage.

Congealing puddles of blood littered the floor. Deep red stains were soaked into the furniture, Claire's white reading chair marred by a giant burgundy apostrophe.

Ben began to shake.

His tortured, unbelieving gaze swept the coffee table where a human hand – this one definitely not Nat Zimmerman's – lay palm up, the fingers curled like the legs of a dead spider. The hand was too large to belong to Julia. But it wasn't too large to belong to his mother.

Behind the couch he spotted a tennis shoe, the toe pointed up. He thought at first it was a man's shoe, but then he remembered his mother's height, her large feet. She'd always been self-conscious about them, hated the fact that her shoe size was measured in double digits. It was his mom's sneaker he was looking at, Ben was certain, but as he drifted slowly around the couch, he realized the rest of his mom was elsewhere. Her leg had been chopped off below the knee. A ragged tube of shinbone, its spiky tip glistening like some gruesome gem, poked out of the bloody hamburger of the wound.

Ben knew he should be mourning his mom, knew he should be

crying her name over and over or praying for her soul or something, but he could only stand there in shock, stand there and take in the state of the room, the walls splashed with blood, the adjoining kitchen in a similar state. On the island lay a large slab of butchered meat. He identified it after a moment as Nat Zimmerman's torso. It had been hacked and mutilated, but the splintered ribs snarled in all directions and the purplish entrails dangling over the edge of the granite island top assured him that, yes, this was a human torso.

Ben turned toward the hallway.

Listened for sounds coming from the nursery.

He did not want to find whatever was behind the door at the end of the hallway, but he forced himself to move in that direction anyway. Whoever committed this atrocity

(*you know who did it*)

had placed one of Nat Zimmerman's legs on the mantle, so that the blood had drizzled out of it and showered the hearth below. Before Ben left the room he noticed the way the hanging Venetian blinds were stirring, the ones that covered the sliding door leading to the deck. He reached out, brushed the blinds, and as he did he saw that most of the glass in the door had been shattered, the spangled spray of shards twinkling dully in the westering orange sunset. Ben pushed one hanging slat of the blinds aside and saw without surprise that the object that had been hurled through the window was his mother's head. Had this not been such a horrorshow of desecration, he might have been spared the indignity of looking into his mother's dead, staring eyes, but even this perverse joke had been inflicted on him. Charlotte Shadeland's kind blue eyes were fixed open in an expression of stunned dismay.

Ben let his hand fall from the blinds and moved toward the nursery door. It was closed, he saw, and though this should have comforted him – Was it possible whoever had done this had spared Julia, had not even bothered with the nursery? – the sight of the closed door had the opposite effect. Dismally, he saw the trail of blood leading to the nursery. What dim hope to which he'd clung vanished at sight of this, the smeared footprints in the hallway, an object placed near the door of Julia's room.

(*you knew this was coming*)

He attempted to brush off the thought, but it would not go away.

(*this is your fault*)

Because it had been in his mind all evening – hell, had been in his mind since his ordeal on the Sorrows.

(*you failed, Ben*)

For a full year he'd fretted about everything, from fire hazards to Joshua's diet to insisting on keeping all poisons on the top shelves despite the fact that Julia was still months away from crawling and Joshua was smart enough not to guzzle window cleaner.

(*you're the worst father*)

And now he'd committed the most egregious error imaginable – he'd left his baby unattended. He'd known what was out there; deep down in the most primal reaches of his brain he'd *known* there was still a danger. The nursery door was closed, though that mattered little. He knew what he'd find. In the lightless hallway he could just make out what sat before the door like a derisive sentry.

Nat Zimmerman's head.

It had been positioned to face the door, and the meaning Ben supposed he'd been meant to draw from this was plain enough: *See, Ben? I'm watching the baby. Just like you told me to.*

Ben could no longer breathe, could no longer think. His eyes blurred, his heart had swollen painfully and was about to blow apart, which was no more than what he deserved. Jesus Christ, he'd been a fool. Why had he left Julia here?

He paused before the door, reached for the knob.

Don't leave her alone, the voice in Ben's head had proclaimed. *Don't leave her alone.* Was that so difficult? Was he so dense he couldn't listen to his gut just that once?

His fingers closed on the doorknob.

Had he listened to his gut a year ago he never would have traveled to the Sorrows; had he listened then he never would've encountered the creature. His best friend Eddie would still be alive. And they wouldn't have incurred the wrath of the thing on the island, the beast that had once been called Gabriel. The satyr, the monster, the seven-foot-tall nightmare with muscles so immense they threatened to burst through its black, leathery flesh.

Gabriel might still be inside the room. Ben pushed open the door and tensed for battle. He watched the door swing open, awaited the same savage blast of carnage that had assaulted him earlier.

The room looked normal.

No, not quite normal, he amended. There were more blood tracks on the floor, these easier to see because in here they'd had carpet installed thinking it would be easier for Julia to crawl on when she learned how.

But she would never learn to crawl because within the crib he was about to find her mutilated remains. The room was so dark Ben couldn't discern Julia's shape within the pooled shadows of the crib. He ached with the deepest recesses of his soul to take back this night, to listen to his gut just this one time and in doing so save his precious baby girl. Knowing he could delay no longer, Ben reached out, flicked on the overhead switch.

The bloody footprints – there was something wrong with them, they were too human – and the humped shadows in the crib…they weren't shaped like a baby. Was it possible…

Ben rushed over to the crib, peered inside.

Nothing.

Julia was gone.

A tide of emotions so powerful swept over him that Ben had to lean on the edge of the crib for support. He was relieved she was alive – or *could* be alive. He was heartbroken she'd been abducted, and not just abducted, but abducted by a monster.

Ben slumped over the side of the crib, sobbing silently. One hand brushed the red-and-blue cushioned Thomas the Tank Engine toy Joshua had picked out for his baby sister, a plush train Julia enjoyed nuzzling. Ben grasped it, raised it to his nose and inhaled. It smelled of his baby, that combination of talc and sweetness that made him so happy he wanted to cry.

Ben froze.

Upon discovering the bloodbath in the house, he hadn't sent Claire and Joshua away because he wanted to protect them the way he should have protected Julia. But he'd been in the house how long? Five minutes? And the

(*beast*)

murderer could have gotten them by now. Perhaps

(*it*)

he had been lurking in the adjacent woods the entire time, biding his time until Ben entered the house, knowing Ben would be transfixed, would give

(*the monster*)

the killer ample time to—

Oh Jesus, Ben thought and shoved away from the crib.

He'd taken two panicked strides down the hallway when he heard Claire scream.

PART TWO
HOMECOMING
CHAPTER ONE

Teddy Brooks arrived at the Shadeland house around eleven-fifteen that night.

The cops had treated him like some kind of derelict when he pulled up outside Shadeland's ranch. That was okay, Teddy supposed. When he quit the force, he'd understood he was probably leaving the fraternity forever, and that now he'd be regarded with the same distrust he'd always leveled at civilians.

So upon arriving, he'd taken the baleful looks and the curt questions in stride, electing to chill out by his car and smoke until Shadeland noticed him. When Ben did, he didn't come over right away, only remained beside Claire and Joshua, who were sitting on a bench at the edge of the yard, the little boy's head in Claire's lap. Claire herself was staring glassy-eyed at nothing in particular, and when Ben knelt in front of her to whisper something, she didn't even nod, just kept staring and thinking whatever unutterable thoughts she must be thinking. Teddy couldn't imagine. He and Tanya never had children, and given the way things turned out, that was probably for the best. Still, Teddy understood that what was happening to Claire Shadeland was every mother's worst nightmare.

Ben came over.

"They have any idea who did this?" Teddy asked.

Ben braced himself against the side of Teddy's trunk, looking like he was trying to overturn the car by sheer strength. "They think they do."

"Let me guess," Teddy said, blowing smoke out the side of his mouth. "Marvin's men."

Ben nodded without looking up.

"You called me because you figured I could confirm it one way or the other."

Ben looked up at him, hopeful and maybe a little scared.

Teddy shook his head. "I haven't seen anything suspicious lately. Certainly not Marvin's thugs."

Ben sniffed, fighting off the tears. Teddy looked away.

Ben said, "It wasn't Marvin."

"You sound pretty convinced of that."

Ben didn't answer, but Teddy could see his shoulder muscles flexing and unflexing through his shirt. The guy was wired and Teddy couldn't blame him. Maybe Shadeland *could* overturn the car by brute strength.

But Teddy said it anyway. "You're not gonna tell me it was the beast, are you?"

Ben let himself into Teddy's car.

Teddy got in behind the wheel and waited.

"Look," Ben said. "There's more to the story than what I told you."

"Shit, I could've told you that," Teddy said.

Ben seized Teddy's leg, just above the knee. Goddamn, it hurt. But Teddy wasn't about to let Ben know that. He stared back mildly at him, Ben saying, "Before I tell you this, I've got to have your word you'll keep it secret, especially from the FBI."

"They'll be here soon," Teddy said, and that was true enough. It was the reason why Teddy had busted his ass to get here so quickly after Shadeland called.

"I know you don't believe me, but what I said about the island, all of it was true. I just left out a few things."

Teddy let the rest go for now. "What kind of things?"

Ben let go of Teddy's leg. Teddy tried not to show his relief.

Ben frowned. "Your clothes are wet."

Teddy shivered a little. "I was taking a shower when you called."

"Claire killed someone."

Teddy hesitated. "Your wife killed someone?"

"Shot him in the face."

"Your wife did. One on the bench over there."

Ben nodded. "Ryan Brady. He flipped out and tried to kill Joshua right after the helicopter crash."

"You're not making any sense."

Ben looked at him pleadingly. "This is why I never told the truth. I was afraid they'd…"

"Afraid your wife would get locked up?"

Ben ran a shaking palm over his face.

"We don't have much time," Teddy said. "Anything else you wanna get off your chest?"

"Can I trust you?"

Teddy dragged on his cigarette, blew smoke out the open window. At length, he said, "I gotta live somehow, Ben. That means I've got to do right by the people who hire me, and if that means betraying someone else's confidence – the someone else being anybody not paying me – I've got to do it."

Ben's upper lip curled as if he'd tasted something sour. "You'll sell out anyone who stands between you and a paycheck."

"Hey, man, I could just lie to you and let you spill your guts and then tell it all to Christina, couldn't I? But I'm bein' straight with you, tellin' you how it really is. You wanna be pissed off at me for that, go on ahead. I'm just tryin' to save you from makin' a mistake."

Ben looked over at him, unmoved. "You're just thinking of me."

Teddy glanced at his dashboard. "Fuck you."

His cigarette had burned only halfway, but suddenly he didn't want the rest of it anymore. Heedless of the cops milling in the driveway, Teddy flicked the smoldering butt into the gravel and said, "I've got to get back to town. Sorry about your daughter." He started the engine.

"Turn off the car."

Teddy shook his head. "We're done playing."

"I'm going to cooperate with the Feds."

Teddy looked up. "How's that?"

When Shadeland didn't answer, Teddy reached down, killed the engine. "What are you talking about?"

"The first two who worked on me," Ben said. "They wanted me to go to the island with them."

"For what?"

Ben looked at him with red-rimmed eyes. "What do you mean, for what? The same thing you've been asking me. They wanted me to reconstruct what happened on the Sorrows."

Teddy stared at him, mouth open. "Man, your daughter just got abducted…your mom got…" Teddy shook his head. "What the hell you wanna…" He trailed off, eyes widening.

Shadeland said nothing, only stared back at him.

Teddy said in a wondering voice, "You think that's where she is, don't you? You think that thing took her to the Sorrows?"

Ben's arm shot out, seized Teddy's shirt. Teddy felt himself jerked over the armrest, his face inches from Ben's. But strangely he felt no alarm, no outrage at being handled so roughly. The only emotion he experienced was fascination. Staring into Ben's tear-streaked eyes, Teddy thought he had never seen such an unholy mixture of sadness and fury.

"*He took her*," Ben said, teeth bared. "*That bastard took her, and I'm going to get her back.*"

"They'll never believe you," Teddy said. "You can't go to the Feds with such a weirdass story, they'll—"

"I'm not gonna tell them about Gabriel," Ben said, releasing him.

"I'm listening."

"I'll say I had a flashback from last summer, that what happened tonight jarred my memory."

"You think they're gonna buy that?"

"No, I don't. But I think they want to get to the bottom of what happened and will be too interested in that to care about why I'm cooperating."

Teddy nodded toward Ben's wife and son. "What about those two? You just gonna leave them alone?"

"They'll go to Colorado with Claire's parents. The beast is resourceful, but it's not going to go a thousand miles to get them."

"Christina will be happy." When Ben shot him a look, Teddy explained, "About us going to the island, that is."

"Us?"

"She owns the damned place. If I know Christina, she'll bring her whole damned entourage. Bodyguards, this medium she consults, the professor."

Ben cocked an eyebrow at him.

Teddy smiled. "That's right. It'll be a regular goddamned *Gilligan's Island*. Only thing we'll be missing is that hot red-haired girl, what's her name? Ginger? We just need a Ginger, and we'll be good to go."

Ben opened the car door, swung a leg out. "The FBI lady has red hair."

Teddy snapped his fingers. "Son of a bitch, you're right!"

Shadeland climbed out, flung shut the door. Teddy watched him cross the yard, reach down and scoop up his son. Moving like a sleepwalker, Shadeland's wife followed him toward their Camry. Teddy assumed the three of them would spend the night in a hotel, and tomorrow Ben's wife and son would be on a plane to Colorado.

Teddy started his car, put it in reverse, then described a slow U-turn through the driveway. Jesus, Teddy thought, moving around the bend into the forest. What a crazy yarn. A seven-foot-tall creature straight out of Greek mythology spiriting away an infant to its island in the Pacific Ocean. Teddy shook his head. Craziest shit he ever heard.

Still, when he came to the stop sign that led to the main mountain road, Teddy put the car in Park, swiveled in his seat and peered into the back to make sure there was nothing hiding there.

When he was sure the beast wasn't hitching a ride to town with him, Teddy slid the car into gear and continued down the mountain. When he reached the bottom of the mountain road, he angled onto the rocky shoulder, shut off his engine and dialed Christina. It was Chad Wayne who answered.

"Hello?" Wayne said in a bored voice.

"Mr. Wayne, this is Alfred. Your tuxedo is ready for the Gotham City Ball."

Silence.

Teddy sighed. He usually enjoyed messing with the big moron, but tonight his heart wasn't in it. "Put Christina on."

"Who's this?"

Teddy could almost imagine Wayne frowning at the phone in his hand, the guy's deep-set eyes crossing a little. "Who the hell you think it is, dumbass? It's Brooks. Put your boss on before some drunk driver comes along and crashes into my ass."

"Are you standing in the road or something?"

Jesus. "Are you gonna put her on or not?"

"Hold on," Wayne grumbled.

There was an interminable pause. It was late, but not so late that calling her would make her mad.

"Here she is," Wayne said.

A second later, Christina Blackwood's slightly groggy voice said, "Where are you, Teddy? Nothing's wrong, I hope?"

"I'm okay, but something's come up."

Careful to leave out the gruesome details, Teddy told her what had gone down at Shadeland's ranch.

There was a gasp and then a protracted silence. Finally, he heard her whisper, "That's terrible."

"It is that," Teddy agreed. "But though I hate to say it, there's a silver lining. At least for you, there is."

"I can't imagine anything good coming from this."

"Ben's going back to the island."

"Why would he do that?"

"He thinks he'll find his daughter there."

An even longer silence. "How would his daughter end up on the Sorrows?"

"You got me," Teddy said, deciding it was best to leave out the part about the seven-foot-tall goat man. "I just know he's going there."

"You think we should go too?"

"That's your call."

He pictured her thinking it over. Chewing on a thumbnail, like she always did when she had to make a tough decision.

"What time should we leave, Teddy?"

Teddy told her as soon as possible. Christina said they'd go tomorrow afternoon, and soon after, they hung up. Teddy sat there a couple minutes wondering why he was so unsettled. It wasn't the slaughterhouse back at Shadeland's ranch, though that hadn't exactly been a cheerful episode in Teddy's evening. It wasn't going to the island tomorrow; if anything, the prospect of finally seeing the castle he'd heard so much about was a little exciting. No, it was something else… something about the phone conversation…

Then he had it. It had been Teddy's own comment, the one about the drunk driver crashing into him. He'd been joking, of course, but it was one of those ill-advised jokes, the kind that left a sour taste in your mouth after you said it. Teddy had a quick, unwelcome recollection of a night ten years ago. It had been a lot like this. Warm, sultry even. He'd been with his wife then. They'd just left Amelio's…

Teddy's fingers twitched. With a spasmodic motion, he gunned the engine into life and spun out onto the road. Enough of that shit, he decided. He had work to do. Preparations to make.

The last thing he needed was bad memories.

CHAPTER TWO

Jessie Gary didn't like it, but her partners on the case, Sean Morton and Troy Castillo, were beaming their approval at Ben Shadeland. The morning was cool and overcast, the stiff breeze adding a chill she normally didn't associate with a California July. Troy Castillo looked a little uncomfortable, his deeply tanned flesh tight with goose pimples. The pink polo shirt and white shorts had no doubt been selected to display his muscular physique, but as she watched him bounce on his heels in his ill-chosen sandals, Jessie suspected Castillo was regretting his wardrobe choices. Morton didn't seem fazed by the coolness. Ben Shadeland showed no sign of noticing the weather either, merely stood staring at them as the wind whipped his sandy brown hair off his forehead.

Jessie took a moment to size Ben up and decided that under other circumstances he'd be a ruggedly handsome guy. But the purple hollows under his blue eyes and the grizzled cheeks lent him a haggardness that made it impossible to forget what he was going through, what he must be feeling.

But it didn't make sense to her. If Ben was so determined to keep his wife and boy near him at all times – they were waiting in a car just fifty yards away – why the tickets to Denver, why the sudden desire to return to the Sorrows, the place where so much horror had occurred?

"Shouldn't take too long to set up," Castillo said.

"No more than a week," Morton agreed.

The two agents continued talking as if Ben and Jessie weren't even there.

"Today," Ben said.

Morton and Castillo stopped talking and stared at Ben. Castillo's grin faded.

"What do you mean 'today'?" Castillo asked.

"We leave today," Ben said, his expression unchanging.

Morton didn't speak, but Castillo's easy smile returned. "Come on, Ben. You're messin' with us, right?"

Ben didn't respond.

Castillo frowned. "Please tell me you're messing with us."

"Mr. Shadeland," Morton said patiently, "we're as eager for closure on this case as you are, but—"

"No you're not."

Morton fell silent. He studied Ben Shadeland as if seeing him anew. Castillo, however, was squinting at Ben as though he were a fool. A thought tickled at the back of Jessie's mind, but it was gauzy and half-formed.

"Let me see if I get your thinking," Castillo said. He ticked off his points, enumerating each on his big, tanned fingers. "We're supposed to procure clearance from our supervisors, get the go-ahead from the owner of the island, find a competent helicopter pilot who can also be trusted on this sort of mission, and pack all our things today? That's absurd."

"That's the only way I'll go with you."

Castillo glanced at Morton in exasperation.

Morton said, "What happens if we can't satisfy your terms?"

"I'll get there some other way."

Castillo gave him a challenging look. "I suppose you can fly a helicopter?"

"No," Ben said.

Morton said, "You could charter a boat, I suppose, but it would be difficult finding one on such short notice."

Castillo made a dismissive gesture. "I say we let him go. He thinks he doesn't need us, he can find his own ride."

"He could go with Christina Blackwood," Jessie said.

All three men turned to stare at her. She detected the ghost of a smile on Ben's face.

"How the hell would he—" Castillo paused. "Wait a minute, why do you think she's going to the Sorrows?"

Morton was watching her. "Mrs. Blackwood hasn't been to the island for decades."

"But she's had a detective trailing Ben for the past year," Jessie said. "She wants to know what happened to her son, and she thinks Ben can tell her."

Morton said, "You think she'd cooperate?"

"Why not?" Jessie said.

Castillo stared at her, arms akimbo. "And where the hell do you come up with something like that?"

"I phoned the Santa Rosa police this morning," Jessie explained. "They said Ben spent some time talking to a man named Teddy Brooks."

"The detective," Morton said.

"How do you guys know all this?" Castillo said. "We just got the file the other day."

"You were to read it immediately," Morton said, all trace of chumminess gone.

Castillo reddened. Jessie suppressed a grin.

Morton turned to Ben. "So we either take you there today, or you go with Christina Blackwood's party. Is that correct?"

"What do you mean her *party*?" Castillo asked, shivering. The wind had picked up and was whipping salt spray in their faces. "We still have jurisdiction."

"The deaths occurred over a year ago on a privately owned island. There's no imminent danger now, so we hardly have the right to restrict access," Morton said. "What I want to know is why Mr. Shadeland wants us to come if he already has a ride."

Castillo turned to Ben, a sardonic twist to his mouth. "How 'bout it, Shadeland? Why do you need us?"

Again, that ghost of a smile played at the corners of Ben's mouth. "Who says I need you?"

"You know," Castillo said, "I don't enjoy being made fun of." He stepped closer, jaw tight. "Is that what you're doing, Shadeland?"

"Given your line of work, I'd think you'd be able to tell," Ben answered.

Then they were standing toe-to-toe, both very broad, but Ben a good three or four inches taller. Jessie didn't know who would win in a brawl, but she suspected it would be worth watching.

"Mr. Shadeland," Jessie said. It took a full five seconds for him to turn from Castillo, but when he did look at her, she could tell she had his attention. "I think you should reconsider sending your wife and son to your in-laws'. They need you now."

In her periphery she saw Morton and Castillo exchange a look.

"I also suspect you need them," she said, but even as she said it, another idea was forming, at first inchoate, but rapidly transforming into a theory.

"Joshua and Claire leave on the 12:20 flight," Ben said. "I want to arrive at the island by four. Do we have a deal or not?"

Jessie's eyes widened. "You want us for protection."

"Protection from what?" Castillo asked.

Still looking at Ben, she said, "From whatever's on that island."

Castillo chuckled. "Nothing's on the island. Just ask the agents who had this duty before us...what were their names?"

"Moss and Early are both on medical leave," Morton said.

"Both of them are?" Castillo asked.

Morton said, "We were brought in not only for our expertise, Agent Castillo, but because there is currently no one on the case."

"So what happened to them?" Castillo said.

Ben said, "That's the first good question you've asked."

"You're using us," Jessie said wonderingly.

Ben eyed her, and she caught a flicker of what might have been guilt. But it vanished in an instant. "I'm doing what you guys have been asking me to do since last summer."

Castillo's eyes narrowed. "What do you think we're going to run into on the island?"

"I'm sure you can handle it," Ben said.

But Castillo wasn't to be put off this time. "We get there tonight, and all of a sudden you say, 'Oh, I remember now.' And then you spring some fanciful story on us, and we're meant to believe it. That about right?"

Ben seemed about to answer, but Morton broke in. "We agree to your terms."

Castillo cocked an eyebrow. "We do?"

"Meet us at Santa Rosa Memorial at two p.m. There's a helipad there."

"How do you know that?" Castillo asked in a plaintive voice. "Was that in the file too?"

"We wanted Mr. Shadeland to return to the island," Morton said. "I didn't think he'd acquiesce this quickly, but I wanted to be prepared for when he did."

"I'll be there at two," was all Ben said.

Morton wheeled and headed up the beach without a word. Ben set off toward his family.

Jessie and Castillo followed Morton. Jessie was halfway to the car when she heard Ben call, "Agent Gary."

He was coming toward her at a slow walk. She glanced back to see if Castillo or Morton had noticed, but they had their backs turned and were nearly to the car.

She hurried across the thick sand to where Ben had stopped.

"I'm not going to ask you to keep this between us because I'm sure you took some kind of oath," he said. He was talking fast, sounding distracted, but there was an intensity in his voice that drew her closer.

"Go on," she said.

"You wouldn't believe me if I explained," he said, "so I'll just skip the why. But I'm telling you, there's something horrible on that island. Worse than anything you can imagine. And it has my baby girl."

Jessie opened her mouth, but Ben hurried on.

"You better come well-armed. It probably won't do us any good, but it won't hurt to be prepared."

He took a step away from her, but paused, a deep frown creasing his forehead. He moved nearer to her again, so near she had to force herself not to take a step backward. Under his breath, he said, "Morton seems okay, but that Castillo is a prick. Believe me, I've met his kind before. Last summer, as a matter of fact." He took a breath, paused as if choosing his words carefully. "The island is like a magnifying glass, but it only magnifies the darkness in a person. The malevolence. We've all got it, but some of us are more afflicted than others. You need to steel yourself against it, because it'll work on you, too. And I'd keep a close eye on Castillo. He's exactly the kind of guy the place preys on."

And with that, Ben headed toward his car.

★   ★   ★

Teddy glanced about the vast marble foyer, more than two stories high, the Corinthian pillars broad and tall enough to prop up the Roman Coliseum. There were expensive-looking paintings on every wall, one of which he was pretty sure was a Picasso. There were freshly cut flowers sprawling out of delicate antique vases. Teddy wondered who was responsible for them. There'd be a full-time gardener, he was sure, for a place this big. He'd never asked Christina about it, but he figured the estate for fifty acres or more, a good deal of that landscaped. Stephen Blackwood, Christina's late husband and one of the corpses from last summer's bloodbath, had inherited the land, but the structure on it, the opulent pool area, the tennis courts, the twelve-car garage full of foreign sports cars – all that had been Stephen's doing. Too bad the guy had been an asshole.

Christina was currently bustling about the foyer, a cell phone in one hand and a drink in the other – Teddy couldn't tell what it was, but from the color, he doubted it was orange juice. Her trendy black skirt billowed around her whenever she turned, providing Teddy with a healthy glimpse of her legs all the way up to her thighs. Woman was fifty-one and a widow, but Teddy wasn't complaining. Her thighs were just fine by him, as were her calves, breasts and her face, the last two items he suspected of having been surgically enhanced.

Her bodyguards were lugging suitcases and boxes of books through the huge front doors, both men with muscles on their muscles. Jorge carried Mrs. Blackwood's personal items. Chad Wayne had been charged with toting the boxes of books from the library to the car.

Professor Peter Grant was on the phone too, carrying on what to Teddy sounded like a hell of a boring conversation with another professor. They were throwing around words Teddy hadn't heard since he was an undergrad at Cal-Poly; just listening to the men discuss paradigms and dichotomies made Teddy want to go to sleep. He felt bad for their students.

The doors opened again and in walked Elena Pedachenko. Teddy felt his malaise lift immediately. Seeing the way her tight little body shifted in the slinky blue sundress, Teddy felt something else lift too. Hot damn, the woman was something. Too bad she was creepy as hell and fond of freaking Teddy out. The few occasions he'd attempted to strike up a conversation with her, she'd ended up making him feel naked, and not in a good way. Naked as in showing up for school without your clothes on and having everybody laugh at you. She knew how to get to him, which was why he mostly avoided talking to her these days. But that didn't mean he couldn't look, did it? When she turned sideways, he caught a glimpse of her sensual profile, the tiny turned-up nose, the full pouty lips, the striking green eyes that might as well have been surgically removed from some cat. Teddy let his eyes crawl down the curve of neck. The silky blue fabric just nuzzled the tops of her breasts, but the sides of them were as bare as her willowy arms. He bet she had the slightest bit of roundness on that little tummy of hers. What he wouldn't give to sprinkle some sugar on it, just like that grating Def Leppard song his ex-wife had always wanted to make love to.

At the thought of Tanya, Teddy frowned. What kind of a black woman wanted to have sex to Def Leppard and Poison rather than Marvin Gaye? He once tried to play "Let's Get It On" to put her in the mood, and she laughed at him. It made Teddy so mad, he'd given it to her as hard as he could, thinking to punish her. Yet she'd enjoyed that, and after a couple minutes, he had too. That was Tanya – prudish most of the time, but when she let loose, the wilder the better. Occasionally wanting to find ways to spice things up, some of them dangerous. Some of them…

Teddy felt a chill, and his erection began to soften.

Elena Pedachenko was looking at him.

"Hey, Elena," Teddy said with what he hoped was a relaxed smile.

Her pouty lips had gathered on one side of her mouth in a look that was both rueful and coy.

"I was just thinking of someone else," Teddy explained.

"Your wife," she said.

For once, the low purr of her voice – just the merest hint of a Russian accent, so slight you wouldn't notice if you weren't listening for it – didn't make every nerve ending in his body tingle. Nope, this time the words she uttered made him want to run away screaming.

But he said, "I miss Tanya sometimes, sure."

Elena smiled her Sphinx-like smile and continued toward the arched doorway leading to the library. Teddy watched her tight butt sashaying beneath the silky sundress, but the sight did little for him.

Christina ended her call. When she pushed back her sunglasses into her thick, dark hair, the welcoming sincerity in her eyes almost pushed away the upsetting memories that had just besieged him.

Almost.

"Teddy," she said, reaching out and clasping his hands.

"How you doing, Mrs. Blackwood?"

Her face darkened in remonstrance. "How long has it been, Teddy? Almost a year? And I still have to remind you to call me Christina? 'Mrs. Blackwood' makes me feel so aged. And," she said, lowering her voice, "it reminds me I was married to Stephen. I'd rather not be reminded of that, okay?"

"Sure thing," Teddy said. Her fingers grasped his, and as he smiled back at her, he marveled at how much like a teenaged boy she made him feel. Teddy was only a couple years her junior, but whenever she turned that sweet smile on him, he felt like Dustin Hoffman in *The Graduate*. In fact, Teddy mused, now that he thought of it, she did sort of remind him of Anne Bancroft in that film. Not quite as worldly and jaded as Mrs. Robinson, but every bit as sultry.

"Anything else you need, Christina?" a male voice asked.

They both turned and saw Jorge Navarro crossing the foyer to join them. Jorge nodded at Teddy. The big Hispanic guy was polite though never overly friendly, but in Teddy's professional opinion, Jorge was a good person to have around. Teddy had a suspicion Marvin and his men were going to make a move soon, and the fact that Christina and her motley coterie of hangers-on were heading to the Sorrows for a week was a relief. At least it would delay what Teddy felt was the inevitable showdown. Marvin wanted his money; Christina refused to pay him. Men like Marvin did not relent, so Teddy figured the man and his henchmen would soon descend on the estate like the jackals they were. If that happened while Teddy was around, he hoped Jorge was on duty.

Christina smiled. "No thank you, dear. You should have some water before you dehydrate."

Jorge chuckled. "You sound like my wife. She's always on me to drink more water."

Christina opened her mouth to say more but was interrupted by the appearance of her other bodyguard.

Chad Wayne came lumbering across the foyer, the sweat streaming down his forehead in runnels. Teddy wrinkled his nose in distaste. Wayne had what Teddy thought of as weightlifter breath.

"How come we have to take all those books?" Wayne asked. He was in his late twenties, but to Teddy the guy sounded like a twelve-year-old being made to mow the lawn. Even his brown ponytail seemed fatigued.

"Peter needs them for his studies," Christina explained.

Wayne was bent over, hands on knees, panting like a water-deprived dog. "Man, those boxes are heavy."

Teddy glanced at Christina, observed the way she was looking at Jorge, and not for the first time had an idea something was going on between the two of them. And if it wasn't, it wasn't because of a lack of desire on Christina's part. Teddy supposed he understood why. Jorge's long black hair and perpetual five o'clock shadow gave him the tough, dangerous look of a hit man. Or a teacher of salsa dancing.

Christina turned as a figure approached from the library and then brightened when she saw who it was. "Elena! When did you arrive?"

The little Russian woman allowed Christina to wrap her up, Christina a full six inches taller than Elena. They embraced a moment, and before they pulled apart, Teddy saw Christina kiss Elena on the cheek. It wasn't a passionate kiss, but it wasn't a peck either.

Christina sighed happily. "Are we all here?"

"All but Dr. Grant," Jorge said.

"What time is it?" Christina asked.

Teddy said, "About five till noon."

"*There* you are," Christina said, and they all turned to see Peter Grant striding toward them. The professor was in his mid-fifties, his graying hair distinguished and neatly trimmed, his thick-framed glasses adding another thirty points to his IQ.

Grant sighed extravagantly. "Sorry about that, Christina, but Professor DeGroote is in possession of a text I desire but with which he steadfastly refuses to part."

"What sort of book?" she asked.

"Oh, just a dusty old tome in ancient Greek. It isn't essential to my studies, but it would be useful for cross-checking a few things."

Christina looked from Jorge to Chad Wayne. "You're certain you two got everything?"

Jorge nodded. Wayne massaged one beefy shoulder. "Unless you want me to grab a couple of those big bookcases from the library and haul them out to the truck too."

"That won't be necessary, Chad. And thank you for all your help today."

Wayne nodded, looking slightly mollified.

Christina looked at Jorge. "And your wife will understand your being gone this long?"

"She understands."

Teddy said, "Could I have a word, Christina?"

He moved a good distance off from the others, Christina leaning toward him solicitously. "What is it, dear?"

"I just want to prepare you," he said. "You know, in case this doesn't go according to the script."

"I don't understand."

"I told you earlier Ben had agreed to cooperate with the feds."

"Yes?"

Teddy gave her an embarrassed grin and rubbed his chin. "He said he'd cooperate with the *feds*, not necessarily with you."

Her smile faltered. "Why wouldn't he cooperate with me?"

"No reason I can think of," Teddy said, "except he hasn't yet, and I don't want you getting your hopes up."

"But if he changed his mind about talking to the agents, why wouldn't he talk to me?"

"I'm not saying he won't. I'm just saying he might not. Given what happened, he might be a bit volatile right now."

"He's met with me before," Christina went on as though speaking to herself. "He was complimentary of my son. If he and Chris got on well, why wouldn't we?"

Teddy opened his mouth to explain, but decided not to push the matter. He smiled. "I'm sure you'll get along fine, Christina."

Her forehead furrowed. "I'm more worried about you. Your other clients won't mind your being unavailable for the next week or so?"

"They can survive without me a little while," Teddy said, not feeling the need to disclose that Christina Blackwood was currently his only client.

As she and Teddy rejoined the group, Christina surveyed each of them in turn and sighed appreciatively. She reached out her hands, linked them with Peter Grant's and Elena Pedachenko's. Peter and Elena grasped Jorge's and Teddy's hands. Then, after a moment's hesitation, Chad Wayne joined hands with Jorge and Teddy to complete the circle.

Christina said, "Then let us return to the place where so much tragedy has occurred. Let's allow our collective energy to edify us against evil.

May our group spirit overcome whatever fell presence resides on the Sorrows. May love and light overcome malice and darkness."

"Let it be so," Elena said.

Peter Grant said, "Indeed."

Chad Wayne merely looked confused.

Jorge remained silent.

Teddy thought, *What in the fuck did I get myself into?*

CHAPTER THREE

Claire sat beside Ben at gate twenty-nine. Joshua lay curled in Ben's lap, sniffling. Last night Joshua had asked her what had happened to Julia and Grandma; Claire had been at a loss for what to say. Perhaps knowing Joshua would figure things out eventually, Ben said that Grandma had joined the angels but that Julia would be back home soon.

Ben had been insistent upon the fact that Julia had been abducted instead of murdered, and that morning as they were driving away from the beach and Ben's meeting with the three FBI agents, Ben had been proven correct. Samples of blood from all over the house had been tested, and none of them had matched Julia's uncommon blood type: B-negative. That wasn't, the voice on the phone had cautioned, confirmation that Julia was alive, but the news, coupled with Ben's insistence on the abduction theory, had been enough to allow Claire to hope that she might someday hold her baby girl again.

Now Joshua looked up at his dad. "Why can't you come with us?"

Ben kissed his son on the top of the head and said, "Look at me, honey."

Eyes wide and brimming with tears, Joshua sat up and looked at his father.

Ben cleared this throat. "I need to tell you something."

"It's about Julia, isn't it?"

Ben only hesitated for a fraction of an instant. "Yes, honey. Someone...took her."

"Why?"

"What I need you to know," Ben continued, "is that Daddy's going to get her back."

Joshua fell silent a moment, thinking. "The one who took her," he said.

She saw Ben tighten. "What about him?"

"Will he...hurt her?" Joshua asked.

Ben swallowed. "No."

Claire looked up to see Joshua nodding slowly, the tears finally starting to streak down his face. "I miss her, Daddy. I miss playing with her."

Now Ben's voice did grow raw. "I do too, honey. Daddy misses her too."

Joshua seemed to remember something. His hands went to his upper legs. "I don't have the boppy. What will I put her on when we get her back?"

Claire smiled through her tears.

Ben said, "You can use the boppy when we're all home."

"When will that be?"

Claire looked up at Ben. She'd been wondering the same thing. Their tickets were one-way.

She could tell by the way Ben glanced down at his lap that he was choosing his words carefully. When he finally looked up, he said, "Not long. A few days at the most."

Joshua nodded at this. Then a new fear seemed to creep into his face.

"What is it, honey?" Ben asked.

"Will you be okay?"

"Of course I will."

"What I mean is…" Joshua's breathing started to hitch.

Claire put a hand on his leg, whispered, "What is it?"

"It was the monster, wasn't it?"

Ben looked like he'd been slapped. He put out his hands, rubbed Joshua's bony little shoulders. "Joshua, he—"

"I *knew* he'd find us," Joshua said in a voice that was nearly a wail. "I knew he'd do something to hurt us again."

"Honey, he can't—"

"He did!" Joshua moaned. "He swam in the ocean and found our house. He'll get you too, Daddy. Please—"

"Now boarding gate twenty-nine," a female voice declared.

"—don't go, Daddy. He'll kill you, I know he will. He already has Julia… He can't—" Joshua's words devolved into violent sobs.

Claire rubbed the back of Joshua's head. She had no idea what to say, no idea how to take his terror away.

Ben had drawn Joshua against his chest. He was caressing his son's back, though his stubbly cheeks had gone rigid. His voice thick, Ben said, "I swear I'll be all right. Julia will be all right too."

"How do you know?"

The corded muscles in Ben's arms tensed. He took Joshua by the shoulders, peered down at him and said, "Daddy doesn't give up, does he?"

"Uh-uh," Joshua said.

"And when things were scary that other time, Daddy didn't leave you, did he?"

Joshua swallowed. He shook his head no.

"Now," Ben said, drawing closer and resting his forehead against his son's. "I don't know how…" His mouth trembled, but he cleared his throat, pushed through. "…how that *thing* found us, but I do know you'll be safe in Colorado."

"But you're going to the castle, aren't you? Back to the island?"

Ben paused, staring into his son's eyes. Then, evidently deciding it was better to tell him the truth, he said, "That's right. It's where I'll find your sister."

"And you'll come back?"

"I came back last time, didn't I?"

Joshua's little mouth worked. When he was finally able to speak, he said, "But it hurt you. You were all cut up—"

"I came back," Ben said. "I came back then, and I'm coming back this time."

"Last call," the cool female voice proclaimed. "Last call for gate twenty-nine, non-stop to Denver."

"I promise," Ben said. "I promise we'll come back."

Joshua reached into his Thomas the Tank Engine backpack and came out with something Ben had forgotten about, an eagle's talon he'd won Joshua at a fair a few months prior.

Placing the long, black talon in Ben's hand, Joshua said, "Take this with you."

Smiling, Ben kissed his son on the forehead, and when he drew away, Joshua leaned up to him with his lips puckered. Ben kissed his son on the lips, then wrapped him into his arms. For the first time in months, Claire felt as she often used to feel − that she was an outsider, a third wheel to Ben and Joshua's special bond. But the feeling disappeared as

Ben reached out for her, drew her into their little circle, and kissed her on the lips too. Then they were clenched in a long embrace, and when it ended, it felt too soon.

"Be careful," she whispered to Ben. He kissed her hard, told her he would.

The airport worker was releasing the doorstop as they approached the gate.

"Just a second," Ben called.

The worker paused and held the door open. The woman working the desk looked a little put out, but took their tickets uncomplainingly. Then Claire and Joshua were moving toward the door. Just before they passed through the doorway, Joshua stopped. He had his Thomas the Tank Engine backpack slung over one shoulder.

"I love you, Daddy."

Ben averted his eyes, and when he looked up, there was a strained smile on his face. "I love you too, buddy. Take care of Mommy, okay?"

Joshua nodded. "Okay. Don't lose my claw."

Claire watched Ben over her shoulder as she and Joshua passed inside the tunnel. Her last glimpse of her husband was brief but poignant: one hand on his hip, the other one raised in farewell. He was trying to smile but failing, and even from here she could see the tears streaking his face. Claire moved away, an unbearable wet heat in her throat. She held Joshua's hand as they moved down the tunnel toward the plane, the picture of Ben standing there etched vividly in her mind.

Claire hoped she would see her husband again. She hoped she would hold Julia again. She wanted more than anything for her little family to be together and safe again. But something more powerful than instinct told her it never would.

★   ★   ★

The helipad at Santa Rosa Memorial didn't work out. There was a single helicopter stationed there, and at around noon, a delivering mother with severe complications had to be lifelined to San Francisco, which left Morton scrambling for a replacement.

The replacement was named Gus Williams.

They'd found him, strangely enough, in the hotel phone book. A freelancer who gave rides over the coast for a hundred bucks an hour, Williams appeared oddly unimpressed with the federal agents.

"You do understand," Morton had said during their brief phone conversation, "this is a delicate situation, one that requires complete secrecy from all parties."

Jessie watched Morton's expression go from bemused to exasperated during the conversation with the pilot, and after meeting him on the scraggly strip of concrete he used for a helipad, she understood why Morton had reacted the way he had to Gus Williams.

While Jessie, Morton and Castillo bustled about making phone calls and trips back and forth from their car, Gus had merely lounged in his rusty red pick-up truck sipping from a dented silver thermos. The only time Gus had left the comfort of his truck was to open the side doors of the old chopper, one of which was apparently held shut with wire.

Now Gus was back inside his truck, some old Doobie Brothers' song wafting slowly toward them as they loaded the helicopter. Her dad had been a Doobie Brothers fan. At least she thought he had been. She hadn't seen him for thirteen years.

Morton shoved a case of supplies under the helicopter seat. "That was clever of you today, Agent Gary."

Jessie hefted her suitcase, slid it into the chopper. "What was?"

"Ingratiating yourself with Shadeland. Telling him not to leave his wife and son."

"I wasn't being clever. I was serious about him staying with his family."

Morton showed no anger, but his tone was brusque, even more businesslike than normal. "In that case it was an unnecessary risk. What if he'd taken you up on your suggestion?"

"His family would still be together."

"And we'd be no better off than our predecessors. Do you find that an acceptable trade-off?"

Morton's pale blue eyes were hard and assessing.

"I don't want to compromise our investigation, but I feel that Mr. Shadeland isn't making sound decisions at the moment."

"Of course he isn't," Morton said. "And we exploited that fact to further our cause."

Jessie searched Morton's face. "Doesn't that bother you?"

Morton seemed to consider. "Let me ask you this: Do you believe Ben Shadeland has been forthright about what happened on the Sorrows?"

"He says he doesn't remember."

"But he remembers being shot in the stomach by Ryan Brady. The pilot, incidentally, who had stolen Ben's wife, was about to take his son from him, and who – if the evidence that has come to light since then is to be believed – was carrying on an affair with Ben's teenaged stepdaughter."

Jessie said, "Maybe Ben got shot because he caught wind of the affair."

Morton watched her a moment. Then his eyes narrowed. "Care to tell me what Shadeland really said to you this morning when Agent Castillo and I were out of earshot?"

Jessie knew Morton would likely ask her about this, but the question still caught her off-guard. She forced her voice to remain steady, knowing if Morton detected a lie, there could be repercussions. "He told me we needed to be prepared."

"Yes," Morton said patiently, "that's what you told us when Castillo asked you about it driving away from the beach." He stepped closer. "What I want to know is what Shadeland *really* said. The truth, in other words."

"He said there could be trouble on the island."

Morton's stare was implacable. "What were his words?"

Jessie shrugged uncertainly. "He said there were things on the island that could be dangerous."

She was sure he'd pursue the matter further, keep battering her with that withering blue gaze of his, but Castillo bailed her out by appearing beside them.

"Old Gus looks half-asleep," Castillo said.

"I'm just glad we were able to find a replacement," Morton answered, apparently dismissing the matter. "At this late hour, I had worried we wouldn't."

Castillo threw a glance over at Gus, whose crossed legs were dangling out of his open truck window. "Hope he gets us there alive."

Morton strode back to the car. Jessie heard a ding from inside her suitcase. The text probably wasn't urgent, but perhaps she still should answer it. She dragged her suitcase from under the seat.

Castillo swung his travel bag up to the helicopter floor next to hers.

"Think it's just coffee in Gus's thermos?"

Jessie had wondered herself. "I'm sure it is."

"If it isn't, I hope you know how to swim."

Jessie said nothing.

Castillo gave her a wry sidelong grin. "You're a hell of a lot nicer to Sean than you are to me."

Jessie scooted her suitcase over, then spun it around so the open door would block Castillo. She didn't want him looking at her underwear.

Castillo chuckled. "Now I get the silent treatment, huh? That's not very nice."

"You're obnoxious," she said, unzipping the suitcase.

"Ah, she *does* talk! That's a relief. I thought you were gonna ignore me the whole helicopter ride."

Jessie reached under her makeup bag and probed for her phone.

"You don't even give a guy a chance."

"Did it ever occur to you," Jessie said, turning and letting her suitcase door flop shut on her wrists, "that you shouldn't be approaching me as a 'guy'?"

He frowned. "What's that supposed to mean?"

"You act like we're at a bar or something, like I'm some chick you're trying to pick up."

"I'm not supposed to find you attractive?"

"Of course you're not," she said, louder than she'd intended. She glanced nervously over at the car, but Morton was obscured from view by the open trunk. She hoped Morton's hearing was obscured too.

"I can't even look? I'm supposed to pretend you're some cow with bad hair and warts all over her face?"

She rounded on him. "Do you hear yourself? Everything you say concerns my face, my body...who cares if I have warts? What does it matter if I'm overweight? Do those things affect the job I do?"

He raked her body with hooded eyes, a crooked grin lifting one corner of his mouth. "You're not overweight."

"For God's sake," she said and turned back to rummage through her suitcase. She tossed open the unzipped door and began peeling back layers of clothes.

"I never figured you for a thong," Castillo said.

Open-mouthed, she seized it and stuffed it against the suitcase wall.

"What else have you got in there? Anything naughty?"

She turned and braced herself on the open helicopter doorway. "You're not the first man I've met at the Bureau who acts like I'm a potential screw instead of a colleague."

He threw up his palms, took a step back. "Hey now, I never said—"

"You didn't have to. You're vulgar, you're narcissistic and your language toward me is a dozen steps beyond inappropriate."

"Just because I'm—"

"I've tried to be patient with you. I assumed you'd take the hint. But it's becoming obvious you're unable to discern between what to say and what to keep in that lewd adolescent brain of yours."

He smiled delightedly. "Hah!"

"And I notice you don't act like this whenever Agent Morton is around. I think it's time he's aware of your behavior."

Castillo's smile evaporated, a look of real concern darkening his face. "Now look—"

"Here he is now."

Morton was treading briskly back over to the chopper. "That should about do it. I assume you have ample ammunition, Agent Gary?"

"I do," she answered, her eyes fixed on Castillo.

Morton stopped what he was doing. "Something wrong?"

"Of course not, Sean. We were just talking things over," Castillo said.

Morton nodded. "I see. And did these things pertain to Agent Gary's beauty?"

When she glanced over at Castillo, she was amused to see he was blushing, which was hard to do given his deep surfer's tan. He was sweating a little too, a first in her experience.

"Your silence is telling, Agent Castillo," Morton said. "Agent Gary and I have worked together several times, and on each occasion I have found her more than capable." He crossed his arms. "You, on the other hand, are an adequate agent who could be a good one if you approached your job with more professionalism."

Looking like a chastened school kid, Castillo shifted uncomfortably but did not answer.

"Focus," Morton said, "is paramount to what we do. Without it, we leave ourselves open to error. In our line of business, errors can lead to death." Morton cocked his head, eyed Castillo meditatively. "Have you ever been in a dangerous situation, Agent Castillo?"

Castillo's tone was sullen. "You mean have I ever been shot at?"

"That qualifies, yes."

Castillo glanced toward the interior of the helicopter, gave a little shake of the head.

Morton said, "I have. Several times. More often than I would have liked." Morton nodded toward Jessie. "On one of those occasions, Agent Gary was with me. She performed admirably. Do you understand me, Agent Castillo?"

Castillo nodded.

When Morton only persisted in staring at him, Castillo exhaled loudly, heaved a petulant shrug. "Of course I understand."

With a curt nod, Morton said, "Glad to hear it." Turning, he squinted toward the road. "And it looks as if the last member of our party has arrived."

Jessie watched Ben Shadeland's Camry roll to a stop. Checking to make sure her underwear had been properly stowed, she went over to greet him.

★   ★   ★

Ben grasped an orange-and-white seat cushion, his fingertips on the vinyl sweaty. *Almost there*, he thought. *Can't be more than ten miles away.*

Gus Williams glanced back at Morton and Jessie. "So y'all are with the government," Gus said. It was the first time the man had spoken since takeoff.

"Federal Bureau of Investigation," Castillo said. With just the right amount of superiority, Ben noticed.

Gus nodded. "You think that'll help you?"

Seated to Gus's right, Castillo turned and frowned at the pilot. "Help us do what?"

"Live," Gus said.

Castillo glanced back at Morton, whose expression could've meant anything.

"I get it," Castillo said to Gus. "You're one of those guys who believes in Roswell, that kind of stuff."

"Of course I believe in Roswell. You saying the town doesn't exist?"

Castillo's frown deepened. "You know what I mean."

"The UFOs," Gus said, nodding.

Ben glanced over, saw that Jessie and Morton were both watching Gus now.

"You think they found little green men," Castillo said, "and the government covered it all up."

"Course not," Gus said. "The government would never do anything deceitful."

Castillo's mouth spread in a contemptuous grin. "Uh-huh. We're the enemy. We're always hatching one sort of conspiracy or another in an attempt to rob people of their civil liberties."

Gus ignored Castillo's remark, glanced at Ben over his shoulder. "You're that composer, aren't you?"

Ben eyed him noncommittally. "Why?"

"You do good work," Gus said. "I liked your *House of Skin* score, but I favor your early stuff."

"*House of Skin* wasn't written under the best of circumstances."

"So I hear."

Ben gave Gus a sharp look, but the man looked as serene as ever.

"I went out there once," Gus said.

Jessie sat forward. "You've been to the Sorrows?"

Gus shook his head. "Never landed there. But I flew some folks over a few years back."

"Who?" Castillo asked.

"That's my business," Gus said.

"Hey, where do you—"

"As I was saying," Gus resumed, "this party wanted me to fly over the island. I'd never done it before, but I'd heard plenty of stories from pilots who had. They said it was like walking through a graveyard on a moonless night."

Castillo grunted. "What a load of crap."

"What happened?" Morton asked.

Gus shook his head. "Nothing."

"But you felt something," Ben said.

Gus grew very still. At length, he nodded. "You could say that."

They all waited, the silence drawing out in the chopper until Ben began to suspect Gus would leave them all hanging.

Finally, he said, "My party – it was a professor and his two assistants – they wanted me to get down close to the castle. You know, hover over it so they could snap some good pictures."

"Did you?" Jessie asked.

"I tried," Gus said. "I've been flying this bird for a good long while, and I know her better than I knew my ex-wife, which I guess isn't saying much since she cheated on me after twenty years of marriage. But as I was saying, I know how to handle this machine better than I know anything."

"Let me guess," Castillo said. "It started to do weird things, and you nearly lost control of the helicopter."

"The chopper worked just fine," Gus said. "It was myself I nearly lost control of."

"What happened?" Morton asked.

Gus gave a nervous little laugh. "I started thinking, that was all. This professor, he was a nice enough guy, and his assistants, they were just ordinary young people. They didn't do anything to me. But I started thinking about how I never went to college and how sometimes people who did had a tendency to look down on me. I started imagining that these three, the professor and his assistants, were mocking me and that maybe they deserved a good scare."

Gus uttered a mirthless laugh. "The door beside you, Agent Castillo, pops open sometimes. I can make it open just by veering sharply. The professor was sitting where you are now. I told him to take off his seatbelt so he could get something out of the back for me."

"You were going to kill him," Ben said.

"I might have," Gus agreed. "I'm not proud of it, but...as I was hovering over that island all I could think about was how condescending people often were to me, like I didn't have a brain in my head. I thought of how easy it would be to take it out on this professor. You know, make an example of him."

"So what happened?" Morton asked.

"I came to my senses is what happened," Gus said. "And thank God for that. One moment I'm getting ready to jerk the controls and send that poor man plummeting to his death, and the next I'm shaking all over and aiming the chopper back east again."

"You know," Castillo said after a few moments. "Admitting to something like that could get you into an awful lot of trouble. Especially in front of a federal agent."

Gus looked at him. "Only if that agent is a dickhead."

Castillo opened his mouth to respond, but it was too late.

The Sorrows lay before them.

As the chopper curved toward the island, Ben double-checked his seatbelt.

CHAPTER FOUR

After the helicopter touched down and they climbed out, Teddy Brooks came through the front door of the castle and met them on the lawn.

Brooks nodded at Ben, flipped his cigarette butt into the tall grass. "How's everybody doing?"

Castillo said, "I don't know who you are or how you—"

"We came in the *Blackie*, Agent Castillo. Ain't that a hell of a name for a yacht? Christina's husband apparently didn't worry about political correctness."

Morton appraised the man coolly. Brooks noticed Morton's gaze and extended a hand. "Name's Teddy Brooks. You must be Agent Morton."

"You seem to know a good deal about us," Morton said. "Your friends in Los Angeles must still hold you in high regard."

Brooks shrugged. "We keep in touch."

"Where are the others?" Ben asked.

Castillo glowered at him. "It doesn't matter where they are, what matters is where they're going." He turned to Brooks. "You've got ten minutes to get off this island."

Teddy chuckled down at his cordovan loafers. "You're going to have a hard time gettin' rid of this party."

"I've got the right of the United States Government, buddy. I say they leave, you can bet your ass they're gonna leave."

Morton sighed. "How many are there?"

"Counting you four and excluding your helicopter pilot," Brooks said, "there are ten people on the Sorrows."

"That's far too many," Morton said.

"Don't worry," Ben said. "The island has a way of thinning things out."

They entered the castle. Inside the foyer Ben peered through the arched doorway to the great hall. It was exactly as Ben remembered it. The hand-hewn rafters lined a ceiling that hovered twenty-five feet above the stone floor. To the far left of the room he glimpsed the capacious fireplace, the one with the snarling lions carved into the stone mantle.

The agents went through the doorway, but Ben had no desire to reacquaint himself with the great hall. What he wanted was to the immediate right.

"Where you goin', man?" Teddy asked.

"Down here," Ben answered without a backward glance.

Ben flicked on the stairwell light, just a dim yellow bulb that brought with it a flood of grotesque memories. His best friend Eddie going insane and shoving Ben down the stairs. The bestial sounds emanating from the sub-basement. Then...

Ben shivered, but started down anyway.

Teddy clomped down the stairs behind him. "Care to explain to me what we'll find down here?"

"Julia."

"You're kiddin', right?"

Ben didn't answer, only continued his descent.

Teddy's voice was solemn. "I guess I didn't realize how serious you were until now."

"You have a gun?" Ben asked.

"Do you?"

Ben didn't see the need to answer. The ankle holster he'd purchased in Santa Rosa felt small and unreassuring, the Ruger it contained only slightly more substantial. Though the main odors in the ancient, echoey stairwell were damp concrete and a faint tinge of sea salt, beneath those Ben fancied he could detect a gamey undercurrent, the musky smell of an animal den. Or perhaps the stink of a long-neglected kennel, a cage in which the mongrels had resorted to eating one another for survival until only the most vicious and bloodthirsty one remained.

A whisper of fear tickled his spine.

"Man, how far down these steps go?" Teddy called.

Ben jumped at the sound of Teddy's voice and compressed his lips. *Don't alert it to our presence*, he wanted to hiss. *Just keep your mouth shut and be ready for anything.*

But he knew such demands would be received in the same manner

Ben's other declarations had. Teddy Brooks no more believed there was a monster under the castle than he believed in the Easter Bunny. Nothing Ben could say would persuade him otherwise. When they did encounter the beast, Brooks would either stand with him or turn tail and run.

"What are you doing down there?" a voice blared down at them, shattering the preternatural stillness of the stairwell.

It had been Castillo who'd shouted. *Big surprise*, Ben thought. The guy had the tact of a sledgehammer.

The agents were hastening down the steps toward them. Teddy favored Ben with a sheepish grin. "Damn near shat myself. I didn't realize how scared I was."

"You're smart to be scared," Ben said.

Teddy's grin faded. Then the agents were beside them.

"What do you think you'll find down here?" Morton asked Ben.

Before Ben could respond, Jessie said, "His daughter."

Morton's eyebrows went up. "Is this part of what he told you this morning?"

"I didn't tell her much of anything, except to be on her guard," Ben said. "You're too pragmatic to believe this, Morton, but what Gus said was spot-on. The Sorrows can affect people."

Morton studied him. "How so?"

Ben started down the steps. "You're aware of the island's history?"

"I know what happened to Agents Moss and Early, if that's the history to which you're referring," Morton said. "And, of course, the nebulous events of last summer."

"Hold on," Jessie said.

Ben turned and glanced up at her.

"It's not lighted down there, is it?" she said.

Ben felt a smile forming. "You're right. I guess I was in so much of a hurry..."

He pushed past Castillo and started up after Jessie.

Castillo said, "Are we going down there or not?"

"Not without flashlights," Morton said.

As Ben pulled even with Agent Gary, he said, "I can't believe I forgot. It's pitch black inside the pit."

"You really think your baby's down there?"

They reached the basement door. Hand poised on the handle, Ben turned to her. "Just make sure Castillo is careful with his gun. I don't want him shooting Julia."

He led her back out to the helicopter.

Gus looked up at them as they approached. "You gonna get your stuff out of here so I can take off?"

"Give us a few minutes," Ben said, retrieving the two flashlights he'd packed.

"No electricity in the castle?"

"No lights in the basement," Jessie said.

She rummaged through one of the supply boxes until she found a pair of big black Maglites.

"No lights," Gus mused, "but maybe quite a few other things."

Ben and Jessie stared at him.

Gus looked away, perhaps trying to play it off. But the man's deeply seamed face betrayed his nervousness. "It's just a feeling I get," he said.

Ben nodded. "I know the feeling."

Gus looked at him.

"Take care of yourself," Ben said, and headed back to the castle.

CHAPTER FIVE

"What are they doing?" Elena asked.

"Getting flashlights," Christina answered.

They stood before one of the casement windows in the master suite. Christina assumed Jorge and the rest were settling into their respective rooms. Chad Wayne was likely still convalescing from a nasty bout of seasickness.

Leaving Christina with Elena Pedachenko.

Watching Ben Shadeland and the female agent moving away from the helicopter, Christina said, "I'm thinking of renaming the yacht. The *Blackie* was my husband's idea."

"Why not call it the *Rosa*?"

Christina's stomach dropped. "Why did you say that?"

"It just came to me," Elena said.

"I don't believe you."

"You can choose not to."

"Well, I don't," Christina said. She'd intended her tone to be authoritative, but instead it came out sounding peevish.

Elena moved away from the window. Christina watched her, the way the afternoon sun glowed on her exposed back, the sensuous shoulder blades. "You should relax, Mrs. Blackwood. It isn't good for you to be so uptight."

Christina chewed the inside of her mouth. "Why do you keep referring to me as Mrs.? Stephen's been dead for a year."

Elena shrugged. "That's how you introduced yourself when you enlisted my help."

Christina sighed, moved over to her suitcase. She began the job of unpacking. "That was three months ago. I would think you'd be a bit more familiar by now."

Elena's voice was low and soft. "Would you like me to be more familiar?"

Christina's fingers paused on an article of clothing. Glancing down she realized it was a negligee she hadn't worn since she and Stephen had been intimate. How long ago was that? Two years? Longer? She wrested it from the suitcase, turned, and stuffed it roughly into a dresser drawer.

"Why are you so afraid?" Elena asked.

Christina paused, wondering the same thing herself. After all, it wasn't even night yet. She had Jorge and Chad to guard her, not to mention the federal agents. Why she should be so skittish—

How about the Rosa*?*

Forcing her hands to remain steady, Christina took a small stack of clothes and deposited them in the top drawer of the ornate mahogany armoire.

Returning to the suitcase, she said, "How does it work, Elena?"

Elena was poised at the foot of the four-poster bed, one finger tracing a delicate line over the curved footboard. "You always ask about that."

"That's because you've never told me."

"It just is," Elena said. "It's been this way since I was a child in Belarus."

"Then tell me about that."

"The first time it happened I was playing in our house. It was an old house. A farmhouse. My mother had recently purchased it. It had a stream behind it and a forest. There was a well."

Christina found the girl's voice soothing. The medium was twenty-four, but despite her small frame and her playfulness, there dwelt something much older in her voice, something knowing. It unnerved Christina sometimes, but now, listening to the lilting cadences of Elena's voice, she found the soft purr taking some of the edge off her nerves.

"I enjoyed playing there," Elena said. "I would hide in the closets with my little brother, and we had much fun."

"How old were you?"

"Abraham was only three. I was five. We were inseparable." Elena caressed the smooth cherry footboard and smiled wistfully. "We had many happy times in the house, yet we always avoided the well."

"Someone died there," Christina guessed.

Elena gave her a sad smile. "It's never that simple. I pick up impressions, Christina. Just impressions." The smile went away. "I picked up impressions when I ventured near that well."

"Impressions of what?"

Elena frowned. "There was shouting. A brutish male voice. It was coarse. Harsh. Made cruel by alcohol. The voice laughed, but it was not a kind laugh. It was full of violence. Full of rage."

Christina reached into her suitcase, encountered the black rectangular box containing her vibrator. Blushing, she wrapped a shirt around it, transferred it to the armoire.

Elena seemed not to notice. "I didn't mention it to my mother that first summer, but the next summer I did. I was six by then and she considered me old enough to draw water from the well. She told me to do so, and I refused. She threatened to punish me, and though I was frightened – my mother was a gentle woman, and I was seldom reprimanded – I remained firm. She demanded I tell her why I was being insolent. I told her there was a hairy man who would hold me over the well. I was afraid he would drop me into its freezing darkness. I wept and pleaded with my mother, but after a time I noticed she was no longer scowling at me. She had a hand to her throat, massaging it. Her face had gone pale.

"'What did I say, Mother?' I asked her. 'Why do you look at me that way?'

"My mother said nothing at first, but she did not persist in making me fill the pail. It was late that night, after Abraham was asleep, that she knelt beside my bed. She whispered because Abraham and I slept in the same small bed. She said, 'You must not speak of the well anymore. There is nothing to fear there.'

"'But the man,' I insisted.

"'There is no man,' my mother said firmly. 'Not anymore. There was once a man who lived here with his wife. His name was Nestor. They lived here for many years. No one visited them because of the kind of man Nestor was. They knew of his habits in town because he would sometimes visit there. But only for drink and sometimes to spend his money at the brothel. Nestor had a way of punishing his wife for her misdeeds. It could be for something she had said. Most of the time it was for something she did not do. Something he had made up. This all came to me from his wife's sister. She was the only one his wife told of his habits.'"

Christina moved over to the bed, waited for Elena to continue. The medium's eyes were shining with a weird, fervent light.

Elena nodded. "Many years later, my mother explained it in more explicit terms. Nestor would hold his wife over the well and make her admit to cheating on him. He would call her a whore and make her confess that she had lain with other men. He would make her wallow in the mud and snort like a pig. He would tell her she was a pig and that she wasn't fit to mate with a pig. He would tell her to slather herself in mud, to put mud in her…" Elena broke off, shivering. "Mother told me that Nestor's wife would comply because of her fear of being dropped into the well. And because she had come to feel she deserved this treatment."

Christina considered this. She asked, "Did he hit her?"

"Not at the well. He scarcely touched her at the well. He did his hitting in the house, in the bedroom, the kitchen. He often used a stout piece of wood."

"And did you feel anything in those places?"

Eyes downcast, Elena shook her head.

"Then I'm not sure I understand."

Elena's green eyes rose to meet Christina's. "Do you believe that words can do injury?"

Christina thought of Stephen Blackwood, who had never laid a hand on her – except for that night here in Castle Blackwood; she hurried away from the memory with an inward shudder – but his sarcasm, his constant and deeply cutting remarks…

"Yes," Christina said. "I believe that very much."

Elena held her gaze a long moment, then moved toward the door.

"You're going?" Christina asked.

Elena opened the door, half turned, then regarded her with a look Christina could return only with difficulty. "Nestor's words are what killed her. Not the club."

★   ★   ★

They got back to the stairwell and Jessie saw the others waiting for them. Ben, Brooks and Castillo started down. Morton had held back, Jessie assumed for good reason. She stood with him, watching the others in the sickly glow of the lone yellow bulb. It blinked and flickered like it might go out at any time.

Morton said, "I don't like bringing the detective down here."

"Tell him to go back up."

Morton nodded. "I might yet."

"Why wait?"

Morton pursed his lips a moment, thinking. "Ben trusts him. God knows why, but he trusts him. Ben trusts you too."

Jessie opened her mouth to protest.

"We need as much trust as we can garner," Morton continued. "Everyone who's spoken to Ben this past year has either attempted to strong-arm him or coddle him. Neither approach has proven effective."

Jessie frowned. "So you want me to string him along? Act like I believe his story?"

Morton looked embarrassed. "Agent Gary. I wouldn't dare tell you what or what not to do. I trust your judgment. But if Ben trusts you, he's far likelier to talk, is he not?"

"I suppose so."

"So you can banish whatever worries you have about my directives. I would no more ask you to mislead him than I'd ask you to use your feminine wiles on him."

She nodded, then thought of something. "I forgot to ask. We're assigned to Ben, but who's watching Marvin Irvin? We think his men are the ones who abducted Julia, right?"

"Huffer and McWilliams. They're back at Marvin's place, staking it out."

Jessie knew Jon McWilliams. Short, handsome, nice eyes. He seemed cautious, and that was good. But the thought of Jacob Huffer, one of the most cocksure agents she knew, standing guard at Marvin Irvin's house filled her with an icy dread. The guy practically lived for conflict, and if none of Marvin's men moved first, chances were strong Huffer would goad them into it.

Morton seemed to read her thoughts. "I don't like it either. McWilliams is a good agent, but Huffer is a bit of a maverick. Even more than Castillo." Morton nodded at Castillo, who was sweeping his flashlight back and forth through the murk of the stairwell. The steps seemed to go on forever. Morton said, "At least Castillo possesses a healthy fear of death."

Jessie grunted. "He doesn't show it."

"He conceals it well. But that's from years of practice. Look closely into his eyes sometime, Agent Gary. You'll see the terror hiding there."

Jessie and Morton continued the descent until they saw Ben, Brooks and Castillo ranged outside a large wooden door that had gone colorless with age.

When Jessie and Morton reached them, Morton asked, "Where does this lead?"

Ben said, "Not sure. But there's no light at all in there, and it's going to smell like an animal den."

Castillo glowered at Ben. "For not remembering anything about what happened here, you sure have a hell of a memory for this castle."

Ben put his fingers around the handle, glanced at Morton. "You ready?"

Morton nodded.

Ben looked at Jessie. "You?"

Jessie said she was.

Ben pushed down hard on the iron handle. Even with his prodigious strength, he had to lean down on it, the tendons of his neck straining, before there finally came a grinding noise and the handle scraped downward. The skin of his arms and face scrimmed with sweat, Ben hauled back on the wooden door, and the whole thing swung inward.

The stench was eye watering.

The back of his wrist shoved under his nose, Castillo said, "What the hell is this?"

Breathing through her mouth, Jessie answered, "A smell like an animal den."

Castillo looked at her with a mingling of annoyance and apprehension. "What kind of animal?"

She glanced at Ben for an answer, but he was already stepping into the veil of shadow.

Jessie and Morton looked at each other.

"Come on then," Morton said.

They followed Ben Shadeland into the darkness.

CHAPTER SIX

Griffin Toomey peered out the displaced curtain beside Marvin's front door; the raucous sound of Jim Morrison singing "Roadhouse Blues" made his ears hurt. Marvin's house smelled of pot, Indian food and something even less pleasant. Something that reminded him of incense and flyblown meat. He'd glanced in the living room earlier, where Nicky had one of his weird drug friends laid out naked on the floor. Flat-chested, her stringy blonde hair like excelsior, the girl scarcely looked eighteen. Nicky had been screwing her, both of them zoned out of their minds on heroin and pot, with Ray Rubio watching. Rubio was smoking a cigar, but from the way Rubio acted, Griffin suspected he had been dosing on heroin too. Nicky and the girl both had zombie stares and moved like people underwater, but Rubio was glitter-eyed and restive. In other words, even scarier than usual.

Griffin worried they were going to kill the girl. A little while ago he'd heard her shout something in protest, and that had been followed by a disquieting smacking sound. Then there were lower-pitched thumping sounds. Griffin had tiptoed over and cast a fleeting glance around the corner to find Nicky again riding her. She looked alive, but there was a glistening trail of blood seeping out of her ear. Ray Rubio watched the sex show, impassive.

Yes, Griffin was worried they'd kill the girl, but he was even more afraid of Marvin coming home. According to Jim Bullington, the boss didn't know Nicky was into drugs again – he'd been arrested on possession and driving under the influence once before – and if Marvin arrived home now and found his son flying high and nailing some bleeding-from-the-ear skank, he might get mad. He might get very mad.

And he might blame Griffin.

Blotting out the thought, he examined the FBI agent through the window, the agent who hadn't left his post in over an hour.

Faintly, Griffin heard Rubio call, "They still there?"

"One of them is."

"What's he doing?"

"He got into it with his partner earlier," Griffin explained, his eyes never leaving the stocky FBI agent who leaned against the silver sedan. "The short one got mad at the bigger one and walked away."

Rubio materialized beside Griffin and shoved him aside. "I asked what the pig was doing now." Rubio peered out the window, making no effort at inconspicuousness.

"What the hell is that?" Rubio asked.

Griffin watched the agent pushing buttons on some small device, probably an iPhone or something like it, sometimes shaking the device, staring intently at it, then either grinning or tossing back his head in disgust. "I think he's playing a game."

"You bet he is," Rubio said in his raspy voice. "Bastard's toying with us."

"That's not what I meant. I meant he's playing a game on that—" Griffin started to say, but Rubio was already opening the door and shouldering past him. Griffin followed, scared to death of what was about to happen, but on some level grateful to be out of the house. Nicky and his unpredictability...Griffin remembered the smacking and thumping sounds from earlier, Nicky likely beating on the stringy-haired girl. The guy was an animal. Marvin, he was scary too, but at least most of the time you could guess what he was going to do, or at least afterward work through his logic. With Nicky there was no logic, only a brooding silence sometimes broken by eruptions of savage violence.

Then there was Rubio...

Actually, as Griffin followed Rubio up the walk, through the driveway and toward the street, he realized no one in the outfit scared him more than Ray Rubio. Bullington was huge and remorseless, but Griffin had never observed him inflicting pain just for the sake of doing it.

Rubio was batshit crazy.

Rubio stalked across the road, no center line but plenty wide, the houses close enough to call it a neighborhood but spaced far enough to provide the illusion of isolation. On the far side of the road Griffin saw the fed leaning against his car, the silver paint in stark contrast to the wooded rise that began just beyond the dusty shoulder of the road.

There was exposed dirt from rain and erosion at the base of the hill, but down the road a ways, where the road serpentined gradually lower, the forest sloped even more dramatically so the road and the trees were on an even plane. Griffin saw a trail there, maybe forty feet away, and wondered where the other agent had gone. Up that trail, down the curving road for an afternoon walk, or maybe somewhere on Marvin's property where he could peer in the side and back windows? The thought filled Griffin's belly with cold lead. He was the assigned lookout, him and Bullington both. If that other fed, the short one with the dark complexion, made his way around the house, he might get bold enough to spy at Nicky through the window, and once he beheld that scene they were all screwed: The Doors piping through the expensive sound system; the flat-chested girl with the pale, crinkly hair and the bloody ear; the water bong positioned right beside the couch where anybody could see it; the hypodermic needles; the baggie of white powder.

Shit. Griffin had to get back inside.

But before he could, Rubio said, "You lookin' for somebody?"

The stocky agent frowned in concentration, but did not look up from his mobile device. In the silence Griffin found himself contemplating the numbers of the situation. There were two feds, and there were four of Marvin's men. He supposed it was good to be in the majority, but neither two nor four were numbers he cared for much.

Griffin was a few feet behind Ray Rubio, technically standing in the road, but though he couldn't see Rubio's face, he could see well enough the way the broad back beneath the navy blue windbreaker expanded as Rubio puffed himself up. It reminded Griffin of the hood of a king cobra. A king cobra with a raspy voice and an affinity for shearing guys' noses off with a mandolin slicer.

"Maybe you don't hear so good. I asked you a question."

"Just a second," the agent said without taking his eyes off the game. He was shaking the iPhone, his tongue poking out of the side of his mouth in concentration. The agent had on a silly-looking white hat with blue little sailboats on it and a royal-blue-and-white Hawaiian shirt. He was a big guy, six feet tall and very broad, and though there was a softness about his sloping shoulders, Griffin also got the impression the man possessed a good deal of physical strength.

The agent stopped shaking the phone, stared at it a moment, then tossed back his head and groaned. "Doesn't that beat all?" he said, grinning sardonically at Rubio. "The machine won again."

Rubio didn't speak, which Griffin took for a very bad sign. When Rubio was talking to you in that raspy voice, you wished he'd stop talking. But when he just stood there and looked at you with those coal-black eyes, you wished you were anywhere else in the world.

The agent smiled at Rubio as if they were old pals. "You believe that?" the agent said. "That's three out of the last four this damned thing has beaten me."

When Rubio continued to glower at the agent in ominous silence, the agent favored Griffin with a sheepish grin. "I always play Yahtzee when I'm waiting. It's a weakness I have. My mom and dad used to make us kids play it every Saturday night, but we secretly enjoyed it. My dad usually beat us all because he had the best luck."

In the silence that followed, Griffin glanced from the agent to Rubio and back to the agent. To break the terrible quiet, Griffin asked, "What are you doing here?"

The agent's eyebrows went up and he nodded as if impressed. "Ahh, I wondered when one of you would ask me that. It turns out I'm waiting for your boss, a Mr. Marvin Irvin? I'd like to talk to him about a couple things."

Griffin swallowed.

He could still smell marijuana. He wondered if the agent smelled it.

"Marvin's not here," Rubio said.

"Yeah, I know that," the agent said. "But I figured I wait here long enough…" He smiled, showing them big white teeth.

Rubio's voice was gruffer than usual. "What if Marvin don't want to see you?"

"Oh, he will." The agent extended his hand. "I'm Jacob Huffer," he said. "And you guys are Griffin Toomey and Raymond Rubio." When Rubio didn't shake, Huffer dropped his hand, unabashed. "How you doin', Ray?" he said in what Griffin assumed was supposed to be a parody of a New York accent.

Rubio stared at Jacob Huffer. There was a pulsing twitch in Rubio's left temple.

Oh crap, Griffin thought. He had moved abreast of Rubio and could now see the soulless void in his eyes. The deadness in Rubio's expression chilled Griffin to the marrow, but if the agent noticed it he wasn't letting on. Or, Griffin realized with escalating terror, the agent saw what was in Rubio's face and was actually daring the big man to do something. *Oh hell*, Griffin thought. *Please don't push him. You don't know what he can do.*

But Huffer said, "That bother you, Raymond? My talking like that? It was actually an homage to my favorite television show. You ever watch *Friends*, Raymond? Or does your sense of humor not turn that way? Maybe you prefer that sicko shit. Stuff about serial killers. *Dexter. Cold Case Files. The Walking Dead* maybe. I'd say *The Twilight Zone*, but that'd take too much imagination."

Rubio's hand moved to his hip.

Jacob Huffer swept back his shirt and brought his fingers to rest on the holster of what to Griffin looked like one hell of a huge gun. That had been the reason, he realized now, for the ridiculous Hawaiian shirt.

"I'd drop that hand if I were you, Raymond. This is a .38, and I suspect you know what kind of a hole it would put in that polyester windbreaker of yours."

Rubio's hand didn't drop. Neither man moved.

"You wanna see if I'll do it?" Huffer asked, looking delighted. "I'm happy to shoot you, Raymond. I know about the stuff you've done. Things so sick and depraved they'd make Ted Bundy cringe. And you know what, Raymond—"

A look of flabbergasted surprise spread over Jacob Huffer's face. He actually smacked his forehead with an open palm. "Shit, man, I can't believe I didn't think of it earlier. Your favorite show is *Everybody Loves Raymond*, right? I mean, it's too perfect not to be true."

Rubio's left hand, hanging at his side, was bunching into a fist. His right hand, the one near his hip pocket, remained poised where it was.

Huffer kept on. "Romano, Rubio. The names are damn near the same. I bet you make a mean pasta, don't you, Raymond?"

Rubio's fingers inched toward the side of his sweatpants. Huffer's eyes widened a fraction, his own fingers closing on the handle of his gun. "You don't want holes in your chest, I'd drop that hand right now, Raymond."

No one spoke for a long moment. No one moved. Griffin didn't breathe.

Then two things happened simultaneously. Down the road a ways, the other agent, the one Griffin had totally forgotten about, appeared at the mouth of the trail. What he'd been doing, Griffin had no idea, but in a matter of milliseconds his expression changed from surprise to steely awareness. He was already coming toward them, a hand closing on what Griffin was sure was the butt of a handgun, the other hand held up in warning.

The other thing that happened was the appearance of a female jogger a good way down the road. The agent approaching them was now forty feet away and closing. The lady jogger − she was probably in her late forties but looked like she was in great shape − was twice that distance away, but she had her head down, fiddling with something attached to her headphones. She had on a bright orange sports bra and black spandex shorts, and though she was chugging uphill, she was making great time.

Huffer still sounded like he was entertaining a group of partygoers with a great story. "Hey, McWilliams! Come on over and meet my buddies. Griffin here's scared shitless, but Ray Romano wants to rumble."

Rubio's hand closed on whatever was in his hip pocket; Griffin was shielded from it, but he assumed it was the same hand cannon he always carried, the Dirty Harry Callahan special, the Magnum something or other.

"*Hands in the air,*" McWilliams shouted. In slow motion Griffin glanced at the woman jogger, sixty feet away now. McWilliams was closer. McWilliams's gun was out and pointing at Rubio, who still hadn't moved. When McWilliams saw Griffin glance at the lady jogger, McWilliams hunched his shoulders as if expecting to be attacked and cast a look behind him. McWilliams halted, threw a hand up at the woman to grab her attention, and shouted, "Get on the ground!" but the lady was still screwing with the iPod or whatever the hell she was listening to.

Then a shot so loud it made Griffin's bladder let go erupted nearby. The one named McWilliams pinwheeled his arms and jerked sideways, and before he went down Griffin caught a glimpse of a huge black hole just beneath his right armpit. He struck the dusty shoulder and arched his back in an ecstasy of pain.

The gunshot had finally gotten the attention of the female jogger, who was standing only ten or so feet away from the writhing federal agent, whose wound was now gushing blood the color of cranberries into the dust. Her palms went to her cheeks in a gesture straight out of some comic book, her mouth a trembling oval. She had dark reddish hair and a lot of makeup – maybe some actress trying to keep in shape between gigs. The jogger gaped at McWilliams a moment; then, when the grisly sight of the dying agent apparently became too much for her, she switched her gaze to the three men standing by the silver car. Huffer finally had his gun out, but he was pointing it at something caddycorner from the lady.

Griffin and the lady watched in horrified silence as Rubio finally produced the object from his hip pocket, which was a nasty looking knife, the kind Griffin imagined you'd use to dress a deer. Rubio took a step forward, raised the enormous knife across his body, and then tore loose with a backhanded slash that unzipped Jacob Huffer's throat. The blade sliced the agent so deep and wide that Huffer's neck looked like a hinged box, only the contents of the box were spraying out in all directions, the hot blood showering Rubio's maniacally grinning face. Huffer pirouetted toward the sedan, going with the momentum of Rubio's ferocious stroke, and after painting the side of the car with gore, Huffer completed his spin and leaned backward against the trunk.

With grim deliberateness, Rubio moved over so he was face to face with Huffer again. "You wanna make jokes about my name some more, you grinning pussy? You *stupid…*" He pumped the knife into Huffer's gut. "*…fucking…*" He yanked the blade upward, ripping through Huffer's flesh and entrails. "*…pig!*" The blade had reached Huffer's sternum and lodged there, but Rubio wasn't content. The agent's unseeing eyes gaped at Rubio as Rubio placed his free hand on Huffer's forehead, bent him backward across the trunk until the base of his skull made contact with the once-silver paint.

The lady jogger moaned, uttered garbled oaths.

Bent backward that way, the throat wound Rubio had inflicted was now splitting open to reveal the agent's severed windpipe, the meaty cartilage of his ruptured throat. Blood spurted over Rubio, but the big man scarcely seemed to notice. He was sawing through Huffer's sternum, finally dislodging his buck knife so he could continue his vertical incision through the man's torso. Rubio was a scarlet hulk now, his wide moonface painted red, his navy blue suit sodden and black.

Rubio might have gone on sawing and hacking all day had Jim Bullington not emerged from the bushes at the southern end of Marvin's property. Bullington had his gun out, his face as expressionless as ever.

Griffin finally realized where the hole in McWilliams's armpit had come from.

As if remembering the other agent too, Rubio disregarded the now moveless form of Jacob Huffer and strode over to where McWilliams lay. Bullington looked on from the middle of the road, throwing occasional glances right and left to see if a car was coming.

The lady jogger stared at Rubio in horror as he approached, the gore-streaked buck knife gripped in one hand. McWilliams lay gasping a mere six feet away from the jogger, and as Rubio loomed over the fallen agent, Griffin heard her quietly sobbing. A black puddle of blood surrounded the dying man.

Rubio stood over McWilliams a moment.

The he plunged the knife into McWilliams's left eye and twisted. The sight of brackish-looking blood bubbling up around the revolving knife was grotesque, but it was the sound of the blade scraping bone that made Griffin retch. He puked all over the road, no longer able to bear the sight of Rubio's butchery.

When he finally finished puking, he stood up, lightheaded. He noted that Bullington was turned away, facing Marvin's house. For a second Griffin thought Bullington had finally reached his limit for carnage, but then he saw Nicky, a silky black-and-red robe hanging loosely on his shoulders, emerging from the sidewalk. He didn't appear at all surprised by the ghastly scene that greeted him. The jogger's paralysis seemed finally to be shattering, her sculpted legs taking jerky backward steps away from Rubio.

Rubio was still immersed in carving up McWilliams's face. He'd connected the bloody craters where the agent's eyes had been via a deep slash across the bridge of his nose, giving the man the appearance of having donned a messy pair of crimson spectacles.

When the lady jogger bolted, she initially started off in the direction she had come, no doubt intending to get the hell home so she could call the police. But Jim Bullington was hulking in the middle of the road, and though he made no move toward her, the sight of him was enough to make her shriek and veer toward the shoulder.

"Hey, lady!" Rubio called in a merry voice. "Come here and dance with me!"

She shrieked again and scampered toward the path leading into the woods.

"Hey, come back!" Rubio said, laughing and starting after her.

His face as bereft of emotion as Rubio's was full of sadistic mirth, Nicky ambled toward them, the robe coming open to reveal his naked body beneath.

The jogger made her stumbling way up the incline, her terror making her clumsy. Moving fast for such a big man, Rubio clambered up the incline after her, and then both were gone into the thick forest. Nicky headed that way too, seemingly in no hurry.

Moments later, the screams began.

Griffin sank to the road, not caring that he was sitting in his own disgorged lunch.

Rubio's laughter merged with the lady jogger's screams. Nicky disappeared into the woods. Smacking sounds could be heard from the sheltering forest, occasional pleas. Soon, the only things Griffin could hear were the noises Rubio and Nicky made.

Griffin sank down with his head on his forearm. He realized he was weeping.

CHAPTER SEVEN

With Ben in the lead, they ventured into the lightless pit, which was about twenty feet wide and slightly longer than that. Ben kept his flashlight aimed at the ground ahead. He was scared, but the fear wasn't as powerful as his desire to get Julia back.

"You guys see anything?" Castillo asked, his voice reed-thin.

"Not yet," Jessie answered.

"Man, what's making that smell?"

"Quiet, Agent Castillo." That had been Morton, who seemed tense but very much in control of his fear. Jessie was doing fine as well. Brooks had grown uncharacteristically closemouthed.

They neared the far end of the room. Ben scanned the walls for some sort of lever. He'd thought it over many times and was convinced there must be some sort of secret door here.

He examined the walls, his breath growing thinner. It had been how long since Gabriel had disappeared with Julia last night? Twenty hours? Julia wouldn't have had milk or anything else in that time, which meant she would be ravenous. Ben jerked his flashlight beam left and right, aimed it at the floor. Nothing. He inspected the ceiling. Nothing there either. What the hell?

"It appears whatever you're looking for is gone," Morton said.

"Can't be," Ben muttered. Turning, Ben pushed past Brooks and Morton. He would walk the perimeter, slowly inspecting the walls until he returned to this spot. If that didn't work, he'd start moving about the room's interior, probing for an opening of some kind. Ben touched the wall, began moving slowly along it, painting the ancient concrete with bright swaths of light.

"Mr. Shadeland," Morton said.

The tips of Ben's fingers scraped over the scabrous surface, the moisture down here making the concrete cool to the touch, almost frigid. His lips pressed together in concentration, Ben reached the corner and continued his inspection. Nothing yet. Nothing but wall, ceiling and floor. No secret passageways.

There has to be a passage.

"Let's get the hell out of here," Castillo said.

"Be calm," Jessie said.

"To hell with calm, I want out of this place."

"Agent Castillo," Morton said.

Ben continued to shine his light along the wall. He crouched, checked the area near the floor. Still nothing.

"Tell you the truth," Brooks said, "I sort of agree with Castillo on this one. This place ain't right."

"It's just a basement," Jessie said, but there was a tightness in her voice that belied her words.

Ben reached the next wall, the one containing the door through which they'd come. There *had* to be another way...

There isn't, a voice declared. *So look somewhere else. You've got time.*

Bullshit! he thought, teeth grinding together. *Julia's been with the beast for a day already. No milk, no warmth—*

"Mr. Shadeland," Morton said. "I think it's best we return to the main level. There's still the matter of the other party. We need to set parameters, insure everyone's safety. We need to—"

Ben rounded on him. "We need to get my daughter back."

Morton stared at him.

"She's on this island," Ben growled. "The beast has her."

Morton's eyes flitted toward Jessie, then came to rest on Ben again. "Mr. Shadeland, there's no one on this island but us and the rest of Mr. Brooks's party."

"Ain't my party," Brooks muttered.

Ben moved closer to Morton. "Your people performed forensics on my house last night, right?"

"That's correct."

"And what did they say?"

"Hey, Ben," Brooks interrupted. "Why don't we go upstairs and talk this over?"

"Shut up," Ben snapped. He turned to Morton. "What did the results say?"

"We haven't received the results," Morton said.

"I can tell you what they'll say. They'll say 'inconclusive,' or maybe something more bizarre."

"Ben," Jessie said.

"What did you think you'd find here?" Morton asked.

"*The thing that took Julia*," Ben almost shouted. "The creature."

Morton stared back at him in the ensuing silence. "Why didn't you say anything about a creature on the mainland?"

"Because you would've looked at me like you are now. Like I'm some kind of lunatic."

"I don't care if he's sane or not," Castillo said. "Can we just go?"

"Mr. Shadeland, we have a good idea who abducted your child," Morton said. "Not only have Irvin's men been threatening Christina Blackwood, they've been keeping you under constant surveillance. Judging from the depravity of the crimes committed last night at your residence, and bearing in mind the reputation of Mr. Irvin and the medieval methods his men employ, it's perfectly reasonable to assume they're the ones who perpetrated the atrocities."

"They didn't."

"I'm goin' up," Castillo said. "You coming, Brooks?"

But Teddy was watching Ben and Morton.

Ben glanced at Brooks. "You think Irvin's guys did that? You think they killed Nat and my mom?"

Brooks regarded his loafers. "It's the only theory that makes sense, Ben."

"Bullshit," Ben said.

Castillo took hold of Jessie's arm. "Let's go, Jessie. This guy's losin' it."

Ben whirled on him. "If I'm crazy, why are you so scared?"

Castillo shook his head and laughed.

Ben turned back to Morton. "What produced this smell, huh? You ever been on a farm, Morton? Owned a dog?"

"I have two dogs," Morton said carefully.

"They smell like this, don't they?"

Before Morton could respond, Castillo broke in, "Anything could make the smell, Shadeland. It could be wild dogs."

"Wild dogs," Ben repeated.

"Sure, why not?"

"How do they get in and out of here?"

Castillo looked away.

Ben stepped closer. "Is there a little doggie door up there I missed? Or do they know how to manipulate doorknobs?"

"Listen, asshole," Castillo said, squaring up to him.

Ben's hands balled into fists.

"Enough of this," Morton said, moving past them. He reached the doorway and halted. "You're hurting, Mr. Shadeland. I understand that. I feel very badly for you and your wife. But we did not venture here to feed your delusion."

"It's not a delusion," Ben said in a thin voice.

Castillo brushed past him. "You've been watching too many movies, Shadeland. Maybe next time you and your wife should pick a nice family film to write the music for. Something about unicorns."

Ben resisted an urge to bounce Castillo's head off the wall.

"I'll come back with you later," Jessie said.

Ben turned and saw her looking up at him. The sympathetic expression she wore was even harder to stomach than Castillo's mocking one.

"You're here to remember, Ben," Brooks said. "It's time everybody got some closure."

"Closure."

"That's right."

"My baby is missing, Teddy. I can't get closure until I get her back."

"Then you're in the wrong place," Brooks said. "I'm sorry to tell you that, but it's the truth. You want your baby, you better get back to California."

Jessie stepped closer. "Ben, if you could just concentrate on—"

"You can all go to hell," Ben said. He crossed to the wall and resumed his search.

"We're trying to help," Jessie said.

Teddy said, "Come on. Let's give him some time."

When they were gone, Ben recommenced his inspection. When that revealed nothing, he began scouring the floor. He'd been on his hands and knees for a few minutes when something began to nag at his memory. It reminded him very much of the way the music came to him when he was writing, so he concentrated hard on *not* concentrating, on mentally looking away from the subtle tremor in his mind so it could swell into an all-out earthquake.

Ben shined his light on the ground, screwing up his eyes to detect a rise in the dirt or an indentation. Maybe a small fissure you couldn't see unless you got down close to it.

The tremor in his mind grew, became a steady vibration. Something about Joshua…about the night the beast had stolen him from the sixth floor studio…

Ben concentrated on the ground, the smoothness of it. As if it had been first compacted and then worn smooth by something enormous and heavy and banded with muscles.

A terrible realization occurred to him.

If Julia were nearby, he would have almost certainly heard her by now. She had powerful lungs, her screams far more strident and earsplitting than Joshua's had been when he was a baby. That had been why…

Why you left her with a sitter.

No.

Why you and Claire left your sweet, defenseless baby behind while you went out for dinner.

No!

Ben shook his head against the thoughts, listening hard for Julia's cries, but there was nothing, only the deafening silence of this pit, of this tomb. Was it possible Julia was sleeping? Or could the beast have—

Ben sat up straight, the thought tremor exploding in his mind.

The night the beast had taken Joshua.

Taken Joshua not to this pit, but taken him somewhere else on the island.

Ben sucked in breath.

The clearing. The redwood grove. The beast had taken Joshua there and had somehow sedated him. That's where Ben and Claire had faced the monster. They'd fought the beast and taken Joshua back.

Ben stumbled to his feet, burst through the doorway and raced up the steps two at a time.

Yes, he thought, heart juddering in his chest. He would find Julia in the clearing. He was alone this time, but he was better armed too. The Ruger likely wouldn't kill the beast – you'd need a missile to do that – but it would sure get the beast's attention. And while it was reeling from the bullets Ben was about to put in it, he would take his baby back. He would return to the castle.

Then the others would have to stand with him.

The others would see. They'd be forced to believe.

The flashlight in one hand, the Ruger in the other, Ben sprinted up the stairs.

PART THREE
MONSTERS
CHAPTER ONE

Griffin sat in the stern of Marvin's boat and told himself he didn't belong. He wasn't a monster. He eyed Bullington, sitting stolidly on one of the benches. The moonlight bathing the huge man's face was pale, ghostly. If Bullington felt any compunction about shooting Agent McWilliams, he didn't give any indication.

You're not one of them, Griffin thought. *You feel bad about what happened.*

Feeling bad's not enough, another voice said. *You didn't do anything to stop it.*

Griffin's throat constricted, his airway thinner than a blade of grass.

Nicky Irvin, seated across the aisle from his father, had swiveled around to stare at Griffin. There was an ugly, scornful gleam in his colorless eyes. "You don't look so good, Toomey. Think you might have to puke again?"

At Nicky's words, Griffin realized that he did feel nauseated. He ordinarily didn't mind being on the water. But of course, he normally didn't witness the slaughter of three innocent people either.

"You shoulda seen him, Daddy. He was barfing all over the place when I went into the woods to join Ray, and he was still barfing when I got back. Stupid son of a bitch was laying right there in the puddle. Chunks of orange and yellow all over his face. Like he was a goddamned toddler who couldn't keep himself clean."

Marvin Irvin, slouching cozily at the wheel, grinned.

Nicky turned back to Griffin. "You probably crapped yourself too, didn't you? Son of a bitch, I bet you did! Hey, Ray. You check Toomey's drawers, see if he dropped a load in 'em?"

Rubio, on what Griffin estimated was his fifth glass of bourbon, eyed him from the bow of the boat. "Check 'em? Hell, I didn't wanna go near the filthy son of a bitch. Bastard pukes at everything."

"I noticed that," Nicky said. He leaned forward, tilted his head at Griffin. "You got some sorta disorder, Toomey? Somethin' we don't know about? Like puking Tourette's or something?"

At this Rubio let loose with a merry gust of laughter.

Griffin had a fleeting recollection of Rubio's gore-spattered front, the red, demented face, the slop and viscera all over his sodden sweatsuit; he found it highly ironic that Rubio found Griffin's vomit disgusting, but he kept the observation to himself.

Nicky returned to the attack. In the pellucid glow of the nearly full moon, his mean eyes glittered like polished onyx. "Puked when we were talking to that bodyguard. Puked when Ray iced that smartass agent."

At this, Rubio reproduced the slashing motion he had used to slit Jacob Huffer's jugular.

Griffin retreated from the memory, closer than ever to getting sick again. Christ, would this nightmare never end?

You don't deserve it to end.

Stop, he thought weakly.

You're as much a part of it as they are.

No!

You could've intervened, but you didn't.

I didn't have a gun.

But the agent did. Both the agents did. When Rubio and Nicky ran off after that poor jogger, you could have picked up either one of those guns. You could've saved that lady. Instead you left her in the woods with those animals.

I didn't do anything to her.

You didn't do anything for *her either, did you? You coward. You goddamn weakling.*

Nicky was imitating him now in a weird, lisping voice. "Please don't hurt them, Nicky! Please don't touch the poor federal agents!"

Rubio threw back his head and brayed laughter.

Griffin turned sideways, stared out blearily at the water. There were a billion tiny glimmers on the churning sea, the wind having subsided but the Pacific by no means placid. The motion was burrowing into Griffin's guts, Nicky's words pushing him closer and closer to tears. He wouldn't do it, though, wouldn't give Nicky the satisfaction of breaking him down.

But Nicky was suddenly standing over him, bent over and hissing into his face, "Look at me, you fuckin' pussy. Look at me!" He jerked Griffin's chin around to face him. "You're only around because my daddy thinks you're smart."

Griffin's lips trembled. Dear God, he *was* breaking down.

"You feel bad for that bitch we killed?" A flat palm smacked Griffin across the mouth. Spittle flew from Griffin's lips, speckled the metal railing. "You think we're a coupla bad guys cuz we had a little fun with her?"

Just leap over the edge of the boat, he told himself. *Drowning would be better than what he's doing to you. Anything would be better.*

"You know what she said to us, Toomey? Right before Ray opened up her belly? She says, 'I got a daughter at home.'"

Nicky's face loomed nearer, their noses nearly touching. "And you know what Ray here says? Tell 'im, Ray."

Rubio called, "I said, 'Invite her over. We'll bang her too!'"

Rubio brayed laughter, but Nicky scarcely moved. He acted like he was trying to hypnotize Griffin with his glassy eyes. "You think it was our fault that bitch came jogging past at that moment?" When Griffin didn't answer, Nicky let go his chin, grasped a handful of hair and gave it a violent jerk. "*Do ya?*"

"What's your point?" Griffin managed to croak.

Nicky's eyebrows went up. "My point, you stupid—" Nicky cut off, let go of Griffin's hair. He made a face, wiped his hand on his pant leg. "Mother of God, Toomey, don't you ever fucking bathe? Your hair's greasier than a homeless dude's ass."

"So what's the plan?" Jim Bullington asked.

Marvin pursed his lips. "I'm thinking we take the castle."

"Just walk in and take it?"

Marvin nodded. "We storm it, like they used to do back in olden times."

Nicky was nodding, his colorless eyes glittering. "I like that. Like a buncha knights with swords."

"Only we'll use the automatic." Marvin leaned back from the wheel, crossed his arms thoughtfully. "I figure the place has more than one entrance, right?"

"It has three," Griffin said.

Everyone turned to look at him. Nicky's expression reminded him of a batter who's just struck out and is about to beat the Gatorade cooler with his bat. Only Nicky would use his fists instead of a bat, and Griffin's head would be the cooler.

"Talk," Marvin said.

Griffin squirmed under Marvin's scrutiny. "I studied up on it this morning."

"This morning when?" Nicky asked.

"When you and the rest were still sleeping," he said, taking care to keep his voice neutral. It felt good though, needling Nicky. Really good.

Just don't overdo it.

Griffin went on. "I typed *Castle Blackwood* into the computer, and though there were tons of articles about the Sorrows, there weren't any floor plans available."

"Then how do you know how many doors there are?" Rubio asked. Like Nicky, he looked like he'd love to take a swing at Griffin.

"Some of the articles mentioned how Robert Blackwood had the place built. He actually tore down the first castle and built a new one. The only thing remaining from the old castle is a tower. It's still there."

Marvin watched him. "Go on."

"The new castle – I mean, it's old now, but compared to the first one it's new. The new one was modeled after a Scottish castle from way back in the 1600s. Craigeivar Castle. It's still there if you wanna see the pictures. Really beautiful place."

They watched him in silence.

"So Castle Blackwood is a replica," he added quickly. "There are minor differences, but the shells are basically the same. L-shaped, six stories tall. There's a door in the front, one in the back, and one at the end of the L."

Marvin gave Nicky a look that amounted to *You see what I mean?* And though Griffin was certain he'd pay dearly for that look later, it felt good to be valued for once. Damned good.

"Tell me more about the layout," Marvin said.

"The main floor is what you'd think it would be. A big room for gatherings – they call it the 'Great Hall' on the blueprint – a gourmet kitchen, a nice-sized dining room. The second and third floors are various sitting rooms, smaller bedrooms, studies, parlors. There's a hell of a big library."

When no one seemed to care about this – shit, he should've known – he continued. "The fourth floor is more bedrooms, but bigger ones. The fifth story is where the family used to stay. You know, and important guests. It's where the master suite is."

"That's where we'll stay, right, boss?" Ray Rubio said. Griffin marveled at the childlike eagerness in his voice, like a little boy asking his dad to camp out in the backyard. It was easy to forget that earlier that day Rubio had disemboweled two people and carved the eyes out of another.

Marvin nodded. "That's right, Raymond. We'll live it up. After we take the castle."

The words sent chills up Griffin's spine.

"You said there were six stories," Marvin prompted.

"The sixth floor is one big studio. The Blackwoods are one of the oldest musical families in America, as you no doubt know, Mr. Irvin. The builder devoted that whole floor to a vast, acoustically friendly room in which Robert Blackwood could play and compose music."

Marvin stroked his chin thoughtfully. At length he asked, "Anything else, my young bird?"

"There's a basement, but it doesn't look like there's anything down there, at least not from the Craigeivar floor plans. There's roof access, but you can only get to that from the studio."

"So it's shaped like an L," Marvin said, leaning forward on the wheel.

"Yes, sir."

Marvin held out a hand, made an L with his thumb and forefinger. "We'll hit all three doors at once. That way there'll be no way they can slip out and strike at us from behind." Marvin glanced at Bullington. "Jim, I want you to take the back door. That's the place where the longest line of the L ends, am I right?" Marvin looked up at Griffin, who nodded. Turning back to examine his hand, Marvin said, "Ray, I want you on the front door, where the two lines meet." He tapped the base of his thumb. "That'll leave me and Nicky to cover the short part of the L, the side door."

When he didn't say more, Griffin cleared his throat. "Where will I be, sir?"

Marvin said, "You've no doubt observed my boy and me have a difference of opinion where you're concerned."

Griffin threw Nicky a quick look but didn't say anything.

"Nicky thinks you're worthless and that I made a mistake bringin' you into the fold. I feel differently, though I do have to admit your habit of turning green every time there's work to be done worries me."

Work, Griffin thought. *Christ.*

"Now, this mission is going to afford you the chance to show me how smart I was in taking you on. And I dare say you wouldn't mind making Nicky here eat a little crow, am I right?"

Griffin didn't even need to look at Nicky to know how bitter his expression was.

"So here's the deal. You stick with me. Prove yourself tonight, you'll stay with us permanently."

Griffin swallowed. "Tonight?"

Marvin grunted a humorless laugh. "Of course tonight. What do ya think we're gonna do, camp out on the beach? Roast weenies?"

"I don't—" Griffin forced the lump down his throat. "I don't have a gun."

Eyeing him steadily, Marvin reached under his jacket, came out with a shiny silver pistol, a squarish, sleek-looking thing that glinted moonlight as Marvin held it out.

Griffin accepted it. He turned it over in his hands, amazed at the thing's solidity.

"You take that Smith & Wesson as a sign of my trust, Griff. You'll more than likely get the opportunity to use it tonight."

Griffin nodded. He'd never fired a gun before, but the thing in his hand intrigued him.

Nicky watched him sourly. "I don't like it, Pop."

Turning back to the wheel, Marvin said, "Give him a chance, Nicky. Griff here's rejuvenated me. I even left my cane back at the house. A guy has that kind of effect on your daddy, least you can do is give him a chance."

The gun in his hand, Griffin returned Nicky's baleful stare and thought, *That's right, Nicky. Give me a chance. And don't turn your back on me, you goddamn monster.*

Griffin gripped the gun tighter.

★　　★　　★

Teddy Brooks awoke at just before midnight. He'd been drowsing fitfully but not really sleeping. Almost like he'd eaten Thai food. Whenever he and Tanya had gotten Thai, he'd had a hell of a time getting a decent night's rest. But Tanya liked it, so they got it often. Whatever Tanya wanted, Tanya got.

The thought of his ex-wife brought him fully awake. Teddy sighed, reached out in the dark and fingered the satiny bedsheets. Expensive. And the bed…shit, it was like lying on one of those mats they used when he did high jump. He always sucked at high jump; it was his worst event because he was too short. But the coach probably assumed because he was black he could jump. Teddy didn't mind though. Some of the prettiest girls on the team were in the event. He'd wait his turn and often stand near the big, puffy mat as if spotting the female jumpers. Looking out for their well-being. When all he was really doing was waiting for them to land in a heap so he could catch a glimpse of their crotches in those tiny track shorts.

Yeah, this bed was almost as big as one of those mats, but that only mattered if you had somebody in bed with you. Lying in the big bed alone he felt absurd, like it was accentuating his loneliness. Shit, how long *had* it been? Six months? Eight? Shaking his head, he realized it was probably even longer than that. And now that he had the image of flimsy little track shorts in his mind, he had a hard-on, and what good was that? Sure, he could take care of it himself, but that would only leave him feeling glum and messy. He didn't even have any tissues. Teddy blew out a disgusted breath. It was a sad thing for a man his age to have to jack off to get some satisfaction. He was supposed to have a wife.

Teddy sat up in bed, glanced out the window. It was relatively early, but he knew he wouldn't be sleeping again for a good long while.

He swung his legs over the edge of the bed, winced as the bare soles of his feet touched down on the frigid wood floor and went over to slide into his loafers. He didn't suppose he looked too manly wearing nothing but a pair of yellow boxer shorts and some loafers, but who was he going to see this late at night?

Maybe Elena. He passed through the door and ambled down the hallway. Yeah, that would be all right. Teddy was still muscular, the slight layer of cushion on his lower belly understandable given his age. But he could suck that in. His chest and arms were hard. Tanya had always loved his legs. Yeah, if he encountered Elena Pedachenko right now, and if she could get past the ridiculous yellow underwear-loafer ensemble, she might be pleasantly surprised by his build.

He started down the spiral staircase.

If he met Elena at this late hour, he was *certain* he'd approve of her outfit. Teddy reflected back on that lovely blue number she had on earlier, the way the sundress showed off her shoulder blades, the delicate line of her backbone. The girl was tiny, couldn't weigh more than a hundred and twenty pounds, and though he normally liked his women with more size on them, there was something irresistible about Elena's tight little body, those pert breasts. He was positive she wore no bra.

Teddy reached the first floor and passed into the pantry.

"*Teddy.*"

His hand halfway to the pantry light, Teddy froze. He gazed into the darkness of the pantry, but it appeared empty.

Yet he'd heard the voice.

"You're goin' crazy, Teddy," he muttered. He flipped on the light.

And bellowed in terror at his wife's face staring back at him from the shelf. He windmilled his arms, backpedaled, swept cans and bottles off the shelves, then tripped over his own feet and fell sideways into the hall. But he could still see Tanya's face eyeballing him, smiling, the face very much alive but ghastly in its unblinking knowledge. Teddy scrambled around the corner, had taken a few panicked strides toward the staircase, when it occurred to him.

Tanya couldn't be in the pantry.

Tanya couldn't be anywhere.

"Come on, Teddy," he muttered, recrossing the hallway. He felt a blast of dread as he stepped into the pantry again, but it was as he thought. Empty, except for the food.

He moved deeper into the pantry and scanned the shelves. Boxes of pasta. Some canned soup. Some protein drink in a big canister. Probably belonged to Chad Wayne. Dude had to make sure he maintained those cartoonish muscles and that rancid stink breath. Remembering the smell of Wayne's breath, Teddy wrinkled his nose, and as he did, he noticed something in the rear of the pantry, where he'd scared himself shitless thinking his ex-wife had materialized between the Rice-a-Roni and the taco shells.

There *was* something stuck between a couple of cans. Minestrone soup and some baked beans, Teddy observed as he edged nearer. What poked out between them was only a small piece of paper, and why that should fill him with such an atavistic dread he had no idea.

"Come *on*, Teddy," he said with even less patience this time. He reached out for the beige slip of paper, thinking it was a scribbled note or maybe a receipt. But no, he thought, his fingers closing on it and sliding it out, it was the wrong kind of paper for that. Too thick.

Teddy saw it was a business card.

He read the name on it, then read it again.

He clapped a hand over his mouth, the card fluttering down to land between his loafers. The card lay face up, the name still easy enough to read even from this distance: LARS HUTCHINSON.

Teddy became aware of a high-pitched moan coming from way down in his throat. He wanted to believe this was a sadistic joke someone was playing, that sassy little Elena maybe, but the hope vanished as rapidly as it had sprung up. No one here would do something like that because no one would go to so much trouble. And even if someone had taken the time to learn about Teddy's past and use it against him, just how the hell would they know to place the card right here where he'd find it?

"*Teddy.*"

Teddy spun around, a scream clotting in his throat. Teddy bolted out of the pantry and dashed toward the staircase. He hurried up the stairs, wishing he could move faster but knowing he was incapable of any more speed. His heart rocked in his chest, the beat like a militaristic snare drum. Teddy expected at any moment to see Lars Hutchinson or Tanya lurch out of the shadows to claim him, and was it any wonder Ben Shadeland had so much fear of this place? Ben feared it, Teddy realized as he clambered higher and higher, because it was a place where anything could happen. Teddy didn't believe that bullshit about a goat man and music playing from a tower that had been walled up for almost a hundred years.

But did he believe the place had a tendency toward the supernatural?

"Bet your ass I do," Teddy muttered and hustled down the fifth-floor corridor. He pushed through his door and heaved it shut with a clang.

Holy shit, he thought. Just how could Lars have found him? How could...

The island is like a magnet, Ben had said.

Yes, Teddy thought as he squirmed under the covers. Ben sure had told him that. Told him a whole lotta other stuff too, and the scariest thing was, the thing Teddy hadn't considered until right now, was that one part being true − that there were spirits on the island − meant the other parts could be true as well.

The covers cinched tight around his throat, Teddy thought it over. He had never believed in the paranormal, supernatural, whatever the fruitcakes like Elena wanted to call it. He didn't want to believe in it now. But...

Lars Hutchinson.

"Son of a bitch," Teddy whispered.

He sat up, pushed off the covers and hurried to get something out of his suitcase. He got back under the covers, the furthest thing from tired.

But the bottle would help. It was Glenlivet, a bit of an extravagance, sure, but worth it. Good Scotch was always worth it. He opened the bottle, took a long gurgling swig. The heat from the Scotch swirled down his esophagus, made his empty stomach tingle. But it felt good. He knocked back another huge swig. The stuff was too expensive to merely get drunk on, but right now sobriety was the last thing he needed.

Yes, Teddy thought, sipping again. He needed to get the hell away from sobriety, needed to enter the land of the anesthetized, the land of the severely sedated.

Drunk was what he needed to be. Drunk and out cold. He'd pay for it in the morning, but he refused to spend the rest of the night listening to every stealthy sound in this old mausoleum.

The thought made him shiver. *Move on, Teddy*, he told himself. *Move on. Drink. Drink until you forget about Lars. Hell, drink until you forget about Tanya.*

As if he could.

But Teddy drank.

Drank and hoped the business card was the only part of Lars he would find.

CHAPTER TWO

The pills hadn't worked. Reading hadn't either. She had pleasured herself with the Rabbit, but even the catharsis her vibrator offered didn't make her drowsy. Sleepless, frustrated, Christina lay awake in the vast, lonely master suite. Part of her wanted to march down to Ben Shadeland's room right now and demand he tell her everything he'd told the federal agents. Of course, there were two problems with that. According to Teddy, Ben hadn't told the agents anything. Even more troubling was the fact that as of eleven o'clock that evening, Ben apparently hadn't even been to his room. Teddy refused to tell her much about their experience earlier in the basement, but what he had shared didn't imbue her with much hope.

She sighed, rolled over and lay on her stomach. Dammit. Why couldn't Ben just remember everything so they could all move forward? She didn't care particularly what she learned about Stephen's death – truth be told, the news of his murder had come as a monumental relief – but she simply couldn't bear not knowing what had happened to her son.

At memory of Chris, her eyes began to sting. She thrust the covers off and got out of bed. To hell with it, she thought. It was time for more pills. They might put her under until well past noon tomorrow, but at least she'd be rested.

She was heading toward the bathroom when a faint voice made her freeze. It had been high and lilting. Familiar. Christina leaned forward, listening.

The sound came from the interior wall of the room, which was impossible. There was no room behind her, only...

Her breath caught.

Only the secret passageway.

Though the walls of the castle appeared to be solid and uninterrupted stone, the castle was actually honeycombed with tunnels that ran between rooms, down hallways and even from one floor to the next. Years ago, upon learning of the tunnels and the two-way mirrors within them, she had been appalled. She'd declared the original builder of the castle – Stephen's great-great grandfather Robert Blackwood – a fiend and a pervert.

But eventually, as her puritanical preoccupations with sex began to dissolve, so too had her contemptuousness toward the voyeuristic tendencies of Stephen's forefathers. One night early in their marriage – this was during their second visit to the Sorrows – she had awakened to find her husband gone. When he'd slipped back through the hidden doorway to their room, she'd confronted him. He'd at first tried to play it off as boyish exploration, but she'd known the truth even before he admitted it. He'd been spying on their attractive cook Rosa as she'd showered. Christina had almost left him then, would have left him had it not been for the prenuptial agreement he'd forced her to sign. But eventually curiosity had replaced anger, and after making sure Stephen was outside walking the grounds, she had entered the hidden door to spy on Rosa herself. She'd never given much thought to her attraction to women, nor had she any sexual experience with them. But when she discovered Rosa under the seething water of the shower…when she'd glimpsed the firm, brown body moving within the cloud of steam…

The memory of Rosa's nude body made her nipples instantly harden and a pleasant warmth spread in her tummy. The noise came from the wall again, the sound of it the perfect counterpart to her erotic memory. Christina realized how incredibly aroused she was. Already she was far more excited than she'd been with the Rabbit. That had been a robotic exercise, an obligatory ritual. Bloodless and bereft of passion.

But the voice she now heard, though faint, was bursting with passion, was oozing with energy.

It was Elena's voice.

Heart racing, Christina hurried over to the wall, her fingers finding the slight indentation unerringly. She swung the heavy wall section open, then pulled it shut behind her. The whole thing was so well constructed that even now, over a century after it was built, the mechanism worked smoothly and silently. Christina scurried quickly through the narrow black passage. No light was necessary, though here and there she discerned ghostly vanes of moonglow cleaving the tunnel shadows. Elena's room was next door, so she didn't have to venture far. Nearing the peephole over Elena's bed, Christina wondered if Elena had already taken a lover here on the island, and if so who it was.

She brought her eye to the peephole, looked.

Elena was alone.

But she was also nude.

Beautifully, gloriously nude, her small, delectable breasts culminating in perfect pink nubs. Her arms were lithe, her shoulders smooth and achingly kissable. On occasion, when she'd drunk several glasses of wine and had gone to bed alone, Christina had pleasured herself and imagined that the vibrator was actually Elena's quivering tongue.

And now…here was Elena. In the flesh. Elena writhing on the bed, the blankets and sheets cast to the floor, Elena with a hand on her sex and the other pressed to her supple mouth, stifling her own cries.

Christina lifted her negligee, began to massage herself.

Through the peephole Christina could hear Elena's moans, very loud despite the index finger the girl was biting down on. The moonlight spilling through Elena's uncurtained window was so intense that Christina could see the tiny drops of moisture glistening in the curls of Elena's pubic hair.

Slowly, luxuriantly, Christina Blackwood masturbated. She rubbed herself faster, imagining what it would be like to sink down between Elena's legs and kiss her inner thighs, her sex. And as the molten heat began to spread through Christina's body, her mind traveled back to Rosa Martinez, back to the only woman with whom Christina had ever made love.

Yes, Rosa had been Christina's lover, but when Stephen discovered the affair, he had insisted on making the relationship a ménage a trois. In the beginning, when it had been just Rosa and Christina, their exploration had been an exhilarating experience.

When Stephen got involved, it became dreadful.

Christina frowned in the shadows of the tunnel, struggling to break loose from the memories. But they charged in upon her, chilling the sweet flame within. She peered down at Elena, whose climax never seemed to end. The girl was undulating now, arching her back, the cries issuing from her mouth full of longing and abandon. But Christina's own climax eluded her.

It had been Stephen, the bastard, Stephen who had ruined what she and Rosa had shared. Stephen with his big gut and his unimaginative ideas about sex. Stephen demanding that he be present whenever Rosa and Christina were in a room together.

Stephen who ultimately murdered Rosa.

Christina jammed her palms against her eyes, as if the pressure there could eradicate the memory of that horrible night from her mind.

Stephen, Christina and Rosa in the master suite.

Stephen first watching with his greedy leer as Rosa went down on Christina.

Stephen fondling his short, thick member as Christina zoomed toward climax.

Stephen interrupting Christina's orgasm by shouting at Rosa, ordering the little woman to bend over before him.

Stephen tupping Rosa from behind in the corner of the room, just feet from the casement windows, which were open to let in the sea breeze.

Stephen's big body pushing Rosa closer and closer to the window.

Rosa spinning around, struggling to loose herself from Stephen's grasp.

Stephen plunging into Rosa, shoving her into the open windowsill.

Stephen choking Rosa, his enormous belly pounding her farther and farther over the edge of the sill.

Christina's only child Chris, fourteen years old at the time, stumbling into the room to discover the murder in progress. Christina, under the influence of some horrible, unfeeling spell, telling Chris to go away. As if nothing at all abnormal were happening in the corner, where Rosa now dangled more than eighty feet off the ground and certain death.

Moments later, Stephen had let Rosa fall.

"No!" Christina screamed.

Clapped a hand over her mouth.

She opened her eyes and saw Elena scrambling off the bed, fumbling for the covers. Elena's eyes were huge, her hunched form backlit by the moon. Christina stared at her through the peephole, terrified that Elena would discover her and realize how lecherous her employer was. Oh God, Christina thought. Elena would think her a disgusting old slut, pathetic and patently unlovable. She stared at Elena, afraid to move, afraid that any sound would betray her whereabouts.

Then the room began to darken. A mountainous shape materialized behind Elena, *around* Elena, and as Christina watched, transfixed, she discerned a set of broad, muscular shoulders, a pair of rippling arms. Elena stood trembling at the end of the bed, facing Christina and totally unaware of the figure behind her, which was rising, expanding, the thing monstrous, the wild stench it broadcast overpowering her even through the wall. The hair on her arms prickled, a scalding acid sizzling the back of her throat. Couldn't Elena smell it? Couldn't she hear the monster's steam-engine breathing?

You have to warn her!

Christina gave a little start, realized it was true. She'd failed Rosa Martinez those many years ago and had never forgiven herself.

Now it's time to make amends.

Yes, she thought, but how? If she alerted Elena to her presence, the beast would simply maul Elena on the spot, and Christina knew the medium would have no chance then.

No, Christina would have to confront the beast.

But before she took a step, she saw a black, hairy hand shoot up and clamp over Elena's mouth. Elena's eyes were horrorstruck. The beast reached down with its free hand, yanked one of Elena's legs sideways.

The beast had white, pupilless eyes, which snapped up and fixed on Christina. The peephole was tiny, had been designed to blend into the wall so it would go undetected. But the beast was looking at her, was unmistakably *leering* at her, the white eyes triumphant.

Oh no, Christina thought. *Please don't. Please—*

Whimpering, Christina pushed away from the peephole and shambled down the passage. Lurching into her room, she cast about for some weapon, something hard with which to batter the beast.

A scream punctured the walls, making Christina stand rigid, hands out, fingers tensed like claws.

Low, chortling laughter.

A wail of pain, the sound of something shattering on the floor.

In an agony of impotent terror, Christina snatched the first object she found off the dresser, what looked like a pewter box. The hard object was about the size and width of a fat paperback novel. She clutched it and crossed the room. On the way out she heard an awful clatter from next door. It sounded like Elena had broken away from the beast and was hurling objects at it, doing anything she could do prevent it from violating her further.

I'm coming, Christina thought. *Hold on a moment longer, Elena. I'm coming.*

Her nightgown billowing behind her, Christina pelted the short distance to Elena's door, hammered on it, the corners of the ornate pewter box leaving deep scars in the old wood. Christina paused, listening for the commotion, for Elena's shrieks.

Silence.

She tested the knob. Locked.

Christina reared back with the box and rammed the door as hard as she could. She listened for voices, but all was silent.

Had the beast murdered Elena?

"Leave her alone!" Christina shouted. "Leave her the hell alone!"

From down the hall came the sound of opening doors, confused voices. She heard Peter Grant asking someone if everything was all right.

It's not all right! Christina wanted to scream. *The thing has Elena and it's ripping her apart as we stand here doing nothing!*

A man's voice, Teddy Brooks's she was pretty sure, called down the hall, "What's happening, Christina?"

Christina couldn't answer, could only beat on the stupid unyielding door with hands that were numb and starting to bleed. Where was Jorge? Where was Chad Wayne, the big freaking ox?

Peter and Teddy were moving swiftly down the corridor, and finally, blessedly, Jorge's door swung open, Jorge looking dazed but rapidly emerging from his sleep fog to kick some ass. She didn't know if there was still time to save Elena, and she highly doubted even Jorge would be a match for the monster behind this door, but at the very least he'd be able to—

The door swung away, Elena gaping up at her in a T-shirt and underwear.

"What is it?" Elena asked.

Christina stared down at her. No scratches, no bruises. No wounds of any kind. And how did she get dressed so quickly?

Christina grasped her arm, jerked her into the hallway. Ignoring Elena's protests, Christina shouted, "Jorge, the thing is in here. You'll need your gun."

"What thing?" Elena asked.

Christina stared at her, thin-lipped. "The thing that was...the creature that was making those terrible noises. The one that..."

Christina realized everyone was staring at her. Elena and Jorge looked incredulous. Teddy was eyeing her closely, but she couldn't interpret what his look meant. Peter Grant merely seemed rumpled, his gunmetal colored hair pointing up at odd angles. Chad Wayne was nowhere to be found. Neither were the agents.

Jorge said, "Mrs. Blackwood, what did you hear?"

She cleared her throat, trying to cling to what dignity she might still retain. "I thought I heard voices from your room, Elena, but..."

No one answered. They only continued studying her like she was some bizarre species of insect recently discovered by science.

"I suggest we all return to our rooms," she said. "I...I must have had a nightmare."

Elena's bemused expression softened. She reached out, touched Christina's forearm. "Would you like me to stay with you?"

The skin of Christina's temples tightened. She heard herself saying, as if from a great height, "That won't be necessary, Elena. I'm perfectly capable of putting myself to bed."

Without another word she turned and set off down the hall. She refused to make eye contact with anyone until she was safely inside her room. When she had made her successful retreat, she locked herself in and slumped against the door.

Great job, she told herself. *If they didn't think you a spoiled, eccentric spinster before, they certainly do now.*

With an enervated sigh, she pushed away from the door and had almost reached her bed when something caught her eye.

Her throat as instantly dry as midsummer chaff, she beheld the secret door. The door she had left open.

The door that was now closed.

It swung shut on its own, she thought.

But she knew it didn't work like that.

Maybe a draft...?

That was stupid too. There was no wind within the passageway because it bordered the interior wall. The only way for it to close was for someone – or some*thing* – to push it shut.

Nervelessly, Christina sank back on the bed. She closed her eyes and remembered the beast rising up behind Elena. Remembered the beast leering at her as it prepared to defile Elena.

Like it was telling Christina, *This will be you soon. Only it will be much, much worse.*

She shook her head to rid her mind of the image, but try as she might, she could not escape those leering alabaster eyes.

Or the sound of the beast's low, inhuman laughter.

★   ★   ★

Peter Grant tossed down the bedclothes with an angry sigh. He knew from experience he wouldn't be going to sleep again any time soon. The commotion Christina had caused minutes earlier forbade an ordinary heart rate, and neither of the usual remedies – reading dull books or ruminating on his next article – would prove equal to the task of putting him to sleep.

Because Christina had seen Gabriel.

Oh, Peter doubted it had been Gabriel in the flesh, the actual corporeal being who once inhabited this island and who might, in some form, still exist here. But Gabriel's *spirit*, his *essence* was so potent that Peter believed he could inhabit dreams if he so chose. Perhaps Gabriel could do much more than that.

And now, he realized with a dawning sense of wonderment, was the ideal time for him to put into practice three decades' worth of study. True, there had always been something of the ascetic in him. He fancied a rural life back in Victorian England would have suited him just fine. Give him his books and a warm hearth by which to read, and Peter would have been more than content.

But this...this was fieldwork!

The notion thrilled him. He'd always been an admirer of Indiana Jones and had often wondered if there might exist in him a rugged adventurer ready to break free of the strictures of academia.

What better time to find out than the present?

Springing out of bed, Peter selected his most adventurous outfit: a red button-down chambray shirt, well-worn blue jeans, scuffed hiking boots – which were scuffed not from hiking but from being stored in the bottom of his closet – and the *piece de resistance*, a leather Stetson hat.

Placing it atop his head and regarding his reflection in the bureau mirror, he fancied he did look a bit like Harrison Ford. He pulled the brim lower so his eyes were shadowed. Oh, what he wouldn't give for a whip!

Heart jackhammering now from sheer exhilaration, Professor Peter Grant plucked his flashlight from the bureau, slipped out his door and stole nimbly down the corridor. There was a moon now, but earlier he had spied ominous thunderheads in the distance. Storms had been threatening back in California for several days now, and he suspected tonight the heavens would unleash their bottled fury.

All the more perfect!

The peal of thunder and the quicksilver of lightning would be the ideal accompaniments for a thorough study of Castle Blackwood. And though the list of spots he desired to examine was expansive, there was nowhere more tantalizing than the pit.

Verily floating down the spiral staircase, Peter imagined how it would feel to have his theories verified, the sheer, unmitigated vindication he would experience. He'd been working on the Blackwood case for so long…

Advancing through the gloom of the main floor, Peter neared the basement door.

Over the years there had been many at the university who had scoffed at his beliefs about Castle Blackwood. Some of these doubters had been discreet about their opinions of him, opting to whisper behind his back or spread slanderous tales about him when he wasn't present. Others had been openly derisive about his obsession with the Sorrows, and though he'd held his own in his exchanges with these puerile opponents, he knew there were many who sided with them, naysayers who'd rather mock him than thoughtfully consider his ideas.

Yes, Peter thought as he stepped through the doorway, flicked on the basement light and closed the door behind him. Listening was a dying art. Much of the time Peter felt like a ninny in front of his classes. And though he'd procured tenure long ago, he knew that Rowena Garth, his shrew of a department head, did him no favors with his class schedule. Last year it had been English 201 and three sections of Basic Comp. This fall it was even more dire: two sections of English 101 and two classes on Pre-1750 American Literature. He wasn't even permitted to teach Poe! And Rowena Garth had reveled in his misery. After their teaching assignments had been sent out and they'd run into each other outside Clay Hall, Peter had sensed a wicked glee in her voice as she'd explained to him that his expertise really was best utilized with freshmen who needed to get their English credits out of the way and that his encyclopedic knowledge of mythology, history, and literature in general could be put to excellent use in his lessons on *Pilgrim's Progress* and the sermons of Cotton Mather.

And she expected him to believe her.

The bitch.

Sighing, Peter tramped down the first long flight of stairs. He might have gone insane or developed a bona fide persecution complex if it hadn't been for Melissa and Mark, his two loyal assistants. Soon they'd be moving onto greener academic pastures, but for the past three years they'd helped him weather the worst of Rowena's iron-fisted tyranny, not to mention the alarming uptick in impertinent undergrads who, perhaps sensing his discomfort with the source material, had taken to challenging Peter's authority like bull sharks circling a bleeding swimmer.

An exchange from the recently completed May term:

HANDSOME BROWN-HAIRED BOY WITH GLEAMING SMILE: Why do we have to write five hundred words?

PETER (good-humoredly): Well, when writing about John Bunyan, it hardly seems fair to limit you.

HANDSOME BOY (staring blankly): I thought five hundred was the minimum.

PETER (sobering, but still a good sport): It is. You're free to treat that baseline loosely, but please do shoot for five hundred or more.

HANDSOME BOY: What about fifty?

PETER: Fifty words?

HANDSOME BOY: Sure. (Gleams a smile at the pretty girl next to him)

PETER: I'm afraid that's a little low.

HANDSOME BOY: What if I'm just really good with words?

(Pretty girl snickers)

PETER: Be that as it may, I think to give the subject a fair treatment you need to—

HANDSOME BOY: What if we think the book sucks?

(Murmurs of assent)

PETER: I think we need to keep the piece in perspective. To the modern reader, Bunyan's language might seem—

HANDSOME BOY: But that's what we are. Modern readers. Is that, like, our fault or something?

PETER: I didn't say—

HANDSOME BOY: It's like you're trying to convert us. I mean, not everyone is a Christian. Haven't you ever heard of religious freedom?

PETER: Um…

Peter reached the yellow bulb, which flickered portentously in the broad, dank stairwell. The flashlight clutched a bit tighter, Peter continued down the stairs and shook his head as if the motion alone could scatter the memory of the handsome boy's smarmy face and gleaming shark teeth. The boy – Peter couldn't remember his name straightaway – was yet another example of what Melissa would call a "hater". Yes, the boy was a hater. And what did Melissa always say about haters?

Haters are going to hate.

A grim smile formed on his lips as Peter's steps quickened on the descending stairs. Yes, haters were common in this world, but the good guys did sometimes win. They had to, or what was the point?

And this, Peter thought as he tromped deeper into the bowels of Castle Blackwood, would be one of those occasions when the haters would be disappointed. Because he, Professor Peter Allan Grant, would be proven correct. Not only about the history of this lonely isle, but about the nature of Gabriel Blackwood as well.

But first things first. He could now see the immense gray door leading into the pit. Just as he'd imagined it! Even the sere gray surface bore the proper sinister aspect it always had in his imagination. Funny, Peter thought, drawing nearer, his heart hammering in his bony chest. How could a board sheltered down here from the elements appear *weathered*? No matter. It was merely the thing's age showing. He hustled down the last flight of stairs and glided across the final landing. He feared for a moment the door might not work, but perhaps because the others had trodden this path earlier, the enormous door swung open easily, though its ancient iron hinges shrieked. The sound was delightful! And the pit…

Peter began to tremble with joy. The pit was precisely as he had envisioned. Peter's middle name had been chosen by his English teacher father to honor Edgar Allan Poe. And as Peter now aimed his flashlight's beam into the stygian darkness of the pit, he recalled many of his favorite Poe tales. "The Cask of Amontillado". "The Pit and the Pendulum".

"The Premature Burial".

No, he thought. *Not that one.*

Stepping through the doorway and allowing the beam to knife through the tenebrous murk before him, Peter made out the stone walls, the grimy floor. And the smell, he thought, nose wrinkling. Yes, the smell in here was revolting. How had he not noticed it before? His eyes began to water as he inhaled the stench, which reminded him of both a petting zoo and a public restroom.

The first tremor of misgiving whispered through him.

But wasn't this exactly what he'd imagined? If his theory – first posited by his mentor, the late Richard Clay – about Gabriel Blackwood was correct, the scent of wild animals was precisely what one *should* smell when exploring this godless domain.

Wasn't it?

Only…while the notion of such an odor was logical and even edifying in the realm of logic and academic theory, the reality of it was a bit overwhelming.

For pity's sake, Peter, he heard Richard Clay saying. *Don't you want to be proven correct? Or would you rather spend your life cloistered in that airless little study of yours, whiling away your time rather than shoving the proof of your beliefs in the faces of those who scoffed at you? Good God, man, don't you want to be right?*

Of course I want to be right.

Then stop being a ninny!

Yes, he told himself. *Stop being a ninny.*

But the odor bored its way through his nostrils, into his head, and seemed to permeate his entire being. Not only was the smell repugnant and, far more disconcertingly, *fresh,* but the sight of the pit's floor suffused him with a spirit-crushing dread. He shined the light at the old stone and thought he could make out tufts of black hair, a large spot near the rear of the chamber that was smoother than the rest, almost as if something had spent many nights sleeping there. And nearer him…on the ground a few feet away. Was that…

Was that blood?

Quit stalling! Richard's voice bellowed in his mind. *Look for the lever!*

Okay, he agreed. *I'll look for the lever.*

He directed the amber beam of the flashlight at the wall beside the door. If anyone hurried in here and needed to pull the lever, it would be in a spot adjacent to the door.

But well hidden.

Yes, Peter agreed. *Concealed from anyone who might follow.*

He inspected the wall to the right of the doorway and found no suspicious ridges. He stepped to the left side of the door and began to run his fingers over the wall. But there was nothing there, no fissures or divots he might—

Above the doorway, he thought.

He reached up and immediately located the small wooden lever.

I knew it! he thought. *I knew it would be near the door.*

Peter wondered what the lever would do.

Pull the confounded thing and find out! Richard snapped.

Peter reached for the dark wooden handle and paused.

But Richard? he thought. *There's just one more thing.*

Well? Richard asked. *Have out with it.*

When you came to the island?

What about it?

You died here.

Richard had nothing to say to that.

Stomach fluttering with dread as well as excitement now, Peter reached up and grasped the lever. The wooden handle was clammy, almost slimy to the touch.

That's just the moisture down here. It's a basement, remember?

Yes, Peter thought. *Moisture. There's no way it's…I mean, it can't be…*

"…animal grease," he muttered.

Peter took a deep breath and pulled.

And the entire floor of the pit began to descend.

CHAPTER THREE

Ben fought off the vertiginous sense of déjà vu that threatened to overtake him as he made his way down the single castle tower, the one from which they'd heard music emanating last summer despite the fact that the damned thing had been walled up in 1925. Having found no sign of Julia in the tower – or anywhere else, for that matter – he again made for the forest.

As he passed under the arched pine boughs and the towering old growth oak trees, he struggled to remember the way to the clearing, the one in which he and Claire had faced the beast last summer and had won back his kidnapped son. He'd crisscrossed the island twice already, and thus far he hadn't located the site.

Ben stopped, a frown creasing his forehead. The song was in his head again, its clarion melody dominating his thoughts. Ben compressed his lips, concentrating on his baby girl's face, the silky feel of her skin. Music was the last thing he needed to worry about right now. Who gave a damn about the deadline? Composing was a job, and what use was a job if the people he worked to support, his reasons for living, were in danger?

But still the music persisted. The melody was subtle, elusive, but all the more haunting for those reasons. As often happened, the creative urge was like a nagging itch in his mind. The longer he waited to let the music out, the more severe the itch became. Until it grew maddening. Until it overwhelmed—

"Enough," he growled.

Aware that he'd spoken aloud, he glanced about the forest, suddenly sure someone or some*thing* had heard him.

So take care of it, an angry voice demanded. *Get the notes down on paper, or at least get your phone out and record yourself humming the melody. The music's like a sickness. Once you get it out, you can concentrate on Julia.*

Ben paused on the path, a rush of conflicting emotions swarming over him. He recognized that voice. It was the one who'd hovered over his shoulder for five years before the change occurred...the change that deprived him of his best friend...

Ben closed his eyes and thought of Eddie Blaze.

He never uttered Eddie's name around the house, at least not when Claire was around. Sometimes Nat Zimmerman would talk about Eddie when they were on the phone, but never within earshot of Claire. To Claire, Eddie's name was anathema. To Claire, Eddie was the boogeyman.

Ben couldn't blame her.

The first time Claire had met Eddie, they'd had an argument at Lee Stanley's party. This had been before the four of them – Ben, Claire, Eddie and Eva Rosales, Lee Stanley's assistant – had traveled to the Sorrows and had apparently awakened an ancient evil.

Before Eddie had seemingly lost his mind.

The Eddie he knew had been arrogant, reckless. He'd been a smartass and a difficult guy to get along with sometimes.

But Eddie had also been Ben's lifeline.

Not only was Eddie Blaze the only one who seemed to understand how Ben's mind worked, and was thus the only one who could help Ben blast through that impenetrable bedrock of writer's block that so frequently walled him in; not only was Eddie an indispensable cog in their bizarre creative machine; not only was Eddie a collaborator and a savvy politician with the studio brass – he was a good friend.

No, that didn't quite capture it either, Ben thought, moving slowly down the path now. He remembered Eddie's cocky smile. His easy laugh. His stupid, goofy sense of humor. Yes, Eddie was much more than a friend. He'd been like a brother.

And now Eddie was dead.

Ben ducked under a low-hanging branch and moved down the path, which trended left and up a steep incline. He'd forgotten how large the island was, how deep these woods were. Gaining the top of the rise, Ben glanced behind him and beheld the dark forest unrolling like a sable rug, the trees only vertical glimmers of paleness on the shadowy landscape. Ben continued on, his footfalls becoming steady, metronomic. He felt the earth under the soles of his sneakers, breathed in the rich piney air.

He realized he was humming.

Ben cut off the sound, aggravated with himself. *This isn't like last time*, he thought. *You're not here to find inspiration. You're here to save Julia. There's no telling what kind of trauma that monster has inflicted—*

Stop fighting it, Eddie said.

"Shut up," Ben spat. He pressed his palms to his eyes, dug into the sockets to get Eddie's voice to go away, to get that stupid music out of his head.

Why do you want it gone?

Because I want my daughter!

What if one could help you get the other?

"That doesn't make any sense," he muttered. He set off at a jog, thinking the motion might knock the unhelpful thoughts loose. He needed to navigate. He needed to look for markers. Anything that might help him remember where that clearing was.

Help you remember, huh? Eddie asked. *Isn't that what you told the agents? Isn't that why you jeopardized Christina and Teddy and their whole party? Isn't that why you brought them all here, as fodder for the beast?*

No! he thought.

Knock off the bullshit, Eddie said. *Something happened to you last summer, but you don't wanna admit it.*

The only thing that happened, Ben thought, *is I almost lost my boy. And Claire. And I don't mean to lose Julia.*

And you'll sacrifice anybody to save her. As long as they can help you achieve your ends, you'll offer them up.

I didn't make them come.

But you sure as hell didn't stop them from coming, did you?

Ben shook his head, but the voice would not be silenced.

You're not that different than I was, Eddie went on. *I wanted a woman, I did whatever it took to get her. I wanted you to write music, I pushed you as hard as I needed to get you to do it. Lacking a killer instinct, you never would do it for yourself.*

"Shut up," Ben said. There was another opening in the forest, one stretching in the direction he thought was west. The redwood grove and the clearing might be in that direction. He set off through the dense underbrush, trying to outrun Eddie's wheedling voice, but the words trailed after him like a stench.

But you've got it now, don't you, Ben old pal? You found your killer instinct.

The music began to trickle in the back of Ben's mind. He gnashed his teeth, kept his eyes on the ground ahead to make sure he didn't trip over a hidden rock or a tangle of vegetation. Weeds lashed at his legs as he passed, branches whipping his knees.

Can't run from yourself, can you?

Ben shoved ahead, the bough of a spruce as big and sharp as the tail of some prehistoric animal whipping the side of his arm. It felt like it had drawn blood, but Ben welcomed it, welcomed anything that would distract him from the music, from Eddie Blaze.

Just look at you, Eddie muttered. *You brought them here and now you're facing the beast alone anyway. What a fool you are. You'll die, Julia will too, and the beast will pick off those unsuspecting sons of bitches one at a time. Great plan, Ace!*

His thoughts broke off abruptly. Ben whirled, listening hard. He'd been so focused on Eddie that the sounds of the forest had nearly escaped his notice. There were the occasional calls of nightbirds. The frantic rustle of small animals fleeing his approach.

There were men's voices.

Ben frowned into the darkness.

He screwed up his eyes, studied the trees, the shadows, the occasional slivers of moonlight.

Nothing. There weren't men over there, he told himself. There couldn't be. Because the voices he thought he'd heard were moving in the opposite direction, moving *toward* the castle.

Ridiculous.

Sighing, Ben proceeded until he reached another trail. It wound for a couple minutes through the woods before he noticed how much better he could now see, how the scant illumination had grown. Now the slivers of moonlight penetrating the forest were incandescent pools.

The trail moved up a steep incline, and beyond that the world seemed to open up. He had reached the ocean.

When Ben crested the hill and beheld the sparkling sea, the beauty of it didn't even register in his mind. The only thing that did was down by the beach.

Next to Christina's yacht, the one called the *Blackie*, was another, smaller boat. This one didn't appear to have a name.

But Ben thought he knew who it belonged to.

It belonged to the men whose voices he'd heard in the forest.

Marvin Irvin and his henchmen.

Ben sprinted for the castle.

★   ★   ★

Peter Grant no longer felt much like Indiana Jones. If anything he felt like Jones's inept sidekick…what was the character called? Marcus. Yes, he thought it was Marcus. The character was entertaining, but when it came down to it Marcus was simply a type: the helpless academic. He was always bumping into things and causing problems. A bumbler of the first order.

Which was how Peter felt now.

The descending pit floor had been a surprise; he'd merely expected a door to open up to some passageway. That the whole floor would descend a full twenty feet was something he decidedly had *not* expected. He would have reversed the gigantic elevator immediately had Richard Clay's trenchant voice not bullied him forward. But after venturing only five paces into the opaque gloom that awaited him down here, what mettle he'd possessed had vanished. For perhaps the first time in his adult life, he wanted his mommy.

The ceilings down here were much higher than he would have suspected, and though there was a dampness, a disquieting fecundity in the air, he was also surprised at how dry the area was overall.

Yet the animal smell was overpowering. If the pit had reminded him of some sort of dog kennel, being down here was like being inside the *dog*. The odor was an incredible brew of diarrhea, vomit, semen and unwashed flesh. With each step Peter took, his sense of foreboding increased. He was out of his depth and he knew it. There was little joy in having his decades of work vindicated. And could one actually be considered vindicated if no one else was made privy to the evidence? Peter didn't think so.

No, the thing to do now was to return to that pit elevator, locate the ascent lever and rejoin his party. And it wasn't as if he'd be returning empty handed either. Granted, they might wonder why he hadn't explored the area more thoroughly, and perhaps they'd even think him skittish, but wouldn't their gratitude at his discovery exceed their contempt? Yes, he thought it would. Furthermore, the federal agents would help him reconnoiter the area. And they were armed.

And even more importantly, it would give him the chance to spend more time in the company of Jessie Gary. What a fascinating person she was!

Yes, going back was just the thing – the only prudent course of action.

Peter was just turning toward the pit elevator when his flashlight beam picked out an opening ahead.

Peter paused, considering.

Would it hurt to do just a tiny bit of exploring before returning to the others?

Yes! a frightened voice within him cried. *It damn well could hurt, could hurt very badly. Could get you killed, as a matter of fact. Now find that lever!*

Ninny, Richard Clay said.

"Damn you, Richard," Peter breathed. Keeping his light trained on the opening ahead, he discovered that the passage turned right. Peter crept closer to the turning until he reached the corner. Taking care to move as stealthily as possible, he aimed the beam down the new corridor.

Ten feet ahead the hallway opened up. Peter felt the sparse hair on his forearms rise.

This wasn't merely a tunnel that wormed its way through the bowels of the castle.

This was a labyrinth.

With a cursory sweep of his flashlight he picked out five, six, seven arched doorways. Whoever had constructed this maze had not spared any expense. Despite the fact that no one had likely glimpsed this labyrinth in perhaps ninety years, the walls seemed in excellent shape. The chances of there being a cave-in were virtually non-existent. And the smell, he abruptly realized, might have nothing whatever to do with the legends. Who knew where the tunnels went? They might honeycomb the entire island.

Yes. But he needed some way to mark his progress. The last thing he wanted was to become lost down here. Every cell of his body alight with a twitchy energy, Peter tapped first one hip pocket, then the other, searching for something he could use for a trail. In one of them he found something.

A pack of breath mints. He always kept them on hand in order to keep his breath inoffensive. He'd made a vow to himself as a young professor to never disgust his pupils with the sort of halitosis many of his own teachers – not to mention a good many of his colleagues – were guilty of broadcasting. Rowena Garth, particularly, had a habit of puffing out clouds of garlic-tinged coffee breath, which made speaking to her even more unpleasant. Like he'd been forced to converse with some unhygienic dragon.

There were ten mints in the pack. If he broke them in half and left them at the various branches of the tunnels, he could do plenty of exploring without fear of being lost.

He made to snap a mint in half, but it was too thick and his fingers weren't up to the job. Instead, he placed it between his molars and bit down until it cracked. Then, his mouth tasting pleasantly of wintergreen, he tossed one half of the mint on the floor and pocketed the other.

Then he made straight for the archway across from him. Peter smiled, thinking of the others' reactions, of the treasure trove of mysteries he was about to unlock. This would be the biggest find of the twenty-first century!

Just as importantly, his students would no longer think him a fool. His colleagues would respect him. And by the time the full import of his discoveries was realized, Rowena Garth and her dragon breath might just find herself answering to him.

Dr. Peter Grant, Head of the Stanford English Department.

It had a lovely ring, did it not?

Almost at a run, Peter passed under the archway.

And crashed into something with immense muscles and wiry black hair. Peter landed on his ass, his shoulders and head smacking the floor, the flashlight skittering uselessly off to the side. Its beam came to rest on the black, gnarled hooves of some giant steed.

Only he knew this was no horse. This was…this was…

"*Come*," the creature growled.

Peter groaned in a paralysis of terror as the beast snagged one of his legs and began to drag him deeper into the labyrinth.

CHAPTER FOUR

Jorge Navarro had one vice. He loved to eat in the middle of the night.

It nettled his wife Lucinda, was in fact the sole point of friction in their marriage. Because Lucinda was a light sleeper, she awoke whenever Jorge rose to make himself a snack, and if she was able to fall asleep after he had gone, she invariably awoke again when he returned. So livid did she become when he disturbed her sleep not once but twice within the same half-hour period that she had occasionally ordered him to sleep on the couch because of his nocturnal feedings.

Jorge whistled as he made himself a peanut butter and ham sandwich with extra peanut butter.

Lucinda found the combination foul, and because she was so vocal about it, their kids had begun to make sounds of revulsion whenever Jorge fixed himself his favorite sandwich. To avoid their censure he'd begun limiting himself to more traditional fare when they were around.

But here on the Sorrows, here in this vast gourmet kitchen with a stocked pantry, there were no kids to gag and groan when he slathered the peanut butter on the ham, no Lucinda to snap at him when the box springs creaked as he climbed off the mattress.

Jorge whistled Kool and the Gang's "Celebration" as he fixed himself a double-decker peanut butter and ham sandwich. Lucinda was a good woman but she didn't understand his devotion to Kool and the Gang either.

Jorge assembled his huge sandwich, took a monstrous bite and described an elaborate spin between the island and the countertop. He knew he'd miss his wife and kids in a day or two. But tonight he was enjoying the high life, eating what he wanted to eat, getting in and out of bed whenever he felt like it and singing the kind of stuff he loved to sing. Jorge took another enormous bite, savored the ham and peanut butter and thought, *I may even go outside and take a long, satisfying leak.* Lucinda hated it when Jorge peed outdoors.

The peanut butter was making him thirsty. He knew they didn't have Mountain Dew, his favorite soda, but maybe they'd have something else like it. Mello Yello maybe. Or at least a Coke. Jorge danced over to the fridge, did a breakdancing move he remembered from an old music video he'd once seen. That was another problem, he thought as he scanned the beverages, his kids thought he was a bad dancer. And maybe he was. But wasn't that the point of dancing, to let yourself go and just have fun? Jorge broke into a delighted smile as he spotted a green two-liter lying on its side on the second shelf. My God, Christina had even made sure they had Mountain Dew!

"'There's a party goin' on right here,'" Jorge sang in a loud, out-of-tune voice. The Mountain Dew bottle in hand, he did a little shimmy. Jorge flipped shut the door, turned with the sandwich in one hand and the two-liter in the other and stared into the cold, impassive face of Ray Rubio.

Who brandished a huge buck knife. "I'm not surprised you go in for that jungle music. You illegals always do."

Jorge swung the two-liter at Rubio's face. Rubio brought the knife up, impaled the two-liter. Mountain Dew sprayed over Rubio's front, dousing the man's moonlike face and making him splutter. Jorge lunged toward the counter, seized the first thing his fingers encountered. From a distance of five feet Jorge hurled the jar of peanut butter at Rubio. It thunked him between the eyes, the hard plastic knocking him backward, his big arms pinwheeling. Rubio went down in a heap.

Jorge scrabbled along the counter, searching frantically for something better than a two-liter bottle or a peanut butter jar. He encountered a wooden rack from which depended cooking implements. A ladle, a spatula. *Dammit*, he thought, gaze flitting around the dim kitchen. He was acutely aware of his lack of clothing. He'd only thought to put on a pair of pajama pants over the boxer briefs he'd worn to bed. No shoes, no shirt. The stupid gun was upstairs in his nightstand drawer.

Jorge shot a look to his right, found Rubio gone. Upstairs? Or somewhere in here trying to sneak up on him?

Jorge wrested open a drawer, found the forks and spoons. Yeah, there were butter knives, but that was like entering the Indy 500 with a go-cart. That damned buck knife Rubio was wielding could decapitate a man. Jorge better find something bigger.

Frantically, he spun around, scanned the kitchen island. *Oh hell yeah*, he thought, rushing to the knife rack. He had just slid the butcher knife out of its holder when a supernova of pain exploded in his ankle. Jorge bellowed, face upturned, and when he jerked his head down and saw the dark shape on the floor he realized Rubio had scuttled around the island to stab him. And the bastard had gotten him good, had plunged the buck knife all the way through his ankle and was now yanking it out of him. *Jeeeezus!* He could feel the blade scraping against bone in there. Bracing himself on the countertop, Jorge swept down with the butcher knife and exulted in the enormous slice it made in Rubio's triceps. The son of a bitch hissed in pain but still ripped his buck knife the rest of the way out of Jorge's ankle. Grasping his bleeding arm, Rubio scrambled toward the far end of the kitchen, where the big double sink was. Jorge made to give chase, but the moment he took a step his bad ankle gave way, and he pitched forward onto the tile.

Peripherally, he saw Rubio stop, spotting an advantage. The buck knife whistled down just as Jorge pushed up onto his side. The knife blade clanked on the hard tile, its tip buried there. Rubio jerked the knife free. Jorge rose on one leg, careful not to overtax his injured ankle this time, and dove at Rubio. As he did, he brought the butcher knife down. Rubio tried to fend him off, but the butcher knife chunked into his elbow, the sound reminding Jorge of an axe striking a tree stump. Rubio let loose with a weird, high-pitched cry and rolled away, the butcher knife whipsawing free of Jorge's hand, the damn thing still embedded in Rubio's elbow.

Somehow Rubio was crouched against a cabinet door now; he sidearmed something in Jorge's direction. Jorge didn't realize it was the buck knife until it caught him in the chest. The knife blade connected almost parallel to his body, so that the length of the blade buried itself in Jorge's big pectoral muscles, but only by about a half-inch or so. He stared down at it in mute surprise a moment before ripping it free. A wave of nausea rippled through him as blood began to weep from the shallow wound and trickle down his stomach.

Disgusted and enraged, Jorge shot a look at Rubio.

Who winged the butcher knife at him. Jorge ducked just before the heavy knife whipped over his head and went clattering against the cabinets.

Jorge started forward, saw that Rubio was fumbling to get at something in the hip pocket of his sweatsuit. *A gun?* Jorge wondered as he stalked toward the big bastard. *Uh-uh*, he decided. The bulge in his hip wasn't big enough. He closed on Rubio, the blood-slicked buck knife raised like the killer in that *Psycho* shower scene. *Oh yeah*, Jorge thought. *I'm gonna carve you up good, you ugly son of a—*

Faster than he would've thought possible Rubio lashed out as Jorge hammered down with the buck knife. Something hit Jorge's wrist, the pain so sudden and bright that he lost his grip on the buck knife. The momentum carried the buck knife's tip down into Rubio's shoulder, but it barely broke the windbreaker's fabric and went tumbling into the sink behind him. Rubio's hand shot out again and set Jorge's forehead aflame. He stumbled backward, a patina of blood drenching his face. Jorge armed blood out of his eyes, blinked through it at Rubio, who advanced on him, Rubio brandishing something slender and glittering. A scalpel, Jorge realized. Rubio had a scalpel. And on the heels of that realization, he thought, *Who the hell carries a scalpel?*

For the first time he understood what an animal he was dealing with, what a sadistic bastard Rubio was. The guy wasn't even human. Was closing on him with a horrid grin on his face, was actually *giggling*.

Icy fear clutched him. Jorge took another backwards step to put some distance between himself and the maniac, but a mist of gray enshrouded him and he staggered, went down. He tried to get up, but he slipped and landed in some cold liquid. Jorge thought at first it was his own blood, but then remembered the Mountain Dew. He rolled over. A searing strip of fire tore through his back, Rubio slashing him from shoulder blade to tailbone. The giggling grew louder. Blood dripping in his eyes, Jorge glanced askance and made out the vague shape of Rubio's legs. Impulsively, he reached out with both hands, yanked. Rubio's feet skated along the slick tile, then left the floor entirely. Growling, Jorge thrust the man's feet in the air, upending him. The back of Rubio's greasy head landed on the floor with a flat, smacking sound. Jorge heard another clatter.

The scalpel. Rubio whimpered. *Not so tough without your blades, are you?* Jorge thought. *Not such a big man now, you psychotic son of a bitch.*

Grinning savagely, Jorge clambered over to where Rubio lay and slashed down at his face with a balled fist. He felt Rubio's cheekbone crunch beneath his knuckles.

Don't like that, do ya? he thought. *Don't want a go at me without your weapons.* Rubio brought up a hand to ward him off, but Jorge knocked it aside, hammered down at the man's face again. This time he got Rubio in the teeth, heard a dull crunching sound.

I'm stronger than you are, Rubio. I work out instead of putting shit into my body. Jorge swung, tagged Rubio in the mouth. There was a brittle crack – hopefully one of Rubio's teeth – and he was about to wallop the man again when Rubio's big fingers began pawing at Jorge's midsection. *Looking for my balls?* Jorge thought. *Sorry, asshole, those are lower.* He swung at Rubio, caught him in the forehead this time, but the blow wasn't as satisfying, and what was more, Rubio's hand was still scrabbling up Jorge's midsection like a persistent spider. He made to brush the hand away but before he could, Rubio's fingertips delved into the slit in Jorge's chest, clawed at the tender flesh within. Rubio's fingers cored in, yanked down. Jorge's gash yawned wider, the muscle fiber within tearing. Jorge bellowed in pain, grabbing Rubio's arm with both hands now to pry off his implacable grip, but as he did he realized he'd miscalculated. Rubio was distracting him, occupying both his hands so he could—

Jorge abandoned Rubio's ripping fingers to stop the scalpel, but he was too late. The sharp blade punctured his eardrum and continued inside. Pain so intense Jorge could only crumple to the floor gusted through him. He thought he was dead then, but Rubio had hold of the scalpel by the handle, using it like a lever to bring Jorge's face up to look at him. In the ear that wasn't punctured Jorge heard muffled gunshots, screams.

Ray Rubio stared at Jorge with eyes that were black and glittering. "Your bitch of a boss is gonna die upstairs. Her and everybody with her. You failed her. I wanna be sure you know that."

But Rubio's words were lost in the increasing roar in Jorge's head. Jorge thought of his kids, of his wife. He wondered how Lucinda would do without him. He wished he were home, even if it was on the couch. As the scalpel was driven into his brain, he closed his eyes and missed his family...

CHAPTER FIVE

A knock at her door. Loud, urgent.

At least it's not Castillo, Jessie thought. *He'd be nonchalant about it, try to sweet-talk his way in here.*

"Who is it?" she called, sitting up in bed.

"Morton."

Jessie sat up rigid. Morton's voice had been as tense as Jessie had ever heard it. She scrambled out of bed, wriggled into her blue jeans. She wasn't crazy about Morton seeing her in the loose-fitting tank top, but there wasn't time to worry about that now. Without thinking she retrieved her Glock from the top dresser drawer, crammed it in her pocket. Buttoning her jeans, she hustled over to the door, opened it.

Jessie's heart galloped harder. Morton had his .38 out, his expression deadly serious. "We have visitors," he said.

Jessie frowned, stepped into the hallway with him. "Are you sure it isn't Ben? I didn't see him after we left the—"

"Down!" Morton shouted.

A ragged *brrrrriiiippp* tore through the quiet of the castle, the stone around them exploding in a stinging rain of shards and dust. Jessie hit the floor, Morton beside her. Someone was firing an automatic weapon at them. Or a semi-automatic. It sounded like a Bushmaster or something like it.

A crashing sound erupted nearer, was repeated three more times – Morton's .38 returning fire. Jessie's eardrums rang, the noise unbelievable. Morton grasped her by the back of the shirt, hauled her up and made for her door, but the deafening scream of the automatic erupted again, the corridor a hailstorm of stone fragments. Morton grunted, fell against her. They hit the ground, scuttling backward to evade the assault. Morton brought up his gun again, fired.

Jessie and Morton turned and bounded for the staircase.

The semi-automatic opened up again.

Jessie felt something whiz by her head, let out a surprised gasp.

Marvin and his men had come.

★　　★　　★

Griffin Toomey hadn't planned on this. He had no idea what he had planned on, but it sure as hell hadn't been this. Marvin could have been heading out to a cocktail party, he was so casual about it. The Bushmaster clutched in one arm Marvin stopped them on the third floor landing and said to Nicky under his breath, "You go up to the fifth floor," then looked at Griffin. "That's where they are, right?"

Griffin flushed, hoping to hell he'd been correct. "That's where the luxury suites are, sir. I'm guessing Mrs. Blackwood would want to stay up there."

"Mrs. Blackwood," Marvin said, smiling. "You don't call a widow Missus, you call her Miz. And *Miz* Blackwood is about ready to find out why people don't fuck with me."

Griffin thought, *She didn't fuck with you, Marvin. She just refused to pay your extortion money.*

Sounds of a struggle from far below. There was a high-pitched squeal, a series of thuds.

Oh man, Griffin thought. *That's Rubio I hear. He must've run into someone.*

Marvin's eyes danced with dark excitement. He nodded down the fourth floor hallway. "They'll have heard that. If they haven't, they'll know we're here soon. We'll—" Marvin's words cut off, his eyes growing very wide. "Get back," he muttered.

From down the fourth-story corridor they heard soft footfalls. Marvin peered around the corner, and Griffin could see the man's mouth open, his tongue licking his lips in a movement that reminded Griffin very much of a ruthless predator getting ready to leap on some lesser animal for a feast. Griffin leaned out to get a better look, but Marvin shot out a hand, pinned him against the wall.

Griffin heard a female voice speaking in hushed tones. The man in the corridor answered her.

Then Marvin opened up on them.

★   ★   ★

Jessie was convinced she would die before they reached the shelter of the fourth-story landing. She considered halting, whirling on the shooter and returning fire, but the automatic weapon's flow of rounds never seemed to end. Thankfully, whoever was shooting at them had thus far missed her completely.

But Morton hadn't been so lucky. He was groaning.

Jessie and Morton moved the final ten feet to safety in a series of lurching, hunched-over strides. Then they were veering around the corner and thudding into the wall, Morton's normally steely demeanor now distorted by pain.

"Where?" Jessie demanded.

"Doesn't matter," Morton said. But in the pooled gloom of the landing, Jessie beheld the dark patch spreading on his left side, wondered how bad the wound was.

"Who're they after?" Jessie asked.

"Think, Agent Gary." Morton reloaded his .38 as swiftly and efficiently as ever. If the wound was severe, it wasn't affecting the way he did his job. "There is only one heiress on this island."

"I thought he wanted Ben Shadeland."

"Only as a means of getting to Christina and her money. Marvin means to take her by force."

Jessie bit down on her lip. How could she have been so stupid? The suddenness of the attack. The ungodly roar of the Bushmaster. She shook her head. It was time to get her mind in gear, to—

"Look out!" Morton called.

Shots rang out deafeningly in the stairwell. In the silverlight flashes from the gunman's shots Jessie could make out the crazed visage of Nicky Irvin, the spoiled and – if all she'd heard was true – completely unhinged son of Marvin. Nicky was staring down at them from fifteen feet above, a maniacal grin contorting his features. Leaning toward Morton, she fired twice, and Nicky, still cackling, darted away from the railing.

"Come on," Morton said. "They'll be going for Christina now. You cover us from the back in case the others try to flank us."

Trusting Morton to gun down Nicky if he popped up again like some homicidal jack-in-the-box, Jessie backpedaled up the stairs, her eyes fixed on the fourth-floor doorway. If so much as a shadow twitched there, she'd hit it.

You were good at training, a dubious voice said. *But that's a far cry from real life.*

No different, she told herself. *No different at all. Remember your training. It's what will keep you safe.*

You really think you're safe? You're surrounded. You're outmanned. It's just you and Morton, and he's wounded.

"Where the hell is Castillo?" Jessie asked in a harsh whisper.

Morton didn't reply, only continued creeping up the steps. Watching him, Jessie's spirits rose a half-notch. Morton was good. If Nicky Irvin appeared again, Morton would kill him. But then again, she thought, Nicky was so erratic, such a nutjob…he could get lucky.

Nicky's rap sheet wasn't very long – just a stint for heroin possession and a DUI – but if the whispers Jessie had heard were true, Nicky was not only a drug addict and a complete waste of life, he was a serial rapist and a killer who got off on torturing his victims. Marvin Irvin was the name everyone knew. But Nicky Irvin and Ray Rubio were just as bad and very likely worse.

Her skin crawling, Jessie proceeded up the steps. She listened for the sound of gunfire, but for the moment, none came. She risked a glance down. Even though the fourth-floor landing was now obscured, Jessie was pretty sure there was no one pursuing them.

Which meant Marvin and the other guy had retreated to the other staircase. They'd ascend to the fifth floor, just as Jessie and Morton were doing.

Then it would be a race to reach Christina Blackwood.

But Marvin had the Bushmaster and they only had handguns.

"Who's out there?" someone called from above.

She turned and met Morton's stare. He mouthed the word *Christina.*

Get back in your room, Jessie mentally urged the woman. *You have no idea what's coming for you.*

They were almost to the fifth-floor landing when Morton swung his .38 up, fired. There was a surprised *oomph* from above but no return fire.

Morton moved around the spiral staircase until they were even with the fifth floor. He kept his gun poised on the stairs above them.

"Nicky?" she asked.

"Sixth story," Morton whispered.

"You out there, Morton?" a man's voice called. It was Teddy Brooks. At least, Jessie thought, there was an armed man with Christina. The only other voice Jessie could hear was the medium's. The young woman sounded frightened.

Jessie couldn't blame her.

"I'll get Miss Blackwood," Morton said. He nodded up the stairs. "You take Nicky."

"He's trying to separate us," Jessie hissed. "You need me here."

Morton fixed her with a fierce look. Speaking through his teeth he said, "There isn't time, Agent Gary. What I need is your cooperation. What I don't need is Nicky Irvin sneaking up and shooting me from behind. *What I don't need is having my orders questioned.*"

Jessie wanted to slap him for his stubbornness, but he was right about one thing – they didn't have time to argue.

Abandoning Sean Morton to deal with the Bushmaster and its owner on his own, Jessie clambered up the steps to the top floor.

Toward Nicky Irvin.

CHAPTER SIX

Teddy heard the gunfire and knew what was happening right away. He stayed in his bed though, suspecting the collective bad karma he'd built up would pretty much guarantee him a slow and painful death if he got involved.

Just stay in your room, Christina, he thought, the covers drawn up around his neck. *Just stay the hell in your room and let the feds handle this. It's what they're trained for, isn't it? I'm just an ex-cop who drinks too much. This is outside my job description.*

More thunder from below. Jesus. Someone had a machine gun down there.

Jorge could handle it, Teddy told himself. Jorge and that musclehead Chad Wayne. Even if Wayne had more muscles than brains, he would protect his boss when push came to shove.

But when Teddy heard Christina's terrified voice in the hallway asking what was going on, he forgot how it wasn't his job to help her.

Blowing out frustrated breath, Teddy shed his blankets and climbed out of bed. As he fetched his gun and slipped on his clothes, he heard another voice in the hall. It was Elena Pedachenko, sounding frightened and bewildered.

The gun at his side, Teddy went to the hallway. Opened the door and turned left.

Saw Christina's distraught face. "What's happening, Mr. Brooks?"

"Marvin got tired of waiting," Teddy said. "Now why don't you get in my room where you'll be safe?"

Christina's eyebrows gathered together in apprehension, but she nodded. That was good, Teddy thought. Still capable of coherent communication.

"Where are your guards?" Elena asked Christina.

Though it was a good question, Teddy didn't want to stand here in the hallway ruminating on it. "Come on," he said and took Christina by the arm.

They had just about reached Teddy's room when shots behind them got his attention quick. Teddy saw shadows there, realized right away the shots weren't being fired at them – someone in the stairwell shooting at someone else instead. But it was only a matter of time, he knew. You took a job offered by a billionaire being threatened by underworld killers, and being shot at was a mathematical inevitability.

What the hell had he been thinking?

"Let's get our butts inside," he said to Christina, gripping her arm and towing her along more forcefully now.

"Get down, Miss Blackwood!" someone shouted from behind them. Definitely one of the feds, Teddy thought. He and Christina were almost to Teddy's room, but ahead of them Teddy saw two figures emerge from the darkness. One of them held a gun that looked like it could take down a wooly mammoth.

"Let's get to your room," Christina said in a tight voice.

Too late, Teddy thought. And pulled her to the ground beside him.

★   ★   ★

Jessie pursued Nicky Irvin up the stairs and chided herself for not checking out the top level of the castle earlier. She'd familiarized herself with the basement and the other five stories, it was true, but this oversight was unforgivable.

She hoped she wouldn't pay for it with her life.

Nicky's footfalls echoed in the spiral stairwell, then continued as the man's feet landed on a different surface. She heard the footsteps accelerate, recede, and wondered if he was simply hustling all the way to the other stairwell so he could descend on the other side to rejoin his father. If that was the case, they'd at least only have to worry about being attacked from one direction. Maybe, Jessie thought as she neared the fifth floor, she could simply trail him, slip down the stairs behind him and take them all by surprise. It would certainly make up for her inaction earlier, her stupid reliance on Morton to save them both.

Her gun drawn, Jessie stepped forward and saw the moonlight pouring through the windows into what appeared to be one large studio. The whole sixth story, she realized, moving into the room, was devoted to a piano and some seating areas.

A foot shot out and knocked the Glock out of her hands. Her first instinct was to go for it, but that was crazy. Nicky was armed too.

She let her momentum from his kick swing her body around, but rather than falling she completed the turn and whipped an elbow at him. His gun went off in the darkness, an unbelievable crashing sound this close to her ears. She went instantly deaf, the only noise in her head an unearthly ringing. No time to worry about that, though. Nicky was lowering the gun toward her.

Jessie thrust a forearm at his wrist, felt it connect solidly. The gun went clattering to the floor.

Nicky went for the gun, and though Jessie's own gun was no farther away than his was, she decided not to chance it. He was bent over, reaching for the gun, his profile to her. She reared back and booted him in the side, the point of her toe catching him in the kidney. Breath whooshed out of him, a hand clamping over his side. He yawed to his right, looked like he was about to fall over. Jessie followed, moving into a position where she could kick him in the face. She reared back, meaning to knock the bastard out so she could retrieve her gun and help Morton.

But Nicky had been lulling her, pretending to be near a fall when he was actually reaching for something near his ankle. When Jessie's foot arced toward his head, Nicky's left arm whipped at her in a vicious backhand. Bright pain scalded the sole of her foot. *He's sliced through my sneaker*, she thought. The pain was so terrible and unexpected that Jessie did what instinct demanded – she grabbed for her bleeding foot. But that allowed Nicky Irvin to slash at her again, this time ripping a hot gash in her bare shoulder.

Jessie sucked in shocked breath, slapped a hand to her shoulder, but the cut was deep, the blood already squirting out around her fingers. She realized she'd left herself unguarded again and all of a sudden understood how different this was from her training.

She was sure Nicky would deal her a death stroke from his knife, but rather than stabbing her or slicing her again, Nicky cocked a fist and brought it crashing down on her nose.

Jessie went down.

"That's a sweet girl," Nicky said. She made out his words, though they sounded as though he was calling to her from a great distance.

"You're a feisty little kitty, aren't you?" Nicky said. "We're gonna have us a great time together, aren't we, kitty?"

Something smashed into her side. Jessie doubled up, moaning. Nicky had kicked her, she realized. Kicked her like some stray dog he'd discovered foraging in his garbage.

Nicky kicked her again, this time right in the throat. Jessie coughed, her throat instantly ablaze. The pain was worse than any she'd yet experienced, indescribable.

"Wittle kitty hurt a wittle?" Nicky cooed.

No, she thought, tasting the blood that filled her mouth. Not like her training at all. Her training hadn't been in a castle. Her training hadn't involved awakening from a sound sleep to be shot at by an automatic weapon. And her training hadn't pitted her against a psychopath in the dark.

Not just a psychopath, she thought. *A torturer and a murderer.*

And a serial rapist.

As though he'd heard her, Nicky reached out, tugged on her sweatpants.

"Oh my land," he said, his voice thick with lust. "Look what we have here."

★   ★   ★

Ben was hustling through the forest – for the moment his terror for Julia was usurped by the more imminent danger of what was about to happen at the castle – when he heard the first gunshots.

My fault, he thought, pushing himself even harder down the trail. The branches and outreaching weeds whipped his body. Ben's skin was lashed in half a dozen places, but the physical pain was nothing next to the guilt crashing down on him, the dread knowledge that it was he who'd led them all here, he who had set them up in this isolated place to be slaughtered by Marvin and his animals. Teddy had told him stories, and though Ben lent them some credence, he hadn't truly grasped the danger Marvin presented until this moment. He thought of Teddy, sleeping peacefully in his room; Agent Gary, who seemed far too human to be working for the government; Morton, who though humorless didn't seem like a bad guy; he thought of Christina Blackwood, whose only crime was being rich. Who'd lost her only child a year ago and who therefore had a far deeper bond with Ben at the moment, one that eclipsed socioeconomic differences.

Christ, what had he done?

Another possibility, this one so dire he wished it hadn't arisen, blasted through his mind: What if the beast had Julia hidden somewhere else? After all, there was no guarantee it had taken her to the redwood clearing. She could just as easily be lying there exposed near the shoreline, in one of the many caves, atop one of the cliffs on the southern side of the island…

…or within the castle itself.

More gunfire, this time announcing itself as some kind of machine gun. The mob guys had brought their heavy artillery to the island.

Nearing the forest's edge, Ben slowed and took out his weapon. He emerged into the brilliant, moonlight-flooded castle lawn, took a few steps toward the front of the castle, then thought better of it. It was true they might have posted sentries at all three doors, but it still seemed more prudent to enter through one of the less conspicuous ones.

Knowing every second mattered, Ben pelted toward the back door. Ben ripped open the door and saw a fist the size of a Christmas ham come hammering down at his face.

CHAPTER SEVEN

Buuuhrrrrip-ip-ip-ip-ip-ip-iiiiiiipppppp – went the automatic, the sound so loud it made the fillings in Teddy's molars vibrate.

The *pom pom pom pom* sound of return fire wasn't quite as loud, but it came from closer to them and was therefore just as hard on their ears. He was splayed out on top of Christina, both of them facedown, and though he'd entertained more than one fantasy about engaging in some extracurricular activities with his wealthy boss, the circumstances made their current intimacy about as sexy as kissing his elderly Aunt Regina. Teddy's midsection pressed into Christina's buttocks, and as the gunfire raged over their heads Teddy became aware of moisture down there. Either he'd pissed himself or Christina had or both of them had. It hardly mattered, and if it was Teddy who'd tinkled on his boss, he didn't think she'd hold it against him. After all, he had saved her life. Or at least saved her life so far. They were far from safe, were in fact in the middle of a fucking war zone. But neither of them had been shot yet, perhaps because neither party wanted them shot.

Check that, Teddy thought, burrowing his head deeper into the crook of Christina's neck. The two groups – the feds behind them and Marvin's in front of them – didn't want Christina Blackwood to die, but he doubted very much either party would fuss much if Teddy got hit with a stray bullet. Oh, the feds weren't aiming at Teddy necessarily, but one less divorced detective in the world wasn't going to make anyone in the Bureau lose much sleep. As for Marvin's men, shit. They'd love it if Teddy got killed. Hell, he wouldn't be surprised if Marvin and that goddamned automatic happened to dip a little and send the top of Teddy's head somersaulting through the air like a bottle cap. Marvin wanted Christina and he wanted her alone. The only other person he might keep alive on this island would be Ben Shadeland, and that was only because Shadeland had a little money too. He wasn't as rich as Christina – he wasn't even in the same zip code as Christina – but he had more money than a private detective, that was for damned sure.

Shouting voices from the gangsters, a returning shout from the feds. Teddy had only seen one agent back there, but more could be there now. Who the hell knew? His body was dizzy with adrenaline, and his ears rang like lunatic church bells. Teddy had to get Christina into his room. Hell, he had to get *himself* into his room.

A new voice joined the chorus of shouting, this one back there with Agent Morton. Teddy risked another look back and discovered, lo and behold, that Agent Castillo had finally shown up. *Nice of you to make time for us!* Teddy thought bitterly.

"Get them to safety," Morton said to Castillo. "I'll lay down cover."

Castillo nodded, though he looked none too excited about jumping into the O.K. Corral this hallway had become. Castillo moved forward, hunched over, and as he did, Teddy saw that he was looking beyond Teddy, in the direction of Marvin and his henchman.

Teddy realized Marvin had stopped firing.

He glanced up at Marvin and saw the man was indeed waiting. It was as though in the middle of the firefight the two men – Castillo and Irvin – had decided to wage a staring contest. What they were waiting for Teddy had not the slightest clue. But the window to get Christina to safety wouldn't be open much longer, of that much he was certain.

"C'mon," he whispered. And drawing Christina to her feet, he lurched with her the final four strides to his door. It was ajar, thank God, and Teddy rammed it with his open left palm. The door banged open, and Teddy thrust them both through. On their heels came Troy Castillo with his arms around Elena Pedachenko, who was wincing in pain. When Teddy strode over to secure the door he saw why. She'd been shot in the left arm.

"You okay?" he asked her, knowing as he said it how stupid a question it was.

"What do you think?" she asked.

He shook his head. "Hey, I—"

"And where were you?" Elena shouted at Castillo.

"Shut up," the agent muttered. "I need to hear what's happening."

The request was reasonable. But even in the dimness of the bedroom, Teddy could see Castillo's evasive expression.

What are you hiding? Teddy wondered.

Then the shooting started anew.

★   ★   ★

Jessie lay on her stomach, her head ringing.

She had never been raped before, had never even had a man try to force a kiss on her. She knew such abhorrent things happened all the time – much more frequently than they were reported – but it was still a shock when she felt Nicky's fingers slither between her legs.

She clamped her legs together instinctively, rolled onto her side and slapped at Nicky's hands, but that only elicited laughter from him, made him plunge his fingers closer to her sex. With a cry of revulsion Jessie jerked her hips around with Nicky's hand clamped between her legs. There was a dull popping sound from Nicky's wrist.

Nicky yelled, "*Fuck!*"

She thought for a moment she could carry him all the way over with the force of her rotating legs, but his hand slipped free, and then he was on his knees next to her, clutching his injured wrist.

Teeth bared, he growled, "Stupid bitch."

Jessie knew she should yank up her pants, but her anger mastered her. She lashed out with the hand nearest him and watched her fingernails rip bloody troughs up the side of his neck.

Nicky bellowed, clapped at his bleeding neck.

Jessie rolled over, but Nicky was on her instantly.

He tackled her, knocked her back toward the staircase and landed on her. His right hand appeared uninjured, and it was with this fist that he set to work, jabbing at her like a frenetic piston, some of the blows missing but too many landing on her cheeks, her chin. One caught her in the mouth and Jessie felt her bottom lip explode in a wet burst of heat.

Nicky hammered her face, grunting out curses as he did. "Stupid… fucking…cunt…" Another blow opened the skin at her temple, the pain immense despite how dazed she felt. "Gonna drill…" A jab. "…that sweet ass of yours…" A blow rattled her jawbone. "…gonna come inside you…" His fist slammed into her. "…then I'm gonna kill you."

Jessie realized he was straddling her so his punching angle would be improved. He'd left himself exposed. She shot a knee between his legs.

It didn't get him square in the nuts, but enough of her leg struck home that he doubled over in pain, which allowed her to shove him off, roll over and retrieve the first object her blurred vision could discern.

Nicky's knife.

As she turned toward him she caught a clear glimpse of the implement – Good God, like a miniature sickle. The thing reminded her of the fillet knife her grandpa had once used to clean the smallmouth bass they caught in his stocked pond, and though Nicky looked up in time to see the blade whistle down at him, he didn't have time to block its diagonal trajectory. The curved blade sliced his left nostril in half, proceeded down through his upper lip – cleaving deeper as it descended – then created a fine slit from the corner of his mouth all the way to his jaw. As he gaped at her and pawed at the slit, she watched the blood, which looked as black as crude oil, first fill the gash and then pour out of it. Nicky's eyes widened in horror. He rose to his feet, swaying, and stared down at the blood dripping out of his mouth, first pattering on his open palms, then spilling over his fingers as the flow grew steadily more severe. He glanced at her as though he couldn't believe she could behave so violently. Then he staggered sideways, teetered like he was about to fall.

Reached down for something on the floor.

Jessie gasped as she realized his intent. Even in his badly wounded state Nicky was still very much a dangerous predator. He lulled you into believing you were safe, even using his gushing blood as a ruse. No wonder he'd killed so many people. No wonder he'd raped so many women. He was made for killing, a heartless machine who reveled in pain, who'd destroyed who knew how many lives.

But not this time.

A feral grin stretching her lips, Jessie strode over to him, and before he could raise the gun, she gripped the knife with both hands and slashed down at him. There was muted snicking sound as the fillet knife tore through the side of his neck. Then a noise that reminded her of gentle rainfall as his carotid artery spurted blood over the studio floor. The gun in one hand, he stood and gaped at her and placed his free hand over the gushing neck wound. The gun began to rise, but she anticipated it, snatched the gun away with her left hand while with her right she swung the fillet knife. A glistening black smile opened in Nicky's throat. The fluid ran in a sheet down his front, his eyes huge and glassy. He stumbled into her, his blood soaking her tank top. With a grunt, she sidestepped and gave him a two-handed shove into the doorway. She thought he'd fall then, but was shocked to see him still walking, zombielike, toward the stairs. The only part of him that seemed fully alive were his hands, which were clawing madly at his gushing jugular.

Gun outstretched, she followed him, wondering how far he'd get before he fell. She knew she should shoot him. There was gunfire below again, and her duty was now to lend Morton aid. But she wanted to see Nicky bleed, was fascinated the dying slimeball could still move.

Nicky had made it halfway down to the fifth floor before he pitched forward and landed face first on the unforgiving stone steps. She thought he'd simply lie there and bleed to death, but his momentum carried him down, his legs and ass flipping over his bloody front so that he somersaulted forward, his boneless body tumbling toward the landing. Jessie followed, wishing she'd retrieved her own gun – who knew how reliable Nicky's was?

When his body finally hit the landing and sprawled into the fifth-story corridor, Jessie was about six feet behind him and still obscured by the landing wall.

But the sound of Marvin Irvin's heartbroken wail reached her without problem.

★   ★   ★

Ben looked up, his thoughts muddled. The man who'd slugged him was one of the largest he'd ever seen. Sure, Ben was a big guy, the type most considered a huge guy. But if Ben was huge, the man looming over him now was a colossus.

The giant stepped through the doorway and groped for him. Ben let the giant grasp him two-handed by the shirtfront, allowed the giant to lift him off the ground. He thought at first the man might toss Ben onto the grass like a toy that had displeased him, but instead he righted Ben, getting him into position.

Face to face, the man reared back.

Ben jerked his head aside just as the haymaker whooshed by his face. He seized the man's shirt, whipped his head at him. Ben's forehead crashed into the huge man's nose.

The giant didn't cry out, scarcely made any sound at all. Nor did he let go of Ben and go reeling away. Despite the pain the head butt must've brought on – hell, Ben's forehead felt as though it had been struck with a mallet – the man didn't loosen his grip on him. Looked, if anything, more resolute than he had previously. The man leaned back, slammed his head into Ben's.

The pain was astonishing.

But rather than dimming his consciousness, the blow brought Ben fully alive, the agony of the blow like the world's worst brain freeze. The giant seemed to understand he'd hurt Ben because he swung at him again, this time from the shoulder. Ben only partially dodged this blow, the giant's ham-like fist smacking Ben in the ear.

This pain was somehow worse than the brain freeze had been, and it made him angry. Jaw tight, Ben swung low and pounded the giant in the ribs. He felt the huge man's body jolt, and though the giant still did not release him, Ben thought he'd finally succeeded in hurting the man. Ben reared back, blasted the giant in the side again, Jesus, like hitting a slab of cold meat.

The giant thumped Ben in the ribcage, the blow so fierce he was lifted off the ground. The man seemed to find Ben's weakest point – right in the side, where his ribs weren't sheathed in muscle. The giant walloped him again, and again Ben's feet were lifted off the ground. The giant reared back to strike him a third time, but Ben grasped him by the shoulders, pivoted and swung him toward the castle façade. The huge man hit the wall shoulder first. Grimacing, the giant squeezed the shoulder that had crashed into the castle, leaving his right side exposed.

Ben moved in, swinging in looping sideways arcs. The sensation of punching a slab of meat recurred, but then the giant shifted, covering his battered ribs.

Ben was ready. He aimed a roundhouse right at the man's face, bashed him right in the cheek. The giant's head whipped sideways, spittle flying out of his mouth. Ben swung with his left arm, but the punch wasn't as accurate and only glanced off the giant's jaw.

Gunshots sounded from above and Ben suddenly remembered the others. They might all be dying while he brawled with this huge bastard on the castle lawn.

Ben made a move toward the castle, but the giant thrust out a big foot and tripped him. Ben stumbled forward, sure the giant would shoot him in the back. Ben had no doubt the man was armed.

He swiveled his head expecting to see the man holding a gun to his face, but the giant was evidently still interested in fighting with his fists.

Ben decided to comply.

He lurched forward, away from the man's grasping fingers, and when the giant followed, Ben spun, planted, then launched his body into the giant's midsection. The giant uttered a low grunt, pushed against Ben, but Ben had leverage, dug his heels in and drove with his legs until the giant was backpedaling, encircling Ben's lower back in an attempt to leverage him off his feet. Ben wrapped the giant up around the man's thick middle, then picked him up, took another couple steps and slammed him onto his back. Despite the cushion of grass, the man's breath whooshed out, his face crinkling in an expression of surprise and pain.

The sweat was trickling into Ben's eyes now, but he ignored it, pushed up to his knees. Half on top of the man, he rammed down with his right fist and caught the giant in the eye. A furious, wounded cry issued from the giant's mouth as he tried to cover his face.

Ben rained blows on the man's head, battering him until he dropped his hands. Blood sprayed from the man's face, his big body going limp.

Ben pushed to his feet, stood panting over the giant. He knew the man wasn't dead – not even close to it – but he had to get up to the fifth floor, where he was certain the battle was taking place. There was still gunfire, but not as much of it now. He hoped Teddy was still alive, hoped the bastards hadn't killed Jessie.

The giant twitched, reached for something under his shirt. Ben stood immobile for a moment, caught between making a run for it and stopping the man's grab for his gun.

Ben grabbed for the gun. He barely made it there, the giant moving nimbly despite the beating Ben had given him. The big handgun rose toward Ben's face, but Ben seized the man's wrist, redirected the gun toward the woods a moment before the deafening blast erupted, stealing Ben's hearing and filling the air with the stink of graphite. Ben pinned the man's wrist to the grass, but the giant was feisty, aiming a haymaker at Ben's face with his free hand. The blow didn't have much behind it, but it angered Ben nonetheless. Ben reared back, pounded the giant in the face. When the giant's left hand batted at him again, Ben jabbed him in the nose. Still, impossibly, the big man was raising his right hand, the one with the gun, with Ben's hand still clutching his wrist. The big bastard was immensely powerful, and Ben realized he wasn't going to escape this lawn without one of them dying.

The giant mouthed something, but Ben couldn't hear it. The only thing he picked up with his ringing eardrums was a distant roar that reminded him of the ocean.

Teeth bared, Ben muscled the gun back down, swatted the man's bloody face with a fist. God, the guy was strong. But now, absurdly, he was mouthing words again, choosing this of all times to attempt communication with Ben.

"What the hell do you want?" Ben shouted.

The man gripped Ben by the shoulder, hauled him lower. Ben began to fight at first before he realized the giant was trying to say something into Ben's ear.

But all he could pick up were the words *island* and *ghosts*.

Frustratedly, he thrashed the man's gun hand on the grass again and again, but the giant would not relinquish his hold on the gun.

The giant yelled again, and this time Ben heard him well enough. "This island is full of ghosts!"

Ben glared into the giant's eyes, their faces only inches apart. "*Let go*," Ben shouted into his mess of a face.

"Uh-uh," the giant shouted back. "Not until you kill me."

Ben was so surprised by this that for a moment he forgot to struggle. The gun immediately jerked up, but it wasn't toward Ben's face that it flew – it rested against the giant's temple.

"You do it," the giant said. "I don't wanna go to hell."

Ben thought of telling the man he'd probably go to hell anyway working for a guy like Marvin Irvin, but decided now wasn't the time.

The man was blubbering, his saliva mixing with blood. "I saw 'em when we docked tonight. I saw all the people I ever killed. None of the other guys did, but I saw 'em. Lined up on the beach waiting for me. Just staring."

When Ben only gaped down at him, the giant grabbed Ben's hand, placed it over the handle and trigger, then covered it with his own big paw. "Please," the giant said. "You gotta! I can't do this anymore."

Gunshots sounded from above. Ben stared into the man's grimacing face, felt the incredible strength still thrumming through the man's body. If Ben didn't kill him, he'd keep fighting. If Ben died, the giant would certainly kill others.

"Please," the giant whispered, red spit bubbling on his lips.

Ben closed his eyes, turned away, and squeezed the trigger.

The boom was muffled this time, but that was probably owing to his already compromised hearing. Blood and other matter splattered everywhere. Ben rose, taking care not to look down at the man's ruin of a face.

Ben moved away from the twitching giant and began scanning the tall grass for his gun. Just when he was sure he'd lost it, a dark object near the castle wall caught his eye. Blowing out a relieved breath, Ben retrieved his Ruger and made for the door. He half-expected another one of Marvin's henchmen to be waiting for him inside Castle Blackwood, but the back entryway was empty.

The gun gripped in one bloody hand, Ben sprinted for the stairs.

CHAPTER EIGHT

Jessie watched it all unfold as in a nightmare.

Her triumph at having bested Nicky faded the moment she saw the expression on Marvin's face. The man and the blond-haired crony attending him had dragged a squat wooden table out of one of the rooms and were hunched behind it. Marvin was still clutching the Bushmaster, the blond guy with him just looking dismayed by it all.

Morton had managed to get the others to safety, apparently. He was leaning out of Christina's door, drawing a bead on Marvin, about seventy feet between them.

Jessie continued down the steps after Nicky, whose tumbling body had finally come to rest half in, half out of the long hallway.

But there was enough of him visible for Marvin to know what had happened.

"Nicky?" Marvin whispered.

Marvin rose up behind the overturned table.

Jessie saw Sean Morton's SIG-Sauer come to rest on Marvin.

Morton fired.

A splash of liquid plopped out of Marvin's shoulder. Morton had been aiming for the heart, but Marvin had staggered a little as he made his way around the table. Morton squeezed the trigger again, but this time there was only a dull click.

She could see, drawing closer to him, that Morton was reloading frantically, his body language making plain how angry he was with himself for committing this error and for missing an opportunity to kill Marvin.

"Nicky?" Marvin asked as if he hadn't just been shot.

"Get down, Sean," Jessie called.

But Morton didn't, instead remained in that half-crouch, reloading his SIG-Sauer.

"Nicky?" Marvin called. As Marvin drew nearer she saw his forehead crease and his bottom lip begin to quiver. "Nicky? OH GOD NICKY!"

Marvin swung the Bushmaster up and began to unload.

Rounds pinged off the inner wall of the hallway, tossing fragments of stone and dust everywhere. Marvin's aim was even wilder than before, his face contorted by grief. Jessie was still a good fifteen feet behind Sean Morton, but she couldn't wait any longer. Stepping sideways to get Morton out of her sightline, she brought Nicky's gun to rest on Marvin, squeezed the trigger. Marvin spun, the Bushmaster spraying bullets around the corridor, taking bites out of the ceiling, the outer wall, shattering a window, then uttering that agitated *vrrrrr* that told her he was out of bullets. She fired twice more, and this time Marvin went down. Then Nicky's gun clicked empty, and she had no ammo with which to reload.

For just a moment she realized Morton had been watching her and Marvin going at it, but now Morton's trance broke, and he rose, gun trained on Marvin's prostrate form.

It was at that moment that Jessie saw the figure rise up from behind the table down the hall.

She'd forgotten all about the other one, the blond guy with hair like some sort of punk rocker, the one who'd done nothing but cower as the firefight raged on, the one who was now inexplicably moving to his feet, a gun rising from his side.

"Get down, Sean!" Jessie screamed. But Morton did not get down, did not even appear to notice the other one, so focused was Morton on his fallen foe. Marvin lay on the floor, sobbing and grasping his shoulder.

Morton leveled the gun at Marvin. The blond guy beyond Marvin strode forward, gun extended. Jessie took a big step to her left, hoping to pick the gunman off before he could shoot Morton, but she was too late. The blond guy had already squeezed the trigger. Morton doubled up, then crumpled to the floor. Jessie fired, but the blond guy had begun running in a stooped position. Jessie fired again, missed. The guy skidded to his knees and threw an arm over Marvin Irvin, like that would protect him. But his other arm was held out, the gun spitting fire at Jessie now. Jessie hit the ground, crawled forward to get to Morton.

Morton's wound was bad, Jessie could see that right away. Not only was blood sluicing over the fingers clutched to his gut, but there was blood pooling on the floor, blood trickling from Morton's lips. He was dying, dying right here in this hallway, and it was the blond guy's fault. He'd stayed out of the fray until everyone forgot about him, then he'd made his bullets count. The bastard.

"Get him into the room," a voice shouted from behind Jessie. She gasped, whipping her head around to see who it was.

Ben Shadeland, looking as though he'd been through hell. Ben Shadeland with a gun aimed at the pair of gangsters. But it wasn't a pair of gangsters any longer, she realized as she glanced back at Marvin and the blond shooter. There was a third now, and this one, like Ben, was painted with gore. Had Ben and the new gangster gone at it? And if so, how had the fight ended without one or the other dying? The new gangster – it was Ray Rubio, she realized – fired on her. The bullet bit the wall to her right. A fleeting memory of Rubio's horrific file flashed through her mind, and despite the adrenaline coursing through her she experienced a momentary chill.

"Here," Ben said from beside her. "I'll get Morton, you cover us."

Jessie nodded. Ben knelt, scooped up Morton like he was a small child and raced for the master suite. Jessie shot at the gangsters, who returned fire. She backpedaled and threw a quick glance over her shoulder to confirm that Ben and Morton had made it into the room alive. Jessie fired one more time before lunging through the doorway behind them.

"How is he?" Jessie asked, locking the door.

"Terrible," Ben said.

Jessie waited at the door, listening for gunfire. But there were only muttered oaths and the sounds of a brief argument. Then the voices receded from the same direction they'd come.

The gangsters had departed.

CHAPTER NINE

Five minutes later, after they'd all collected in Christina's room, Teddy heard footsteps outside the door. Teddy reached out, plucked his gun from the table. Agent Gary had hers ready too.

The door creaked open.

"Everything okay?" a timid voice asked.

Teddy exhaled trembling breath, exchanged a weary look with Jessie.

Chad Wayne stepped into the room.

"The hell you been?" Teddy asked him.

Wayne scowled at them. "I was in my room."

Ben said, "You figured we had it under control."

"I was scared."

"We were *all* scared," Jessie said. "But that doesn't mean we hid."

"Hey," Wayne said, palms up, "I didn't sign on for all this. No one said there'd be shooting."

"What kind of a bodyguard are you?" Elena asked, a hysterical edge to her voice.

"I don't wanna die any more than you do, so why don't you just—" Wayne caught sight of Morton's stomach. "Oh shit."

"Make yourself useful," Jessie snapped. "Get some more clean towels."

Wayne's skin had gone a sallow hue, his chin working.

Teddy hustled into the bathroom. There was only one towel left, so Teddy grabbed it and a small stack of washcloths. When he got back to the bedroom, Morton's legs started to spasm. Morton coughed and blood bubbled up over his teeth. He coughed again, and the blood sprayed out the sides of his mouth.

"Holy shit," Wayne said. He turned and puked.

"At least use a waste basket!" Elena shouted. But Wayne remained stooped over beside the dresser, his big back heaving.

"Everybody accounted for?" Castillo said.

Christina shook her head. "Jorge is still missing. Peter's gone too."

Jessie said, "Could someone get another towel? A big one?"

Still bent over, Wayne glanced up at Teddy.

Teddy glared at him. "What am I now, the towel boy? We in the antebellum South all of a sudden?"

"Oh, for God's sakes," Elena muttered, and went toward the door.

"I wouldn't do that," Castillo cautioned.

"You wouldn't do anything," she answered and stormed out of the room.

Castillo looked up at Jessie. "What the hell's that supposed to mean?"

Without looking up from Morton's wound, she said, "It means we could've used you earlier, Troy. Where were you?"

"I was exploring the castle," he said. "Jesus, is that some sort of crime?"

"But why did it take you so long to—" Jessie broke off. Glancing down, Teddy saw why. Morton's eyes were open and staring at Castillo.

"What is it, Sean?" Jessie asked.

Morton's lips worked, but no sound issued forth. More blood trickled from the corners of his mouth.

Jessie drew closer, her face only a few inches over Morton's. "Say it again, Sean. I couldn't...what?"

Morton's lips moved. Then, though it obviously cost him an effort, he said, "You..."

Morton coughed, his body racked with pain. He turned his head away from Jessie, and blood drooled out in a messy string. Stuff was so red it reminded Teddy of acrylic paint.

Jessie glanced up at Teddy. "What's he saying, Ben? I can't—"

"He's delirious," Castillo said. "Too much blood loss. We need to get him sedated."

"Are you insane?" Jessie said. "Lower his heart rate any more and he'll die."

Morton's eyes riveted on Castillo. "You...son of a *bitch*," Morton hissed. The words were unmistakable, but they set off another torrent of coughing. The pain on Morton's face made Teddy's heart hurt, the poor man obviously dying. Teddy'd only seen one other man gutshot, one of Teddy's former LAPD buddies by the name of Dan Herbert. Dan had died only a minute or two after being shot in pursuit of a carjacker. Morton had survived longer than Herbert had, but Teddy didn't think

Morton would last another five minutes. His face had already gone pale, and if anything, the crimson blooms on the towels seemed to be spreading faster rather than slowing down.

Jessie moved her hand aside as Ben pressed another towel atop the others. "I've got it," he said quietly.

Jessie took her hand off Morton's hemorrhaging stomach and caressed his wan cheek. Her fingers left bloody contrails on Morton's face, but Teddy didn't figure the man would mind.

"…knew…" Morton whispered to Jessie.

Cradling his head, Jessie said, "Knew what? What are you…" She glanced pleadingly up at Ben and Teddy. "What's he talking about?"

Ben shook his head. Teddy had an idea but resolved to keep it to himself for now.

"My God, that looks like it really hurts," Christina said, glancing at Ben's face.

Chad Wayne glanced up at the gaping gash on Ben's cheek and his eyes widened. Groaning, he vomited again.

"Could someone please get him out of here?" Jessie said. Teddy could see tears in her eyes.

"Come on, pal," he said to Wayne. Careful not to step in puke, he put his hands on the man's waist and steered him toward the door.

"I don't wanna go out there," Wayne moaned.

"They're gone," Teddy said, hoping that was true.

"But what if they're not?" Wayne asked in a small voice.

"Well, then you just toss your cookies again and they won't want to come near you."

"*Awww man*," Wayne moaned.

Teddy guided him out the door, and once they were out there, made the mistake of glancing at Wayne's face. His lips were creamed with vomit, the long hair that had fallen into his eyes also sticky.

Teddy gave Wayne an unsentimental shove toward Teddy's room. Stumbling, Wayne advanced a few steps, stopped and began to dry heave.

Teddy returned about the time Elena got back with a fresh stack of towels. When they got inside, Teddy knew right away what had happened.

Jessie stared down at Sean Morton's slack face with tears streaking her face. Ben had a hand on her shoulder. Castillo's back was to Teddy, but when Teddy moved deeper into the room, he saw Castillo watching Morton's motionless body with what looked like guilt.

Or maybe that was Teddy's imagination.

★   ★   ★

Jessie heard Brooks saying they should make sure the castle was secure, but she couldn't take her eyes off Morton's bloodless face. Someone touched her arm. She looked up, realized it was Ben Shadeland.

"We need to make sure those bastards are gone," he said.

Jessie regarded him a moment, then gave him a hollow nod.

"I'll go with you," Teddy said.

"Uh-uh," Ben said, leading Jessie to her feet.

"What do you mean 'uh-uh'?" Teddy asked, scowling after them.

Ben opened the door slowly, his gun at the ready. He poked his head into the dark corridor, Jessie huddling close behind him. When he appeared sure the gunmen were gone, he led her into the hallway.

Teddy followed them. "Why should I stay here?"

Ben spoke under his breath. "You trust Castillo?"

"Hell no, I don't trust him. Why you think I wanna come with you?"

"You notice Castillo didn't volunteer to search the castle?" Ben said.

"I noticed," Teddy said.

"That strike you as odd?"

"I'll tell you what strikes me as odd," Teddy said, closing the door behind them and moving them farther into the hall. "Castillo looked at Marvin like the two knew each other. Like they were old pals."

Ben searched Teddy's face. "You think Castillo tipped them off? That's how they knew we were here?"

"I think it's possible," Teddy said.

Both of them looked at Jessie, but she only frowned. "I don't know. Castillo's a jerk, but to do that...to set us all up..."

"Either way," Ben said, returning his gaze to Teddy, "do you think the ladies should be left alone with him?"

Teddy shrugged. "There's Wayne."

Jessie said, "He needs protection more than the women do."

Teddy blew out disgusted breath. "Fine, I'll play watchdog, but you two owe me."

Ben and Jessie moved down the hallway, guns at their sides. Jessie peered into the arched doorway that led to the stairs but could pick out nothing but an amorphous mass of shadows.

"How are you feeling?" Ben whispered.

Like Morton's death is my fault.

She turned to him. "Did you…"

He shook his head. "I came up the stairs just as Morton was falling, but even then I could see you didn't have a clear shot."

A lump threatened to choke her breathing. She fought to swallow it back.

They paused at the doorway, Ben putting out an arm and making to move her behind him.

She grasped his forearm. "Who's in charge here?"

"You just lost someone. I figured—"

"I'm fine," she said, moving past him. "I need a distraction."

At length, he said, "You really want to take your mind off Morton, I've got a story that'll do it for you."

"Last summer?"

"You won't believe it, but there's a beast on this island. Not a beast like Rubio or Marvin. I mean a real beast…" And as they moved slowly down the stairs, following the droplets of blood that Marvin had left behind, Ben told her the story. She could tell he was leaving out some of the details, but the way he told it made it hard to dismiss.

"You think it's crazy?" he finally asked.

She considered. "I can't believe in something like that until I see it. Though if it does exist, I doubt I'd want to see it."

He chuckled softly.

"Hey," she whispered. "I forgot to ask. What happened to you? You look like you've been through a cage match."

"I have. There was this mountain of a guy standing guard outside."

"Jim Bullington?" she asked.

"I didn't ask his name. I was too busy trying not to get killed."

"What'd he look like?"

"A little taller than me. Bigger and broader than me. Late forties."

"That's Bullington," she said. "Did you kill him?"

A troubled look crept into Ben's face. He nodded, as if he was replaying the man's death in his mind.

"Good," she said. "That means there are only three of them to deal with."

"That we know of."

She shook her head. "Marvin doesn't keep many associates. He came at us with everything. He's down to three men now."

"And two of them are hurt."

"Two?"

"Did you see the other guy? The one who got there last?"

"Ray Rubio," she said. "What about him?"

"He was covered with blood."

"Doesn't mean it was his."

Ben stopped. "You think it was Jorge's?"

"Who else could've fought him?"

Ben compressed his lips. "Damn."

They proceeded down the spiral staircase until they reached the main story. They could've stopped on every floor and checked the rooms, but what was the point? The trail of blood – both the bloody sets of footprints and the droplets of blood that had likely spilled from Marvin's wounds – kept to the stairs, and they'd examined the landings and found no blood.

Yes, the gunmen had moved down the stairs and had hopefully fled the castle. But they had to be sure.

Jessie led Ben through the shadowy great hall, her fingers white against her Glock. Behind her she could hear Ben's footfalls, which were relatively light for such a big man. She had no idea if he knew how to handle a gun or not, and part of her blanched at the idea of navigating a potentially dangerous situation with a civilian. But Ben had already proven trustworthy; without his help, she might not have gotten Morton's dying body into the bedroom.

Who are you kidding? a taunting voice in her head spoke up. *He saved your ass. You only killed Nicky Irvin because your survival instincts kicked in. Look at how you failed Morton. Or how you failed your family.*

No, she thought. She wasn't going to go there. Not now. Not ever if she could help it.

But as she moved around the corner of the great hall toward the kitchen, from which the bloody footprints led, the images flashed through her mind anyway, unbidden, as vivid as they'd been on the night it had all happened. The night she'd awakened, three weeks shy of her seventeenth birthday, to hear male voices echoing up the stairs of her parents' house. There'd been three men's voices. She'd heard them whispering as they crept up the stairs. Heard them shouting as her father confronted them. A single gunshot. The sick thump of her father collapsing.

"Oh hell," Ben said.

Jessie started, realized she'd been drifting. She peered into the darkness of the kitchen, looked up at Ben, who nodded toward the far end of the center island. After a moment she spotted it, the glistening hump of what looked like a butchered cow laid out on the expensive tiled floor. The only thing she recognized of Jorge Navarro's body was the longish black hair, the ponytail held in place with a rubber band. None of the man's other features were discernible. Moving closer, she saw how mutilated his body was, what a state of disarray the kitchen was in.

"Must've been a hell of a fight," Ben murmured.

Jessie silently agreed. She didn't know a great deal about Navarro, but she knew he had a wife at home and children who'd never see their daddy again. *Senseless*, she thought in mute fury. *Totally senseless.*

A flash of memory strobed through her mind: her father's body.

Another: her mother's body.

Again: her older sister, just home from college and expecting a summer spent with friends. Not expecting to be raped and murdered on the same bed where her mother was raped and murdered.

While Jessie cowered in her secret place.

While the three monsters raped and cut and laughed. Jessie heard her mother's screams, her sister's wails. But most of all the laughter. That monstrous, luciferian laughter.

"Don't look at him," Ben said, putting an arm around her and drawing her away.

"Get the hell away from me," she snapped.

He recoiled. "Hey, I was just…" He swallowed. "Come on, let's check where those drops of blood lead."

She turned and moved away. They came out of the kitchen, Jessie picking up the pats of blood right away. Marvin might live, she decided, but she'd gotten him good anyway. She had no idea how badly Rubio had been injured in his battle with Jorge, but Jessie's group had better health and superior numbers on its side.

Unless Castillo's really in with Marvin, she thought. *Then no one is safe.*

She stepped forward, moving parallel with the drops of blood and throwing frequent glances up at the doorway ahead. There was only the occasional ghost of a bloody shoeprint now, which made sense. Rubio had tracked Jorge's blood up the stairs during the gunfight. By the time he'd returned down here most of it would've been rubbed off.

"Careful," Ben reminded.

When they stepped into the foyer, she wondered briefly if the three gunmen had taken refuge in the basement. But she realized after a moment's inspection that the droplets of blood, which had grown sparse, led to the front door.

"Get back," she whispered to Ben. Reaching out, she opened the door as stealthily as she could, her gun out and ready to blast the blond-haired freak who'd killed Morton.

The front porch was empty. Stepping out onto it, she spotted a drop of blood on the sidewalk leading away from the castle.

"They're out there," Ben said, moving up next to her.

"Where though? Would they have gone back to the mainland?"

Ben shook his head. "Not those guys. We've killed two of them."

"I killed the boss's son."

Ben nodded. "I wasn't going to say that, but you're right. Marvin's not going to let that pass. They'll be gunning for us."

Jessie stared out into the night, thinking of the killers that lurked somewhere in the darkness. As she thought of them, she tried not to hear the cackling voices of the three monsters who'd slaughtered her family.

But she found that the voices would not subside.

PART FOUR
RECKONING
CHAPTER ONE

When Griffin got the boss situated in the cave, his hands began to tremble wildly, as if he'd been storing up all his terror until the battle was over. But it didn't matter, Griffin realized as he knelt beside Marvin. The crime lord was in too much pain and grief to pay Griffin any mind. Rubio would have no doubt found Griffin's jitterbugging hands hilarious had he not been so carved up. The guy looked like he'd taken on a lawnmower and had only escaped after being run over six or seven times. But the bastard deserved that and worse. And look at Griffin, not a scratch on him and feeling good.

Yes, Griffin realized, he felt very good indeed. And not just good. *Incredible.* The nutty part was, he had no idea how it had all happened. One moment he had been feeling the way he'd always felt – sick, terrified, alone. He remembered quailing behind Marvin as the mob boss unleashed the automatic, looking unnervingly like Al Pacino at the end of *Scarface*. He had been hunched down behind Marvin, doing his best impression of a floor tile, when he'd heard Marvin grunt in pain. He'd looked up, seen Marvin lying there on the floor, and then…what?

Griffin took off his shirt, wrapped it over Marvin's shoulder and tried to recall how he'd felt. There'd been the grunt, the glimpse of Marvin falling and then Griffin had felt something…*change.* He'd heard of out-of-body experiences before, but this was different. This had been like remaining in his body while someone else drove. He'd been hyper aware of everything around him, but instead of being unnerved by it, he'd been confident. Arrogant even. *Take your best shot*, he'd felt like saying as he strode toward the federal agents. *Take your best shot and see where it gets you. But I warn you, I'm not afraid of your guns. I'll rip your guts out, you stupid pigs, and—*

Griffin paused in the act of tightening his rolled-up shirt around Marvin's shoulder. Those thoughts had been in his mind at the time – thinking of the feds as pigs that deserved to be slaughtered – but the thoughts were not Griffin's. He'd never thought that way. In fact, when Nicky and Ray had gone insane at Marvin's house yesterday, butchering the two agents and then that poor woman, Griffin had only harbored hostility toward Nicky and Ray. He'd never thought of feds or policemen or even security guards as anything but normal people, and here he was shooting one right through the belly. And *celebrating*. He was a…he was a…

A murderer. The word clarified like a bloated animal rising up from the depths of a sludgy pond.

No. He bared his teeth, tightened the shirt.

Marvin gave a little gasp.

"Sorry," Griffin muttered.

"You did good tonight, kid."

Griffin looked up in surprise. He hadn't realized Marvin was watching him.

"I'm gonna get that bitch," Marvin went on. "The one killed Nicky. I'm gonna do her worse'n anyone's ever been done. I'm gonna do it slow and nasty and make her turn all sorts of colors."

"Let's get 'em all," Rubio said from a few feet away. "We shouldn'ta run away. They were off balance."

"We didn't run away, you asshole, we regrouped." Marvin cringed, placed a hand over the already bloody wrapping. "They don't know where we are, but we know where they are. They're down two men."

"So are we," Rubio said. When he saw the stricken look on Marvin's face, he muttered, "Sorry, boss."

Marvin took a moment to collect himself. He said, "We don't know we're down two. Bullington might still be alive."

"He woulda been here by now," Rubio said.

"Not necessarily," Griffin said. "We never set a rendezvous point. He probably doesn't know we're here."

"Then why didn't he help out at the castle?"

Griffin didn't have an answer for that.

Marvin said, "Raymond's right. We gotta assume Jim's dead." Marvin eyed Rubio. "You killed the Mexican, right?"

Ray grinned. "He was a tough son of a bitch. Most bodyguards I know, they strut around and talk shit, but I never met one as tough as that guy."

"You got him though, didn't you," Griffin said.

Ray's mouth spread in a sly grin. "Bet your ass I did." He appeared to consider. "And you got that fed. That was a good shot, kid."

Griffin kept cool, but inside he felt like a boy whose strict father has just given him a rare compliment. But *should* he be feeling that way? Should he be flattered by Ray Rubio's approval?

Or revolted?

"Ray's right," Marvin said. "I wouldn't have made it out of there if not for you. I gotta be honest, I'd begun to think Ray here and…" His voice grew thick. He cleared his throat, his eyes shining. "…and Nicky were right about you. But all along I suspected there was more. I bet on you, kid, and you pulled through. Consider yourself one of us now. When we get back home, things are gonna be good for you."

Griffin smiled. He couldn't help it. And as much as he hated to admit it, there had been satisfaction in shooting the federal agent, satisfaction in walking right out in the open and taking aim. Man, it'd been just like a movie. He could scarcely believe it was him that had done it. No wonder the guys were impressed.

It wasn't you, a faint voice whispered.

Griffin brushed it off. Of course it was him. Who the hell else would it be? Clint Eastwood? The ghost of Wyatt Earp?

"We're gonna need some things," Marvin said. "Supplies from the boat."

Rubio got up, but you could tell it cost him an effort. He'd lost plenty of blood in the fight with the Hispanic bodyguard. "What do we need, boss? More guns?"

"Guns, yeah, but we'll need food too. Fresh water."

Rubio frowned. "I don't get it."

"We're not goin' back to the castle right away. We'll take a few hours to sort things out. Then we'll head over there and get the rest of 'em."

"You mean kill them all?" Griffin asked.

"All but Mrs. Blackwood."

Rubio shrugged. "I still don't get why we don't—"

"I know you don't get it, Raymond. That's why I'm the one makes the decisions."

Rubio looked like he was going to press the matter, but Marvin sat up, waved him over. Rubio stepped over to kneel beside Marvin. The moment the big man was next to the crime lord, Marvin clutched a handful of Rubio's shirt and yanked him closer. "You think anybody wants those bastards dead more than I do?" Marvin asked. He glared into Rubio's face, and for the first time Griffin saw uncertainty in Rubio's eyes.

"Then why wait?" Rubio asked.

"They killed my boy," Marvin growled. "They took my Nicky. He was all that mattered to me. This whole operation, all of what I did was so Nicky could take over some day. Once he got through his wild stage." Marvin drew Rubio closer, so their noses were almost touching. "And those sons of bitches, they took him away from me. They took my boy."

Marvin turned to Griffin. "You go to the boat. But be careful. They might be looking for us, and I don't want you getting shot."

"We'll see them before they see us," Rubio said.

"You're staying here."

"Huh?"

"I can't risk letting both of you go. Way I feel now, I might pass out any second. I don't wanna be laying here by myself when those assholes happen by."

Rubio made a face, looking like a sulky child. "But why do I gotta play nursemaid?"

"And if I sent you for the gear, you'd be complainin' about bein' made an errand boy. So just do it and shut the fuck up, all right?"

"What do you want from the boat?" Griffin asked.

"Remember all those totes I had you stow in the cuddy cabin?"

Griffin nodded.

"They were full of food and bottled water. Get 'em. And some guns. As many as you can carry."

★   ★   ★

Minutes later Griffin was picking his way through the forest, moving in the direction he thought the boat was in. He had the Smith & Wesson, the same Smith & Wesson with which he'd shot and killed the federal agent.

For some reason, the thought made him frown, so to get rid of it, he quickened his pace down the winding trail. He was out of shape, there was no questioning that, but he felt good tonight, as if that other who'd ridden along in his body earlier was still endowing him with extra vitality. His bare chest was slicked with sweat, his hair sticking up in wild, damp tufts. But he felt good. *Strapping*. That was a word he'd always liked but had never felt applied to him. His mom had always used words like *wiry* and *lanky*, but Griffin knew those were just nice ways of saying *scrawny*. But tonight he felt strapping.

He heard the creek well before he saw it. It surprised him despite the fact they'd crossed it earlier in the evening. What really surprised him now was the bridge spanning the water. When they'd crossed earlier, they'd merely hopped over the creek, its banks being shallow and close together. But at this point the creek was nearly broad enough to be called a river. It bubbled and undulated under a shaft of slanting moonlight, but the bridge itself was steeped in darkness. Griffin slackened his pace and screwed up his eyes to make sure the boards weren't rotted through. That would be a hell of a thing, wouldn't it? To break through the bridge and get stuck down there with a busted leg?

Griffin put a toe gingerly down on the first plank and tested it. It was soft, but there didn't seem to be too much give. He put his weight on it, taking care to keep hold of the wooden rail. He'd have grasped both sides of the bridge, but it was a couple feet too wide for that. He stepped forward again, tested the next plank. This one was fine too. He decided he'd—

"*Griffin*," a throaty voice called.

Griffin's legs turned to liquid. The sweat on his skin froze to a sheet of ice.

The voice had come from under the bridge.

He forced his legs forward, but he'd only made it a couple more steps when he heard it again, the same throaty speaker calling out his name. The voice was awful, like a swarm of insects forming words in unison. A buzzing, wheedling voice like that of a lifelong smoker in the last stages of throat cancer. It reminded him of...of...

Oh God no, he thought, and then looked down between the warped wooden slats.

And saw only turbid water.

But that wasn't where he'd heard the voice, was it? It had come from behind him, nestled down on the bank in the bunched darkness, the kind of place where a homeless person would build a fire. Or where a fairy-tale troll would exercise his dominion. The mental image this conjured made him smile. He'd long ago read a book to his little sister, a *Dora the Explorer* book, the kind where you could lift the flaps. In it there had been a troll under a bridge, a silly, cartoonish troll that had stolen a chocolate egg. It was the reader's job to help Dora retrieve the missing egg. He remembered how Ashley would make him read that book over and over, and because he could never say no to his little sister, he'd always complied. Griffin snorted laughter, remembering it.

"*Get down here, boy!*"

Griffin threw out an arm to keep from falling. His heart banged in his chest, the fear so powerful he felt as though he'd faint. It wasn't possible that the voice could be who he thought it was, but he had to know. His whole body a nerveless lump, Griffin leaned out over the railing and craned his long neck down until he could see under the bridge.

Baleful white eyes stared at him from a hideous black face. "You waitin' for an invitation?"

"Holy shit," Griffin said in a toneless voice. Automatically, he retraced his steps to the beginning of the bridge, continued on around the edge of the railing and stumbled down the embankment. His feet got tangled near the bottom and he landed in the sand at the creek's edge. He peered up at the figure under the bridge, the face caged by shadows. But the legs...he could see the legs all too well, legs he'd recognize anywhere. They belonged to Eliza Carol Little, formerly Eliza Carol Toomey, only that had been her husband's last name, and she'd divorced that good-for-nothing long ago.

Griffin's mother watched him from under the bridge, and the more he looked at her the more he realized her legs were now her best feature. Those legs used to scare the shit out of him, squiggled with purple varicose veins and gone a sickly yellow hue from the jaundice, but now they were the closest features to normal his mother possessed. Because her face…dear God, her face was a blackened, wrinkled pouch that reminded him of spoiled fruit. If not for the whites of her eyes, he wouldn't have believed her alive at all.

Yet she couldn't be alive. Griffin hadn't been there for her funeral, but Ashley had somehow tracked him down, had left a message on a recorder: *She's dead now. Not that you care.*

Griffin's mother gave him a moody glance. "Happy to see me?"

Griffin swallowed. "Of course I'm glad to see you. But I don't get… how are you, you know…"

"Alive?" she asked. "Didn't I always tell you things have a way of working themselves out?"

He didn't respond to that. It was too much like the crap she always used to say.

"Oh, I forgot," she said in her wheedling, cancerous voice. "You don't believe in all that nonsense, do you?"

It is nonsense, he almost said, but an atavistic fear of her still prohibited speech. He'd never argued with her. Look at his dad. Dad had argued with her, and she'd gotten rid of him. Griffin didn't want to be gotten rid of. Until he couldn't stand it anymore. And then he'd left and hadn't seen her again.

"Nothing to say to your mother?" she said.

Griffin observed with a rise of disgust that her hands were blackened too, the skin eaten away in several places to reveal ulcerous red sores.

"You're not real," he said.

"There you go again. Questioning things that are meant to be." She made that little clucking sound she'd always made when she was proving a point. Which was bullshit, because she never proved anything. Only used her astrology and her numerology and her absurd faith in superstition and fate to justify her theories.

He couldn't take it anymore, the clucking and the superiority and the complete lack of logic. "You're why I left, you know. I was tired of waiting on things to work themselves out. You always said that, 'Things will work themselves out,' but all that really meant was that you were lazy."

She twisted her mouth into a nasty sneer. "Why didn't you take Ashley with you too? That way you'd have stolen everything from me at once."

"I would've taken Ashley, but she was a member of your dumbass religion." Griffin smiled. God, it felt good to finally tell her off. "You looked at those stupid astrology magazines and read the horoscopes you thought suited you. Everything that happened was a sign or a good omen, 'Mars is in Venus rising this month', or 'Your minor sign is aligned favorably with Pisces'."

"The numbers don't lie."

"They're just numbers!" He clambered forward in the sand. "Don't you get it? Not everything has to mean something. Every time I got a new locker combination, you acted like it had some deep significance. Every time we got a new license plate, you acted like it was a turning point. But they're just numbers, Mom! They're just numbers!"

"So why are you working for a bookie?"

That stopped him.

"Why were you at that blackjack table the night you met him?" She leaned forward, holding up one rotten banana peel finger. "Better yet, how were you able to kill that man tonight?"

Griffin licked his lips. "I killed him because I took a chance and did something, which was more than you ever did."

She smiled, her horrible black cheeks crinkling. "No, Griffin. You succeeded because two of your five had been slain. You went from an evil number to a powerful number. Haven't I always told you there's power in three? There's courage in three?"

Griffin buried his hands in his hair, pulled on clumps of it until pain flared. "How can a number mean courage, Mom? *It's just a number.*"

"Every religion from the beginning of time put faith in numbers," she said in a maddening singsong voice. "Even the Greeks recognized their power."

Deep within him, some switch was tripped by her words. "The Greeks," he murmured.

"We've taken their gods and made of them bedtime stories and children's movies. Yet there's still immense power there. Enormous *potential.*"

Griffin found he could no longer speak. But he was thinking. Thinking rapidly and with some new, momentous understanding.

"You know what I'm talking about, boy?" she asked.

"I think so," he said.

"You've heard about this island?"

"Not really. Only the stuff everybody knows."

Mother surprised him by reclining further and drawing her legs up so they disappeared from the moon's glow. "You were pleased tonight in the cave," she said.

Griffin squinted at her. It occurred to him that she couldn't possibly know what had transpired in the cave, not having been there herself. But there was something else bothering him. It seemed her legs had lost their jaundiced hue. The shadows even seemed to mask her thick varicose veins.

Mother went on. "You liked having your boss proud of you."

"Yes," Griffin said.

"There is another authority on this island. Far greater than any man."

"Far greater," Griffin said in a soft, inflectionless voice.

"He wants you to serve him. You've served him already, as a matter of fact, and he is well pleased. He reveled in the death of the federal agent. The agent was a bringer of order. His death gives chaos a greater reign."

Mother's voice had grown guttural, like a newborn creature from the sewer trying out its vocal cords and attempting to mimic human speech. Griffin discovered with little surprise that where Mother's legs had been there were only pale mounds of sand. But the eyes remained, those lucent white orbs in the blanket of darkness beneath the bridge. He leaned uphill, squinting to make out her shape.

"Will you serve him?" Mother asked.

Griffin took a step up the hill. "What does he want me to do?"

"A god needs followers," she said. "You may not have believed in my 'rubbish' as you so meanly called it the day you abandoned us—"

"Mom—"

"—but the underlying truths remain the same. A god possesses power, but the more devoted his followers are, the more formidable his power grows."

Now the eyes were difficult to make out in the veil of shadow. Only the suggestions of pale orbs remained, and the black, wrinkled mouth scarcely moved at all.

"Don't go, Mom, I'm sorry for leaving you and Ashley—"

"Ashley is dead."

Griffin stood rooted to the spot. He wanted to somehow explain her words away. But in his bones he knew they were true.

"What happened to her?"

"Why do you care?"

"Mom, I have to—"

"A man," his mother said offhandedly. "A man broke her heart and she slit her wrists."

"*No*," Griffin said in a choked voice.

"Oh yes," Mother said. "A man very much like the ones in the castle right now. He was a brawny fellow, very into his body. He made a plaything of our Ashley and when he'd compromised her and made a fool of her, he went a step further and publicly called her a whore."

Griffin couldn't breathe.

"She might have recovered from the humiliation, but you know how small towns are. And she had no big brother there to protect her, so she became a laughing stock."

Griffin hung his head, his chest hollow and burning.

"There are three men like that in Castle Blackwood. The Master would like it very much if you destroyed them. Ashley would like it very much."

Griffin stared up at Mother hopefully, but all he could see now was a quiver of black under the bridge. Not even the shape of her head was discernible.

"There are three of you," Mother went on, though now her voice was almost lost beneath the trickle of water behind him.

"Three of us."

"There is power in three."

"Power."

"Serve the Master."

Griffin nodded. "Yes."

He remembered how it had felt to murder the agent. The way it felt for Marvin to treat him with respect.

"Mom, how do I—" he began but stopped when he realized there was no movement at all from under the bridge. He scrambled up the embankment and trailed his hands through the sandy soil but encountered only useless mounds and a few scattered weeds. He'd imagined the whole thing. Of course he had. The idea that his dead mother could have taken up residence under an island bridge in the middle of the Pacific Ocean was an idea too ludicrous to believe. Yet…

...yet he believed it. Yes, he realized. He truly did. He believed his sister was dead, believed some meathead had broken her heart, believed the men up in the castle were just as vain and cruel as that man had been.

Serve the Master.

Yes, Griffin thought, nodding. And what if it was true? What if the master of this island was a creature of myth? What if the wild stories he'd heard about the Sorrows had a simple but incredible explanation?

Griffin climbed up the embankment and made his way across the bridge. Though he didn't run, he moved with greater purpose. He would fetch the supplies for Marvin. Then he'd go hunting at the castle. They'd post a guard, he was almost sure of it. And whoever it was would soon find out what happened to guys who messed with nice girls.

For Ashley, he thought, nodding. *I'll do it for you, sis.*

And for the Master.

CHAPTER TWO

From a sixth-story window Ben watched the clouds swallow the moon. They had chosen the studio because none of the others felt secure down in the great hall. Ben thought it was a lousy place to talk, with entrances at both ends of the room, but apparently the agents felt the elbow room was more important than the vulnerability that came with it.

"So the first thing we gotta do," Teddy said, "is come up with a schedule."

Wayne shook his head. "Screw that. I'm gettin' the hell off this island."

Teddy, sitting next to Ben and across from Wayne, said, "And how you propose to do that?"

"*The boat*," Wayne said, as if Teddy were a stupid child. Wayne jerked a thumb at Teddy and swept the others with a look of disbelief. "What's he think we're gonna do, swim home?"

"The boat," Jessie explained, "is on the other side of the island."

"So we go get it."

"With those fellas in the woods," Teddy said.

Jessie said, "And remember, Ben isn't leaving the island."

"Not leaving the island?" Wayne said. "Why anybody would stay here after—"

"I'm not leaving either," Christina said.

Everyone turned and looked at her. She and Elena sat on a loveseat they'd pulled up to fill in the north side of their makeshift circle.

"Then you're nuts too," Wayne said.

"I thought you worked for the woman," Teddy said.

"Not anymore," Wayne declared, leaning back in a plush green chair. "After what happened tonight, I'm gettin' into a different line of business."

Teddy said, "With that strong constitution of yours, maybe you could do autopsies."

"What do you think?" Jessie said, and it took Ben a long moment to realize she'd been addressing him.

"I'm going to find my baby."

"Another loon," Wayne grumbled.

"Mr. Shadeland, I think it's time you joined us here in reality," Castillo said, leaning forward in his chair. The deep vermilion brocade gave the chair the appearance of a throne, and like a king, Castillo's tone implied he was the one in charge here. "I can appreciate your desire to get your daughter back—"

"Oh you can, huh?" Ben asked.

Castillo rolled his eyes. "I get it. Because I don't have kids, I can't relate. Is that about right?"

"That's got nothing to do with it."

Castillo's eyebrows rose. He spread his hands and leaned back in his seat. "Then how about you enlighten me?"

"I'll try," Ben said. "But I doubt it'll do any good."

Before Castillo could respond, he continued. "There's a paternal urge in some men, but not all men have it. You see, it's different for a man than it is for a woman. A woman bonds with her baby when it's in the womb. There's a relationship there, so when the baby's born, they're already bonded emotionally."

"Fascinating," Castillo said.

"But a man doesn't always feel bonded right away. He doesn't shoot his sperm and immediately start caring for the child he's helped create. For the dad, it sometimes starts after that, and then the emotion grows."

Castillo gave him a listless look. "You don't say."

"It's why," Ben went on, "there are stepdads who're better fathers than the biological fathers could ever hope to be. Because if the stepdad has the paternal urge, he turns out to be ten times the father the biological father ever was. For a man – though this probably applies to women too – it's less about biology and more about what's in your heart."

Wayne was frowning, but the big ape actually seemed interested. "So how do you know if you've got it or not?"

Ben eyed Castillo. "A lot of it comes down to selfishness, and whether a man's able to put others before himself. If he's able to, if he cares more about the child than he does his own desires, there's a good chance he'll be a great father. And that's why I know, Agent Castillo, that you'll never have the slightest clue what I'm talking about. You're a smug, selfish prick who couldn't care less if the rest of us died as long as you get off the island in one piece."

Castillo's jaw had tightened into a knot. The others watched him expectantly. Ben readied himself for the fight he figured would inevitably come.

But it was Wayne who broke the silence. "So even if you're not a dad, you can still have the paternal urge?"

Without taking his eyes off Castillo, Ben said, "Theoretically."

Teddy said, "Does he have to have a functioning brain too?"

Wayne squinted at Teddy.

"This is all very interesting, but I need to rest," Elena said. "My arm hurts, and I need to know I can close my eyes without being shot."

Jessie said, "I think Mr. Brooks's idea of forming a schedule makes the most sense. Mr. Wayne, you'll take the first shift."

"Huh?"

"This is your chance to make up for abandoning us earlier."

"Hold on, I said I was—"

"What you do after you return to California is your business, but you're here now, and we need you to do more than hide in your room."

Wayne's mouth worked for a moment; then he seemed to shrink as the unsympathetic faces of the group only watched him in silence. He cringed as thunder rumbled in the distance. "What do I have to do?"

"Walk from one end of the ground floor to the other. There's the long hall, and there's the one branching off from it. We need you to make sure no one's trying to break in. If you hear anything, you're to come directly upstairs to alert the rest of us."

"Do I get a gun?"

Jessie hesitated, but Castillo said, "Of course."

Wayne sat there mulling it over, his small eyes narrowed in concentration. "How long do I have to watch?"

Jessie regarded the others. "Three hours?"

"Sounds about right to me," Teddy said.

But Wayne was staring at her, astonished. "Three hours? I gotta walk around that whole time?"

"It's already…" She consulted her watch. "3:07 in the morning. I'll relieve you at six."

"I can take Agent Gary's place at nine," Teddy said.

Castillo nodded, "And I'll relieve Brooks at noon."

Elena shook her head. "I don't understand why we have to stay here. There's already been so much death." She shivered, rubbed her arms, then winced when she accidentally brushed her bandage.

"Are you okay?" Christina asked.

"No, I'm *not* okay," Elena said. "I'm terrible. I've never…this is an insidious place. I've never experienced the sort of sensations I'm picking up here."

"You're right to be scared," Ben said.

Castillo snorted laughter. "Jesus Christ."

But Christina was watching Ben closely. "Mr. Shadeland, have you recalled anything since returning to the island? Do you remember what happened to my son?"

Don't tell her a thing, his mind warned. *Don't let those floodgates crash open. Because if you do, there'll be no going back. You screwed up telling Teddy about it. You went too far talking to Jessie this morning. Don't make the mistake of trusting anyone else.*

He said, "I'm going to find my daughter. When I get back, you and I can have a talk."

Castillo said, "You're not going anywhere."

Elena turned to Castillo. "Please don't do this. Don't let this become some silly contest about who's manlier."

Teddy said, "I think Ben's manlier."

"Shut up," Castillo said.

"And more polite," Teddy added.

"One more word and I'll kick your ass," Castillo said.

"Touch him," Ben said, "and you'll have to deal with me."

Teddy leaned forward. "That's sweet of you to defend my honor, Ben, but I'd rather kick his ass myself."

"Would you please *stop*?" Elena shouted. "I want to leave! Let's just get on the boat and go. There's no way three of those guys can stop—"

"Unless they already disabled the boat," Teddy said.

Everyone stared at Teddy. In truth Ben had considered this possibility, but he'd decided not to verbalize it.

"Shit," Castillo said.

"I can check it when I'm out looking," Ben said.

"If it still works, we can leave, right?" Elena asked.

Jessie was watching Ben. "I don't think you should go alone."

"Come along if you want."

Teddy made a pained face. "There you two go again, runnin' off without me. You know, if I were a more sensitive type, I'd be in a lot of emotional turmoil right now. Abandonment issues and everything."

"You guys are gonna get eaten alive," Castillo said. "Or have you forgotten what mad dogs Marvin's men are?"

"It's a big island," Elena said, her eyes imploring each member of the group. "They might not even see us going to the boat."

"If we can hold off until afternoon," Jessie said, "we can take another way home."

Elena inhaled sharply. "The helicopter pilot."

"Gus," Jessie said.

"Gus. When did you say he's coming back?"

"Three o'clock," Jessie said.

Elena bit her lip. "We're stuck here till then?"

"We've all got duties to fulfill," Ben said, rising. "Even you, Chad."

Wayne made a face. "I told you—"

"I know what you told us," Ben said, "but it doesn't work like that. You were hired to protect Christina, and you're going to do it. You're going to take the first shift and you're gonna shut up about it. You spend enough time working on your body, now it's time to use it doing something productive."

Wayne's face went tight, but he didn't argue.

"You," Ben said to Elena, "were also brought here to help Christina. So do your job."

Elena leaned forward, her pretty heart-shaped face fierce. "You don't understand, the vibrations I'm picking up here are unspeakable. We're in terrible danger, and not just from the bad men. There are spirits—"

"I understand better than anybody, but it changes nothing."

He glanced at Christina. "Work with Elena, see what she can learn about your son."

Christina watched him with a look Ben could scarcely stomach. Was it cruel to delay the news of Chris's death and her husband's descent into psychotic behavior? Should he *ever* tell her the truth? He turned to Teddy Brooks, grateful to be loosed from Christina's depthless gaze.

Teddy tilted his head. "You're gonna tell me I had my courage all along, right? That I didn't need to see the wizard of Emerald City to find it?"

Ben smiled, looked down at Jessie. "I need to remind you why you and Castillo are here?"

Castillo's mouth trembled into a sneer. "You're not in charge, Shadeland."

"Ben's right," Jessie said. "It's time we stop acting like lost sheep and focus on doing our jobs. One, we keep these people safe. Two, we continue our investigation."

Castillo leaned back in his chair, massaged his forehead. "It's been investigated."

"By a forensics team that couldn't recreate what happened."

"And the agents that came here last fall?"

"They vanished."

Everyone stared at Jessie. Castillo said, "Early and Moss got reassigned. Everybody knows about them, I don't know why—"

"They disappeared," Jessie said. "Morton told me before he died."

Teddy said, "So nobody knows anything."

"Except this prick," Castillo said, nodding at Ben.

Ben's fingers twitched. He felt a dark heat building in the pit of his stomach.

"Didn't like that, Shadeland?" Castillo asked, eyeing him from his deep red throne. "Don't like being called out for your selfish behavior?"

"Go to hell."

"Hit a nerve, did I? You lecture me about how selfish I am, but look at you. You're the one endangering everyone on this island. Morton, Professor Grant. That guy Jorge? Their blood's all over *your* hands, not mine."

"You ever meet Marvin before, Castillo?" Teddy asked.

Castillo's eyes narrowed. "What's that supposed to mean?"

"Never mind," Teddy said, his eyes never leaving Castillo's.

"Here's what we're going to do," Jessie said. "Right now we start the shifts. Ben and I will go to the boat to see if it's been tampered with. If it's functional, I'll take it back to get help."

Castillo had been listening to Jessie with an increasingly nasty grin on his face. "It sounds like you're pulling rank on me."

Jessie turned to him, her expression bland. "How many years have you been an agent?"

Castillo's grin turned nastier.

"That's what I thought," Jessie said.

Jessie had started to move when Castillo reached up, grabbed her forearm.

"Don't touch her," Elena said.

"Shut up," Castillo answered.

Jessie struggled in his grasp, but Ben could see Castillo wasn't letting go.

"Let go of her," he said in a low voice. "Now."

Castillo eyeballed Ben a moment. Then he released Jessie, sidled between chairs so he was standing in a large, open area of the studio.

Ben followed him.

"Please don't do this," Christina said.

Castillo ignored her. "You should know, Shadeland, that I was an All-American wrestler at Iowa, second in the nation. Our team came in third that year."

"I never did like the Hawkeyes," Teddy muttered.

Castillo was shaking out his arms, limbering up. But his eyes stayed locked on Ben's. "Know what weight class I was in? Two eighty-five. You know how much I weighed? Two nineteen."

"That what you still weigh?"

Castillo shrugged, hopping in place to get loose. "I weigh a little more now, but it's muscle weight. If I wrestled the two-nineteen version of myself now, I'd annihilate him."

Ben nodded. "I chase my son around the yard quite a bit, hold Julia while she's crying."

"Guess you should've held on tighter, huh?"

Ben's stomach did a flip.

"Uh-huh," Castillo said, grinning and rolling his shoulders. "That's what I like to see. Drop the bullshit and get to the real thing."

Ben told himself to breathe, to keep on top of his anger. *Don't do anything stupid. Wait for him to move.*

"You're a real dick, you know that, Castillo?" Teddy said.

But Castillo ignored that. "One of the first things I learned at Iowa," Castillo said, beginning to pace around Ben in a slow circle, "was how much posturing guys did. See, the reason I told you my weight and class is because the one ninety-seven group has the largest range. They go one twenty-five, one thirty-three, one forty-one, one forty-nine, one fifty-seven, one sixty-five, one seventy-four, one eighty-five, one ninety-seven, all the way up to the next one. Guess what it is."

Ben didn't answer, merely pivoted so Castillo couldn't get an angle on him.

"Two eighty-five," Castillo said. "You believe that? Most of the groups, they go up in increments of eight, nine pounds. But the guys in one ninety-seven, they gotta wrestle the monsters weighing two-eighty, two eighty-three. You know what those huge guys do?"

"Drop weight until they're just under two eighty-five."

"Exactly! Now if that's fair, I'd like to see what their idea of unfair is."

"The guy you lost to," Ben asked. "He one of the monsters?"

Castillo pooched his lips, nodded. He'd just about completed his revolution around Ben. "You got it. Dude was two seventy-nine, down from two ninety. Son of a bitch shook the ground when he walked. I came in low, meaning to take his legs out from under him. The bastard just sat on me. Felt like there was a Sherman tank parked on my back. Could barely breathe, heard my coaches shouting. The crowd going nuts." Castillo shook his head, lost in the recollection.

"He pin you?"

"Uh-uh. But he beat me on points pretty easily. I couldn't budge him."

"Second place isn't bad."

Castillo had returned to his original spot, coming toward Ben now. "Unless the one in second place dies." And darted in at Ben's waist.

Ben was on his feet one second, toppled onto his back the next. Castillo was scrambling over him, the guy moving like some kind of crazed panther. *Damn*, Ben thought. *He wasn't lying about the All-American thing.*

Castillo had him down with an arm locked under his chin. Ben flared his neck out and lowered his chin as much as he could, trying to dig it under Castillo's iron grip, but the agent was bearing down on him, going for the chokehold. Ben crested on a wave of panic. He could hear the others shouting at Castillo and wondered if the man really would kill him. Then it would be the rest of the survivors against the mob guys, with Gabriel – the true threat – prowling the island. Forget rescue. They wouldn't make it through the morning. And Julia would die with the beast.

It was the thought of Julia that galvanized him. Ben's breath was all but choked out. He was able to jerk forward, tuck his head a little in an attempt to roll Castillo off him. But the agent stayed grafted to Ben's back like another layer of skin, both of them doing a half somersault and ending up with Ben on his back with Castillo under him, the guy's unshakeable arm cinched under Ben's neck more tightly than ever. Desperately, Ben shot an elbow into Castillo's gut, and with a surprised whoosh of air, Castillo let go. Ben rolled off, gasping, and Castillo pounced to his feet looking more energetic than ever.

Castillo wore a hungry smile. "That was a cheap shot, Shadeland. I didn't expect you to fight that—"

Before he finished he lunged at Ben's waist again, but this time Ben saw it coming. He took a bracing backward step, swung down hard at Castillo's head. The blow was a solid one, tattooing Castillo in the left temple and making his head do a violent jag. When Castillo again wrapped Ben up, Ben could tell plainly that the punch had stunned the agent. He drove into Ben, but to Ben it felt like he was propping Castillo up as much as Castillo was pushing Ben backward. Ben backpedaled with him, but as he did he tore down at Castillo's exposed back with three bone-rattling jabs. Castillo grunted and continued forward, but the arms had gone away from Ben's back. Ben stepped out of the way and Castillo blundered face first onto the dusty studio hardwood. Ben strode over as Castillo pushed to his knees. Ben looped a right hook at the agent, cracked him in the back of the head.

"What the hell?" Castillo shouted. "You wanna play dirty, Shade—"

Ben waylaid him the moment he stood up. The punch would've knocked out the average man, but Castillo merely went stumbling back. Ben followed him, grimly intent. The darkest corner of his mind whispered that he should end matters once and for all. But that wasn't who he was. He didn't kill unless he had to.

What about Bullington?

No choice, Ben answered. But he couldn't get the guy's doomed expression out of his head.

Castillo put out an arm to fend Ben off, but Ben thrust it aside with his left hand and heaved an uppercut with his right. Castillo's jaws clacked together. This time the agent did fall—

(*Kill him too, just like you killed the last one*)

—and Ben was on him, straddling his chest, raining right-handed blows and using his left hand to keep Castillo centered, make sure the bastard couldn't thrash out of the way. Blood swirled on Castillo's face. Ben imagined that face as a cut of meat he was tenderizing, his fists the cudgels that would

(*just like Bullington*)

reduce his face to pulp, to something that resembled corned beef hash. Castillo's hands weren't even up now, were splayed

(*yes, kill him*)

out like he was crucified, his face a pinkish mess that occasionally spat out a fresh gout of blood, the agent's features slack now, unconscious and

(*a few more jabs*)

seeming to welcome death—

"BEN!"

Ben froze, the reality of the situation racing back to him in a horrid suck of disbelieving gravity. He relaxed his fist, the knuckles of which were flayed open and pulsing blood down his fingers. He stared down at Troy Castillo in horror, the man's face a blasted moonscape of craters and welts.

Hands were on Ben, shoving him roughly off Castillo. Ben was faintly aware of Teddy saying something to him, but it was Jessie's face Ben couldn't unsee, the red-haired agent with a hand to her mouth and her eyes crammed with accusation. Ben got up unsteadily, moved past Elena and Christina and past Chad Wayne, who looked as confused as ever.

"Wait a minute!" Jessie shouted after him. "You can't just leave the scene like this."

The scene? Ben thought and fought a wild urge to laugh. What he was walking away from actually constituted a *scene*?

He was nearly to the stairs when Brooks pulled up alongside. "This is serious stuff, Ben. You just assaulted a federal agent."

"It was battery," Ben said. "When you actually hit him, it's battery." He started down the steps.

"The hell you think you're talkin' to?" Brooks asked, following. "I was LAPD for fifteen years, you don't think I know the difference?"

Ben didn't answer, swiftly crossed the landing and began to hustle down the staircase.

"Listen, man, no kiddin' around. We're talkin' serious jail time, man."

Ben did what he could to remove the afterimage of Castillo's devastated face from his mind. He needed to stop off at his room, get his gun, extra ammunition—

"You think you're helpin' your daughter by getting arrested? You think it's gonna do your wife and your little boy any good if you go off to jail?"

"You think he's clean?" Ben asked without turning. He reached his room, went in.

"Man, of course I don't think he's clean. But all we got are theories right now and the fact that the man's an asshole. That ain't gonna get you anywhere, this thing goes to court."

Ben chuckled humorlessly. He plucked the Ruger out of his top dresser drawer, furious with himself for ever having let it leave his sight. He still wore the ankle holster, so he slid the gun down into it, the heavy feel of the nine-millimeter against his flesh reassuring.

Teddy swatted him on the arm. "Man, you even hear what I'm tellin' you?"

Ben shook his head, opened up the box of ammo. "You don't have a clue, do you?"

"Enlighten me."

Ben pocketed the rounds, palmed several more and stuffed them in his other pocket. "You talk about going to court, about what a judge might do to me. Do you have any idea what's coming? That thing – the one you think I fabricated to account for all the killings that went on here last summer? – that thing makes Marvin and his men look like Boy Scouts. I saw the beast climb along the castle façade, moving faster than anything moves on the ground. I saw it make a jump of about twenty-five feet from the top of the castle to the helicopter. I watched it pick up Chris Blackwood and bite his head off, the way monsters do in low-budget movies. Only this wasn't a movie. This was something that almost destroyed my family. *And it's still trying to destroy my family.*"

In Teddy's face Ben saw a mixture of pity, uncertainty and what might have been nascent belief. Or maybe he was just stalling Ben long enough for Jessie to arrest him.

"I'm going to look for Julia," Ben said.

Teddy followed him out the door. "If what you say is true, isn't it possible you're gonna run into the creature?"

"I plan to," Ben said.

"Well, shit," Teddy said, moving up beside him.

"What are you doing?"

"Comin' with you," Teddy said. "I'm damn sure not gonna sit here in the castle waitin' for those mob guys to come get us."

CHAPTER THREE

Of all the things in the world Chad Wayne might be doing, and especially of all the *places* in the world in which he might be doing it, standing guard in Castle Blackwood was his absolute last choice. He was doing what Agent Gary had instructed, walking up and down the halls of the first floor, testing the exit doors every time he passed and peeking into each room just to make sure the windows weren't being jimmied. After Ben had beaten Castillo to within an inch of his life, Agent Gary had enlisted Chad to lug the federal agent's heavy body down to Castillo's room. Conveniently, Brooks and Shadeland – the A-hole responsible for Castillo's condition in the first place – had taken off and left Chad as the only conscious male in the castle. That meant that he was to be ordered around by not one, not two, but *three* women, and man, if that wasn't bullshit, Chad didn't know what was.

Then Agent Gary had strapped the damned ankle holster on him, which embarrassed him even worse. It wasn't enough the thing had some sort of double strap that looked like a freaking garter belt, but she also made him hike up his pajama leg so she could put it on. If there was one body part Chad was self-conscious about – other than his penis – it was his skinny ankles. He never went to the gym in shorts because of this, because when the other guys caught sight of them they made all sorts of jokes, calling him animated character names like Gru and Mr. Incredible.

And now look at him. Keeping a monotonous watch and holding a gun he had no idea how to use.

He passed the great hall and threw a quick glance toward the kitchen. He didn't like to look that way because even though Shadeland and Agent Gary had dragged Jorge's body to a closet out of the way, there was still a hell of a lot of blood in there, and Chad fancied he could smell it in the air.

He came to the dining room, reached in and flicked on the light.

Everything looked okay in here. The table was barren except for a few place settings at the far end. The ceiling was painted ivory and featured all sorts of inlaid designs. There was what looked like some sort of butler's station in one corner, with a good-sized table with a blood-red cloth draped over it. Next to that there was a smaller stand with a blue-and-white vase on it, a short stretch of wall covered with flowery wallpaper, then the windows overhung with ivory curtains, one of which was billowing from the storm. Chad continued his scan of the room, wondering if he should go back to the kitchen to get a snack. His stomach was growling, and he couldn't remember the last time he'd eaten. He supposed he could...

Chad's thoughts trailed off, his eyes moving to his left again.

Back to the billowing curtains.

Oh Jesus Christ Almighty Jumped-Up Jehoshaphat. The freaking window was open. Wide. Fucking. Open. And that meant someone, anyone, could be in the room.

His mind instantly sought the refuge of rationalization. Ben had opened it. Or Teddy had. Right before the men had left the castle, one of them had opened the window to let some air into the old-fashioned dining room. It was musty in here. How long had it been since anyone had aired it out?

Last summer, a voice from nowhere whispered. *They aired it out right before they all died.*

Holy shit, Chad thought. *Holy holy shit.*

He'd never been more scared in his life. Okay, that wasn't quite the truth. He had been more frightened when the shooting had started up a few hours ago. One of the reasons it had taken so long for him to come out of his room to look for the others – other than the fact that he actually *had* been under his bed – was that he'd pooped himself after the second or third gunshot. Finally, his debilitating fear of spiders had driven him out from under the bed.

But now he thought he might fill his drawers again. Holding his breath, Chad gazed down at the long dining room table and beneath it, praying silently to no one in particular that he wouldn't spot a huddled shape, the toe of a work boot. He didn't think the mob guys were wearing work boots, but that's what his imagination dressed them in just the same. Work boots and heavy, grungy work clothes.

And what else? A fucking hockey mask and a machete?

He would have laughed at the thought if he hadn't been so utterly suffocated by fear. He didn't think there was anything under the table, but he couldn't bring himself to crouch down to check.

His eyes drifted to the butler's table. The red cloth draped over it. That stupid freaking cloth hung almost all the way to the floor, which meant anything could be hiding under it. A mob guy, a ghost, even a machete-wielding psycho. Oh, what the hell had those stupid women gotten him into?

Not since that police detective had shown up at the club three years ago had Chad been so overcome with dread. He swallowed, thinking of it now, and though he welcomed the distraction of another train of thought he was pretty damned sure this was not the thought train he wanted to climb aboard. He didn't want to think about Rex Holder.

But he was. Yes, he was thinking about him all the same.

Thunder crashed outside, making Chad yelp in fright and perform a spastic air dance. The storm was really howling now, and like the four-year-old Chad used to do, he found his mind irrationally begging the rains and the thunder and the magnesium flashes of lightning to cease.

But they did not. Neither did the memories of Rex Holder, a nondescript guy who'd shown up at Chuck's Gym, where Chad had been a trainer, and had promptly developed a man crush on Chad. No, the guy hadn't been gay, though for some reason Chad found the gay dudes seemed to come on to him more than they did other guys. Maybe it was the ponytail. But Rex had come up to Chad and asked if Chad could spot him on the bench. *Why not?* Chad had answered, it was his job after all. Of course, he hated it when people asked him for a spot because it took him away from his own workout. But he'd stood there behind Rex just the same, knowing right away the man had not a freaking clue about the bench press just by the way he gripped the bar and let the damn thing bounce down off his chest. Plus, as Chad expected, Rex had loaded too much weight on the bar, even though it was only one seventy-five. Rex was barely able to squeeze out two reps with crappy form. Hell, if Chad hadn't put the clips on for him, the discs would've slid right off the bar and injured them both.

So after damn near killing himself with the bench press, Rex had annoyed Chad further by striking up a conversation. Making small talk. If there was anything in the universe Chad hated more than being interrupted from his workout, it was being interrupted from his workout by some dipshit wanting to make small talk.

"How long have you worked here?" Rex asked, as if interviewing Chad for the school newspaper.

"Awhile," Chad said, eyeing the lat pull machine he'd been on but which was now occupied by another gym member.

Rex frowned and said, "Oh yeah," and the way he said it, it was like he and Chad were old friends. Like they'd been at Chad's house the other day drinking beers together and Rex had forgotten to bring something up.

"I've been meaning to ask somebody," Rex went on. "Why is this gym called 'Chuck's'?"

Chad sighed, looked around. "No idea."

"Is that the owner's name?"

"His name is Mike Adams," Chad answered.

"Is Chuck his nickname? Do they call him Chuck?"

"They call him Mike."

Talking to Rex was about as pleasant as getting a rectal exam. Chad finally got away from him, but the next afternoon, there was Rex asking Chad for a spot on the bench again. Chad made little show of friendliness this time, and when Rex ambled over Chad told him he couldn't help him.

"Oh, are you helping somebody else right now?"

"You're not supposed to work the same major muscle group two days in a row," Chad said in a monotone. "Fast twitch muscles are okay. Abs, calves. But not slow twitch muscles like pecs. You do that, your body won't have time to recover."

Rex nodded thoughtfully, as though Chad had just solved all the secrets of the universe for him. "Hey, you sound like you know a lot about this stuff."

"What they pay me for," Chad said, starting away.

"Do you know anything about steroids?"

Chad paused, a hundred different thoughts caroming around in his head, none of them charitable. He glowered at Rex thinking, *Of course I know about steroids. How you think I got this big? You think I stuck an air compressor up my bunghole, made my muscles stretch like balloons?*

But he said, "Steroids are illegal. They can damage your liver and cause heart disease."

Rex favored him with an infuriating *Aw shucks* grin that indicated plainly that he knew better, that they were old buddies – hadn't Chad spotted him on the bench, after all? – and that good old Chad needn't hide the truth from him.

Rex said, "I've been doing a lot of reading, and I understand the risks."

Sure you do, Chad thought. *Sure you know about the way it makes you feel like you wanna jump out of your skin, how it gives you headaches, how it makes you so cranky you often feel like killing somebody. You know all about the bad breath and the inexplicable increase in armpit sweat. You know it can make you feel weightless and truly screw up your night if you drink too much alcohol the same day you juice. You know how it makes your penis do weird things, which is especially scary if you've got some insecurities in that area to begin with. How it can makes your stools turn to stone and your nuts ache. You know all these things because you read about them. Right.*

"Not to mention," Chad said, "that 'roids are unregulated. There's no way of knowing what you're putting in your body. It could be anything."

What a waste of time, he thought. He knew the type. The shortcut hunters. They spent all kinds of money on supplements, but they never got big. Because to get big you actually had to, you know, *do the fucking work.*

"See, that's what I keep getting stuck on," Rex said analytically. "The articles all say what steroids do, they say how they can affect your body. But they don't tell you where you can get them."

Chad opened his mouth to tell this wanker to get lost. But just as he was getting ready to, he noticed the man's watch. It was a Rolex. Now in one way this annoyed Chad even more. Because who worked out in a Rolex? But in another way it made him see Rex in a completely new light. He'd watched the guy pull up through the gym window earlier. In a light blue Porsche. And before changing into his workout clothes, hadn't Rex been wearing an Armani suit? Yes, Chad thought. He believed Rex had. Living in Malibu and driving a car like that, Rex must be doing awfully well for himself.

And the truth was, Chad could use the money. He drove an old Ford Taurus and shared an apartment with another trainer at the gym. And, if Chad was being honest, he did sometimes act as middleman in deals like this.

Rex raised his eyebrows. "You don't know anyplace I might find something like that, do you?"

Chad shrugged, keeping it casual. "If I did, I wouldn't talk about it here."

The way Rex's smile changed then, Chad could hardly look at the guy. It was as if Chad had just confessed to some terrible crime, one that Rex had suspected him of all along. In a way, Chad guessed this was precisely the truth.

"And where would you be inclined to discuss such a transaction, if indeed you knew about such matters?"

Chad didn't like that word at all – *transaction* – it sounded too much like prison doors clanking shut. *Transaction* meant this was getting serious. *Transaction* meant Chad was officially in this thing, a part of some sinister machinery.

So keep it casual, he reminded himself. *Rex is the one wriggling on the hook, remember? So chill.*

He told Rex he'd meet him at a beach he often went to, one just down the road? Rex said he knew the beach well, he'd surfed it when he was younger.

Well, whooptie-freaking-doo, Chad thought.

So they met there and talked it over and agreed on a price, which was much higher than anyone who really knew about steroids would pay. Rex said he wanted to do a cycle of Deca, which Chad usually charged about eight hundred for, keeping half for himself. But he figured, Armani suit, Rolex, Porsche...how about three thousand?

"Three thousand?" Rex asked, eyebrows raised.

"Of course," Chad had answered. "You wanted a full cycle, right?"

Rex had frowned and said yes, and at that point Chad knew Rex was completely full of shit. Sure, the guy knew Deca was a popular steroid, but that seemed the extent of his knowledge. Three grand was highway robbery, but it would mean Chad's cut would be huge. Hell, two months' rent.

Chad told Rex he needed the money up front, and Rex paid him in cash the next day.

★　　★　　★

Then Chad's source wouldn't answer his phone calls. Rex got antsy. A week went by and Rex's chummy demeanor vanished. He demanded Chad deliver the stuff. They were in the locker room of all places when Rex threatened him, guys milling about in their skivvies and some of them with their schlongs hanging out, fat old men who seemed to enjoy being naked in front of each other.

"Are you going to refund my money or do I tell your bosses?" Rex said loudly enough for one naked guy with his belly hanging over his privates to hear.

Chad felt cold sweat on the back of his neck. "I told you, I'm gettin' it."

"Forget about the 'roids," Rex said. "I want my goddamned money back."

In truth Chad had spent it. He'd intended to get ahead in his rent but had instead bought himself some new clothes, a pair of sweet sunglasses, and had taken two different women out on nice dates. He'd gotten laid both times, but now the money was gone.

At length, Rex said, "That's it. I'm talking to your boss."

"Hold on a second," Chad said.

"Fuck off," Rex muttered, moving toward the door. Chad had liked it better when Rex was trying to be his buddy.

Heart thudding, Chad snagged Rex's forearm and spun the man around. "You don't wanna do that."

Rex stared up at him in astonishment. "Are you actually threatening me? Are you really that dumb?"

That set off a blaring horn of fury deep inside Chad. That D-word. It was the quickest trigger he had, probably because he'd heard it so many times and for so goddamned long. He suddenly wanted to kill Rex Holder. Not strike him, not maim him. *Kill* him. Kill him with his bare hands.

"I'm not threatening you, Rex," Chad said in a low voice. "I'm telling you you're twenty minutes away from getting what you paid for."

"Twenty minutes," Rex repeated.

"Sure," Chad said. "I just have to get it from my car."

They were standing very close together in the entryway of the locker room. Someone brushed past them on the way out, but neither of them broke eye contact.

"It's in your car now?" Rex asked. His voice was skeptical, but from his eyes Chad could see he wanted to believe it. Because in Rex's mind what was in those vials would transform him in a few short weeks from a scrawny guy with a concave chest and arms like pipe cleaners to a guy that looked like Chad, with muscles on his muscles, the kind the ladies would go wild for. Chad noticed that Rex's hair had begun to gray at the temples. The crow's feet around his eyes. He adjusted his mental estimate of the man's age to mid-forties. More importantly, mid-forties and *single*. And Rex didn't want to be single any longer. Rex wanted to snag himself some hotass babe in her twenties, the kind with tits that didn't sag a bit when she unleashed them from her bra. Or else one of those plastic surgery bimbos who looked a decade younger than she was, the kind who not only wanted her man to drive a Porsche, but to look like a professional athlete as well.

Chad could see Rex thinking all these things and realized he'd bought himself a reprieve. But he wasn't out of the hot seat yet.

Chad said, "It's in my trunk, but I can't very well give it to you here, can I? There're security cameras all over the place."

"Where then?"

"The beach."

That glint of suspicion reappeared in Rex's eyes. "You're just putting me off."

"Honest to God I'm not."

"Fine," Rex said, nodding toward the door. "Let's go. I'll ride shotgun."

Chad gave him a humoring grin. "We can't ride there together. That would be just as bad as doing it here."

"You just want me to go?"

"I'll be there in twenty minutes."

"Or maybe you won't show up."

Chad's grin spread. "Where am I gonna go, Rex? You know where I work."

Rex didn't seem satisfied, but he went along with it. Which left Chad with twenty minutes. Shit, he thought. Hardly any time at all. He should've given himself an hour.

But he waited for Rex's baby blue Porsche to roll out of the parking lot, then jogged out to his own shitbox of a car. There were indeed vials in the trunk, but they were used ones. Chad had tossed them back there a few days ago intending to discard them in a public trashcan, but he hadn't gotten around to it, which gave him the idea back in the locker room to recycle them with Rex. The only problem, he realized as he crammed the eight empty vials into his pockets, was that he had nothing to put in them. There were ten unused hypodermic needles still in his trunk, so luck was with him there. He figured if he ever got pulled over he'd tell the cops he was diabetic.

Sweating badly now, Chad reentered Chuck's Gym, bypassed the locker room and headed straight for the trainers' office. Chad didn't come in here often because the only things in the office were some canisters collecting dust and a mustard yellow couch with a broken leg.

Okay, Chad told himself. *What does the stuff in the vials look like?*

Liquid, but slightly thicker than water. And a little translucent maybe. It was tough to tell because the vials were a dark amber color. Chad thought the steroids he used were clear, but then again maybe the liquid was a bit milky. Funny, he'd been putting the stuff in his body for a good five years now but had never taken the time to really examine what it looked like.

He opened a cabinet door and a black, furry spider clambered out. Chad screamed, did his air dance, his heart whamming in his chest. Trembling now, he scanned the canisters. They were all a faded ivory color, very few of them labeled. He examined the strips of masking tape with faint letters scribbled in ballpoint pen. WHEY, one of the peeling strips proclaimed. SOY, read another.

Chad frowned at these, thinking they sounded too mundane. They surely wouldn't fool Rex. A guy like that was probably college educated.

HYDROSYLATE, the next one read. Better, but something about the name scared him. Too much like a substance you'd find in a laboratory. He wanted to fool Rex, not turn him into a lab rat.

BONAMI, the fourth canister said. Now that was more like it. Chad had never heard of it before, but it sounded exotic and didn't make him think of test tubes and Bunsen burners. He guessed the name was Italian or maybe Japanese. He didn't know a lot of Italian or Japanese bodybuilders, but then again Rex wasn't going to be a bodybuilder anyway.

He unscrewed a vial, sprinkled a pinch of the powder in, and filled it with water. But when he shook the vial up, the mixture still looked pretty much like water. He added more BONAMI, shook it, and then sprinkled in some more for good measure.

He glanced up at the clock. Ten minutes had passed.

Shit. Working hurriedly now, he sprinkled a goodly dose of the protein powder into the remaining seven vials, filled them with tap water and capped them. Then, taking care to mop off the excess water with some paper towels, he stuffed the vials into his pockets and hustled back out to his car. He was five minutes late arriving at the beach, but Rex was still there just as Chad knew he'd be, the guy too excited about his free ride to the land of ripped physiques and big-breasted women to fret over five measly minutes.

"You got it?" Rex asked through Chad's open window. Jesus, not even letting him get out of the car.

"Here you go," Chad answered, in truth not really wanting to get out. The only thing he wanted to be was gone. He'd never been a great liar, and he feared if he stayed too long Rex would know he'd been given an innocuous protein drink rather than a real steroid.

Of course, that was what Chad had believed.

Until the day one of the other trainers asked him if he'd heard about the guy from the gym who died in his expensive oceanfront condo.

Chad's mouth had gone dry. He didn't even have to ask what the guy's name was. Shaking, he'd slipped into the trainers' office and opened the cabinet door. He spotted the canister, repeated the name to himself, though he really didn't have to. He remembered BONAMI well enough.

He didn't dare ask anybody about it. What could he say anyway? *Hey, what would happen if you were to inject BONAMI into your bloodstream? Could that kill you?*

He was careful. He went to the public library that night rather than using his roommate's computer. He typed in *bonami protein powder* and didn't get a single hit about the stuff. He did, however, get thousands of websites mentioning a kind of cleaning chemical called *Bon Ami*.

Chad spent the night under his bed. And the night after that.

He'd gone to work though, figuring it was more suspicious to not come in. He thought of those vials. If the first one had killed Rex Holder – and Chad was pretty certain it had only taken one dose of the poison to do the job – that left seven more vials in Rex's condo. Were Chad's fingerprints on them? He'd wiped them off after filling them, but then he'd handled them while putting them in his pockets and giving them to Rex.

But no one came to the club asking questions. Chad was safe.

Yet now, standing immobile in the doorway of the dining room of Castle Blackwood on an island everybody said was haunted, Chad had that sick feeling in his gut again, that dreadful sense of foreboding. And it was something about that stupid red tablecloth that was making him feel this way. Because the tablecloth was moving, the crimson fabric undulating with the breeze. Chad wanted to rush over to the windows and shut them, but that would take too long, and more importantly it would carry him too close to the table. Anything, he realized, might be under that table. There could be one of the gangsters. There could even be a ghost.

No, Chad thought. *Not that.*

And now he fancied he saw something small and glistening just under the lip of the red fabric, something amber-colored and cylindrical…

The crimson tablecloth billowed in the breeze, and Chad beheld the fingers next to the vial.

Chad dropped the gun. He scarcely heard the loud *thunk* it made.

Oh my God, he thought.

Chad focused his whole will on backpedaling out of the room. He wanted to be away from the table, away from the bloodless fingers he'd glimpsed.

Chad turned and expected to run right into Rex Holder's leering corpse. But the great hall was empty, the foyer beyond that seemingly empty too. Chad knew he should retrieve the gun, but suddenly the only thing that mattered to him was getting the hell out of the castle. He would make a break for it – now – and he wouldn't stop running until he reached the beach. Then he'd fucking swim back to California if that was what it took. This place was as haunted as they said, only it was worse, because this wasn't just a place of ghosts, it was your *own personal ghosts* that resided here, and it had only been one goddamn mistake. Did he deserve to die because of it?

Whimpering, Chad broke into a run halfway through the great hall, and amazingly, there was nothing there to impede his progress. He wrested open the front door, lurched through and was met with the sight of a pointed object hurtling at his chest. Instinctively, Chad jerked sideways, the spear grazing his chest rather than impaling him. Gasping, Chad stumbled backward through the doorway and gazed up uncomprehendingly at the man who'd just tried to kill him, a skinny blond guy with a crazed expression on his face. One of the gangsters? The guy raised the long, slender object again – not a spear, but something like it – looking for all the world like some deranged native from one of those old Tarzan movies. The guy jabbed at him, nailed him right in the upper thigh this time. Yelping, Chad kicked the guy in the nuts. The guy staggered back, yanking the sharp implement out of Chad's leg with a sick slurping sound. Whimpering, Chad scuttled backward through the doorway, grabbed hold of the big wooden door and flung it at the guy. The maniac lunged forward at the last second, but the door banged shut just before he made it there. Shaking with terror, Chad pushed to his knees and shot the bolt.

What the hell? Had the guy just been standing out there waiting for him? And what was up with the freaking spear? It looked like some sort of old-fashioned gardening tool, its end bifurcated like the tongue of a snake. Why use something that primitive? Why not just shoot him?

Because the rest would hear it, Chad thought. *Then they'd come running. And the gangsters want to pick us off one by one.*

Well, he thought, at least the door was locked now. There was no way he'd be getting—

The dining room. The windows in there were open.

Chad was on his feet instantly, his desire to get the windows closed now even greater than his pain and his terror. If the guy had been outside waiting for someone to walk out the front door, there was a good chance he knew about the dining room windows. Even now he'd be pelting around the castle to beat Chad there. But Chad had the more direct route, and more importantly, he had the gun. It would be right where he'd dropped it, right beside the dining room table. When Chad limped through the great hall and reached the dining room he saw this was true – the gun lay a couple feet from the long wooden table.

He'd grab it in a moment. But first the windows. He didn't like it, but he had to venture near the butler's table and that horrid crimson tablecloth to draw the windows shut. But what he'd glimpsed there... that was just the guilt talking. And after all, there was no guarantee Chad was the one who'd killed Rex. First of all, Chad thought as he pushed down the first window and thumbed shut the window lock, guys like Rex were classic candidates for cocaine abuse, for heroin, for all sorts of designer drugs. Maybe the reason no one ever investigated Chad was that Rex never even took the poison in the vials, or if he did, its effects had been negligible. He reached out, closed the second window, now watching the castle lawn a few feet away to make sure that bastard mob guy wasn't about to skewer him with the garden spear. Chad thumbed the lock. One more window to go. He reached out, telling himself that even if the cleaning powder had been the cause of Rex's death, it had been Rex who'd taken the stuff, not Chad, and Rex was an adult who could live – or die – with the consequences of his actions.

Chad got the last window closed, tightened the hasp lock. He exhaled tremulously.

He froze, remembering the butler's table. Suddenly sure Rex's moldering corpse would emerge from beneath it, Chad glanced down.

Nothing. But all at once he needed to be sure. Chad wrenched the tablecloth up. What he saw made his limbs go limp.

Then he was bent over and chuckling with relief. Someone – he had no idea who and didn't really care – had left an empty prescription bottle of pills under the table. Chad frowned, reading the name: TANYA BROOKS. Was that Teddy's wife? Chad couldn't remember if Teddy was married.

Still shivering with relief, Chad made his way around the table and reached down for the gun, and it was then that a hand darted out from the shadows and clamped over his wrist. The bones there splintered. Chad's mouth hinged open in a soundless scream. He pitched forward toward the misshapen face, Rex Holder's face, the skin dark red but the eyes glowing a hideous fluorescent white. Rex was grinning, reeling Chad steadily nearer, and then Rex's other hand came up grasping a handful of what looked like dark orange pieces of jewelry. But they were vials, and they were overflowing with tiny black spiders. Rex crammed the vials into Chad's gaping mouth, the spiders scurrying over Chad's tongue and tickling the back of his throat. Rex's iron fingers grasped Chad by the top of the head and the underjaw and made him chew the amber glass and the black furry spiders, and Chad tried to scream again and made only a wet, meaty gargling sound, the blood choking him the same way it had choked Rex, and then the spiders were scuttling under Chad's eyelids, biting his eyes, and Chad could only cough more blood as he choked on glass and spiders.

CHAPTER FOUR

"This is nice," Teddy said. "Just me and you. I thought I'd never get you alone."

They were picking their way along the muddy forest trail, Teddy's feet occasionally slipping on the slick earth. He made a mental note to bring hiking boots if he ever visited a haunted island again during a stiff rain.

"I don't get it," Ben said. "The redwood grove should be right around here."

"That what we're looking for? A bunch of redwoods?"

Ben scowled, hands on hips, and surveyed the forest.

Teddy shivered. "I thought redwoods were the biggest trees on earth."

Ben didn't answer him, but his scowl deepened.

"There been any lumberjacks vacationing here?"

Ben still didn't respond. The afterimages of Castillo's bloody face were still emblazoned on Teddy's memory, but as so often happened he found he couldn't control his mouth.

"Maybe David Copperfield came out here. He figured, 'Hey, I tackled the Great Wall of China. I made the Statue of Liberty disappear. Why not try a whole forest?'"

Ben looked at him. "Let's pretend what I'm saying is true."

Teddy arched an eyebrow. "You mean…"

"I mean all of it. The deaths, the spirits, the beast. Just to humor me, I want you to pretend it's all real."

"That's askin' a lot," Teddy answered. "I used to make believe I was Willie Mays when I was a kid, but that was the extent of my imagination. I didn't even get into G.I. Joes. Not enough racial diversity."

"Are you finished?"

"Probably not, but let's get movin' anyway. My balls are shrivelin' into acorns, it's so damned cold."

Teddy started down the trail again, but Ben made no move to follow him. Teddy exhaled wearily and said, "All right, man, so we stand here. You get my circulation going with a good ghost story."

"You've got to make an effort to believe."

"Okay, an effort I can do. I think you sound like that freaky Pedachenko chick, but I'll listen to you anyway."

Ben scanned the upper reaches of the trees. "Have you ever seen *The Shining*?"

"Shit," Teddy chuckled. "Jack Nicholson? '*Here's Johnny*'? That naked dead bitch kissin' him in the bathroom? Course I've seen it."

"In the novel Stephen King describes the Overlook Hotel as a psychic battery. It absorbs all the evil thoughts and deeds of its inhabitants through the years and bides its time, awaiting the arrival of a vulnerable individual to pour all that malice into."

"And Jack Nicholson was that vulnerable individual?"

"The character's name is Jack Torrance, but yeah, because of his drinking and his temper he's the ideal candidate for the hotel to prey on."

"You realize we're talking about a book here, right? A novel? I would think a guy like you, writes music for made-up stories, would know the difference between make-believe and reality."

"I'm using King's metaphor."

Teddy thought about it. "So all those people on the Sorrows last summer were Jack Torrances?"

"Not exactly."

"They were alcoholics?"

Ben shot him a sharp look. "I thought you were gonna make an effort."

"Takes a hell of an effort when you keep feedin' me Stephen King books."

"It's just a starting place," Ben snapped. "For Christ's sake, would you bear with me?"

"Okay, okay. Take it easy, would ya? I don't particularly want those mob psychos hearing us out here, come try to finish the job."

"They're the least of our worries."

Teddy grunted noncommittally, waited for Ben to finish.

Ben said, "Imagine this island is like a psychic battery too, only it doesn't just absorb the evil that's already in a person when he comes.

It sends a signal to the spirit world – heaven, hell, wherever it is that people go after they die – and those spirits, they're summoned to the Sorrows. It's like…it's like a telepathic link between them. A supernatural conduit."

"You're losin' me."

"It's simple. You live a good life, don't kill anybody or treat anyone too badly, the only thing the island can do to you is magnify your flaws." Ben's expression grew troubled. "Of course, sometimes that's enough."

"This place do somethin' to you?"

"I have a temper," Ben said.

"No shit," Teddy said, thinking of Castillo's mangled face.

"It's easy to contain under normal circumstances. Manageable, at least."

"But not here?"

Ben nodded back the way they'd come. "You saw it. I started in on Castillo, but that breaker that's supposed to shut me off before I really lose it, it was just gone. I hardly even remember what happened. Just this dark cloud coming over me, and the next thing I know everybody's staring at me like I'm a serial killer."

"You see Castillo's face?"

"I didn't need to."

"That what happened to you last summer, Shadeland? That breaker malfunction then too?"

Ben nodded. "I almost killed Ryan. I would have if Claire hadn't stopped me."

"So the island turns a guy into the Hulk even if he's mild-mannered to start with."

"It's not just anger, Teddy. It's all the sins. Vanity, greed, lust."

"I thought you said it only did that to the people without skeletons in their closets."

"It does that to everybody. Amplifies their shortcomings…preys on their weaknesses. But some people come here with more baggage than that. More skeletons."

Despite the fact Teddy was already shivering, a deeper chill took hold of him.

Ben was eyeing him steadily. "Yeah," he said, "I'd imagine a cop of all people would have skeletons."

Teddy clenched his jaws. "I told you I wasn't a cop anymore."

"You told me," Ben said. "But you never told me what it was that made you quit."

"I don't need—"

"Or why it is you and your wife got divorced."

"Now just shut it right there, okay? That's private information neither you nor anybody else needs to know."

Something dawned in Ben's face. "It's already happening, isn't it?"

Teddy bounced on the balls of his feet, tongued the inside of his cheek. "Man, I don't give a damn whether you're all beefed up or not, you keep talkin' shit about my wife I'm gonna knock you on your sorry, deluded ass."

"Who was it?" Ben asked.

Teddy made a face. "Man, who was *what*?"

"The one you killed."

Teddy started down the trail. Fuck Ben Shadeland. Fuck the mob guys too. They wanted to ambush him, they'd have their hands full. Way Teddy felt, he'd like to take them all on himself. Shadeland too, the asshole.

Teddy stalked down the decline, slipped, then caught himself by planting a palm in the mud. Straightening, he wiped his hand on his pant leg. He was about to continue on when a hand fell on his shoulder.

Teddy whirled and slugged the hand's owner in the face.

Ben staggered but did not fall.

Surprised at his own violence, Teddy nonetheless took a step forward. "You wanna go at me, man? Show me how uncontrollable your rage is, what a bad man you are? Well, come on!"

Ben rubbed his underjaw, touched his lips, inspected his fingertips. But when his gaze again settled on Teddy, his expression was thoughtful rather than enraged. "You don't want to come clean, that's up to you. I'm just trying to help."

"Like hell you are. You're just using me to get your daughter back."

Ben nodded. "It'll use your suspicion to turn us against each other."

"Aw, man, not that psychic battery shit again."

"Eddie Blaze was my best friend," Ben said. "He didn't tell me anything he was feeling, any of the uncanny things he experienced. I had to piece it together later. But once I did, I started to wonder if I could've saved him."

Teddy spread his arms in mockery. "You couldn't have saved him because the island didn't want him saved. Man, you act like this place has a mind of its own. Like the spirits are in league together."

"Maybe they are."

"That how you explain the redwood trees going missing?"

"Could be."

"Yeah, that'd have to be it," Teddy said. "It couldn't have anything to do with it being pitch black, getting hit with torrential rains, and the fact it's goin' on four in the morning."

Ben looked unperturbed. "Have it your way, Teddy."

Teddy looked around. "So where you wanna go? Back to the castle? We best get there before the island decides to hide it too."

"The dock," Ben said. "If the boat's there we can at least get you guys home."

"'You guys,'" Teddy repeated. "What about you? You gonna shack up here, redecorate the castle?"

Ben stared back at him.

"You're gonna wait until the island gives you back your girl," Teddy said.

Ben set off down the trail.

It was answer enough for Teddy.

★   ★   ★

And most of all it kept Teddy out of that castle. Out of that pantry and away from all those other shadowy places Castle Blackwood seemed to be comprised of. Teddy hadn't heard his late wife's voice since last night, and he hadn't found another one of those damned business cards since then either. But what he'd seen and heard last night had been enough. Enough to persuade him to stay with someone else at all times, enough to make him feel even more frazzled than he had during the investigation a decade ago. So as Ben trudged through the forest and the windswept night, Teddy found himself thinking about a restaurant, about his wife looking absolutely gorgeous – even finer than she ordinarily looked, which was very fine indeed. *Finer than frog hair*, Teddy would have said at the time.

Lovely dark legs shifting under the silky black sundress she'd worn to Amelio's restaurant that night, the beige interior of his white Honda showing off those legs to stunning effect.

Aren't you going to start the car? Tanya had asked.

Eventually, he'd responded. If you don't mind, for now I'd just like to look.

She'd made a pleased humming sound, the one she made when she was good and turned on, when she was eager for his attentions. She called him oversexed sometimes, but Teddy never thought it a crime to be attracted to his wife. You rather I stare at other women instead? he sometimes asked her. No, she answered, but sometimes you make me feel like it's the only thing you care about. That wasn't fair and Tanya knew it, but tonight she wasn't in her prudish state, was instead in one of her naughty moods. Which was fine with Teddy. More than fine. Because he was too. He could feel the closeness of the Honda, the heat trapped in here bringing him to a sweat. He keyed the engine, thumbed down their windows, and Tanya nestled into her seat, groaning with pleasure now that the sultry summer air was kissing her toned arms, caressing her splendid brown legs. Tanya leaned against the window, dipping her short black hair toward the warm breeze, and as she did the black sundress hiked up a little, showing a good deal of thigh. Teddy was already eager, the crotch of his twill pants constricting him, demanding he make adjustments for his throbbing erection.

Apparently Tanya noticed too. Looks like someone's ready to play, she said.

I need a playmate though, Teddy answered, tilting his head toward Tanya, his radiant dark goddess. I don't suppose you know anyone would oblige me?

Drive, was all she said, so Teddy slipped the Honda into gear and pulled out of Amelio's.

On the freeway he asked her, You gonna sit all the way over there, taunt me like that the whole way home?

You mean you can't wait? she asked, but she was smiling broadly, and even more importantly, she'd allowed the sundress to hug her hips so much that the smallest V of aquamarine panties peeked through at him from the cleft of her thighs. He couldn't see much due to the darkness of the night, but with the warm wind whipping through the Honda, the sundress kept flapping and undulating, the panties beneath playing peekaboo with him.

Roll up the windows, she said. I want to hear some Luther.

Teddy obeyed, thinking some Luther Vandross would be just fine. She picked out one of his favorite tracks, "A House Is Not a Home," and then she was leaning over the console, her mouth breathing deliriously tropical air over his ear. God, just the way he liked it.

I'm surprised at you, Darlin', he said to her. Gettin' me all riled up and still thirty minutes from home. Some might even call that cruel.

Her luscious red lips kissed his neck, the area behind his ear. Then the breath again, the tongue licking his ear, a sweet warmth that sent electric sparks of excitement through his body. Teddy reached over, nuzzled his fingers between her thighs. He massaged her leg so that his hand pressed against the crotch of her underwear, which was already hot and moist.

Someone's ready, he said, smiling at the freeway ahead but dying for them to be home in bed, writhing naked on top of the sheets.

How long till we're off the freeway? she asked through her achingly warm kisses.

Turn-off's up here, he muttered, but we've still got a lotta miles to go.

I know how to make the time pass faster.

His whole body tingled. You do, do ya?

Her hand closed over his crotch, her touch gentle, maddening.

Uh-huh, she said.

He swallowed. That feels pretty nice.

Pretty nice? Her eyebrows rose, taking it as a challenge.

Yeah, he said. You know…

The pressure on his shaft increased, the fingers massaging, kneading.

That's real nice.

Yeah?

She unzipped his pants, drew down his underwear. Lord, like being let out of prison.

Let's see what we can do about this, she said, head lowering.

Sure, you want…

Uh-huh, she said, and her lips closed around him.

Teddy's breathing went husky, his eyes a trifle bleary. He decided to take the back way home so they could avoid the highway traffic. She worked on him a good ten minutes, using her mouth but also her hand, the way he liked it. Teddy could scarcely breathe, it felt so good. They kept decelerating, his foot unable to maintain a constant speed. He was getting close, but she liked him to warn her. He was about to tap her back when her head slowly rose, the sudden coolness on him almost enough to make him spurt. She gazed out the windshield at the foliage overhanging the tortuous mountain road.

Took the indirect route, huh?

He tried to speak through the thickness in his throat. I figured it'd be safer.

Always a good cop, she said, smiling and swinging a leg over him.

What're you doing? he asked, stupidly he knew. Because it was obvious what she was doing. Tanya was like that, she'd act like a Puritan for several months and then, inexplicably, she'd turn wildcat on him, shock him with her enthusiasm.

Just go slowly, she said. I'll lean over so you can see.

But she'd unsheathed her succulent breasts, and the temptation was too great to plunge his face into them. God, they'd been married for fifteen years and she still made him crazy with his need for her. But this, he thought, this was beyond their prior experience. She liked to do some things he considered inventive, but they were always in the house, secret between them and confined to four walls.

This was dangerous. Even though he'd only passed a couple cars since leaving the freeway, there were hairpin turns up here, places where the shoulder dropped away into nothing and the guard rails were old. Teddy was getting ready to point this out to her, but then she lowered her hips onto him and his fears were forgotten.

She put her mouth to his ear. I want you to come inside me, she breathed.

Teddy nearly fainted it felt so good. Tanya was doing all the work, her sex hot and slippery and darkly persistent. Teddy braked as they came around a curve, made the curve easily, and as the road straightened out he felt that magnesium-bright heat build up from the hollow of his lower back, his belly, his whole body alight with the exquisite pleasure her pistoning hips were kindling in him. The road was nice and smooth and straight, the next curve a goodly ways up, and he abandoned himself to the moment, Tanya breathing heavy and moaning now too, their tongues wrapped together, huffing into each other's wet mouths. The geyser in Teddy built, built, rocketing higher and hotter, his whole self—

Blinding lights filled the world, the soul-destroying blat of a horn, and then they were smashed against the steering wheel, the dash, the Honda tilting on its side like a nightmare carnival ride, going over, the two of them lying broken amidst the steam and the still-blatting horn, which was somewhere far behind them.

★   ★   ★

His name was Lars Hutchinson. He was a lawyer of all things.

Or *had* been a lawyer. Until the night Teddy's Honda Accord had crashed into his cherry-red Ferrari.

Of course, Teddy hadn't known this at the time. All he'd known was what his friend, Officer Jeff Catlett, had told him at the hospital. Tanya was in shock, and perhaps that was for the best. She seemed healthy enough, Catlett said, but who knew? When a hotshot lawyer gets drunk and drives too fast, people get killed. Catlett was just thankful it had been the lawyer who'd died and not Teddy or his wife.

Come again? Teddy had asked. His back was all screwed up, his head muzzy. But as Catlett had spoken, all the fogginess in Teddy's brain had dissipated.

Which part? Catlett said.

The part where you said the lawyer's dead.

Died on impact, Catlett said. I'm sorry, Teddy, but it's his own damned fault.

Teddy stared at Jeff Catlett, letting that sink in. Teddy said, Hutchins was drunk?

Hutchin*son*, Catlett corrected. Well-known accident lawyer. I'm surprised you haven't heard of him.

Accident lawyer, Teddy repeated.

Catlett chuckled. I know, right?

Teddy felt the suffocating noose of dread around his throat begin to loosen. You say he was driving too fast?

Hell yes, Catlett said. Guy's been collared twice on DUI charges, and from what I hear that number'd be a lot higher if all the times he's been pulled over actually stuck.

Teddy said nothing. As Catlett spoke, Teddy felt a strange emotional doubling. On one hand what he was hearing could very well mean Teddy would get off without a hitch. But for that to happen he would need to get to Tanya before the police did.

—and the people back at the golf course, Catlett was saying, told the same story. The guy who runs the…what do you call it, the place where they hang out?

The pro shop, Teddy said.

Yeah, the pro shop, he says Hutchinson had at least four drinks before he even went out to eat with his buddies.

Teddy licked his lips. You say Tanya's still out cold?

Catlett nodded. She's sedated, but the doc thinks she's okay other than maybe a concussion.

I need to see her, Teddy said, sitting forward.

Hold on there, buddy, Catlett said, putting his hands on Teddy's shoulders. Seeing Teddy cringe, Catlett said, Sorry about that, but you need to stay put, let the nurses take care of you.

Teddy stared Catlett in the eye. Will you do something for me?

Catlett shrugged. Of course, buddy, you name it.

Tell Tanya not to say a word about what happened, okay? She's not to talk to the police until she talks to me.

Something about Catlett's manner seemed to stiffen, something bemused or maybe even wary creeping into his face. But he shrugged and said, Sure, Teddy. Whatever you want, right?

Still, Tanya nearly caved. It turned out she had muttered a few things in her post-accident delirium, which proved enough to arouse some suspicion on the part of the cops investigating the crash, guys who were decidedly not biased toward Teddy Brooks.

The detectives asked questions, posed theories, hounded Teddy and Tanya day and night, but it all came down to three immutable facts:

One: Lars Hutchinson was a convicted drunk driver who was known to drive recklessly.

Two: Lars Hutchinson was undoubtedly drunk the night of the crash. Not only had eyewitnesses corroborated this fact, but subsequent tests on Hutchinson's mangled corpse had indicated a blood alcohol level nearly three times the legal limit. Hutchinson had been blitzed.

And three: It had been Hutchinson who'd come around the blind curve at an unsafe speed. The location of the crash and what evidence the investigators could cobble together suggested that Lars Hutchinson had been at fault on that terrible summer night in the mountains.

Except Teddy knew better. Even worse, Tanya knew better.

When the investigation was finally closed and Teddy cleared of all wrongdoing, their marriage had disintegrated with startling rapidity. Tanya resented what she termed Teddy's bullying with regard to her story.

What about Lars's family? she sometimes asked.

What about them? Teddy had challenged.

Is if fair for them to think Lars was at fault when it was really us?

First of all, where's this Lars shit coming from? You didn't know him from Adam. Secondly, the guy was an asshole.

Says who?

Says everybody! Teddy shouted. Guy like that? Richer than hell and a total jerk to his family? His wife was probably dancing a jig at his funeral.

You wouldn't know, would you? You didn't even attend.

Of course I didn't attend. Why the hell would I wanna do something like that?

Oh, I don't know. Maybe because you're the one who killed him?

Nothing Tanya could have said could have cut him more. Because she was not only saying he was a liar, or that he'd turned *her* into a liar; she was saying she didn't think much of him as a man anymore. That he was a coward for saving his own skin and letting Hutchinson's family think Lars was the guilty one.

It ate away at Teddy. His work suffered. He decided, at his captain's urging, to take a leave of absence. He took to drinking, an irony that did not escape him. He couldn't sleep. He ate less.

But Tanya…

It ruined Tanya.

The first time he found the needles she wasn't home. She hadn't been home much lately anyway, but on this particular night he was really worried about her.

Okay, in truth he was really pissed off at her. He'd noticed her car

– a sweet little Mazda convertible they could barely afford – had a big hole in the front fender, like she'd driven right into a piece of rebar or something. She'd been asleep when he noticed it – when she was home she was usually sleeping. And by the time he'd returned from the liquor store the Mazda was gone. So he got into her dresser to see what else she was concealing, and there, my oh my, he'd found the hypodermic needles, the remains of what could only be a heroin stash. And Teddy's first thought, though he was ashamed to admit it, was of his job, how if his superiors found out he would almost certainly be fired. Sure, beneath the selfishness there were the feelings of concern for his wife, the sense of loss that came from how far they'd drifted apart. But above all had risen his self-interest, his indignant reproach. So that when she came home at around two a.m. he was waiting for her on the bed, the needles and the baggie in his hands.

She walked in, stoned on something, at that point it didn't matter what. She just looked at what he had in his hands with those new dead eyes of hers. He asked her to explain herself. She rubbed a hand over her face, mumbled something about feeling a lot of stress lately, and as she did Teddy noticed the needle tracks in her arms. He couldn't believe he hadn't noticed them before. He saw for the first time – really saw – the ashen hue of her skin, the gauntness of her cheekbones and the hollow pits of her eyes. But rather than feeling concern for her he just felt rage and contempt. He didn't know how it happened but he was shoving her into the bathroom, jerking her by a forearm over to the mirror. Just look at yourself! he shouted over her shoulder. Look at that haggard bitch you've turned into.

Her lips were trembling, something of her old self in her frightened, tear-filled eyes, but it wasn't enough for Teddy. Not at that point. He was growling out curses at her, telling her what a weak, unappreciative bitch she was. He twisted on the shower and whipped open the curtains. She was crying and pleading with him by then, but he wasn't having any of that shit. He reached down and grabbed the bottom of her silver sequined dress – man, who the hell wore that kind of dress anyways? – and despite her entreaties he thrust it up and wrestled it over her arms and off her head, the armhole actually ripping one of her gaudy faux pearl earrings out.

She shrieked in pain, but when he discovered what was underneath the dress, for one measureless moment he lost the ability to think.

For one thing, there were no panties. That was bad enough because she'd been gone all damned evening and she sure as hell hadn't been out with him. But what made it worse were the dark purple marks that dappled her belly, her thighs. Even, he saw as she twisted away from him and fell against the toilet grasping her bleeding ear, the cheeks of her ass.

Tanya? he asked in a voice not his own. What are those?

Leave me alone, she said, bawling.

Tell me those aren't hickeys.

She mumbled something he couldn't make out.

Tanya?

It's your fault, she said, her voice clearer this time.

It's my fault you're out screwin' other men, sticking yourself with these needles?

You killed Lars, she wailed. You killed him.

Fuck Lars, he said.

You killed him.

I should kill you.

She turned slowly, a fathomless terror in her eyes.

I will too, he said. 'Less you get your filthy ass out of my house.

Her gaunt face stared up at him with fear and regret and longing.

Teddy, please. I'm sorry, I'll stop—

You'll stop stinkin' up my house, you filthy whore. Now get the fuck out.

Whimpering, she packed a suitcase, and ten minutes later, with Teddy standing in the garage, the Mazda pulled away.

He never saw the car again.

Never saw her again either, save one time in downtown L.A. It had been a year since he'd thrown her out, and at least six months since he'd left the force. He was grabbing some carryout from a Chinese restaurant he liked.

On the way in he'd seen an old lady rummaging through the Dumpster out back of the restaurant and hadn't thought much of it until he paid for his food and returned to his car. For some reason his eyes were drawn to the figure now sitting cross-legged beside the dumpster, a carton of some kind of slop between the old lady's feet. Absurdly, the lady was using chopsticks to stuff the slop into her mouth.

Teddy froze.

It was the clumsy way the old woman grasped the chopsticks that cinched it for him. Teddy had always kidded her about it, but she'd insisted on using them despite how difficult it was for her.

Tanya? he asked.

The old woman stopped moving. A pair of rheumy eyes swung up to fasten on his. The skin was worse than ashen. It was the color of stagnant gutter water.

Oh God, Tanya. I'm so…I'm so…

Hi, Killer, she said. And as she'd said it, she'd grinned, revealing a mouthful of rotting nubs, a good many of her teeth having fallen out.

CHAPTER FIVE

Ben and Teddy came over the ridge at the same moment, but Teddy's eyes must've been slightly better because Teddy said right away, "Son of a bitch."

A moment later, Ben distinguished what Teddy had already seen. Christina's yacht, still tied to the dock but now tilted at a morose angle, the thing half swamped and looking like it would only take a good-sized wave to sink it entirely.

"Shit, man," Teddy said on the way down the grassy hill leading to the dock. "I didn't like the boat's name, but I sure as hell didn't want anyone to sink the damned thing."

Whoever had swamped the *Blackie* had done a good job, much of the starboard side underwater. Teddy moved onto the dock, Ben trailing. Though Ben was acutely aware of how exposed they were here on the long, battered strip of dock, he didn't think any of the three gangsters was lurking nearby. The weather was too inclement to stand still in any one place for long, unless of course the sentinel they'd posted was impervious to the rain and wind.

Teddy uttered several curses under his breath, hunkered down next to the *Blackie*. "What'd they do to it? Shoot up the hull?"

Ben moved past Teddy to the end of the dock. "I don't know, but this isn't the worst of it."

"Ain't the worst of it? Man, are you insane? What the hell could be worse than being stuck here with three guys wanna kill us?"

"Having our only other hope of rescue taken away."

Ben was standing at the edge of the dock watching the rain needle the ocean. The black surface of the water looked like it was being machine-gunned, but there was one place where the raindrops deflected, a place where something white floated languidly toward the dock.

The dock creaked as Teddy moved up beside him. "What is that thing?"

"A seat cushion," Ben said.

"From the *Blackie*?"

Ben shook his head. "The helicopter."

"There you go again, tryin' to be Sherlock Holmes."

"I held that cushion on the way here," Ben said. "I have bad associations with helicopters. Because of last time."

Ben knelt on the dock, leaned over to fish the cushion out of the water. Straining, he snagged it. Towing it closer, he examined it. Orange on top and bottom with white sides.

Teddy regarded the cushion dubiously. "Positive I.D., I suppose."

"I'm pretty sure, yeah."

"Couldn't be another cushion. In the whole Pacific Ocean there couldn't be another one like it."

"Washing up at this dock at this particular time?"

"Let me guess," Teddy said. "The island wanted it to happen."

"I didn't say that."

"The hell you didn't. All of a sudden this place not only turns people into bloodthirsty maniacs, but it commands the sea too?"

"I'm just saying it looks like the same one."

"What about the *Blackie* here? Damn thing's swamped. Couldn't it've come out of that? That makes a hell of a lot more sense to me than some kind of intelligent tide, Poseidon-controlled sea, whatever the hell you wanna call it."

Ben sighed, tossed the cushion onto the dock.

"Look," Teddy said, "I think we need to start facing the situation as it really is."

"What's that supposed to mean?"

"Whether the chopper is coming back or not, there're three guys out there who want us dead. We might think we're fortified within that castle, but who the hell knows? There could be tons of other ways to get in, stuff we don't know about. But let's assume we're safe in there, I mean really safe. What about when the helicopter comes? We just gonna waltz on out to it with those assholes takin' aim at us? They could shoot up that chopper so bad it might blow up all over the castle lawn."

"The helicopter's not coming."

"All right," Teddy said. "Let's say you're right about the cushion.

The chopper's in the ocean, no one's comin' to rescue us and worst of all, your little girl is still missing."

Ben looked at him sharply.

But Teddy stepped closer, the shorter man staring fiercely up into his face. "I'm on your side, don't you get that? I'm saying what we're doing is not gonna work. Guarding this, checkin' on that. What we need is to *sort this out.*"

Ben shook his head. "I don't get you."

Teddy grinned, but there was nothing humorous about it. "They wanna kill us, right?"

"They want Christina's money."

"Sure, but they'll kill us to get it. And they're the ones with the boat that isn't sinking."

"So what do we do?"

"We go hunting. They're probably on that boat right now. It's the safest, driest place. Either that or in some cave, and if that's the case the boat won't be far. So we get them and take their boat."

"'Get them'?"

"I need to spell it out for you?"

"So we walk the coast until we find the boat."

Teddy nodded. "Whole damned perimeter. Thing's bound to be docked somewhere."

"Why do I feel like you don't want to be in that castle at all?" Ben said, searching Teddy's eyes. "Like there's something you're not telling me?"

Teddy made a disgusted sound. "So we're back on that again." He strode away, arms akimbo. "Jesus Christ."

"No," Ben said. "I get what you're saying. Let's go get those bastards."

Teddy gave him a sidelong glance. "You serious?"

Ben just watched him.

"All right," Teddy said. "Let's kill us some gangsters."

★   ★   ★

Troy Castillo lay in his room, a melting baggie of ice dripping on his swollen eyes. He thought he was alone at first, but then he noticed a face staring down at him. Christina Blackwood. It was as though she was the lever that controlled the flood of pain. Because now that his bleary eyes distinguished her pretty features, the agony crashed down on him with unspeakable force. And with the pain came the memory of how it had happened, how Ben Shadeland had sucker-punched him and refused to relent until Troy had lost consciousness. Bastard probably continued to wail on him for a good while afterward, had maybe even left him for dead after his gutless attack.

Troy realized the Blackwood lady was speaking to him. As though rising through the turbid depths of some reeking cesspool, Troy climbed nearer and nearer to awareness so he could understand her.

He attempted to mumble a question, but his lips were so swollen he couldn't form the words. His tongue felt furry.

"Can you hear me?" Christina asked.

Forgetting for a moment his inability to sound like anything other than an idiot, Troy attempted to answer her. When he could only generate a feeble-sounding moan, he settled for a nod. But even this drove a hot spike of pain into the base of his skull. Son of a bitch, Shadeland had done a number on him. It was like a thousand savage hangovers rolled into one.

The soggy bag of ice was removed, so at least Troy was able to see her through the narrow slits of his swollen eyelids.

Christina nodded. "Agent Gary gave you some sort of injection. You've been out for a while. How's your pain?"

How was his pain? What kind of a stupid question was that? He hadn't looked in a mirror yet, but if his pain was any indication, he probably looked like the goddamned Elephant Man.

When at last he was able to open his eyes again, no one was staring down at him. He didn't know if that meant Christina had left the room, but the notion that he wasn't being gawked at provided a modicum of relief.

He couldn't believe Shadeland had done it. Troy had been involved in quite a few skirmishes in his life, most of them on the wrestling mat. Those were the ones he felt the best about, the ones that made sense to him. Senior year in high school he'd gotten state runner-up. Senior year in college, he'd been one win away from becoming national champion. Winning runner-up was a great honor, he knew, but it still galled him. Hell, he hadn't even been Big Ten Conference champion because the heavy bastard who would eventually beat him at nationals also happened to wrestle in the same conference. The bastard had wrestled for Michigan, and while he despised Michigan and especially the heavy bastard who'd beaten him twice his senior year, he could at least respect the guy because he'd played fair.

Ben Shadeland hadn't played fair.

Troy realized he was grinding his teeth and that this was making his pain even worse, so he gave off the teeth gnashing and contented himself with clenching and unclenching his fists. They didn't hurt the way his head did.

Of course they don't, a hectoring voice said. *You didn't use them.*

Not yet, he thought. *But I will. The moment I get out of this bed I will.*

You can try, but it'll be the same thing. Ben Shadeland will whip your ass. And you'll come in second place.

No, Troy thought.

Oh yes. Just like high school. Just like college.

Shut up, Troy ordered.

You can't take a hit.

Shut up!

That's why you wrestled instead of playing football. You could use your strength and quickness and leverage on the mat. You could get comfortable because there wasn't the danger of being blindsided by someone running at top speed. You're plenty tough when you don't have to worry about being hit.

God…DAMMIT, he thought. And despite the way the floodgates opened and doused him with monstrous, splitting pain, he got up off the bed and shambled to the dresser, where the huge old mirror revealed to him just how badly he'd been beaten. My God, it looked like Shadeland had taken a Louisville Slugger to his face. Never in all his life had Troy wanted to kill somebody worse than he wanted to kill Ben Shadeland now. Not the kid who'd trounced him at state. Not the blue whale from Michigan whose lardass had prevented him from winning nationals.

Troy staggered away from the dresser, having seen more than enough of his ravaged face. Wincing, he collapsed on the edge of the bed and began wiggling on his sneakers. After an eternity, he got them on, though they were still untied. Screw it, he thought. He could walk around with unlaced sneakers for a while.

Troy had gotten to the door when he heard the knob turn and

found himself gazing down at the hot little Russian woman, the one who claimed she talked to ghosts. She was gaping at him in surprise, and though he considered her a total fraud – anyone who claimed to have experience with the so-called paranormal was a goddamned liar, in Troy's opinion – he had to concede he'd like to nail her sweet little ass to the wall.

"Why are you out of bed?" she asked.

"You wanna get in with me?"

But something was wrong, he realized. He was favoring her with his patented lopsided grin, the one chicks – especially foreign chicks – found irresistible. But rather than mirroring his good-natured expression, she was watching him with a combination of bemusement and disgust.

Then Troy remembered that his patented lopsided grin was now a literal lopsided grin, his face something out of a carnival freak show thanks to Ben Shadeland. It would cost Troy a good time with this gorgeous Russian. Troy had no doubt she would have gone to bed with him otherwise, but now there was no chance.

His fury toward Shadeland grew.

"You don't need my help," Elena said, turning.

"Sure I do."

She kept walking. Shit, look at her. Like he was a leper now.

He took a step into the hallway. "Where's Agent Gary?"

Elena turned, but she kept backpedaling away. "The ground floor. We can't find our guard."

"Wayne?" Castillo said. "Where the hell is he?"

"Don't know. Maybe he ran away." She turned, continued walking.

"Ran away? Where the hell's he gonna go?"

Elena merely shrugged. A few seconds later, she was gone.

Troy balled his fists. You believe that? he thought. Girl treated him like he was nothing now, just because he was a little banged up. But that's how women were. Only interested in how a guy looked. For Troy's money, they were even shallower than men.

Okay, Troy thought. *Deal with her later. For now, get your gun.*

Go find Marvin.

CHAPTER SIX

When Elena came in, Christina didn't turn, but she could sense Elena's agitation just the same.

Without turning her eyes away from the leaden gray dawn, Christina said, "What's wrong?"

A pause. "How do you know something's wrong?"

Christina laughed softly. "You're not the only one with intuition, you know."

"Agent Castillo left his room," Elena said.

Christina wasn't surprised. She shifted her grip on the thing she held in her fingertips. She didn't want to smudge it.

"Is that what you think I do?" Elena asked. "Use my intuition?"

Christina turned to her, gave what she hoped was a reassuring smile. "Of course not. Why else would I have brought you here?"

Elena didn't budge from the doorway. "I don't know. I don't know much of anything now."

"Come here," Christina said. "I need you to see something."

Elena tarried in the doorway a moment longer.

"Please close the door," Christina said.

Real wariness in Elena's eyes now, the Russian girl nevertheless did as she was bidden.

When Elena was beside her, Christina showed her the picture she held. "This was Chris at his fourteenth birthday party. We brought him to the island."

"He looks like you."

Something deep in Christina tightened, making it suddenly difficult to breathe. The breeze from the storm still soughed through the window, but it did little to take away the febrile sweat dampening her hairline and making her shirt stick to the middle of her back. She badly needed a shower.

She eyed the picture fondly. "Chris was a fun kid. He was a trifle out of control sometimes, but part of that was our fault. I should've told him no more often." Her expression darkened. "And Stephen wasn't a very involved father."

"May I hold the picture?"

Christina glanced sharply at the younger woman, unaccountably fearful of what Elena might learn. But wasn't that why she'd employed the woman and brought her all the way to this accursed place? And furthermore, did she truly believe Elena could unravel her deepest, darkest secrets merely by grasping an old photograph?

Still, handing the picture over took an effort. Elena stared at the photo a moment before closing her eyes and heaving out a long breath. At first, nothing happened. Elena's respiration was soft and even. In the scant light of early morning, the medium's face was beatific.

Then, Elena's forehead creased, a deep furrow forming between her eyebrows.

"What is it?" Christina asked.

Rather than answering, Elena's eyes began rolling under her closed lids, her fingers tightening on the photograph.

"Elena?" she asked. "What do you see?"

Elena's fingers began to whiten from the pressure, the picture crumpling where she gripped it. Christina reached for it, but then Elena's eyes flew open. She relinquished her hold on the photograph, took several backward steps. The eyes fixed on Christina were huge and frightened.

"What is it?"

"I saw her."

The tightness in Christina's chest increased. "Saw who?"

"Rosa."

Fear misted along the base of her spine, but she worked to keep her voice steady. "Rosa's been dead a long time."

"I saw her with you."

The chill gripped Christina harder.

"What did she…" Christina licked her lips, tried to breathe. "What was she—"

"She was more than your cook."

Christina's lips moved but no sound escaped them. She shook her head, took a step toward Elena.

"Don't," Elena warned.

"Elena, please—"

"You haven't been truthful with me," Elena said. She rubbed her arm where she'd been wounded. "I told you I needed one thing from you – honesty. Yet you haven't given me that."

The medium had retreated nearly to the door.

"Please," Christina said. "I'll tell you everything from now on. It's just...what happened is so terrible."

"What happened to Rosa?"

Christina chewed her bottom lip. "She...she died here."

"Everyone dies here."

Christina shook her head. "No, not like the others. Not like..."

"Rosa was murdered," Elena said.

Christina's throat seemed to close off. The way the medium said it, it wasn't a question. "Did you..." she said in a small, choked voice. "Did you see her die?"

"It was hazy," Elena said. "Diffuse. I saw a man reaching out for me, clutching me by my shoulders. He was making love to me, only it wasn't gentle. He was...it was like he was trying to hurt me."

Christina averted her eyes. "Stephen..." She glanced up at the medium. "Wait a minute. You mean you saw this from Rosa's point of view?"

"It's often that way," Elena said. "Sometimes I witness events from above...like a sparrow perched on a branch. Other times I see from the victim's perspective." She massaged her bandaged arm. "I've even viewed death through the eyes of the killer. Those are the worst. To feel that malice boiling inside me..."

Christina stared down at her interlaced fingers. "My husband..."

Elena nodded at the casement window in the corner. "He pushed her."

Christina didn't answer.

Elena said, "You were watching."

Christina couldn't meet the medium's gaze.

"You didn't stop him," Elena persisted.

Christina's eyes began to sting. At length, she said, "I was over on the bed."

"When he pushed her to her death."

"Yes."

"You feel responsible?"

Christina glared at her. "Of course I do."

"You loved her."

Christina stared at the medium gape-mouthed. "I…"

Elena moved toward her. "If you promise to tell me everything, I'll contact Rosa."

Christina swallowed. "You can do that?"

"Perhaps we will learn what happened to your son as well."

Christina nodded. But somewhere deep inside her, she was no longer sure she wanted to know.

★   ★   ★

Troy was having a difficult time seeing, Shadeland's fists having pummeled his face so badly. Man, he couldn't wait to kill that bastard. That's what the guy was, too. An unctuous, artificial piece of dog shit. Troy didn't buy that devoted father crap, either. Sure, a dad could love his kids, but to act like the whole world had come to an end because his daughter turned up missing? Come on. The guy was milking it, probably to impress the women.

Troy made his faltering way through a thicket of trees and down to the beach. He had no doubt it was all a show. Shadeland didn't advertise his attraction to Jessie overtly. But that was part of the guy's game. He acted like he wasn't interested in her, but he put out this subtle vibe that she evidently found irresistible. Troy had no idea why. Shadeland was nearly old enough to be Jessie's father, or her uncle at least. What she ever saw in Shadeland when Troy was right there in front of her he would never understand. Maybe she had some sort of weird kink about older men.

Yeah, Troy thought, ambling along the thick, moist sand. That actually made a bizarre kind of sense. Her dad had been killed when she was still in high school, her mother and sister gang-raped and murdered. Maybe that had messed with Jessie's wiring, caused her to seek out a father figure when she really should've been seeking out a husband or at least a good lay. But those daddy feelings had gotten mixed up with her womanly urges, and the result was terrible taste in men. She ignored the good ones and sought out ones who reminded her of her deceased father. Troy chuckled. Her dad had certainly seemed like an asshole.

Troy still remembered the way the guy begged them to leave, the way he pleaded with Troy to put down the gun, as if Troy was going to stop in his tracks, clap an embarrassed hand over the mouth hole of his ski mask, and say, *Oh, you don't want a home invasion tonight? Our mistake! Sorry for bothering you, Mr. Gary, and have a pleasant evening.*

The guy blubbering about his wife and daughters. Man, it had been pathetic. And then the mom had started in, the woman almost as bad as her husband. Troy hadn't been the one to kill her — that had been David Rasmussen, Troy's best friend — but Troy had been first to rape Jessie's sister.

And the one who killed Jessie's dad.

It was why Troy had left Santa Barbara to take the full ride Iowa offered him for wrestling. Not because of guilt over what he'd done but fear of being discovered. Troy had never been questioned about the crimes, probably owing to the fact that he had no direct connection to Jessie Gary or her family. The one with the connection had been David Rasmussen.

Funny how things unfolded…

David had gone through the drive-thru where Jessie worked. Some barbecued chicken place. David told Troy he'd never seen a chick so hot. Red hair, green eyes, killer body. So they returned the night after as a trio — David, John Farrell and Troy — and despite his compromised vantage point from the backseat, Troy had decided David's assessment of Jessie Gary was spot-on.

David's idea was to wait for her until after work, but that was too direct for Troy. After all, what was in it for him? The satisfaction of knowing he'd helped David score with a gorgeous chick? To hell with that noise.

"Naw, let's do her like the others," Troy had said around his barbecued chicken leg.

Both David and John had stopped in mid-bite, neither one making eye contact, but neither one protesting either. David and John had both sworn they'd never do it again, but Troy knew better. Once you had the taste, you had to keep going back for more, kind of like an alcoholic, only instead of drinking whiskey you killed people and, even more excitingly, raped them.

Troy raped his first girl at age fifteen. She was two years older, and he'd felt she should put out. She'd asked *him* out, hadn't she? So he made sure he took what he deserved from her and afterward, as if he'd rehearsed the script in his head, he told her if she ever said a word about it he'd strangle her.

She never said a word. Neither did the next one, a girl his own age during the summer before his junior year in high school. But she had gone to the same school as him, and that had made his junior year very nerve-racking. He'd sweat seeing her in the halls, try to change his schedule if they shared a class. Even avoided going to social events he knew she'd be attending.

It was a real bummer.

He'd needed a release. So one night he and David and John had been driving downtown and had seen a woman in what looked like a pink halter top and shiny pink spandex. The Bubble Gum Girl, they'd called her.

David pulling up to the median on which she stood. Hey, Bubble Gum Girl, you wanna party with us?

Smiling around a wad of – what else? – pink bubble gum, she'd said, Sure honey, what you got in mind?

Shit, Troy remembered thinking, what a whore.

Troy leaning out the back window. Why don't you get in, talk it over with us?

Sure, sugar, she said, her curly black hair and deeply tanned skin in striking contrast to the fluorescent pink outfit. But first we gotta set some ground rules.

Ground rules? John Farrell had asked.

She means price, Troy said loudly enough for Bubble Gum Girl to hear. She didn't protest, which told him all he needed to know.

Minutes later she was heading to the coast with them, the woman taking nips from the Jack Daniels bottle Troy offered her. Less than half an hour later they were skinny-dipping in the ocean, the headlights of David's white Escalade illuminating her tan-all-over body, her sweet narrow stripe of black pubic hair. Only ten minutes after that Troy was banging her on the shore, David and John taking turns soon after. And approximately ninety minutes after they'd picked her up in downtown Santa Barbara, Bubble Gum Girl was dead.

It hadn't started off that way, of course. They had the money to pay her. David's family was rich enough to pay the salaries of every hooker in Santa Barbara County for a year.

Looking back, Troy decided, it was the girl's *compliance* that had set him off. She'd let Troy shoot his load in her and then hadn't even closed her legs before David climbed on. Man, that disgusted Troy. And then she'd repeated the same ritual *again* with John Farrell.

He remembered sitting on the sand that night, the dregs of the whiskey boiling in his throat, the now-empty bottle clutched too tightly in his hand. He was watching John Farrell's big ass cheeks flex as the boy took his sloppy thirds from Bubble Gum Girl. And she simply lay there the entire time. Not because she had a voracious sexual appetite but rather as though she didn't really give a shit. Boys will be boys, he could almost hear her think. Let them have their fun. Then John Farrell tightened up, his body ramrod straight and the jeans around his ankles quivering like was being electrocuted. Then John, all two hundred and ninety pounds of him, slumped over on top of Bubble Gum Girl. She merely lay there, languid and content, under John's enormous bulk. Eventually he climbed off and, white butt cheeks agleam in the moonlight, leapt into the water like a humpback whale.

But Bubble Gum Girl just laid there, her knees apart and her snatch shining. The sight of it turned Troy's stomach, all those folds and flaps. It reminded him of spoiled roast beef.

But still Bubble Gum Girl just...*laid there*. Man, didn't she have any shame? Any fucking modesty? And as the Jack Daniels took hold and fanned the flames of Troy's edginess into something much more dangerous – something lethal – that contempt for Bubble Gum Girl seemed to condense into a throbbing, pounding knot of hatred, a hatred that narrowed Troy's vision and directed every cell of his being toward that glistening snatch of hers. That dirty, ugly, roast-beef-looking stinkhole. God, he wanted to rid the world of it. And still it refused to go away, only hung there suspended between those dark underthighs of hers, taunting him, expelling its filth at him. He fancied he could see the tracks of John Farrell's spent wad on the bottoms of her buttocks, like snail tracks. It was all he could do not to retch. It was the thought of all that semen inside her that finally got him moving, got him weaving across the beach toward where Bubble Gum Girl lay. When he stood over her she didn't even seem to notice him, only stared up stupidly at the blaze of stars overhead.

Hey, he said.

No answer. Just a stupid, trout-like grin.

Hey, he said, louder this time.

Mm? she asked, still not making eye contact.

Look at me, he said.

Why?

The lethal heat in him rose another notch, that throbbing orb of hatred now expanding and contracting in a red, nearly audible beat.

Because I told you to, he said.

Of all the things she could have said at that moment, Troy would later muse, there might not have been anything that would have saved her life. But of all the things she might have said to him, nothing could have made him angrier than the words she uttered.

Finally shifting her stupid doe's gaze up to his, she said, Why? You ready to tear yourself off another one?

Troy's eyes flew wide. A noise escaped him that was part gagging sound, part roar. Falling, he brought the thick bottom of the bottle down as hard as he could on her nose. The sound she made was enough to startle him out of his rage, a choking rattle that reminded him of television static turned up full blast, and to make matters even more macabre there were her outstretched arms, fingers scrabbling in the air as if she were fighting a downward skid on a gravelly mountainside. Blood bubbled up like a red pond in the mashed reservoir that had once been her nose, and the runoff from the blood poured into her mouth, which turned the static into a gurgle, and then a choking, convulsive cough. And still the hands and fingers stretched heavenward, blood spraying, the eyes huge and glazed. Bubble Gum Girl looked like she was an extra in a George Romero flick, only instead of shambling after human brains she simply lay there imploring the sky to drop some brains into her open mouth. The thought actually made Troy giggle.

What the hell you laughin' at? David Rasmussen demanded, but he was grinning in spite of himself, and that made Troy laugh harder, and soon they were doubled over together right there in the surf, where John Farrell found them. John, a serious D1 football prospect on the offensive line, was at first a Nervous Nellie, begging them to stop laughing and blubbering about how his future was ruined. But when Troy had staved in Bubble Gum Girl's skull to stop her weird choking noises and then explained to John how easy it would be to let the tide take her body out to sea, John had relaxed pretty quickly.

Troy had not killed again until his senior year in high school, and that time had been the best.

Jessie's family.

Troy sighed, becoming aware again of the stinging rain, of the windswept island. He'd been so wrapped up in his memories he'd totally neglected to pay attention to what he was doing. Which was why he didn't hear the man sneak up behind him.

"Put your hands up, you don't wanna die," a raspy voice said.

★ ★ ★

Troy did as he was bidden.

"Now move your ass," Ray Rubio said.

Without turning, Troy muttered, "You wanna frisk me, you can, but you better not take my gun."

"I'll take what I wanna take," Rubio said. But the Glock remained in Troy's ankle holster. "Move," the voice commanded, and something hard and pointed nudged Troy in the middle of the back.

"I said *move*," Rubio commanded.

Troy took his time about it, the fine needling rain actually sort of pleasing on his upturned face. It helped the swelling, reminded Troy he'd return to normal soon. They walked for several minutes. Troy was about to ask where he was being taken, but at about that time he spied a series of black caves eating into the rocks up the shore to the right. There were several of them, but one in particular seemed to call to him. He headed in that direction and when the voice behind him said, "Lucky guess," Troy said he had a knack for finding the right way.

"Then why are you so bad at picking football games?" Rubio said.

Troy didn't have an answer for that. When they reached the cave entrance he saw how it was right away. Marvin had his blood up, was itching to do battle.

"You're lucky to be alive," Marvin said. The small man was a bit pale and there were purplish half-moons under his eyes, but other than those things – and the way his shirt puffed out due to the bandages – Marvin Irvin looked the way he always did. Mean and ready to make people pay.

"You're lucky too," Troy said.

"Don't tell me what I am."

"Which one shot you?"

Marvin gave him a look. "Who gives a shit?"

"The red-haired bitch got him the worst," Rubio said. His upper lip rose in a snarl. "Your buddy."

"She's not my buddy," Troy said. And she wasn't. He didn't know what Jessie was. An obsession? Sure, she was that. An object of fascination and mind-searing frustration? Yeah, that too. But what she was most of all was a loose end. Unfinished business. He wanted nothing more than to tie that loose end up, and quick. Her and Shadeland.

"She's the one killed Nicky," Marvin said. He had what looked like a .44 Magnum Smith & Wesson revolver out and was eyeing the chambers. "She killed my boy and I want her preserved till after we're done with the Blackwood lady."

Troy felt a queasy tremor of excitement in the pit of his belly. "Preserved? You're not gonna kill her?"

Marvin finished with the .44, pocketed it. He sat down heavily on a broad hump of dark-colored stone. "Oh, eventually. I'm gonna do the honors myself. But that's after I make her sorry for what she did."

Troy glanced from Marvin to Rubio and felt the advent of a serious issue. Rubio was a psychopath who got his rocks off torturing people. He'd want in on whatever they were going to do to Jessie. Marvin had a vendetta against her, and he would *certainly* want to be the one dishing out the punishment.

So where did that leave Troy?

It left him holding his dick. That's where it left him.

Unless…

Troy said, "Somebody want to let me in on the logistics of the plan?"

Marvin grunted, exchanged a wry glance with Rubio. "Plan? The plan, Mr. Corrupt Federal Agent, is to storm that fucking castle and kill everything in there that breathes."

"Seems like you tried that last time and it didn't turn out too well."

Rubio's snarl reappeared. "Tell that to your buddy from the Bureau, ask him how good our plan worked."

"You're down to three," Troy said. "They've still got plenty of healthy bodies."

"We may be down to two," Rubio said.

"It's three," Marvin muttered.

"What happened to Griffin?" Troy asked.

Rubio said, "He's acting crazy."

You're one to talk, Troy thought. "Crazy how?"

"He'll be fine," Marvin said.

Rubio became animated, obviously glad to have an audience to whom he could unburden his concerns. "He comes drifting in here a little while ago – this was after bein' gone half the night, mind you – and he says to us in this robot voice, 'The other bodyguard is dead.'"

"Chad Wayne?" Troy asked. "Big, strong guy, not too bright?"

"That's the one," Rubio said. "I says to Griffin, I says, 'How'd you do it? You shoot him?' Griffin looks at me like he doesn't know me, his eyes like black glass. He says, 'I didn't shoot him. But I wounded him with the daisy grubber.'"

Marvin was sitting still now, listening carefully. Trying to make sense of what he'd seen, Troy realized. Wanting to convince himself there was really nothing wrong with Griffin's behavior.

"What's a daisy grubber?" Troy asked.

"Who the hell knows?" Rubio said. "I looked at him a long time, waiting for his explanation, but he didn't give me none. So I says, 'If you didn't kill him, who did?'"

Rubio had a hand in the pocket of his sweatpants, gesturing with his other hand like some kind of seedy nightclub comedian. "Guess what he says to me. He says, 'The spirits took care of him.' You fucking believe that? '*The spirits took care of him*'?"

"He's all right," Marvin said, though he spoke with little conviction.

"He's losin' it," Rubio answered.

Marvin looked up, tapped his chest vigorously with an index finger. "He saved my goddamned life, Raymond. And *I* say he's fine."

"He's a fruitcake's what he is."

Before Troy could blink the revolver was out and leveled at Ray Rubio. The barrel of the .44 quivered with rage, or maybe it was just the unsteadiness brought on by Marvin's injuries. Whatever the case, he was glowering at Rubio as though nothing would be more satisfying than to shoot him right in the nose.

A baffled expression had overtaken Rubio's pitted face. His hands were up as though Marvin were robbing him in some back alley. "What's the matter with you, boss?"

The barrel quivered. "You don't know when to shut up, Raymond. That's always been the problem with you."

"Hey, don't get all riled."

But Marvin didn't lower the revolver. "I'll decide what I wanna be."

Rubio nodded, his expression saying Marvin had responded in a perfectly reasonable manner.

Troy cleared his throat. "What I was saying, Marvin, I was wondering if maybe we shouldn't do this another way."

Marvin finally let the revolver ease off Rubio's face, but he did it reluctantly, like killing his chief henchman was still very much on the table.

Maybe that's a good thing, Troy thought.

Or maybe not. Because this was a chess game Troy had to play exactly right. If he didn't it would mean death or prison, which came to the same thing. A guy like him in jail, hell, that *was* a death sentence. No matter where they sent him, once the other guys caught wind of what he'd been before, they'd kill him on principle.

If Marvin did shoot Rubio, that could be helpful. Rubio was one sadistic son of a bitch. In the years Troy had been with the Bureau he'd heard about a goodly number of fiendish individuals, but if the rumors about Rubio were true, none of the other scumbags held a candle to him for sheer viciousness and soul-shattering depravity. Marvin killing Rubio meant that Troy wouldn't have to, so in that respect it would be a boon. But would Troy and Marvin be enough to take out their adversaries?

There was Shadeland, Teddy Brooks and Jessie. He didn't count the other women. They were as helpless as lambs. And Professor Grant? That effete windbag would be easier to kill than the ladies. That is, if he was still alive. Brooks? A bit of a wild card. He was small, but he'd once been a cop, and from what Troy had seen, Brooks could handle himself all right.

Which left Ben Shadeland. Troy decided not to think of Ben

Shadeland right now. If he did, his thinking would become clouded. Dominated by homicidal urges. And for now that wasn't what he needed. He needed to be a strategist.

Marvin had gone back to inspecting his revolver. Rubio just looked relieved to not have it pointing at him.

Troy said, "How about this, Marvin? How about I go back and make sure Agent Gary is occupied?"

Marvin stopped inspecting his revolver, his gaze riveting on Troy. "Occupied how?"

"I tell her I know where you guys are, I get her away from the group to work out a plan."

"She gonna listen to you?"

"Of course she will."

"I figured you'd had a falling out with your friends."

Troy pursed his lips, regarded the cave wall. "Naw, nothing like that."

"Then why's your face look like the Dodgers used it for batting practice?"

Troy waved that off. "Shadeland sucker-punched me. I'll take care of it."

So Troy told them his plan, which was utter bullshit. But he needed Marvin and Rubio to think they would be the ones in control. He even promised Rubio he could have Elena Pedachenko to himself.

Rubio licked his lips. "Holy shit, you mean it?"

Sure, Troy thought. *I'll let you have some fun with Elena. But the moment you turn your head, I'm going to kill you, you insane motherfucker. And by that time, Marvin will be dead too. And the only one left will be Jessie Gary. I missed out on her thirteen years ago, and I'm sure as hell not missing out on her again.*

Grinning savagely, Troy accompanied the other two killers into the rain.

CHAPTER SEVEN

The two women sat across from each other, cross-legged.

"I need you to breathe deeply," Elena said, "and not just like you do at the doctor's office."

Christina arched an eyebrow. "What other kind of deep breathing is there?"

Elena scooted forward. "Here, take my hands. Breathe in through your nose. Now out through your mouth."

"Feels like yoga."

It did too. Nestled here between the bed and the windows, the thick, luxurious rug beneath her, it was almost possible for Christina to forget that only a few hours ago there had been four deaths in the castle – five if you figured in Peter, who had vanished.

"Deeper," Elena said.

Christina drew in air, but it felt like a concrete wall had formed behind her lungs, prohibiting a truly satisfying breath.

"You're not trying," Elena said.

"I am."

"Look at the way you're sitting. No wonder you can't breathe."

"But—"

"Hold on," Elena said, crawling beside her. The woman's hands were on the small of Christina's back, her belly. "Sit up straight. You're hunched over like a bell ringer."

Elena pushed her erect, the younger woman's strength surprising. "How can you expect to get the emotional part of it when you can't even master the physical part?"

Christina grinned wryly. "The emotional part of what? Breathing?"

"In a manner of speaking," Elena said. She placed a hand between Christina's shoulder blades, pushed. Christina felt her breasts stretching the material of her tank top. She'd not bothered putting on a bra earlier, and now she felt a blush of self-consciousness at how hard her nipples had become. It was the chill in the air, she told herself. Not the pressure of Elena's fingertips. Outside, the winds continued to whip, the storm charging the air that skittered through the open casement windows.

She drew in another breath and found the improved posture did help.

"Keep your back straight," Elena reminded. "Now, when you think your lungs have filled, I want you to raise your shoulders, as though a giant balloon were inflating within your chest cavity." Though Elena spoke flawless English, her accent seemed to have grown more pronounced; her Ys had begun to sound like the Z in *azure*, and her vowels had become subtly clipped. "Breathe in…shoulders higher… breathe out. Feel the difference?"

Christina nodded. Her lungs did feel fuller. More malleable. The hand on her back described soothing circles, the fingerpads tracing her spine, the top of her buttocks. The hand on her belly had relaxed so that the fingertips rested lightly against the black fabric covering her navel, the younger woman's delicate wrist lying on Christina's thigh. A kind of drowsy complacency began to take hold of her. She was suddenly grateful for the sultry air, the intermittent rain spray the open windows permitted.

"Breathe," Elena said. "Breathe in…inflate…higher…then out…"

"That's nice," Christina said.

"It's only part of it."

Christina glanced over at her.

"Eyes closed," Elena said, scowling with good humor. Laughing softly, Christina faced forward again and complied. "Keep breathing this way until you no longer think about doing it. It must become habit before we continue."

Between breaths, Christina said, "You take this very seriously, don't you?"

"You think I could charge so much if I didn't?"

The hand on her lower back continued to massage, the fingers nudging the waistband of her silky black shorts.

"Feels good," Christina said.

"Concentrate."

She concentrated. After perhaps another minute of this, Elena's fingers left her skin. Christina opened her eyes and forgot for a moment to mask her disappointment. Elena sat cross-legged in front of her, a knowing smirk on her full lips.

"We must focus on contacting your son," Elena said.

Christina blushed. She wished it were darker in here so Elena could not see how worked up she'd gotten. She hated this feeling, like she was some horny old woman. Was that how Elena viewed her?

Elena took her hands, said, "It's all right. I'm used to this."

Christina swallowed, pulled her hands away. "I didn't mean…"

Elena pushed up to her knees and leaned forward, her lovely face hovering alarmingly nearer. Then her lips were on Christina's, warm and wet. Christina sat unmovingly, but she didn't pull away. Elena held the kiss a moment longer, just a hint of tongue playing lightly over Christina's lips. Then she drew away slightly and stared into Christina's eyes.

"It's natural, okay?" Elena said, smiling broadly. The lovely face only inches from hers, she could smell Elena's summery breath, could still taste a faint tinge of peppermint on her lips.

Elena searched her face. "You are all right, no?"

Christina nodded.

Elena showed white teeth, sat back. "Good. Now let's connect with the spirits."

Taking Elena's hands, Christina began to breathe. But the spirits were very far from her mind.

★   ★   ★

The music, Ben thought. The confounded music. Of all times for it to start up again, why did it have to be now, when music was the least important thing in the world to him? It was the same thing last summer. The mystery of the island had been deepening, Eddie's behavior altering subtly with every hour they spent on the Sorrows. Of course, they had come to this place for musical inspiration, and though Ben had found it here, that revelation had not come without a cost. Who knew how differently things might have happened had Ben been less engrossed in the music and more attuned to his best friend's moods? But Eddie was gone now, and the only thing Ben could do was concentrate on finding his baby girl, who'd been without food or water for…how long now? Ben began to calculate, then forced himself to stop. The math told a dire story, and he already felt bleak as it was. He didn't need to make matters worse by mourning Julia prematurely.

An unbroken ceiling of clouds hung over the island like a sooty bonnet. He and Teddy had been forced to move inland about twenty yards or so because they'd run out of sand; the coastline was now a sheer cliff wall against which the waters surged and dashed themselves with untiring masochism. Teddy was afraid they'd miss spotting the boat if they strayed too far from the coast, but Ben pointed out that it would be even more unhelpful for one of them to take a fall from the cliff. So they'd compromised, keeping as close to the cliffs as possible without actually risking life and limb.

"I thought this island was supposed to be small," Teddy said. "It feels like I've been walkin' for hours."

Ben opened his mouth to answer, but again the melody pulsed through his brain, scattering his thoughts and replacing them with a haunting run of notes, slightly atonal but spellbinding just the same. Ben grimaced, fought to displace the melody, but predictably he remained its slave.

Teddy eyed him. "You wiggin' out on me?"

"It's nothing," Ben lied. He had a hard enough time explaining the creative demons to Claire; how could he possibly articulate the sensation to someone who hadn't the slightest inkling about music?

"Worried about your girl," Teddy said.

Ben nodded, relieved Teddy had opted not to badger him about it. Ahead, the cliffs barred further progress, another rock wall rising straight into the sky. But before they moved inland, they edged out to the lip of the bluff and peered down to make sure the boat wasn't tucked in some unseen alcove.

Meanwhile, the music grew more insistent. The melody expressed itself in strings, but it played out an octave lower than most of Ben's recent stuff. There was something feverish about it, impatient, in this way utterly dissimilar to the music for *House of Skin*. That one had been Hitchcockian, an interesting amalgam of Bernard Herrmann's *Vertigo* score and the eerie foreboding of some of Rachmaninoff. But this song…this melody…

A higher counterpoint began to overlay the strings. The lower register, he now realized, wasn't the melody at all but was instead an intricate bass line. Unconsciously, Ben nodded his head to the rhythm, even began to hum it under his breath before he caught himself and bit down on the sound with an agitated grunt.

"Ben?" Teddy said, an apprehensive edge to his voice. "I need to be worried about you?"

Ben blinked at him. "I…"

Teddy nodded impatiently. "I, what?"

I don't know how to say it, Ben thought. *I don't know how to tell you what's happening, except now I'm not so sure it isn't important – vitally important. Because it isn't just the music that I'm hearing. It's what I'm seeing. It's…it's…*

Something clicked in his head.

"The castle," Ben said.

Teddy drew back. "Man, what are you—"

"Now, Teddy. We've gotta go back now. They're moving on us."

Teddy frowned. "You don't know that."

Ben averted his eyes, his gaze turned inward. "We've been gone too long. They're coming to finish us."

"Man, how can you *know* that?" Teddy demanded.

Without answering, Ben turned and set off. To their left was a sharp rise and a thick run of oak trees. There was just enough room between the trees and the rock wall for them to sprint without turning sideways. Teddy was still barking out questions, but Ben had no time for them. He noticed as he ran that the path was verging right, wrapping around the wall like a muddy bracelet. They pounded down through a dip in the path and reached a gradually rising incline. The trail straightened out then, Teddy seemingly too winded to quiz Ben further. Ahead the forest became coniferous, the low spruce boughs encroaching on the strip of dirt and forcing them closer to the rock wall. Ben knifed through the dwindling gap, paying little mind to the sharp spruce needles that left stinging welts and pinpricks of blood on his arms. He bounded up a rise, veered left, then right, the path corkscrewing like some sylvan roller coaster. At last the cliffs gave way to intermittent crags inset along a gradual slope. Ben scampered down the declivity, which tended right and brought them nearer the coast. The rains had picked up again, and now, as the path abandoned the forest for a closer view of the ocean,

Ben caught a glimpse of something down the shoreline. He immediately slowed, but moved to the left side of the path. Teddy moved up on Ben's right, his back to the ocean. Teddy bent over, gasping for air, but he was clearly grateful for the respite.

"What is it?" Teddy asked, his voice thin and strained.

"Nothing," Ben said. "Let's get there before those bastards do."

Ben took off and worried for a moment that Teddy wouldn't follow him. But soon he did, and for that Ben was very grateful.

From where Ben had been standing a moment ago, he'd been afforded a view of the beach down below, as well as a small bay. Standing with his back to it as Teddy had been, the detective hadn't seen what Ben had, but even if Teddy had been facing the same direction, Ben didn't think he would have glimpsed it. Ben was more than half a foot taller than Teddy, and Ben could just make out a hint of something shiny.

Dashing down the lane with Teddy just behind, Ben stored the information away for later use.

Marvin Irvin's boat might just be their only means off the island.

CHAPTER EIGHT

"There's a song in the tower. It's music I've heard before."

Christina opened her mouth to ask a question, but the unnatural appearance of Elena's face somehow forbade speech. It wasn't that the medium didn't look like herself – she did – but it was as though the lovely woman's ordinary facial expressions had been replaced by someone else's. It took Christina another moment to realize whose expressions they were.

But when Elena said, "I'm in the tower. I see them," Christina knew the expressions belonged to Christina's son, belonged to Chris.

Christina forced herself to keep breathing.

"There's...there's a man without a mouth. The man is fused to a pair of others. They're...oh God. The man is playing the music...the man cannot stop...and – someone is coming up the steps."

Christina could make no sense of what the medium was telling her, but she had a fairly good inkling of who was ascending the tower.

Elena said, "It's Dad, Dad's coming. He's...he's got a gun. He's pointing it at me. He's..."

Elena began to shake her head slowly, her forehead wrinkling the way Chris's used to when he was a small child about to bawl. Chris cried often when he was younger, and because Chris's father viewed this habit as a sign of weakness, it invariably fell to Christina to console him.

Abruptly, Elena's eyes opened.

"What is it?" Christina asked.

"Your husband," Elena said.

"Yes?"

Elena made a pained face. "You're sure you want to hear this?"

"Yes! For goodness sakes, it's why I brought you here!"

Elena withdrew her hands, her expression sobering. "Your husband tried to murder your son."

Christina could only gape.

"There's more," Elena said.

Christina waited.

Elena studied her face a moment, then apparently deciding Christina was suitably prepared, she said, "Your son escaped because of the spirits. One was named Gregory…another was Rosa – *your* Rosa…"

Christina felt hives forming on her throat and brought up a hand to cover them.

"The spirits, they attacked and…tore your husband apart. He died horribly."

"Good," Christina said at once.

Elena watched her steadily. Then she nodded and frowned at the floor. "Your son then escaped from the tower."

Christina drew in shuddering breath. "Then what?"

"You are ready for this?"

Christina made a vague gesture. "Of course I'm not ready. How could I be? But tell me anyway."

Elena eyed her uncertainly, chewed the corner of her mouth.

Christina offered her hands, palms up. "Come on. Let's get this over with."

Elena took her hands, closed her eyes, and began to breathe slowly. Christina followed suit, and it was as Elena had said it would be, a habit now rather than an effort.

After some time, Elena said, "I am…I am holding a gun on… Gunderson?"

Christina's eyes shot open. "Granderson," she said.

Elena didn't react. Christina saw that the tortured childhood-Chris expression had come back into Elena's face. *Breathe*, she told herself. *You won't do yourself any good by breaking down now. This isn't your son; she's a medium. And she's about to give you what you came here for. So breathe.*

"I shot him," Elena said in a tight voice. "I shot Granderson. He's dying. I…" Elena's mouth worked for a moment as though she might speak. Then the tortured expression transformed into something hideous, her mouth hinging wider, a mask of horror contorting her features. She thrashed her head, gasping. She appeared to rise an inch off the floor.

My God, Christina thought. *Levitating.*

Elena screamed, batted at something, and then her Adam's apple started to bob, her face leaning backward as if to avoid some unseen menace. Her hands balled into fists and pummeled something directly before her.

Christina's trance broke. "Elena!" She clambered forward, saw with disbelief that the medium's whole body was indeed hovering several inches off the ground, was still rising, rising, her head thrashing, a ghastly choking sound issuing from her mouth. Elena's blonde hair whipped from side to side, her face a livid red, now purple. If Christina didn't do something, Elena was going to asphyxiate right here in the bedroom. She seized the medium's feet, which had risen to chest level with Christina, but the small woman rose higher, a horrid cough barking out of her blue lips. Christina got her around the legs, but they too began to kick and scissor, one knee smashing Christina in the jaw. It broke her hold, sent her crashing sideways into the wall. And when she turned and looked up at Elena she was stunned to see the medium rising eight feet off the ground, her body parallel to the floor. Floating, she now saw, toward the open windows.

"Oh Jesus no!" Christina gasped, stumbling over and trying to crank the nearest window shut. But Elena's body kept floating farther down the row of windows, toward the same one, Christina now realized, out of which Rosa had once fallen. And underneath the tempest of horror churning in Christina's mind she could hear a familiar melody play, one she hadn't heard since the night Rosa died. Christina raced to the window, climbed up onto the sill, got a hand on Elena's floating shoulder just as the medium's body began to breach the invisible barrier between safety and death. She clutched the flesh beneath the woman's short-sleeved shirt, but the body kept drifting, drifting, her whole torso hovering over open space now. Christina was dragged out with it, now leaning back in the window frame, one hand clutched against the inner sill. They were both going to die, both of them would tumble five stories to their deaths, and beneath the white noise of fright filling her mind, Christina heard "Forest of the Faun," the song she'd heard that long-ago night when Rosa was being murdered and she, Christina, had done nothing at all to save her.

Elena's body went slack and the medium crashed down on her. For a moment Christina thought they would both fall, that the collision would send them plummeting toward the castle lawn. The medium's limp body flopped back into the room, but Christina hung half in, half out of the window, her upper legs on the sill but her buttocks pressing the downward slanting concrete outside. She had a hand hooked around the inner part of the frame, her torso yawing out over the precipitous drop. She would have screamed had she still possessed the strength, but now, though it was the worst possible moment, she felt herself drained of energy, a kind of resigned torpor shadowing her like a nimbus cloud. She heard Elena coughing and gasping on the floor. Christina's body slid gradually, inexorably backward, her grip on the frame ebbing to three strengthless fingers. She felt her body going, her thighs sliding over the sill, her fingers losing hold—

Hands clutched the belly of her tank top, jerked hard. Christina snapped her head up in surprise, stared into Elena's grimly resolute face. Something of the medium's resolve seemed to communicate itself to her and roused her from her fatalistic lethargy. Christina wrenched her shoulders forward – grateful for the yoga and the ab work she'd been putting in – and was able to brace herself on both sides of the frame. Teeth bared, Elena drove her little feet against the wall beneath the casement window, and they were soon tumbling onto the floor, Christina beside the smaller woman, whose body seemed gripped by an uncontrollable spate of coughing.

She pushed to a sitting position and rubbed the medium's back. Elena's body continued to tremor with the raw, croupy coughs. Christina winced and helped Elena sit up, a hand on her back to steady her. Elena's cough persisted, a mixture of blood and saliva leaking from one side of her mouth.

"We were so stupid," Elena muttered. "We almost let it claim us."

Christina couldn't seem to find her voice. What was there to say? The medium had saved her life, such as it was. What there was to live for…

Elena's coughing slowly dissipated, but her eyes were red-rimmed and watery.

"It's okay now," Christina managed to say. "You saved us."

"You saved me first," Elena said.

"Deep breaths," Christina reminded her. "Don't try to—"

"Your son was killed by a monster," Elena said.

Christina shook her head. "Stephen?"

"Not your husband. A beast. Something from a nightmare."

"You're not making any sense."

Elena tilted her head. "You're lying."

"I don't—"

"You've seen the creature. I know you have."

Christina's stomach did a slow, sick roll. She thought of the vision she'd witnessed through the peephole. The beast appearing behind Elena...

She swallowed. "You think that...that creature killed my son?"

"I know it did."

Christina allowed it to sink it. When she regained the power of speech, she said, "What do you propose we do?"

"We arm ourselves," Elena said. "We go to Jessie right now and demand weapons."

Elena got up, went over and slipped on her shoes.

Christina watched her. "You know how to use a gun?"

"No," Elena said, "but Jessie can show us. Now get up. I think the bad men are coming."

★　★　★

In the back hallway, Jessie eyed the women and told herself it was a bad idea. But Chad Wayne was nowhere to be found, and the others had gone off who knew where. Castillo was in bad shape, and besides, she no longer trusted him. Maybe arming these two was the right move.

But still, she hesitated. "You know you both stand a greater chance of harming yourselves than you do one of Marvin's men."

"Don't insult me," Elena said. "You wouldn't think twice about arming one of the men. Chad Wayne was provided a gun, was he not?"

Jessie dropped her gaze.

There came a resounding thud from the front door. Another. Someone pounding, but doing it slowly. Like a threat rather than a polite request for entry.

"Give me Morton's gun," Elena said.

Jessie listened to the persistent thud and told herself it was Ben or Teddy. After all, she had bolted the door after Wayne disappeared. Maybe Ben and Teddy needed back in. Maybe it was Professor Grant.

Professor Grant is dead.

No, she thought. *That's just paranoia.*

Then where is he?

"The gun," Elena insisted.

"Wait here," Jessie said and started past her.

Elena stepped sideways to bar her progress. "I will not wait here. Give me the gun."

"Or what? You're going to take it?"

Elena stared up at her. "Sure. I'll fight for it." She gestured down the long hallway toward the heavy front door. "What if that's Marvin? What if Castillo is with them?"

"Agent Castillo wouldn't do that," Jessie said, but even to her own ears her voice lacked conviction.

"You know he would," Christina said quietly.

Jessie glanced at her. "What about you? What'll you do if I give Elena Morton's .38?"

Christina shrugged. "Let's worry about that later. What are you doing about this?" And she nodded down the hallway at the thudding door.

Jessie sighed. She held out the gun. "The safety is here. Keep it on until you're ready to shoot, but more importantly, don't shoot unless you absolutely have to. And even if you have to, be cognizant of what's behind your target. Got all that?"

Elena nodded, held out her hand.

But Jessie said, "Don't rest your finger on the trigger. Treat it like the safety's off even when you know it's on. When you are ready to fire – and again, only if it's absolutely *imperative* that you fire – put your finger on the trigger, aim a little low because the gun will kick and when you squeeze, make it slow and smooth."

"Slow and smooth, got it," Elena said.

Jessie handed her the gun. "Follow me," she said and made for the back staircase.

"Aren't you going to see who it is?" Christina asked.

"Yes, but from a safe distance. They might try to shoot through the door."

They bustled after her. "So where—" Elena began.

"The studio," Jessie said. "It's the one place with a panoramic view."

They began ascending the staircase.

Christina said, "What if they're aiming at us? Guys like that are experienced shots."

"We're not going to be dangling out the window," Jessie said with a wry grin. "You two hang back. I'll check everything out."

"I can't wait to get out of here," Elena said as they hustled up the stairs. "This place...this whole island...I've never felt energy like it. It's like a geyser through which the flames of hell are pouring. It's concentrated evil."

Nearing the fourth floor, Jessie said, "You think the castle is haunted?" She tried to make it sound like a joke, but the quaver in her voice betrayed her.

Because it is haunted, a voice in her mind whispered. *If any place in the world is haunted, it's Castle Blackwood.*

"Haunted isn't a strong enough word," Elena said. "I've dealt in the supernatural my entire life. Even as a child, I was in contact with many types of spirits. Beings who were never even human. Creatures who make the darkest imaginings seem harmless."

They were nearly to the fifth floor, only one more to go. Below them the slow thudding went on. Whoever it was must have a bloody fist.

They passed the fifth floor landing. Jessie tried not to remember the way Nicky's dead body had flopped into the corridor, Marvin's squeal of anguish.

"What's here is worse than anything I've ever encountered," Elena said.

"Shut up," Jessie said in the studio entryway. "You two stay here. I'll check out the front door."

"We're not staying anywhere," Elena said. "We'll be right behind you."

"Will you be able to see from up here?" Christina asked.

"We should," Jessie answered. "The porch isn't covered. We'll be looking directly down at whoever it is."

They moved swiftly to the front of the studio, Elena on her right and Christina just behind her. When they neared the window, Jessie put a finger to her lips to remind Elena to keep her mouth shut. She'd begun to like the little Russian woman, but there was such a thing as too much spunk.

Jessie reached the window box, knelt on top of it and slowly brought her face to the clear glass pane.

A tall man with a wild tuft of blond hair stood on the stoop, his fist bludgeoning the door in slow, metronomic thuds.

It was Griffin Toomey. The one who'd shot Morton. She itched to lean out over the sill, take aim and put one in his brain. But with the gusting wind and the rain she didn't trust herself to make the shot.

Quit kidding yourself, the voice in her head taunted. *You can make that shot in your sleep. You're just scared of him.*

Jessie compressed her lips. She hated the voice but knew it carried at least a kernel of truth. She might not get a better opportunity than the one she had right now. She reached out, began to crank open the casement window. They were nearly a hundred feet away, Jessie estimated, and Toomey seemed immersed in what he was doing. The chances of him noticing her were small.

Slowly, she cranked the window. She brought her head forward, leaned out slowly over the lawn. The entryway was slightly to her right, which allowed her a partial view of Toomey's face.

What she saw did not reassure her. Jessie had seen many images of drug addicts, and had even made arrests while on a case in Phoenix with Sean Morton. The look on Toomey's face was very much like the zoned-out expression she'd seen on the faces at the Phoenix bust, but with Toomey there was something more, something purposeful and robotic about his movements that unnerved her more than his drugged expression did.

Abruptly, Toomey stopped thumping and just stood there.

Elena asked, "What's he doing?"

Jessie fluttered an impatient hand at her. Toomey took two steps back from the door, his eyes still straight ahead. It was at that point that Jessie spotted the gun in his other hand. And then everything happened very quickly.

Eyes never leaving the door, Toomey swung the gun up and fired at them. There was a feeling in her scalp like she'd been stung by a thousand wasps. Gasping, Jessie stumbled back into Elena. The second shot pulverized the lintel, and then the bullets whined and pinged four times in quick succession, the castle façade absorbing the rest of the punishment. Dumbfounded, Jessie fingered the top of her head and was shocked at the viscous mass of gooey hair she encountered.

Christina was watching her, horrified. Elena was talking to her, asking her if she was okay.

Sure, Jessie thought. *The top of my head feels like raw hamburger, but absent of that I'm right as rain.*

Then Jessie heard a muffled crashing, the shouts of male voices.

CHAPTER NINE

Elena was dragging Jessie to her feet. "Let's get to one of our rooms," Elena said.

"That's insane," Christina said. "We'll be trapped there. It's just a matter of time before they break in."

Shambling together through the studio toward the back staircase, Jessie tried to think straight, but her thoughts were a disjointed stream of bizarre images. Toomey moving like some kind of sinister robot. Rubio's hideous jack-o'-lantern grin. Jorge's savaged corpse. Nicky Irvin's obscene leer. And beneath it all, noises from that horrible night thirteen years ago replayed in her head like the discordant notes of some infernal music box.

Elena was shouting at Christina. "You know this place better than they do. Is there anywhere they won't—"

"Of course!" Christina said. "The walls."

"The what?" Elena asked as they hustled down the staircase. Jessie tried to keep up, but her legs felt sluggish, as though she were slogging her way through a deep marsh.

"There are passageways in the walls," Christina explained. "It's how I knew you were—" She cut off abruptly, shook her head. "Oh, just follow me."

Christina pulled ahead of them as they hurried into Christina's room. Dimly, Jessie heard male voices. They were shouting at each other, one of them telling the others to keep it down for chrissakes. It sounded like Rubio and Marvin, but that quieting plea...could that have been Troy Castillo? She thought it was.

Christina pushed the wall and the secret passage appeared. Did the forensics team even know of the passageway? Jessie wondered. They hurried inside, and Christina hauled the door closed behind them. They were properly hidden now, Jessie knew. But that didn't mean they were safe.

What if Griffin Toomey knows about the passageway? the wheedling voice in her head whispered.

Of course he doesn't! she snapped. *If the others don't, he won't either. He's just a lackey, after all, how would he know more than Marvin himself?*

Did you see the way he shot at you? He didn't even look.

Jessie's throat constricted, and she was instantly, painfully reminded of her injured scalp. As she followed Elena down the dark tunnel, she brought her fingers up to inspect her wound. Not nearly as bad as she'd thought before, but still a mess and something that needed attending to. When and how that would happen were questions for another time, however, because now they were in danger of being killed, and a grazed scalp was the least of her worries.

Elena barked her elbow on an outcropping pipe, sucked in breath, and Jessie realized two things. One, they had pulled even with a restroom. Two, there was enough light for her to see the other women. Not much, but enough. So where was it coming from?

A moment later her question was answered. She peered into one of the bathrooms via a peephole situated within a shower stall.

Jessie looked around. "Where does this lead?"

"These tunnels snake around the entire castle," Christina said. "I've never explored them all, but my son once did, and he said there are ladders going from floor to floor."

There was a silence as they considered this. Jessie listened for Marvin and his men, but at the moment the only sound was the distant roar of the storm.

"We could take the ladders down, make our way out of here," Christina suggested.

Elena scowled. "And let them have the castle?"

"I'm talking about finding somewhere safe," Christina said.

"And where is that?" Jessie asked. "If the castle isn't safe, where is?"

"The boat?" Christina answered.

"Ben and Teddy went to check on the boat," Elena reminded her, "and they haven't come back."

They fell silent as Elena's words sank in.

Christina seemed to bounce in place. "So we just...what? Wait here? Hope they don't find us?"

"Let's surprise them," Elena said. "Let's wait until they get near the master suite—"

"We only have two guns," Jessie interrupted, "and we have to assume Castillo's on their side."

"Shit," Elena said.

"Let's just find the ladder," Christina said and had actually started to move again when they heard a male voice call, "You say they're up here, Griff?"

They froze. Jessie glanced at Elena, whose nerve seemed to have abruptly dried up. When Jessie looked at Christina, she sensed an even deeper fear.

"Hold on," Toomey answered.

Jessie sidled past Christina and peered through the shower peephole. It was actually a rectangle of tinted glass about four inches wide and two inches high. They hadn't moved far, so Jessie assumed this was Elena's bathroom.

Footsteps in the hall outside. Against Jessie's arm, Christina's body shuddered. Jessie put a hand out, took Christina's.

The footsteps grew more distinct before stopping.

"You sure they're here?" Marvin asked.

Judging from the clarity of the mob boss's voice, the killers were inside Elena's bedroom now.

Rather than answering, the footsteps started anew, coming closer, closer, then stopping. From where Jessie watched, she could only see the translucent blocks of glass that comprised the shower stall. Thus far the lights weren't on in Elena's bathroom, but Jessie thought she'd be able to discern any shapes moving on the other side of the glass wall anyway.

"The bitches in here or not?" a raspy voice demanded. *Rubio*, Jessie thought. There was no mistaking that voice. If Satan's voice were ever caught on tape, Jessie decided he'd sound very much like Raymond Rubio.

"Give him time," a different voice said. Marvin.

A long silence. As they waited, Jessie could hear the other women's respiration. She hoped the men couldn't hear it too.

"Man, what're we waitin' for. They're probably escapin' out the back or something."

"Raymond, shut the—"

"What if they take our boat? How're we gettin' home then?"

"If you say another word, so help me I'm gonna—"

"Where's he goin' now?"

Jessie's heart dropped. Not only were the footfalls growing more distinct, but she thought she could see a shadow swarming on the glass block wall.

Light flooded the bathroom.

"Oh no," Christina whispered.

Jessie squeezed her hand to quiet her. Elena had moved up on her other side to peer through the slit of window. There was definitely someone just beyond the shower stall, a tall, slender shape moving slowly but purposefully toward the open shower entrance on the right. Jessie remembered the way Toomey had shot her without sighting his target. Almost like he was...what? Being controlled by someone else? Someone far more dangerous? Someone with a thorough knowledge of Castle Blackwood and its secrets?

Toomey stepped into the shower stall.

Elena stood rigid. Christina sucked in air, the hand clasping Jessie's like a vise.

Toomey was examining the wall, which, if Jessie remembered correctly, appeared from his side like large blue tiles of beige and navy blue, only one navy blue tile contained a two-way mirror. But Toomey couldn't know that.

Could he?

"Look at him, boss," Rubio said. "What'd I tell ya? Skinny bastard's checkin' out the shower instead of findin' the women." More shadows moved along the glass behind Toomey. Rubio called out, "Hey, Griff. There ain't no naked ladies in there now!" This was followed by a gust of lunatic laughter, the sound almost as chilling as the sight of Toomey's zoned-out eyes scrolling over the surface of the wall, doing slow vertical sweeps almost as though he were honing in on their whereabouts.

That's impossible, Jessie thought desperately. *He can't—*

Toomey stared straight at them.

Jessie recoiled involuntarily. Christina uttered a strangled moan. Elena didn't say a word, but in the enclosed space Jessie felt the medium's body shaking.

Without looking away, Toomey said, "They're right there." And pointed at them. And though Jessie wanted to look away from that accusing index finger, she couldn't move at all, could only remember a movie she'd once seen with Donald Sutherland. *Invasion of the Body Snatchers.* When the body snatchers spotted you, their mouths unhinged, their eyes became full moons, and they pointed just like Toomey was pointing now. And even if he wasn't screeching the way the body snatchers did, Jessie had never been surer of anything in her life than she was of the fact that something else was inhabiting Griffin Toomey's body, something

(*Gabriel*)

ancient and monstrous and craving nothing less than blood and ripped flesh and the souls within, and then the men were talking in raised voices, Toomey telling them exactly how the women had gotten into the passageway. There were heavy footsteps hastening out of the bathroom, Toomey's eyes rolling completely white, holding Jessie transfixed, though Elena was tugging on her arm now to get her moving.

Light flooded the tunnel behind them and jolted Jessie back to her senses. Marvin or Rubio or both were coming now. Jessie got moving, Elena and Christina close behind her.

"Oh yeah. This is it," Rubio said in a voice that echoed down the passageway.

"How you know?" Marvin asked.

"I smell their pussies," Rubio answered.

"Oh my God," Christina whimpered.

"Keep moving," Jessie said.

They hurried deeper into the darkness.

★　　★　　★

"Marvin's men are up there," Ben said.

"Man, how the hell do you know that?" Teddy demanded.

"I can't explain it," Ben told him, "but regardless of where they are, we need to get in there too, right?"

Teddy looked away, but he didn't argue.

Keeping low, they hustled out of the forest and made it to the front door. Ben tried it, but someone had barred it from the inside.

"The back?" Ben asked.

"They locked this one, they'd lock the other ones," Teddy said.

Ben fell silent, agonizing.

"We could break a window," Teddy suggested.

Ben nodded, dashed around to the east side of the castle with Teddy flanking him on the inside. The kitchen window seemed too high, the ground dipping a bit there, but the dining room window…

"Looks like someone already had your idea," Ben said.

Teddy eyed the shattered window. "We're gonna have another shootout, aren't we?"

Ben nodded, reached up and began hauling himself through the jagged frame. "But at least," he grunted as he climbed through, "we're not going to be taken by surprise this time."

"If you keep your damn voice down," Teddy whispered, taking Ben's hand and allowing him to help him through the window.

Ben glanced about.

"Where to now, Mr. Sixth Sense?"

Ben had no idea, so he moved through the dining room until he discovered the blood smears on the floor.

"Whose do you suppose those are?" Teddy asked.

"Hopefully one of Marvin's guys."

"What if they're not?"

"Does it make a difference?"

"I suppose not, though it would change our odds one way or the other."

Ben moved slowly into the hallway, his Ruger up and clutched against his shoulder.

"Where'd you learn to hold a gun like that?" Teddy asked. "Old cop shows?"

Ben scanned the corridor that opened to the great hall. Nothing moved, but there were too many shadows, too much furniture for someone to hide behind. Ben had an unwonted memory of a time he'd agreed to a team BB gun fight with three other kids. When it had come time to figure out who would go hide and who would be seeking, the opposing pair of boys had been eager to hide. Ben hadn't pondered why at the time, but as he and his partner had crept into a copse of trees crammed with hiding places, he'd realized why the other boys had wanted to go first. Moments later, Ben and his partner had been running and yelping, their chests and butts peppered with BB welts.

He felt very much the same way now, clumsy and conspicuous and certain at any moment that their opponents would be opening fire on them, only this time their retreat wouldn't be full of laughter and curses; this time there wouldn't be any retreat at all, only a sucking chest wound or a fatal headshot.

"See anything, Magnum P.I.?" Teddy asked.

"*Would you shut the hell up?*"

"Hey man, I'm not the one with second sight. I'm just followin' your lead."

"Then you figure out what to do," Ben said in a harsh whisper.

"You go on up," Teddy said, "and I'll wait down here."

Ben stared at him. "I'm waiting for the punchline."

Teddy rolled his eyes. "The women gotta be somewhere, right? We stay together, we only cover half the ground."

"We also don't run the risk of bumping into each other by accident and blowing each other away."

"Way you hold that gun, the only thing you're gonna blow away is your face. Get the damned thing down, would ya?"

Ben shifted the Ruger.

"Okay," Ben said. "I go up, you stay down."

"I ain't staying anywhere," Teddy said. "I'll take the first, second and third stories, you take the upper three."

Ben nodded. "All right. Good luck."

"We survive this," Teddy said, "it ain't gonna be luck."

Ben watched him a moment longer.

Then he bolted for the stairs.

CHAPTER TEN

Troy Castillo stood in the master suite, mutely agonizing over which way to go. He still couldn't believe the castle walls concealed secret passages. Christ, like some old-fashioned horror movie. If he followed Rubio and Marvin into the tunnel, he'd be tethered to the scumbags. Worse, he'd be competing with them for Jessie. Granted, Rubio would likely be content to have his fun with Christina or Elena, but Marvin had his heart set on Jessie.

And not just to rape her either. No, Troy had the distinct impression Marvin was about to get medieval on Jessie, and that simply wouldn't do. Not until Troy took what he was owed from her.

He hated it, but there was only one thing to do. Biting back his pride, he jogged into the master bathroom and found Toomey just inside the room staring at him.

Troy felt a chill ripple through his body.

The idea whispered in his head, *It isn't Toomey.*

Troy pushed the thought away, made himself stare into Toomey's crazed eyes. Was it Troy's imagination, or had the irises shrunk? And not just a little either. They were half the size they'd been.

His voice thin and weak, Troy said, "Where are they going, Griffin?"

Toomey's grin broadened.

"I need to know," Troy pressed. "Are they stuck in there? Or is there another way out?"

"Library," Griffin said in a voice that bore no resemblance to human speech.

Had Toomey not been watching him like some sort of werewolf – my God, look at those eyes! – Troy would have shaken his hand or at least thanked him. But he was grateful to get away from that gruesome leer, elated to have somewhere else to go. He hoped Toomey was right about the library. If so, it might even be possible for Troy to smuggle Jessie into some secluded place where he could make good on his fantasies. Oh, how he would revel in her fear, her pain!

Giggling at the thought of her terror-stricken face, Troy gained the back staircase and raced toward the second floor.

★   ★   ★

"Hurry!" Elena called down the ladder.

Jessie shot a glance up and saw how slowly Christina was moving.

"Come on," Jessie urged. They'd reached the third floor, but at any moment Marvin and Rubio would begin their descent too.

Christina descended the rungs a bit faster, but she was still too slow. Jessie was sure the men would be visible above them any second now. Christina reached the third-story passageway and reached up to help Elena down.

"Let's shoot them when they're right above us," Elena said.

Jessie considered. The idea wasn't half bad. But what about the other two, what about Toomey and that traitor Castillo? Jessie and her companions would be stuck in here and the others could simply wait them out. And who was to say they'd be able to overcome both Rubio and Marvin? Once the shooting started, anything was possible. Better to get to a safer place...

"Listen," Jessie said. "They'll be down here any second now, so there isn't time to argue. You two head that way" – she nodded down the passageway – "and I'll continue down to the second floor. They'll see me, but if you two are quiet they won't see you."

Elena opened her mouth to protest, but Jessie leaned forward and said into her face, "There isn't time. I'm going to lure them down and shoot them if I can. You two go to the end of this tunnel, find the way out and then take the back staircase out of the castle. Make for the coast. If luck is on our side, we'll meet up there and get the hell off the island together."

Christina was shaking her head, but Elena seized the older woman by the wrist and dragged her down the third-story passageway.

Less than three seconds later, a voice from straight above Jessie said, "I hope you ladies are feeling romantic today."

Rubio. The wretch.

"Come on then!" Jessie yelled up the ladder. "If you think you're man enough to get it up."

Rubio laughed delightedly. "Oh sister, I can't believe you're teasin' me. You must be a fantastic lay."

Jessie began descending the rungs. She was glazed with an icy sweat, but it seemed the two gangsters were going to take the bait. She reached the second floor, and then, making sure Rubio and Marvin were still following her, she began probing the walls for a place where she could push through. Almost immediately she spotted a vertical sliver of light. It had to be one of the trick walls. Suddenly sure one of the gangsters would grab her before she could escape the tunnel, Jessie put her hands on the wall next to the illuminated sliver and shoved. The wall moved easily, revealing a large room lined with dark bookcases. It was the library, of course, one of the many rooms she'd searched last night. Relief flooding through her, Jessie plunged into the murky room.

Straight into Troy Castillo's chest.

She would have fallen backward had he not slapped an arm around her. He hugged her to him, grinning horribly. Jessie had holstered her gun, and now she reached down for it. But Castillo had his Glock in his other hand. He aimed it at her nose.

"Hey there, old friend."

Jessie spat in his face.

Troy squeezed her against him, the arm like some terrible trash compactor. The man's strength was unspeakable.

"You better wipe off my face, Jessie. You don't spit on me."

"Go to hell," she said.

He squeezed her tighter. "Oh, are you gonna be sorry—"

A voice interrupted from behind her. "Thanks for the help, Castillo."

Castillo spun her around and pressed the gun against the side of her head. Marvin stepped into the room, his revolver at his side and a devilish grin on his face.

"Maybe you didn't hear me," Marvin said, circling them slowly. "I said thanks for holding her. Now hand the bitch over and leave the goddamned room."

Jessie's terror was already extreme, but a new realization made her heart race even faster. Rubio was not entering the room behind Marvin. Which meant he had followed Christina and Elena.

"I don't need long, Marvin," Castillo said. "Just an hour or so, then I'll let you have her."

Marvin's grin became incredulous. "An hour? Are you *nuts*? I want her *now*, Agent Castillo, and if you don't wanna give her to me, I'll make you give her to me. We clear on that?"

Against the top of her head, she felt Castillo's face move back and forth in negation. "I've waited too long for this."

Marvin raised his gun. "The girl."

"Sorry. You're gonna have to get in line."

Marvin showed his teeth. "I said to hand her over, you cocky little prick."

Castillo grunted laughter. "Says the five-foot-nothing guy to a man who could break him in half."

Marvin's eyes glittered. "You have any idea what I could do to you?"

She felt Castillo hesitate. "You can have her when I'm done. I promise I'll leave her alive."

In the meager light of the library Marvin's eyes looked like black stones, the eyes of some deep-water predator. "I'm done talking. You give her to me or I'll skin you alive."

She thought Castillo might give in to Marvin then, but Castillo flexed his biceps, compressing Jessie's windpipe. The gun ground into the side of Jessie's head.

Marvin did not lower his gun.

For what seemed an endless moment, no one said a word.

Then Castillo chuckled. "Well, this is certainly a strange situation."

A shot exploded to Jessie's right and then Marvin was flailing backward, his feet tangling. He half turned as he fell, his chest gushing a merry red color, and his head cracked the side of a coffee table. Jessie figured the knock on the head wouldn't bother Marvin too much. He'd been shot through the heart.

She and Castillo turned at the same moment and beheld Teddy Brooks, who shifted his gun toward Castillo.

Brooks said, "That's how I deal with a conundrum."

Castillo's powerful arm squeezed her tighter, the gun digging into her hair like some burrowing animal.

Brooks nodded. "Now if you don't mind, Agent Castillo, I think it's time to let the lady go."

"Sure, Teddy," Castillo said and jerked the gun at him and fired. Brooks dove behind one of the reading chairs. Castillo tore off four shots before yanking up on Jessie's underjaw and backpedaling them both toward the open passageway. She and Castillo thumped against the tunnel wall, then Castillo reached out with his gun hand and, using two strong fingers, drew the wall closed.

She heard Brooks shout something at them, but the wall clamped shut and she was swaddled in shadow. Castillo moved the gun under her chin, dug the barrel into her soft underjaw. Jessie stifled a groan.

Castillo said, "Have I got a surprise for you."

Jessie swallowed, told herself no matter what happened she wouldn't cry.

But Castillo pushed his groin into her rear end. His sour breath puffing across her face, he said, "You'll never guess who it was that killed your daddy."

Jessie's eyes widened in horror.

★   ★   ★

"Nothing like the chase," the raspy voice said. "I can't wait to see which one of you's a better screw."

Christina suppressed a whimper. Elena was dragging her on through the tunnel, but what did it matter? Since stepping foot on this island, the feeling had been growing in her that all this was fated, that the manner of her death was merely a formality, that her doom had actually been sealed all those years ago the night she'd permitted her husband to murder Rosa Martinez. Didn't Christina deserve this? Didn't she deserve to be killed off by a man who was in some ways just like her husband? No, Stephen Blackwood had never murdered anyone before that night – at least not to her knowledge. And it was obvious that Rubio was a monster, the kind of man who reveled in others' terror and got his kicks inflicting pain. Yet it hadn't taken much to nudge Stephen into the same sadistic behavior. Nor had Christina lifted a finger to intervene. Not when Stephen was bludgeoning Rosa with his fists, not when it became apparent—

"Move, damn you!" Elena growled.

It brought Christina back to the present. She scampered through the tunnel behind Elena, the huff of Rubio's breathing behind them amplified by the enclosed space.

"Where are we—"

"Up the ladder," Elena said.

They reached the terminus of the passageway, and then Elena was climbing, skittering up the iron rungs like some sort of weightless spider. Christina mounted the ladder as well, did her best to follow. They scrambled higher, back up to the fourth floor, and kept going. Below, Rubio's steam-shovel breathing drew ever closer. Elena passed through the floorhole to the fifth floor. Moments later, Christina followed. She could hear Rubio behind them, the iron rungs creaking under his weight. She was halfway up the fifth-floor passageway when a hand clamped on her ankle. She screamed. In the semidarkness of the passage she saw Elena glance down at her in horror, and then Rubio was hauling Christina down, spinning her as she clanged down the rungs, fruitlessly attempting to cling to each one as Rubio's inexorable strength brought her into his arms. Her heels hit the floor and she would've fallen had Rubio's big arms not encircled her, his ursine form instantly pinning her to the iron rungs. His tongue trailed sluglike over her cheek, his breath like sewage on a torrid day. His corpulent gut drove her against the ladder, his hips already dry-humping her like some horny adolescent.

"Aw, lady," he groaned between sewage-smelling licks. "I never had one as rich as you. I cut up your boy once, you know that?" His stinking tongue flicked, smeared. "Now I get to stick it in his mom. This is gonna be AWWWWWW—"

His head jerked away, a shadow passing over their heads. He blundered back from her and fell clumsily onto a twisting figure.

Elena. She'd climbed down the rungs, seized Rubio's black hair and leaped over him without letting go. The pain had been severe enough to break Rubio's hold on Christina, but now the small woman was trapped beneath Rubio's heavy body. Elena was clawing and slapping him, but he shot an elbow back and caught her hard in the side. Elena slashed at his face with whirring hands, but Rubio was turning, regaining the advantage.

Christina lunged forward, reached between Rubio's legs and seized his testicles. Rubio's legs banged together, but Christina's arm was slender enough it didn't matter. She squeezed and tugged at the same time, exerting every bit of her strength in an attempt to tear Rubio's scrotum off. The big gangster was doubling over, completely unmindful of Elena now, but beyond him in the murk, Christina could see what Elena was doing.

Christina gave Rubio's balls, a final yank – Rubio screeching in a voice that sounded like a power saw cutting through sheet metal – then dove toward the base of the ladder.

"You fucking—" Rubio had time to say, then the blast erupted in the narrow passageway, bathing them all in a brilliant flash of light. Rubio's arms flew up as he stumbled forward. His big body rammed into Christina's balled-up form, but he wasn't trying to violate her this time. He slumped onto his side and arched his back in agony. His feet scrabbled like startled hermit crabs, one big arm impotently pawing his lower back.

Where Elena had shot him.

"*Aw Jesus*," Rubio groaned. "*Aw Christ, lady.*"

Christina squinted as a column of light appeared to her left, Elena opening the hidden door to one of the bedrooms. The master suite, Christina realized with a jolt.

"It's not fatal," Elena said. "At least not right away."

"Shoot him again," Christina said. "Kill him so we can get out of here."

But Elena shook her head. Her expression in the pale bar of light made it plain she had no interest in fleeing the tunnel.

"What then?" Christina asked.

Instead of answering, Elena took two strides toward Rubio, raised one shoe and stomped on the side of his head.

Rubio let loose with a string of obscenities. They were all familiar to Christina, those words, but spoken by Rubio's raspy, pain-racked voice, they were somehow filthier and infinitely more objectionable.

"*...fucking cocksucking bitches,*" Rubio howled. "*Oh, you stupid cunts!*"

And that did it. Christina wasn't a prude, but there had always been something about that last word that set her teeth on edge and made her want to hurt the person uttering it.

Without thinking, she stood, raised a heel and stomped on Rubio's nose. There was a crack, and then Rubio was buzzing out a phlegmy scream, the bullet in his back momentarily forgotten.

"Shut up!" Elena shouted and delivered another kick, this one to the meat of his lower back.

Bent nearly backward, Rubio warbled in anguish. Christina made a fist, punched him as hard as she could in the gut. Rubio sobbed. Christina felt a flush of pleasure at this and decided to follow it up with a smart kick to the head. Rubio covered his face, exposing his stomach again, the shirt hiked up to reveal a fish-white midriff. On the instant Elena leaped into the air and came down with both shoes on Rubio's white belly. The big man doubled up and broke loud, explosive wind. That set both of them off in gales of laughter, and as they laughed they braced themselves on the sides of the passageway and stomped on Rubio's convulsing body. His struggles began to abate, so Christina dropped to her knees next to him and began hammering at his face. She sliced her knuckles open on Rubio's teeth, but soon they were torn free of the gums and Rubio was choking on them, coughing against the torrents of blood gushing into his throat. Elena fell to her knees beside her, joined her in pulping Rubio's head. They continued to work on him, bashing his vile face into a glistening soup, and at some point Christina realized she was still laughing and screaming now too, and beside her Elena was slathered in the dead man's blood, her shirt torn open to reveal blood-slicked breasts. Elena stared back at her, her eyes gleaming with joy and ferocity. On impulse Christina lunged forward and planted her mouth on Elena's, and Elena buried her hands in Christina's long hair, Christina driving Elena backward, their bodies rising, Christina pinning Elena to the wall, her hand plunging under the waistband of Elena's sweaty pajamas, cupping her sex, grinding her. Elena's tongue wrestled with hers, their faces jammed together, Elena's hands grasping Christina's large breasts, squeezing them, twisting her aching nipples, but Christina was on fire, she needed more, all of it. She ripped down Elena's pants, her underwear, and then her mouth was clamped over Elena's sex. In moments Elena came, her climax a shuddering, tortured moan that went on and on. Christina started to rise, but Elena shoved her backward, away from the ruin of Rubio's body. Christina watched with languid eyes as Elena got on her knees before her, clutched the sides of Christina's shorts. Christina raised her hips to help the shorts off, then she lay back as the medium began to pleasure her, teasingly at first, the supple, pouty lips dotting the insides of her thighs with kisses, then the head settling in between her legs, the throbbing pressure of Elena's lovely tongue.

When it was done, Elena climbed on top of her and joined her in a slow, lingering kiss, their bodies locked together tenderly. Christina realized she was crying a little. Elena smiled broadly and kissed her again.

CHAPTER ELEVEN

Ben pounded up the steps. He didn't know for certain where the women were, but the same mysterious instinct that had beckoned him back to the castle seemed to be urging him upward. But the moment Ben reached the fifth floor, he knew whatever had happened was over, that the women had either lived or died on their own. Ben lowered the Ruger, a tight coil of dread tightening in his guts. Something was very wrong up here. Something…

Then he heard it. Moaning. From the direction of the bedroom Claire had taken last summer, the bedroom in which he and Claire had made love for the first time.

Ben stepped cautiously forward, probing his memory for the identity of who was sleeping in that room now. It wasn't Christina or Elena. It wasn't one of the bodyguards. Which left Teddy or Professor Grant.

As Ben neared the open door, he realized there were two voices, one female, the other male. The female voice was familiar, though the moaning was so wild and loud Ben had a difficult time attaching an identity to it. The male voice…

Oh hell, Ben thought. He'd heard that voice before, had heard it the night Eva had been defiled by the beast down in that horrible pit.

Ben's gut felt weighted down by lead. His scrotum shriveled.

Because the voice was not only the same – there was no mistaking the voice of the beast – it was groaning with something that might have been passion. But as repellant as the beast's voice was, it was the other voice that made Ben dizzy with fear and something that might have been betrayal.

No, he thought. *It can't be.*

You know it is. You'd never mistake that sound.

No! he mentally screamed. *She would never…she would die before—*

Don't kid yourself, Ben. She already did. She summoned the beast as surely as Eva did. Both of them were wanton—

Shut up.

—lustful—

Shut up!

—whores. Claire is no more faithful than—

"Stop it!" Ben shouted. He stood immobile, realizing he'd given himself away, but the voices from Claire's old room continued in unbroken bliss.

He burst through the door and found them on the bed. His wife. Claire Shadeland, formerly Claire Harden. Naked. Undulating. Moaning and writhing beneath the gigantic, bestial form of Gabriel Blackwood.

Ben stared at his wife, his body gone hollow with shock and heartbreak.

Her legs were splayed wide, her feet bobbing with the beast's thrusts. Her tummy glistening with sweat, Claire ground her hips into the beast as though insatiable for its sex. Her lovely breasts tremored each time the beast slammed into her; her eyes were closed, but there was a delighted, pouty cast to her face that Ben had seldom seen. Only on those rare occasions when she'd been totally divested of her inhibitions had her face even approximated that expression, but he knew she'd never experienced this level of ecstasy with him. The beast's curled horns rose and fell, their scabrous yellowed surfaces the color of arcane parchment. Claire raked her nails over its shoulders, cried out again and again, implored the beast to fuck her harder, harder. Sneering with exaltation, the beast complied. Ben felt sick tears crawling down his cheeks, and though he knew he should do something about this degradation of his wife, what really could he do? She was a willing accomplice, an eager pawn in Gabriel's game. She had thrown away their marriage, their love, all the promises of a happy future for a rut with a monster.

"You're seeing what she did last summer," a voice behind him said.

Ben gasped, spun toward the speaker. Griffin Toomey stood leaning against the far wall, watching him with a cagey grin.

"It's a lie," Ben said.

"Don't you see?" Toomey asked. "Don't you realize what this means?"

"It doesn't mean anything," Ben croaked. "It means this place is trying to get to me. It's trying to make me doubt my wife."

"Julia is the spawn of a monster," Toomey said, a taunting grin transforming his mouth into an abhorrent red scar. "Claire had sexual dreams about the Master, and she enjoyed them so much she invited him in. She begged him to take her."

"Shut your mouth," Ben said. He noticed with little surprise that the figures on the bed were gone, in their place a tangled mound of sheets and pillows.

"You've known it all along," Toomey said. "From the moment she told you she was pregnant."

"Shut up," Ben demanded. His free hand was bunching into a fist; there was a constant twitch in his temple. The gun in his hand trembled.

But Toomey continued to grin at him imperturbably.

Ben frowned. "What did you say about your master?"

Toomey shook his head. "Not *my* master. *The* Master. The one who got your whore of a wife with child."

Ben was across the room in an instant, the gun shoved against Toomey's beaklike nose so that the cartilage of its tip lay against a cheek. "I'll fucking kill you now," Ben growled. "I swear I will."

Toomey eyed him over the Ruger, his expression maddeningly blithe. "Sounds to me like you're under his spell too, Ben. He's only coaxing out what was already in you."

"Bullshit."

"How long did she wait? Three months to tell you she was pregnant? You knew that was abnormal. Your first wife told you right away, right after the positive test. But not Claire…she was terrified of how you'd react."

"You can't know—"

"You hugged her, but you didn't laugh until several minutes later. That's how she knew you suspected her."

"If you've got such an inside track to the…" – he couldn't bring himself to utter the name – "…to the beast's thoughts, then you know where my baby is."

Toomey laughed. "Of course I know."

"Tell me, goddammit!"

"She's very weak now," Toomey went on. "I wouldn't give her more than another two or three hours. Not unless she gets food and water right away."

Ben raised the gun, bashed Toomey in the nose with its blunt handle. Though Toomey immediately covered his bleeding face, Ben tore loose again, ramming the gun butt down on the crown of Toomey's head. That took him down, the blond man landing so ungracefully that Ben was momentarily sure he'd knocked him unconscious, and that sure as hell wouldn't do. Not with Julia's life at stake. He didn't trust Toomey for a second, but he was nevertheless positive what the man had told him about Julia being alive was true. If anything it provided a measure of relief. Ben had begun to believe it was hopeless, that Julia couldn't possibly survive an ordeal like this. But somehow she had. Somehow she had lived through the beast's abduction of her and was still clinging to life, albeit weakly. But how, Ben wondered, how could he force this snake to reveal her whereabouts? What button must he push to make him talk?

Toomey rose, still smirking. He leaned against a dresser, tapped his fingers.

"You're going to forsake the women?" Toomey asked. "Right now, when they need you the most?"

"I'm not forsaking anybody."

"You'll leave your wife too."

Ben felt a gale of fury blow through him, did his best to ride it out. Careful to keep his voice level, Ben said, "Why would you serve him? Why would you willingly help a monster destroy people's lives?" Ben's voice grew ragged. "Risk the death of an innocent child?"

"She's the Master's child," Toomey said.

Ben clenched his jaw. "She's mine."

"Did you ask the doctors about abnormalities?" Toomey said. "Or were you too terrified of what they'd say?"

"I trust Claire."

"You weren't even dating when the Master defiled her."

"Stop saying that."

"But it's true," Toomey said and tapped his fingers. "She was the classic good girl just itching to be corrupted."

"Tell me where Julia is," Ben said, but his voice was distant, distracted. Something about Toomey's restless fingers had triggered a memory deep in Ben's mind. He'd once heard that everyone was a trifle OCD, that everyone was somewhere on the obsessive-compulsive spectrum. Ben knew a good deal about that because as a child he had engaged in meaningless rituals himself. He would hop a certain number of times, put his basketball away only after making a specific number of shots. It had all been nonsense, of course, but it had always relied on some obscure and completely arbitrary numeric code, one that only made sense in Ben's young mind.

"I'm not telling you where she is," Toomey said. "So you might as well stop hoping."

Ben scarcely heard him. Because each time Toomey tapped his fingers on the dresser, they were the same three fingers in the same order. Not index finger, middle finger, ring finger, the way that would seem natural. No, Toomey would begin with the ring finger, follow that with the index finger, and end with the pinkie. The middle finger and thumb remained static during the bizarre operation, the other fingers tapping out their idiot rhythm with mindless regularity.

"Nothing to say?" Toomey asked.

"Three times," Ben answered. "And never with the middle finger."

Toomey frowned. "What are you talking about?"

"Your tapping," Ben explained.

Toomey actually glanced down at his hand, used it to make a dismissive gesture, then hid it in his pocket. "Just a way to pass the time."

"Is it because the middle finger's naughty?"

Toomey's frown deepened. "What are you—"

"You never use it. And it's always three taps in the same order. Your parents teach you that?"

"Don't talk about her."

"*Her?*" Ben asked, and it was his turn to smirk. He turned it up another notch, making his expression as nasty as he could. "Mama's boy, are you?"

Toomey's hands came out of his pockets, his slender body stiff with rage. "Don't you dare—"

"Didn't she teach you to defend yourself, Griffin? Did the other kids bully you?"

"She was a good woman!"

"So she's dead," Ben said, delighted. "I don't suppose you were much of a son, were you? Did you ever call her, ask her—"

But Toomey had remembered the gun in his pocket. Toomey had wrestled it halfway out, but then Ben was on him, the skinny man instantly pinned on the floor.

"You're still scared of her, aren't you, Griffin?" Ben said in his ear. He had each of Toomey's wrists pinned, the skinny man straining up against him. "That's why" – Ben stopped, eyes widening – "that's why you joined up with Gabriel. You think he'll make you stronger."

"*He did make me stronger!*" Toomey yelled in that same shrill voice. "I killed that agent, I made that big bodyguard run back inside so the spirits could get him!"

"You think you're any different?" Ben asked. "Do you really believe you're anything more than a pawn for your master?"

"*Shut your fucking mouth!*" Toomey screamed. And then, impossibly, he did shove Ben off. Ben tumbled backwards, appalled at the scrawny man's sudden strength. Toomey reached for the gun, but Ben had his Ruger up and aimed at him.

"Don't do it," Ben warned.

"I'll show you strength," Toomey said, and Ben received another shock. The scrawny man's voice wasn't so shrill anymore. Was, if anything, lower than Ben's. Toomey stepped forward, the gun at his side and a venomous grin on his face.

Ben extended the Ruger. "I'm not going to ask you again. Put the gun down."

"Scared?" Toomey asked, but it wasn't Toomey's voice anymore. It was rough, guttural. A sound that set Ben's teeth to chatter.

Ben found himself edging toward the door.

"Why don't you shoot?" the thing that was no longer Toomey asked.

"Last chance," Ben said, but he knew the words were meaningless. This thing was no more frightened of bullets than it was willing to tell him where Julia was.

The Toomey-thing lowered its head a moment.

Ben held his breath.

The Toomey-thing's face swung up and leered at Ben, the eyes as pupilless and white as Gabriel's. Snarling, it lunged for him. Ben squeezed the trigger, caught it in the throat. The thing was three feet away now. Ben got off two more shots, and though both of them made the Toomey-thing's head snap backward, it kept coming. It crashed into Ben, drove him across the hallway. The back of his head cracked the large window, the Toomey-thing crushing Ben against the outer wall. He was dimly aware that if the large corridor window gave way, the shards that crashed down on him would be as heavy and sharp as guillotines.

But this danger was easily surpassed by the snapping menace that was now bearing down on him. The creature's strength was diminished by the three slugs Ben's Ruger had spat, but it was still absurdly powerful. Its hands closed over Ben's shoulders, its face looming closer, the teeth snapping. Ben pulled his head back, crammed the Ruger's barrel into its stomach, and unloaded the rest of the clip. The Toomey-thing jerked with the slugs, the grasping fingers weakening but not letting go of him entirely. No matter. It gave Ben the opening he needed.

He dropped the gun, drove his fingers into the messy pool of the Toomey-thing's belly. His hand slid inside effortlessly, the Toomey-thing squealing in outrage. It gave off its attack entirely and pawed at Ben's arm, but despite the way the flailing fingernails gashed his flesh, Ben drove his hand deeper, his wrist disappearing inside it, several inches of forearm. As he shoved his hand higher, the Toomey-thing rose up to its tiptoes, as if by doing so it could avoid Ben's probing fingers. But then he grasped it, the Toomey-thing's pulsing heart. The Toomey-thing slapped wildly at Ben now, scoring the sides of his head with its frenzied fingernails. Ben didn't mind. He'd been attacked before. Grasping the Toomey-thing's heart, he wrenched down with all his might while pushing its chest away with his left hand. With a meaty slurp the heart tore free. The Toomey-thing stumbled backward, its eyes human again, and slumped against the inner wall of the corridor, a scarlet sheet of blood spreading over its lower body and forming a lake around its sticklike legs. A look of stupid surprise stretched Griffin Toomey's birdlike features.

There came a dull thud from down the hall. Ben was out of ammo, but he assumed Toomey's gun was still loaded. Ben hustled over and retrieved the gun. Ignoring the slimy feel of the handle, Ben hurried down the hall.

More sounds. They seemed to be emanating from Christina's room. If it was Rubio or Marvin, Ben wouldn't bother with the questioning again. He'd just shoot.

Ben heard voices, brought the gun up to rest on the open doorway. But then two figures stepped through and all Ben could do was gape.

Christina and Elena stared at him. They were slathered in blood. They were naked.

"What…" Ben shook his head. "What happened?"

Elena raised an eyebrow. "We could ask you the same thing."

★   ★   ★

Castillo smuggled Jessie down the passageway until they reached another of those narrow slivers of light. He muscled open the door with one arm but kept the gun against her head with the other. They shuffled into the room like that, Jessie realizing with grim disgust that Castillo was erect against her. Once into the room he shoved her forward, but before she could grab her gun, he ripped it out of her pocket. Tossing it across the room – which appeared to be some sort of servant's quarters – he rammed the main door closed and shot the bolt. Jessie performed a cursory scan of the room, but the only things she discovered apart from the bed were an end table with a big white lamp and a few scattered hangings.

"I've waited too long for this," he said, flipping on the light and rounding on her. "There's no way I'm doing it in the dark."

"Troy, please, I don't know—"

"Yes you do know," he said. "You just don't wanna believe it."

Jessie shook her head, told herself it simply wasn't possible, but with every word Castillo confirmed it.

"Yours was the first family we did," he said. "The only family we did."

Jessie's gorge leaped. "What are you talking about?"

"'*What are you talking about?*'" he mimicked in a childish singsong. "You know exactly what I'm talking about, you stupid bitch."

"You bet with Marvin, didn't you?"

Something dangerous glimmered in his eyes. He grinned a virulent grin, white teeth showing. "That's what I hate most about you, Jessie. You're a clever girl, I'll give you that. But being clever is more than just figuring out a problem." He stalked closer. "It's knowing when the hell to keep your mouth shut."

The gun was aimed at her abdomen. She imagined him squeezing the trigger, her entrails vaporizing in a body-racking crash of pain.

Down the hallway outside, she heard a door open, someone calling out in a harsh whisper.

Teddy Brooks.

If she could stall Castillo long enough, Brooks might just help her get out of this. "What do you want from me?"

"First of all, I want you to take off your clothes."

"I won't do that."

"Your sister did," Castillo said.

Jessie knees threatened to unhinge. "You're lying."

"Am I? Wanna know what your dad said before I shot him, Jessie?"

Footsteps padding down the hall. Another door creaking open, the room right next to them.

Castillo went on. "He said, 'You can take me with you, but leave my wife and daughters alone.'"

And the tears came then. Because Jessie remembered her father's voice that night, her father's exact words. At that point she'd been near her door, listening. Her father had been weeping, but he'd been brave nevertheless. He'd faced the intruders and done his best to protect his family.

He'd been the opposite of Jessie.

And now she was back in her secret place, the hidden door in the back of her closet. It was just large enough to accommodate her curled seventeen-year-old body. She'd hidden there often as a small child, and when her father had been murdered it was the only place she could think to take refuge. Yet afterward, she'd still been able to hear her mother's and her sister's wails, the laughter of the three assailants.

Troy Castillo's laughter.

"Your dad's head splattered when I shot him, Jessie." Castillo chuckled. "That actually surprised me. I'd killed by then. Killed plenty. But I'd never seen a head just...*explode* like that. It was like some sci-fi movie. Or like that old comedian, Gallagher? His head just blew apart all like one of those watermelons under the sledgehammer. I hear you out there, Brooks!" – Castillo continued without stopping – "And then your mommy, she was wearing these white cotton panties. I'll never forget it because as strange as this sounds, they sort of turned me on. My friends, the two guys who were with me, they laughed at her—"

"Let me in there!" Brooks shouted.

"—but they didn't laugh when they got to take their turn on her. And your big sister…aw, man was she something. She screamed through the whole thing, but I think she secretly enjoyed it."

"You got five seconds, Castillo!" Brooks said.

Jessie glanced left and right, searching desperately for some kind of weapon.

"But what I've always wondered," Castillo went on, seemingly oblivious of Brooks's shouting, "is where you were that whole time. I found out later—"

"One!" Brooks yelled.

"—you were in the house. And everybody knows how you became an agent so you could make amends for being such a coward and letting your family get slaughtered like a bunch of pigs."

"Two!"

"But what I don't get is where you hid. I mean, we scoured your room. You weren't under the bed—"

"Three!"

"—or in the closet. It wasn't like it was an oversight. Hell, Jessie, you were the whole reason we were there. My buddy David Rasmussen dated you—"

Jessie felt like puking.

"Four!"

"—and we even scoped you out at the drive-thru. You were the reason we showed up—" And without pause Castillo whirled and fired three shots at the door, the wood there splintering in a line at about waist level. She waited for the wail from the other side of the door, waited to hear Teddy Brooks baying in agony, but he must not have been hit.

Or if he had been hit, the wound was fatal.

Castillo had his back turned.

Jessie leaped on him.

Though Castillo was a large man, he'd clearly not been expecting Jessie to attack him because upon contact they both went stumbling toward the door. Castillo hit head first, Jessie clinging to his waist like a parasite. He heaved an elbow back that, had it connected, would have knocked her unconscious. But Jessie anticipated it and jerked aside just in time. He gathered himself, made to spin at her with the gun, but before he could do that she swiped at the back of his neck with her fingernails. Morton had often joked that she kept them far too long for a federal agent, but Jessie knew, deep down, they could be used for protection in a pinch.

No, she thought. *Not for protection.*

For attack.

Castillo slapped a hand over the back of his neck, which had already begun to seep blood, and as he turned, Jessie balled her hand into a fist and cracked him as hard as she could in the nose.

Castillo's head snapped back, knocked a glancing blow against the door. She tore loose with her fingernails again in a vicious sideswipe, and when her nails furrowed Castillo's throat he finally relinquished his hold on the gun. The gashes were deep, Castillo clamping both hands over his throat now as if the whole thing would unzip and splash out on the floor. Jessie dropped and retrieved the gun, but as she started to turn in order to blow the miserable son of a bitch away, Castillo fell on her. His entire weight bore down, crushing her, and Jessie knew if he got her all the way to the ground it would be over. He could strangle her three times before Teddy ever got the door locks blown off. She could hear Teddy asking if she was away from the door, but she had to block out that noise now, had to focus on Castillo.

When the agent's big body had first landed on her, it had draped limply over her back like a still-warm corpse. Now, though, that limpness had been replaced by a twitchy energy that chilled her, the muscles hardening as the big body drove her down. Jessie had the gun in her right hand, but one of Castillo's hands was clamped over hers. She braced herself in a sort of push-up on the floor, but her elbow gave and they both crumpled. They grappled for the gun; Castillo was stronger, but Jessie had a better angle. She muscled the gun up. Castillo brought up a hand to stop her and she squeezed the trigger. Three of Castillo's fingers were vaporized by the slug. Blood jetted out of the pulpy wound. Castillo flopped off Jessie and shrieked like a man who'd been set on fire. Jessie spun around, jammed the gun in his crotch, and squeezed the trigger again. Castillo let loose with a buzzing hailstorm of noise that threatened to shatter Jessie's eardrums. Castillo convulsed on the floor, his face a livid red, every tendon in his neck straining with the raw-throated shrieks. He looked like some heavy metal headbanger in the thrall of a great mosh, his eyes bugging out and the blood sluicing over his remaining fingers.

"Jessie!" Brooks yelled. "You okay in there? Don't tell me that son of a bitch shot—"

"I'm fine," she said.

Castillo's legs scissored like a dog chasing rabbits in a dream.

"Jessie?" Brooks called.

"I'm fine," she repeated.

"*Oooo ooo oooooo-oo-oo-oo-oo-ooo*!" Castillo howled. Standing over him, Jessie watched Castillo's thrashing without pity. He sounded like a basset hound in heat.

"Jesus," Brooks said, "is that Castillo I hear?"

Castillo's voice became a hoarse, breathy groan. A long drip of bloody slaver drooled out of the side of his mouth and pooled on the floor.

"That was for my family," she said.

She raised the Glock to put him out of his misery, but a voice behind her spoke up.

"Bring him in here," the voice said.

Jessie's breath caught in her throat. Now she knew she was cracking up because there was absolutely no way that voice had been real. Because the owner of the voice had died last night, had been shot and killed before her very eyes, though it had taken several minutes longer for the bleeding to end his life.

"Now, Jessie," the voice said, not unkindly.

Jessie turned and stared through the bathroom doorway and beheld, sitting on a small wooden chair, Agent Sean Morton. His face was bleached of color, the hollows of his eyes a doleful purple. But absent of that he seemed the same man she'd counted as a friend and a mentor.

"Quickly," Morton said, "before Brooks comes in."

Heart whamming, Jessie pocketed Castillo's gun, moved around to grab hold of his feet, but they were kicking so rapidly she found grasping them difficult. Finally, she snagged them, and though Castillo thrashed in her grip, she began the job of hauling him to the bathroom.

"He hurt you at all?" Brooks called.

Jessie didn't answer, only continued towing the jittering, frothing agent toward the bathroom. When she passed through the door, she paused, sure the spectral version of Sean Morton would be gone. So when she glanced backward and discovered him sitting there, she nearly wet her pants.

"A little farther," Morton instructed.

Jessie pulled on Castillo's legs until the agent's maroon-colored face was well inside the bathroom.

"Now leave him," Morton said.

Brooks was beating on the door and bellowing her name. She wanted to go to him before he ruined his hands, but she had to ask Morton something.

"What are you going to do?"

"Supervise," Morton said.

He had risen and was looming over Castillo now, a grim look on Morton's ghastly, pallid face.

Jessie shook her head. "What do you mean, 'supervise'?"

At that moment something moved within the glass block shower. She hadn't been aware of the figure's presence until now, but there was undoubtedly someone in there, someone who was now emerging from the shower. The figure moved jerkily, like a marionette controlled by a drunk, and Jessie caught a whiff of something terrible, something that reminded her of the underside of a dock at low tide.

"Who…" Jessie began but was unable to finish. Because the gagging fish odor had grown indescribable, the figure smelling of something left rotting on the ocean floor for weeks, maybe years. The odor of something that had been chewed on but not devoured by the bottom feeders in the sunless depths.

"In life her name was Genevieve Cariaga." Morton's dark eyes fastened onto Castillo's writhing form. "But Agent Castillo here referred to her as Bubble Gum Girl."

The figure shambled into view. The hair was swamp black, rotten skeins of seaweed threading through it like vomit-colored extensions. The skin was so devoid of color it looked ashen, the lips a deep purple that verged on black. The body was naked, though it was so mutilated by the depredations of marine life that it scarcely resembled a human being. The flesh along her left hip had peeled open like a bouquet of flowers, the breasts so chewed up they resembled scalloped potatoes. There were no eyes, only tendrils of wormy flesh dangling over pits as dark and shiny as caviar. The woman turned to Jessie and favored her with a green, scummy grin. Gagging, Jessie clapped a hand over her mouth, reeled toward the bathroom wall. The woman's grin broadened and something that looked like a plump brown centipede wriggled out of the corner of her mouth and disappeared into her noxious forest of hair.

"He's here," Morton said.

Genevieve Cariaga – aka Bubble Gum Girl – regarded Morton with an unreadable expression, her glittering eyeholes almost accusing. Then she followed Morton's gaze down to the prone form of Agent Castillo, who by now had inclined his head to stare up at the rotting woman.

Castillo's eyes were huge with something far deeper than mere physical pain, his mouth stretched so wide Jessie believed his lips might just split from the pressure. A rictus of absolute horror took hold of Castillo's handsome features as the rotting woman shambled forward to stand over him. The dead woman straddled Castillo's head, her fulsome juices dripping onto his upturned face. Jessie watched the dead woman's labia opening wider, wider, and then something that looked half like a human baby and half like a carnivorous fish began to slide out of her vagina. Castillo gaped up at it in an ecstasy of terror. The thing dropped out, snarling, and had just begun to tear apart Castillo's face when Jessie stumbled out of the bathroom and lurched to the bedroom door. Brooks hadn't ceased his hammering, and when Jessie slid back the deadbolt and ripped the door open he nearly punched her in the chest. Then she was weeping in his arms, her legs driving both of them out of the room and into the hall. And though she knew there was no safe place in Castle Blackwood, she'd never been more grateful to be anywhere as she was to be in this dreary corridor.

Brooks held her, but he had his gun up and leveled at the open doorway of the bedroom. "He still alive, Jessie?" Brooks asked.

Against her, Brooks's body went rigid. She realized why a moment later, the wet smacking sounds and the muffled screaming becoming audible beneath her sobs.

She pulled away, looked at Brooks's sweaty forehead, his frightened eyes.

He took a step toward the bedroom, but she seized his shirtfront with both hands. "Don't, Teddy."

He cringed as the noises grew louder, messier, something plopping on the floor with a wet smack. "What's going on in there?" he asked.

"Let's find Ben," she said. "Please, Teddy. I can't stand here a moment longer. Anyway, Castillo's dead."

She heard a meaty gasp, then another one of those wet plopping noises. "Or at least he'll be dead in a few moments," she added.

Brooks looked at her. Then, without further delay, he moved with her toward the stairs.

PART FIVE
THE DEAD
CHAPTER ONE

Teddy had never needed a drink more in his life.

It was a few minutes before ten a.m. After Teddy and Jessie had run into Ben on the fifth floor landing – Teddy damn near shooting Ben in the face out of sheer jumpiness – they had decided to confirm that the gangsters were all dead. Before showering the blood off their bodies, Elena and Christina had assured Ben that Rubio was in fact dead, but Ben insisted on checking the body to be sure.

Teddy and Ben had checked it, and then they'd been sure.

In fact, Teddy had never seen a body deader.

Soon after that, they'd checked on Marvin's corpse too. He was as dead as Rubio and Toomey.

Then Ben had suggested they head down to the great hall. So they arranged themselves on the antique furniture that formed a semicircle around the vast stone fireplace, Jessie having supplied them each with bottles of water.

"Okay," Jessie said, "let's talk about our options."

"What options?" Elena said. "We take the yacht back to the mainland as soon as possible, right?"

Ben and Teddy exchanged a glance.

Teddy said, "That's not gonna happen."

"And why not?"

"The *Blackie* sank," Teddy said.

Christina opened her mouth in surprise, but Ben headed her off. "We saw it at dawn. Someone put a good-sized crater in its hull.

It hadn't gone completely under at that point, but there's no way it'll get us home. Besides, I'm not leaving without my daughter."

"You're still convinced she's here," Jessie said wonderingly.

"Toomey confirmed it," Ben said.

"If he knew where Julia was, why did you—"

"He changed," Ben said, glowering.

"I don't doubt that. But—"

"I didn't have a choice," Ben said. "The beast's powers have grown since last summer. I think…" He shook his head. "…I think because it had been dormant for so long, last summer was just its awakening."

Teddy said, "Like a warm-up lap?"

Ben nodded. "The beast…it was incredibly strong when I faced it, but I was still able to survive. Maybe in the back of my mind I knew I'd need help. Maybe that's why I let everyone come."

"You wanted to put warm bodies between yourself and the beast," Elena said.

Ben didn't argue.

"You're stronger than you were last summer though," Teddy reminded him. "Tougher. You've gotten in shape, learned—"

"But I'm still just a man," Ben said. "This thing is…well, something far stronger. It can do more than influence now. Earlier, it…it was controlling Toomey."

Christina's voice was low but firm. "Peter believed the same thing. It was his life's work. He told me we would find things here that would make us doubt our sanity."

"That pretty much nails it," Teddy said.

"That's another reason we can't leave," Ben said. "We don't know Professor Grant is dead."

Elena scowled. "You're just trying to keep us here."

"So what if I am?" Ben said, voice rising. "You're going to abandon an infant on this island? Sentence her to death?"

Christina said, "That's not fair."

"None of it's fair," Ben shouted. "But we either do what's right or we don't. Otherwise, what the hell's the point?"

Jessie asked, "Did you find Marvin's boat?"

Teddy said they hadn't, but he noticed Ben hesitate.

Jessie noticed it too. "You saw it, Ben?"

Ben clenched his jaw, took a slow drink of water, then nodded.

"Why the hell didn't you say something?" Teddy said.

They watched, amazed, as Ben reached into his pocket, took out the keys he must've gotten off Marvin's dead body.

"So where's the boat?" Teddy asked.

Ben eyed the keys and seemed to deliberate.

"Where's the boat?" Elena asked, her tone urgent.

"If I tell you, will you all leave?"

"Going back for help isn't the same thing as leaving," Christina said.

"How long did it take you to get here?" Ben asked.

Christina frowned. "I don't know, a few hours?"

"And it'll take a few hours to get back."

"That's not long," Elena said.

"And how much longer to wrangle up the authorities, persuade them to come out to the Sorrows to help us?"

"Another hour," Elena said.

Teddy arched an eyebrow. "That's a trifle optimistic."

"Late afternoon," Christina said. "We'll bring help back by early evening at the latest."

"Gus's helicopter will be here at three," Jessie said.

"Not necessarily," Ben said.

"What do you mean?"

Teddy told her about the seat cushion and Ben's theory.

"What color was the cushion again?" Christina asked.

"Orange and white," Ben said.

"We had those on the *Blackie*," she said. "Several of them."

Teddy crossed his arms. "I still don't like that name."

"Look," Jessie said, "I think Ben's right. It's fruitless to talk about when you'll return to the island when we don't even know if the boat still works." Elena opened her mouth to protest, but Jessie overrode her. "And then there's the matter of driving the boat, of navigating the Pacific Ocean all the way back to California."

"At least we'll be safe on the water," Christina said.

"Who says you'll be safe?" Jessie snapped. "Have any of you ever driven a boat?"

"I drove my grandpa's fishing boat when I was a kid," Teddy said. "But that was a little outboard with about fifteen horsepower."

"I don't care," Christina said, her voice fraying. "I want off this goddamned island!"

Teddy shrugged. "Look, maybe we should wait. If the chopper comes…"

But he never finished. Because at that moment they all heard a sound that made Christina leap to her feet and the rest of them freeze. The noise was faint, barely audible. But as they listened, Teddy knew there could be no mistaking it.

It was Professor Grant.

$\star$ $\star$ $\star$

Christina said, "That's Peter."

Teddy nodded. "Sure sounded like him." And it did. Christ, not only did the voice sound like Peter Grant, but to Teddy it sounded like he was being stretched on a torture rack.

Christina chewed her lip. "What do we do?"

Ben got up. "We get him."

"All of us?" Elena asked.

Ben gave her a cool look. "No, you'll be staying here."

"But where is he?" Christina asked.

Ben shook his head. "Sound is strange here. Something far away can sound like it's in the next room, and something nearby can be totally concealed."

Elena uttered a breathless laugh. "Concealed how?"

Jessie was watching Ben steadily. "What do you have in mind?"

"The two of us go downstairs, and Brooks stays with these two." Nodding at Elena and Christina.

Ben was already moving toward the foyer, so the rest of them followed.

Teddy pulled out his .38, made sure he'd reloaded it. He had, of course, but with the lunacy of all that had happened and the sleep deprivation he'd endured, he didn't trust his own judgment.

Especially not after what had happened back in California.

Teddy sat rigid as an icy wave of terror crashed down on him. Somewhere, deep in his subconscious mind, he'd thought about what happened the night of Ben's daughter's abduction, but until now those thoughts had been inchoate, suppressed by some internal psychological filter. But as the images began to strobe through his mind, Teddy knew his suspicions were more than that. Those vertiginous, soul-shattering moments he'd endured between sleeping and waking, when that psychological filter had been least effective in sheltering him from the truth...those were real memories, not just nightmarish images spawned by whatever guilt he felt about Lars Hutchinson and Tanya.

Teddy realized he was alone in the great hall.

No, not quite alone. In the far corner, something rustled.

He swallowed. There was a huddled shape back there behind the furniture, obscured by the shadows and the dark wainscoting. The shape...it was moving. To Teddy it almost looked like shoulder blades – cadaverous shoulder blades – draped in some sort of dingy robe.

He glanced toward the doorway and saw the others were already gathered in the foyer, devising a plan to rescue Professor Grant. Teddy wanted to go to them, but at the moment his feet refused to move.

Reluctantly, he turned back to the figure.

It had risen, its upper body hunched over something it was apparently eating. Teddy wanted so badly to move now that he started to whimper, but his feet remained moored to the spot.

The figure began to turn, but it stopped, its profile too dark for him to make out in the midmorning gloom.

Teddy followed the figure's gaze toward the kitchen and beheld Lars Hutchinson, a bottle of whiskey clutched in one rotted hand. The dead lawyer was a reddish-black sack of meat. When the corpse lifted the whiskey bottle to its mouth for a drink, the brownish liquid gurgled through gill-like slits in its throat.

"Hey there, coward," Lars croaked.

Despite his advanced state of decomposition, the lawyer chortled and actually raised his bottle in a mordant salute. "Didn't think you'd have to face me again, did you? You managed to bullshit your way through the investigation, but you never thought about my family... my kids thinking their father killed himself with drink." Lars took another step toward him, the light of the great hall now showing a black scrim of blood covering one side of his head like a disarranged yarmulke. "Come to think of it, you managed to throw your own family under the bus too, didn't you? Your wife was a better person than you. She actually felt guilty for killing me. And you fucked her up good, Teddy. You may as well have shot her up with the needles yourself."

Teddy braced himself for more, but it was to the hunched figure that Lars spoke next. "Don't worry, darling. He'll be one of us soon."

Teddy shifted his gaze to the figure, whose mouth was now visible, a horror of emaciated gray flesh and rotting corn-kernel teeth. It was slobbering over some gobbet of meat clutched in its walking-stick fingers, and as it turned toward Teddy and leered its hideous jack-o'-lantern grin, he gagged and bit down on a palsied knuckle.

It was Tanya under the dingy robe, Tanya naked and stripped of most of her flesh. There were earthworms wriggling in the putrefied sinews and veins of her forearms, flies buzzing in the stinking pile of guts oozing out of her belly. Maggots squirmed in her dripping nest of pubic hair, and what looked like a horde of pill bugs teemed over the gleaming maroon muscles of her fleshless thighs.

But it was the thing she carried in her bony fingers that made Teddy wish he'd died that night ten years ago. The sight of it got him moving, but he knew that even if he survived this ordeal he'd never be able to live sanely again. Not after the sight of his dead wife feasting on a writhing infant.

He made it to the group just before Ben and Jessie headed downstairs. The basement door held open, Ben took in Teddy's agitation at once. "Hey, man, are you—"

"I'm going with you," Teddy said.

Ben glanced at Jessie, began to shake his head.

"Man, I don't give a damn what you say," Teddy said, his voice only half a step from all-out panic. "I'm going down to get the professor, and there's nothing you're gonna do to stop me." He shouldered past them, took a few steps down and glanced back. "You comin' or not?"

Jessie shrugged. "I guess I can stay here and make sure everybody's safe."

"You do that," Teddy mumbled, and continued down.

There was in him an urgent desire to flee this castle, but the thought of being out there alone with the rain and the lonesome cliffs, the dark forests and the general feeling of wrongness…there was no way he was going anywhere by himself. He'd been caught alone in the great hall and just look what happened then.

"You sure you're okay?" Ben said.

Teddy peered up at him and was nettled to see Ben hadn't followed him down the steps. "Man, Shadeland, you need a written invitation or something? Get your ass down here so we can get the professor."

Ben came then, and unexpectedly, Teddy saw a rueful grin forming on Ben's face. "You know, if not for the difference in color, I'd swear it was Eddie Blaze talking sometimes instead of you."

Teddy tried to smile. "This Blaze must've been a hell of a smart guy, he sounded like me."

"Sometimes he was," Ben agreed. "He was arrogant, though. He never believed he was wrong. That's what got him into trouble."

Moving next to Ben now, Teddy said, "I know when I'm wrong. Believe me, Shadeland, I know it."

Above them the door closed with a metallic thud. It sounded to Teddy like a prison cell door, or perhaps some sort of cage.

It's where you belong, Lars insisted. *You're a killer, Teddy. You not only took my life, you desecrated my memory.*

Anyone would've done the same, Teddy answered, but he knew what a feeble defense this was.

Is that so, Mr. Brooks? And would anyone have done what you did to your wife? Bullying her into silence despite the toll it took on her psyche?

Teddy felt a scream rising in his throat and did his best to choke it back.

But Lars wouldn't be silenced. *You're walking to your doom, you realize. And no one deserves damnation more than you do.*

Stop, he pleaded. *I'm begging you, just leave me alone.*

But the damning words came anyway.

You'll be one of us soon.

He tried to stifle a sob but made a poor job of it.

Ben asked, "What happened to you back there?"

Nothing happened, Teddy wanted to say. But he just shook his head, afraid if he started talking he wouldn't be able to stop himself confessing everything.

Like a condemned man being led to the gallows, Teddy Brooks continued down the increasingly gloomy staircase.

★   ★   ★

Ben worked to override a growing sense of unease. He couldn't shake the memory of last summer. He'd been just outside this door before he'd gone in with the axe and found Eva, beautiful, voluptuous Eva, drenched in her own blood and disfigured beyond recognizing. He'd gotten her out of that room, sure, but then he'd turned and seen the beast for the first time, all seven feet of him. And then they'd fought, and it was a miracle or dumb luck that Ben had survived.

Teddy looked like he was about to come unraveled. They crept down the final few steps to the big wooden door. Professor Grant's plaintive wail sounded again, the voice anguished.

Just like Eva.

Ben paused, tried to choose his words carefully. "I know this is rough, but as long as we stick together, we'll get him out of there without getting hurt."

Teddy laughed. "You think I'm afraid of your monster hurtin' me? I'm damned as it is."

"What's that supposed to mean?"

"Man, don't you get it?" Brooks demanded, a strained grin on his face. "You're a smart dude, haven't you ever considered the logistics of the situation?"

"What logistics?"

"The *abduction*, man. What the hell you think I'm talkin' about?"

"You know something about Julia?"

Teddy went on as though Ben hadn't spoken. "To get to your house, the monster would have to swim across eighty miles of the Pacific, move inland twenty more miles, and do a good bit of that during the daylight to commit the murders and kidnap your daughter during the right time frame."

"I've thought of all that," Ben said.

"No you haven't, Ben! No you haven't! Because it only leaves one conclusion: Gabriel couldn't have done all that by himself. Don't you see? He had to have help. A big goat man like him could swim like a shark without being seen, but he couldn't move over land in the daylight, could he?"

Ben's chest had gone very tight. He fought off a growing suspicion he was talking to a madman. Because in some terrible way, he felt he was finally seeing the real Teddy Brooks.

"I thought you didn't believe in Gabriel," Ben said.

Teddy lowered his head, laughing. He ran a palm over his eyes, and then, terribly, Ben realized Teddy was crying. "I didn't believe in him. Not before."

"What changed?" Ben asked, though he now thought he might not want to know after all.

Teddy put out a trembling hand, grasped a handful of Ben's T-shirt. "Don't you see? *I* changed, Ben. *I changed.*"

Ben's chest was now a throbbing ache. He placed a hand on Teddy's arm, but Teddy pulled away. Standing a few feet in front of the door, he said, "You don't wanna touch me, man. I don't even wanna touch me."

"Teddy, whatever it is—"

"I woke up on the beach the other night," Teddy said. "Night your baby was abducted? Musta been ten o'clock. You hadn't called yet."

Ben could hear his heartbeat in his ears. "Teddy, I don't—"

"I woke up, it was like back in the days when I was drinking heavy. After my wife… But when I woke up, I couldn't remember anything. How I got there, what I'd been doing…" Teddy was breathing hard, his shoulders heaving with barely controlled sobs. "…where I'd been and who I'd been with."

Ben threw a glance up the stairs. The glow of the yellow bulb seemed a world away. Ben had a flashlight, but he was too overcome with dread to retrieve it from his pocket.

"I had blood on my shirt," Teddy said. "Blood all over my pants, my shoes, even my fingers. I'd killed people, even though I couldn't remember it. And not just killed them, Ben *butchered* them. Your mom, that other guy—"

"I don't believe—"

"*I'm* the one took your daughter and drove her to the coast. And when I woke up from the trance I was in, I saw tracks leading away from me on the beach—"

"Teddy—"

"—they went *toward* the sea. They were hoof prints, Ben. Big, deep impressions like some giant bull or something had come down to the water for a drink, but these—"

"I can't hear anymore—"

"—were far apart like a man's feet, a really huge man, only that couldn't be, you know? *Because they were fucking hooves.*"

"This is crazy, Teddy."

"I know it is!" Teddy shouted. He gave Ben an anguished, pleading smile. "I *know* it's crazy, but it happened. He used me. And the worst of it was the thing I saw when I looked out on the water. It was dark by then, but I could still make it out. There was this thing made out of twigs and sticks and stuff. It was like a woven basket, only it looked more like some kind of enormous bird's nest." His chest hitched, the tears streaming down his face. "Only it wasn't a bird inside. It was... it was..."

"Jesus Christ."

"*It was your baby being taken away.*"

A wave of nausea rolled through him.

"And underneath the nest," Teddy raced on, "I saw a black hand with long talons holding it up. Like whoever was supporting it was underwater and moving as fast as a shark and—"

From the other side of the door there came a deep thud. A slow, horrible scraping noise. And then the rhythmic click of approaching footsteps. Teddy, five feet from the door, looked up at Ben with huge, terrified eyes. Ben looked back at him.

The door crashed open.

Gabriel stood in the doorway. Seven feet tall, dark yellow horns curling into tapering points. The black flesh, the white pupilless eyes. The tufted hair and the satyr's monstrous grin.

Gabriel shot out an arm, snatched Teddy off the ground and through the doorway. With his other arm Gabriel seized the open door and, his eyes never leaving Ben's, slammed the door shut with such force that it splintered off its hinges, wedged out of shape in the jamb.

CHAPTER TWO

"*NO!*" Ben screamed and darted forward. He got hold of the handle, hauled back, but there was no give at all. From the other side of the door came a frantic gibbering and a prolonged, ear-shattering howl of agony. Then blood began running in thick rills beneath the door and pooling around Ben's sneakers. Ben jerked on the door handle with everything he had, but it remained wedged. There came an inhuman snarling nearly as loud as Teddy's anguished cries, the sickening sounds of smacking lips and snapping bones. The door juddered as something rammed against it, but Teddy's wails were diminishing in strength, growing wet and more akin to a gurgle than a scream. And the door would absolutely not open. The creature had crashed it shut with such shuddering force that there was no budging it. Ben would need a chainsaw to get through. He could hear Teddy's gruesome death throes growing ever fainter.

Still, Ben beat on the door, bellowed for Gabriel to open up and tell him where Julia was, but other than the smacking sounds of the creature feasting on Teddy Brooks, the pit was hopelessly answerless.

"Ben?" someone cried down the stairwell. Giving the mangled door one final tug, Ben wheeled and bolted up the steps. He couldn't save Teddy, but he sure as hell wasn't going to let Gabriel get away.

"*Ben?*" the voice came again.

Jessie.

Ben didn't answer, instead barreled up the steps.

"Where's Teddy?" she asked.

"The beast. It got him."

"What do you—"

Ben hurried past her, moved through the door, which Christina Blackwood held open.

"Where are you going?" Jessie called after him.

"There's an equipment shed around back. There was a chainsaw here last summer…"

"Chainsaw? Ben, what happened to Teddy?"

"He's dead," Ben said in a flat voice. "But Gabriel's the one who has my baby."

He dashed around the corner of the castle and found what he was looking for – the aged wooden sliding door set into the rear of the building. Ben spotted the chainsaw right away, stored on a sturdy metal hook on the wall over the workbench. He had no idea if it would run, but—

Ben stopped, his arm outstretched over the workbench.

Behind him, Jessie asked, "What is it?"

"Do you hear that?" he whispered.

He glanced back at her. She only frowned at him and said, "There's nothing, Ben. Just the storm."

"Underneath that," Ben said, moving out of the enclosure. There was still rain, but it was light now, hardly a sprinkle. "Can you hear it?"

But she obviously couldn't. Hell, Ben could scarcely hear it. But it was there, beneath the soft patter of the rain on the soil.

It was Julia's voice.

"Please tell me what you're thinking," Jessie said. But Ben barely heard her.

You know where Gabriel is. Now go down to the pit and face him.

Julia's not down there.

What if this is a ruse? What if the voice is meant to throw you off?

Ben knew that was possible, but as he considered it… No, he didn't believe it was all some cruel and elaborate decoy. Gabriel was cunning, but to so precisely capture the shrill wail of his infant daughter…?

"What's happening?" someone called.

Ben turned and glimpsed the others coming around the corner of the castle. But there wasn't time to explain. He bolted for the woods.

Julia's voice was raw and weak, but Ben pelted through the forest, letting his hearing guide him. He wondered if what Julia had endured would inflict permanent damage on her body, if not her psyche. They said that children couldn't remember their births, nor could they recall their earliest childhoods. Never in Ben's life had he more passionately hoped that were true.

Undergrowth lashed his face and striped his arms with angry red weals, yet Ben scarcely noticed. The cry, though faint, persisted.

He followed it grimly, exploded through a snarl of wiry branches crisscrossing the path. Behind him he heard Jessie doing her best to keep pace, but Ben was possessed, the voice infinitely more spellbinding than a Siren's call. He veered left and spied a large clearing. He realized he'd bypassed the graveyard because it reminded him of Claire, and in a strange way he felt guilty for his mental accusations toward her. But it was ridiculous, wasn't it? Believing the beast had somehow visited Claire in her dreams, believing Gabriel had rutted with Claire in the small hours of the night…believing Julia was Gabriel's child…

Ben wended his way through the rocks and saplings that littered the verge of the forest. Then he was under the open sky, surrounded on all sides by decaying grave markers. He'd spent time with Claire here sitting on a blanket, and later, after the helicopter crash, he'd helped bury his ex-wife and the pilot here. With all its negative associations, was it any wonder he'd avoided the cemetery?

But he was here now, and the sound of Julia's voice compelled him onward. She wasn't in this part of the graveyard… No, he thought as his steps once again accelerated, Julia's cry was coming from the far edge of the cemetery…back in a dreary section to which he and Claire had never ventured.

Jessie's voice made him jump. "What is it? Did you see something come this way?"

Ben motioned for her to be silent, though her words did strike a blow to his confidence. So he was the only one who could hear Julia's cry. Did that mean it was all in his head? That Gabriel was simply torturing him or throwing him off Julia's scent?

No, Ben thought. It couldn't be. To what end would the beast lead him away from the castle? And if Gabriel didn't want to face Ben, why kidnap Julia and bring her all the way to the island?

Julia's voice, reedy and strained to begin with, grew fainter.

Ben moved through the overgrown cemetery, his eyes roving the gravestones for some sign of Julia.

Maybe she's already dead.

NO! Ben answered the voice. *She's alive, alive, and I'm going to save her…*

But why a cemetery, Ben? Why would you be drawn to this place, and why can't Jessie hear her?

Stop it.

Because she's already dead, genius! You're too late, you've failed.

He had nearly reached the border of the graveyard, and he'd seen nothing to imbue him with further hope. The rain drizzled down on him in mockery. His shoes were sodden from tramping through the wet grass. Julia's voice had vanished altogether, the only sound the patter of droplets on the gravestones.

"Julia!" he shouted. "Daddy's here, honey! Please let Daddy hear your voice!"

Nothing. Only the soft padding of Jessie's shoes, and far behind them, the murmur of Christina's and Elena's voices.

Ben stood in the rain, a hopeless sob forming in his throat. The tears would start soon, he knew, yet he still clung to his guttering belief that she was somewhere near.

Jessie touched his elbow. "Ben, don't…"

"Julia!" he yelled.

There came no answering cry.

Christina and Elena were arguing about something, but Ben hardly heard them. He searched the graves, the trees, the blackened soil for movement, for a glimpse of something stirring, for some sign of Julia. Yet the only thing—

Julia wailed.

Ben sprinted toward the sound.

He raced through the remainder of the graveyard and was almost to the forest when he spotted a small rectangular marker half buried in the grass, only sixteen inches long and lying on the ground with its inscription facing up.

BEN SHADELAND, it read.

Ben swallowed, closed his eyes. He listened for Julia.

The cry was weak, muffled, but it was coming from the marker. Ben grimaced. How could it be? Was this, after all, some infernal joke? But the cry…he could hear Julia even now, her voice becoming fainter…

Someone had buried her here.

"Oh my God," Ben muttered and dropped to his knees. He began to claw at the ground, ripping tufts of grass and wet clumps of earth. He tossed them aside, his hands never ceasing.

"Ben…" Jessie began.

"You hear her," Ben said, his hands assaulting the soil.

"I hear *something*," she answered, "but how can it be your..." She left the thought unfinished.

"It's my baby," Ben said, redoubling his efforts. "It's Julia. I know it is."

Jessie stepped beside him. She said, "Do you know whose grave this is?"

"It's mine," he grunted.

"Look, Ben."

Without stopping, he did.

GABRIEL BLACKWOOD, the stone read.

Ben didn't answer, didn't stop digging. He yanked away the dirt, his fingernails cracking and snapping off on the rocks he encountered, but the soil was still sodden enough to make progress rapid. He'd worry about the implications of the gravestone later, because now he had to save Julia. Her cries grew more distinct the more he dug, and though he knew that wasn't possible, it was true nonetheless. Jessie was saying something but her words didn't register. Other voices had joined her, Elena and Christina, and he did hear one thing Elena said – that she believed there was something beneath the soil, which Ben could've already told her. One of the women gasped – *She'd heard Julia too!* – but Ben never paused. He kept digging, clawing, scratching at the moist soil, his hands bleeding now in a dozen places, his nails jagged. Ben dug, dug and then—

Then there was nothing. One moment he was tossing a handful of dirt behind him, the next he was plunging forward into the shallow hole he had dug. Just when he was sure he'd discovered some hidden sinkhole by tumbling bodily into it, his fingertips caressed something solid and large and much too smooth to be a rock. Frantically, he tore at the narrow funnel he had carved, and now the gap was wide enough for him to see the wood beneath, its dark polished surface reminding him of a violin's base. But this – oh Jesus Christ – was no violin. This was...this was...

Ben let out a harsh sob.

This was a coffin.

But not an adult-sized coffin, he realized as he expanded the hole. No, this was smaller. Much smaller. Jessie had seen it and was helping him now, but if he was about to find what he thought he'd find...if the crying voice had merely been an obscene joke from Gabriel, yet another torture devised by the unholy ruler of this island...

All four of them were ranged around the hole now, Elena and Christina watching in dour silence. Working together with Jessie, Ben tore up the last muddy clumps of earth and saw the entire thing, about three feet by two in size, and without pausing Ben grasped the edge of the door and drew it open.

And beheld Julia. His baby girl.

She wore the same light blue pajamas he'd put her in two nights ago, not knowing that the next time he'd behold her beautiful face, it would be moveless, the eyes closed, the mouth permanently fixed in that innocent, pursed-lipped expression she sometimes wore when in the thrall of a really peaceful sleep.

She wasn't breathing, she wasn't moving, she was—

Julia's eyes fluttered open.

★   ★   ★

Sucking in breath, Ben reached for her, but at that moment the coffin slipped down, falling at least a foot. Ben groped for her pajamas but the coffin sank again, and Ben realized with new horror that the rain was loosening the soil around the wood, that the coffin had been placed atop an open tube of earth that went down and down. Ben had crawled into the hole to his waist, but Julia was still beyond his reach, and dammit she was sliding lower, lower, clumps of earth spattering into her coffin, and even as she fell she began to cry for Ben. She recognized him, he knew, and she was reaching for him now, groping for him even as the terrible wooden box slipped lower. The women were pawing at his legs in an attempt to keep him from falling on top of his daughter, but Ben clawed his way downward, nearly perpendicular to her, only his ankles above the rim of the narrow pit.

The pit.

With a jolt of revelation, Ben realized where Julia was heading. He could still see her, the earthen tube swallowing her like a monstrous gullet. She was four feet away from his seeking hands. Five. And it was growing darker. But because the opening was so narrow Ben was able to climb downward and stop him himself from simply crashing down upon her. If he did that he might well kill her himself, and wouldn't that be the ultimate, ineffable conclusion to this sick nightmare? The copestone of Gabriel's blasphemous tower of evil? Julia was sinking faster now, the corners of the coffin dipping and jouncing as she descended, but never flipping over, never ejecting her from the satiny white lining of the coffin. Ben could barely see her now, and taking no heed of the danger, he began to let gravity do its work. He plummeted three feet before throwing out his hands and legs to grind his body to a halt. Again he dropped, and as he did he realized the tunnel was curving back in the direction of the castle. Yet the drop was still a nearly vertical one, and Julia's coffin continued to slip. Ben persisted, clawing down, tumbling, catching himself, and though it was now utterly dark down here he could still hear Julia's frail whimpers, could vaguely make out the slither of the smooth wood down the earthen throat. He heard sounds behind him, and with something like astonishment he realized that Jessie and the other two had followed him, were even now navigating the same treacherous descent Ben was. Below him he heard a soft crack, like a snapping branch, and a muted thud. He winced, sure the sounds had been Julia's coffin landing on whatever floor lay below them. Ben made his way lower, sometimes easing himself down with limbs splayed, at other times allowing himself to fall. There came a cry of surprise from above him, but Ben forced himself to maintain a methodical pace.

Then the bottom opened up beneath him.

It was a short tumble, perhaps four feet, and the surface on which he landed was a congealed pudding of mud. He landed over the coffin, his left hand actually coming down on the open lid. He realized he was draped over the coffin, and suddenly sure Gabriel had scooped Julia out of it before Ben landed, he reached into the murk for where he thought her little body would be.

He touched the soft material of her blue pajamas. Felt the feeble writhing of her weakened body within.

"Oh my baby," Ben cried. He gathered her into his arms and pressed her to his chest. "Oh my God, oh my God," he whispered. "Oh my baby." He kissed her downy hair, her soft cheeks. She was crying, but it was the most wonderful sound he'd ever heard, the most blessed sound. "Thank you," he said. "Thank you." Ben rocked his daughter and wept.

Above him there were several voices crying out, the squelch of skin against soil. With Julia clutched to his chest, Ben crouched, his head scraping the low ceiling, and yanked the coffin toward him. A moment later there came a loud, crunching thump and a sudden illumination. In the tangle before him Ben distinguished three writhing bodies. They were muddy, the voices either breathless or angry, but in seconds they were untangled and resting a few feet apart. One of the bodies, the one holding the flashlight, got to its feet and moved up beside him.

"Oh my God, Ben. She looks like you," Jessie said.

"She looks like her mother," he answered and shielded Julia's eyes from the flashlight's glare.

"Sorry," Jessie said, lowering the light.

"It's okay." He put his lips on Julia's cheek, kissed her again. Hearing her pitiful whimper brought him back to his senses. "Do any of you have water?"

Elena made a pained face. "In my room."

Christina shook her head.

"She's dehydrated," he said. "Half-starved. It's a wonder she's lasted this long."

No one said anything, and in the silence Ben felt his alarm grow. "You three shouldn't have followed me."

Christina gave him a wry smile. "We didn't. Well, Jessie did. She climbed down after you. I don't know what we would've done, but the ground under Elena and I just sort of gave way."

Jessie gave Julia's hand a gentle squeeze. "We're here now. Let's figure out how to get out of this hole."

For the first time Ben remembered he too had a flashlight. Feeling foolish, he fished it out of his pocket, clicked it on and inspected the area. The low-ceilinged room was about ten by ten feet, but ahead there was an archway leading into a tunnel.

"Will that take us back to the castle?" Elena asked.

Jessie shined her beam down the tunnel as well. "The castle's in that direction. But there's no way to know how direct the route is."

"How far are we from the pit?" Ben asked.

Jessie frowned. "I don't know. A couple hundred yards if it's a straight shot, but we can't—"

Ben started toward the archway.

"Shouldn't we try to go back up?" Christina asked.

Ben stopped. He massaged his daughter's back as he spoke. "We fell about thirty feet. There's no way we'll be able to climb back up that hole, not with how muddy it is." He nodded toward the tunnel. "This is the only way out."

Jessie said, "Why do you think this leads to the pit?"

"It's the only explanation," Ben said. "The beast has supernatural powers, but he's bound in some ways by the same natural laws we are. He can inhabit others' flesh...bend them to his will..."

Jessie began to say something, but Ben overrode her. "But he can't just appear in one place and teleport himself to the other side of the island by magic."

Jessie said, "Last night when we were in the pit we couldn't find a way through. You stayed and searched yourself."

Ben turned and began shuffling toward the archway. "That doesn't mean there isn't a way. It just means I didn't find it."

"Peter did," Elena said.

They all turned and regarded her.

"He's down here," she said. "I sense it."

Ben set off again. "What else can you sense?"

Elena frowned, the skin furrowing between her eyebrows. "Darkness. Just...unspeakable hatred."

"That's about right," Ben said. He moved forward, keeping Julia's frail body nuzzled into his chest and shoulder. "And Jessie?"

"Yeah?"

"If something happens to me..."

"I'll get Julia to the boat."

Ben nodded. Ahead, the tunnel forked. Ben turned left, in what he hoped was the direction of the castle.

CHAPTER THREE

Jessie's fingers were slick with mud and perspiration, the Glock heavy in her grip. She could hear the others' breathing in the dank tunnel, and occasionally baby Julia would utter a cry that sounded to Jessie like a frightened chipmunk. Her mud-caked tank top clung to her skin, the bra beneath it terribly uncomfortable. Her shorts and underwear were soaked through as well. It was her shoes and socks, however, which bothered her the most. They squelched with every step she took, not only making her feel even more miserable, but potentially alerting the beast to their presence.

They had walked for only a couple minutes before they heard the sobbing from somewhere on their left.

Ben paused and Jessie drew up beside him. "That sound like Professor Grant to you?" he asked.

She nodded. "Let me go first."

Ben didn't argue. That was good, but it also put her back in the lead. Exposed. The first line of defense against Gabriel. Against the beast.

Ever since she'd first heard Gabriel's name uttered, she'd been trying to imagine what the beast might look like, but thus far she could only form vague intimations of its cruel features. The curling horns, the furry haunches. But the prospect of actually confronting it now sent cold shivers down her spine, made her every bit as fearful as the night her family had been slain.

Only this time you won't be able to hide.

She clamped down on the thought. She'd already laid those demons to rest, dammit. Troy Castillo was dead. And when – not *if,* she reminded herself – she returned to California and after all this mess had been sorted out, she would find David Rasmussen and John Farrell and make sure they were charged with the crimes they'd committed thirteen years ago. The cases would be cold no longer. And even if something happened to her, she'd told Ben about Castillo's terrible confession earlier.

It's a good thing you told someone, because you'll never make it back to California.

I will, she thought. *I will make it back.*

Professor Grant's voice grew clearer. He was muttering to himself, pleading for someone to help him.

Jessie stopped. "Hold this a second," she said to Elena, who was just behind Ben. Jessie handed her the flashlight. Then, switching the gun to her left hand, Jessie wiped her shooting hand on the hip of her shorts.

But it did little good. When she returned the gun to her shooting hand, her palm was almost as slick and muddy as it had been, and what was more, she'd been given a fresh reminder of just how scared the others were.

Elena had been holding Ben's flashlight, and when she'd also taken Jessie's for a moment, the medium's hand had quivered like a frantic moth. Behind her, Christina Blackwood's face was morose with terror, the heiress pale and moon-eyed and regarding Jessie with an unseeing stare reminiscent of a soldier with post-traumatic stress syndrome. But the real battle hadn't even begun. They'd killed Marvin and his men, but their new foe was incalculably more dangerous. If what the others said was true...if the thing really was some sort of mythological beast...

"Jessie," Ben said.

She glanced sharply at him, then realized she'd been stalling. Not consciously, of course, but somewhere deep in her psyche, the terror had cored down into her and was switching off the instincts that had thus far kept her alive.

"Sorry," she muttered and set off again. This time, despite the chills plaiting down her spine, she made sure she was doing it all correctly. Her weapon was ready, the flashlight's beam keeping what lay ahead steadily illuminated. If the beast did attack, it wouldn't catch her unawares.

A preternatural silence permeated the tunnel. Jessie's heart stuttered in her chest, but she stayed focused, reminding herself to breathe, to see everything, to use every bit of sensory input she could to make decisions.

They were coming to another archway, and as they did Professor Grant's voice came into sharper clarity: "Who is that? Oh please don't hurt me anymore. Please. I've told you all I know. Now please leave me alone!"

Jessie hurried forward and entered a large, circular chamber with multiple archways and a ceiling she estimated was twelve feet high. In the center of the room lay Professor Grant, his arms and legs shackled to the dirt floor.

"Oh please help me," he gibbered. His eyes were blinking and terror-stricken. "Please get me out of these chains."

They knelt on either side of the professor, except for Ben, who was cradling his baby. Elena held one of the flashlights, and she was aiming it at one of Professor Grant's wrists. Jessie could see how the manacle had caused his wrist to bleed. Jessie shined her light on his other wrist and found similar damage. Yet it didn't look to Jessie like Grant had been physically tortured. At least no place where the damage was apparent.

The thought made her squirm.

As if reading her thoughts, Christina said, "Has the…thing been hurting you?"

Professor Grant gulped, nodded his head.

Christina surveyed the professor, a pained expression on her muddy face. "But what—"

"*My mind*," he said, his voice hoarse. "He's in my *mind*!" He shot a glance at Jessie. "I told you he was a god. I told you Robert Blackwood had meddled with forces far beyond imagining."

Christina took his hand. "Peter, please don't—"

"All my research has been duplicated," Professor Grant hurried on. "If I don't make it, find Mark Brown at Stanford. He's my lead assistant. He'll know what—"

"Enough," Ben said. "How do we get you out of here?"

Grant glanced at his bonds. "I don't know, can't you…can't you shoot the chains?"

Ben shook his head. "That'll bring the beast."

"What if he's here already?" Christina said.

"I'll shoot the chains," Jessie said. "Ben, get everybody out of the way. I—"

A low growl reverberated through the chamber.

Grant's eyes widened, his wet lips open and trembling.

Jessie glanced at Elena, but she was already doing a slow scan of the chamber, her flashlight probing each of the myriad archways. Jessie knew she should use her light to aid the search, but she had risen at Ben's side and, like him, she was leveling the gun at wherever Elena's light shone. Every time the beam shifted to the next archway, she expected the towering horned figure to be grinning back at them, but so far—

The beam splashed over a large, huddled shape.

"What is that?" Christina asked in a tight voice.

"Dunno," Ben muttered. "I'll check it out."

"The hell you will," Jessie said, edging past him. "You keep Julia safe. I'll go."

Ben started to protest, but Jessie hardly heard him. The archway was on the other side of the chamber and directly opposite from where they'd entered.

"That's the way he brought me in," Professor Grant said in a hushed voice. "See the breath mint?"

Jessie motioned for him to be quiet, but she needn't have worried. The eerie silence had again taken hold of the chamber. Just inside the archway the tunnel turned, and it was near this veering that the huddled shape lay.

Jessie heard a cracking sound, froze and shined her light on the floor where she had just stepped. There, broken into three pieces, was what looked like a white-and-green breath mint.

She shook her head and returned her attention to the shape huddled before her. Jessie kept her index finger firmly on the trigger. The shape wasn't moving, but if it did she would blast a hole in it before it could lunge at her. Jessie stepped closer, closer, was nearly to the tunnel entrance now. This close to it, no more than fifteen feet away, she could tell the shape was humanoid. She spotted hints of flesh. She moved under the archway. Keeping her light trained on the shape, which she could now see was tan but not all that hairy, Jessie inched closer. She held her breath, her finger trembling on the trigger. She distinguished dark hair...what looked like a shoulder...

Then all at once she knew who this was.

This was Chad Wayne.

Was he, after all, alive? Wayne wasn't moving, but his muscular shoulders and his burly weightlifter's neck did not seem damaged. She reached down, tugged on his shoulder. Wayne slumped sideways, his face swinging toward her. Jessie gagged, took an involuntary step backward. Where his face had been there was now a lurid red nest of blood and chewed flesh. The meaty ruin was acrawl with tiny black spiders.

Behind her there came a wild, trilling scream. Jessie spun around, the flashlight beam strobing over Professor Grant, Ben Shadeland, Elena. When Jessie finally got control of herself she aimed it at the place where all three of them were staring. Something – holy God, it looked like a corpse that had been decomposing for many years – had Christina Blackwood pinned to the chamber floor. The thing was leering down at her, its black, wormy sockets somehow triumphant.

"*I'm sorry, Rosa!*" Christina was shrieking. "*I never meant to hurt you.*"

Jessie took aim, fired. Even from this distance she caught the corpse in the side of the face. The thing's right cheek opened up and began vomiting some kind of black, syrupy discharge.

"Leave her alone!" Elena shouted at the thing.

Ben had his gun up but did not fire, perhaps because he had an infant against his chest. Jessie fired again, but though this shot nailed the corpse woman in the throat, the thing's leer stretched wider, revealing long, tapered teeth. Something resembling a giant black leech plopped out of the corpse's mouth and landed on Christina Blackwood's chest.

Jessie shot the corpse a third time, but it did no good. It lowered its face toward Christina's. Christina bucked to escape it, but her hands were pinioned hopelessly to her sides, the corpse's grip unbreakable.

As they all looked on, horrified, the corpse woman bit down on Christina's face. Christina's shrieks degenerated into a horrible, caterwauling moan. Elena was screaming, but Ben was staring straight ahead. Not at Christina's thrashing body, Jessie realized, but at something beyond it. Something *above* it.

Jessie followed Ben's gaze and saw the beast emerging from the darkness.

★　　★　　★

Ben took a step backward. The beast's eyes were fastened not on his, but on what Ben held against his chest.

On Julia.

The beast moved past Christina and the little, zombie-like woman who was feasting on her. The beast's massive body trembled with boundless rage and virility.

Elena moved against Ben, and together they retreated toward the archway under which Jessie stood. The beast neared where Professor Grant wriggled in his bonds.

"Please don't let this go on," Grant begged the beast. "Please release me."

Without looking down at the professor, the beast raised one massive cloven foot and stomped on his face. Peter Grant's limbs went ramrod straight, then sank slowly to the ground. There were no death spasms, no twitches of feet and hands. Only a revolting soupy mess that had once been the professor's head. To Ben it looked like a red pumpkin someone had smashed.

The creature's face became a hateful rictus as its gaze fixed on Ben. The pupilless white eyes darted to Julia.

The beast uttered one word: "*Mine*."

Ben raised the gun. He didn't want to fire it, not this close to his infant daughter's ears. No matter how securely he tucked her head into the crook of his arm she would still be terrified by the blast, her hearing permanently damaged.

But Jessie shot the beast first.

The slug caught the beast between the horns and tore a patch of bloody scalp from its head. The beast hardly reacted. Ben continued to backpedal, and against his side he felt Elena tense.

"Ben...look."

He scowled down at her. She was staring at something to their left. Ben followed Elena's gaze and at once understood why she'd called it to his attention.

There were figures in the archways. In *every* archway. As Elena swished the light from arch to arch, Ben took in their zombie-like gazes. Some were familiar to him – Stephen Blackwood, Ryan Brady, even Teddy Brooks. Some he'd never seen. There was a woman who looked homeless and damn near skeletal. There were many ghosts, zombies, whatever the hell they were, clad in the garb of long ago, cravats and opulent jewels and three-piece suits and evening gowns. Out of an archway straight ahead of them came Lee Stanley, accompanied by an immense black dog. To their immediate right stepped Nicky Irvin. From the archway beside that one emerged Ray Rubio, the gangster so disfigured he was scarcely recognizable.

And from the one next to that appeared Eddie Blaze.

"Hey, old buddy," Eddie croaked.

Eddie was attended by a tall blonde woman who was badly burned in several places. Eddie carried a baby, which was drowsily gnawing on the innards that spilled from Eddie's mutilated abdomen. "Decided you wanna join us here? You and your half-breed daughter?"

Ben wanted to tell Eddie to go to hell, but he realized at once that Eddie was already there. And what was more, Ben didn't think he could speak if he wanted to. It was all he could do not to faint from the mind-numbing terror that had enveloped him.

He and Elena had reached the placed where Jessie stood in the archway. As if they were connected via the same mental wavelength, all three turned to flee down the tunnel.

But Chad Wayne's corpse was blocking their way, its enormous, spider-bitten arms stretching toward them.

Jessie raised her gun, but Ben shoved her arm aside, and careful to keep a secure hold on Julia, stepped sideways and aimed a ferocious kick at the corpse's chest. He nailed the Wayne-thing in the sternum, and the corpse went staggering backward. Without pause they darted past it, and just when Ben was sure they were in the clear, Elena screamed. He tightened, glanced back and saw the Wayne-thing had hold of her ankle, was reeling her down toward its spider-infested maw. The spiders teemed over his arms, began clittering up Elena's bare ankle. Ben stepped over, raised a shoe and stomped down on Wayne's forearm. There came a dull crack as the Wayne-thing's ulna snapped. Sobbing, Elena stumbled away, and then they were racing into the darkness, Jessie and her flashlight in the lead, Ben pushing Elena ahead of him so she wouldn't be attacked. He could hear the sounds of the dead things growling and chortling in the chamber, their abhorrent voices drawing inexorably closer.

Ahead of him he could hear Elena's tortured breathing. Jessie muttered something, and before he knew it he was following the two women through a smaller chamber and then, hardly breaking step, through another archway. Ben discovered with grim humor that Professor Grant had indeed marked the way with a breath mint. Ben kicked it aside as he passed and hustled ahead, a terror of being left behind in this stygian gloom lending added speed to his steps. In moments he'd caught up to Elena, who was only five or six feet behind Jessie. Perhaps they really could shake the beast and the horde of animate corpses. Perhaps with the late professor's help they really could find their way out of this labyrinth.

They came to a fork in the tunnel, and after a momentary scan of the ground, Jessie selected the tunnel to their right. They followed that into another chamber, studied the ground again, and almost immediately Elena picked out the tiny white-and-green disc with her beam. "There!" she called, and they all pelted under the archway.

They reached another room, this one nearly as wide as the one in which they'd found Professor Grant. Jessie found the correct archway, and they dashed through it. Even if the route they'd taken through these subterranean passages had been circuitous, he was certain they must be nearing their destination. Even more heartening was the fact he could no longer hear footfalls behind them. Absent of their own racing footsteps and labored breathing, the tunnel was silent.

And there was something else now, Ben realized, that suggested they were nearing their destination. He could smell the animal hair, the gamey musk that attended the beast and the unwholesome undercurrent of fecal matter it projected. Yes, it was the odor of the pit, only it was far more powerful here. Wherever they were, they were getting closer to—

"Look out!" Jessie shouted.

Elena uttered a frightened shriek. There was a commotion ahead of them, one of the lights going out. Though the remaining flashlight beam was swinging wildly around the tunnel, Ben caught a glimpse of Jessie's strained features, a pair of arms twining together. He reached the women and realized Jessie was grasping Elena, preventing her from falling into the hole yawning before them. Ben saw the chasm opened to a long decline before veering right and disappearing. It was from this downward-trending tunnel that the animal odor radiated the most powerfully.

"It's where he lives, isn't it?" Jessie muttered.

"I don't care," Ben answered. "You okay?" he asked Elena.

She nodded, seemed about to speak, but she froze, her eyes vast and starey.

"What the hell is that?" Jessie asked in a breathless little voice.

Before Ben could answer, he too heard the demonic muttering of the corpses. As Jessie aimed her light behind them, the tunnel wall began to shift, change color. Materializing, Ben understood at once, into a human figure. The solid earth seemed to bend and swirl, as if the wall had become malleable.

Nicky Irvin's vicious, bleeding face leered at them from the wall. The body began to push through. From farther down the tunnel, they heard the rustle of many footsteps. The corpses were coming.

"Go," Ben said.

They ran. Before long they came to another fork. They turned left without breaking stride and pounded down the corridor for half a minute before it opened into another chamber. Only this one, Ben realized with a flood of dread, contained no visible archways, no means of continuing their flight.

"We're trapped," Elena moaned.

"No we're not," Jessie said, painting the chamber walls with her flashlight beam. "We'll find the way out if we can locate the lever."

Elena whimpered. "I don't—"

"*Think*," Jessie snapped at her. "This whole place is riddled with secret passageways. We've just got to find the trigger."

Ben moved over to the wall, began patting it, knowing how fruitless and haphazard a method it was but knowing also it was better than doing nothing. Against his body, Julia shifted restlessly, and though he knew it was because he'd awakened her with the constant jostling, he took any motion from her as a positive sign. God, she so badly needed food, water.

"What if we can't find it?" Elena asked in a whisper.

Jessie shined the light directly into her eyes. "You're the goddamned psychic, why don't you tell us where it is?"

Jessie continued to probe the wall, but Ben turned and stared through the dimness at Elena. "Can you find it? Mentally, I mean?"

She stared blankly at him a moment, then a vestige of rationality seemed to pervade her anguished features. "I don't know…maybe I can. But it's so hard to concentrate. I don't think—"

"Just do it. Now. Just block everything else out and think."

"But it makes me susceptible to them," Elena said. "What if they… you know, *inhabit* me?"

"I don't know," he said, teeth clenched. "I only know they're coming. Would you rather die the way Christina did?"

Elena blanched, then nodded quickly. "Okay," she said, inhaling. She blew out a long breath. "Okay." She closed her eyes.

From the way they'd come, Ben heard the sifting of soil.

Elena opened her eyes, let out a terrified whimper.

"Don't think about it," Ben ordered. "You can do this. Please, just concentrate."

Elena looked nauseated with terror, but she did as she was bidden. She closed her eyes again and began to regulate her breathing. Jessie continued searching for the lever. Ben knew, though he refused to linger on the possibility, that this might indeed be a dead end. If it was, this would be the site of their last stand. Ben's Ruger was fully loaded, and he assumed Jessie had some rounds left in her Glock. But they weren't facing human foes any longer, bookies and henchmen. They were facing creatures who'd already passed into the realm of death and, seemingly, damnation. What damage could guns possibly inflict on them?

Ben returned to the walls and resumed his search. He probed the wall with his fingertips, always keeping Julia secure in the crook of his left arm.

The sifting sounds intensified, and soon after, Ben heard the shuffling steps of a multitude of creatures. He thought of Eddie Blaze, the monstrous child and burned woman attending him like an unholy nuclear family. He thought of Teddy. Poor, butchered Teddy. Ben had a sudden memory of Teddy's shocking confession just before his death, and with a titanic effort managed to blot it out of his mind.

From across the chamber there came numerous stirrings, places where the solid earth had begun to shift and alter. He glanced at the medium, knowing it would do no good to rush her. She'd either locate the lever or she wouldn't.

The faces in the walls began to take shape. First came Lee Stanley, then the giant black dog at his side. Another, larger figure materialized – Jim Bullington, Ben saw. Next came Marvin Irvin, the crime lord looking much as he had in life except for the patch of congealed blood on his chest.

Ben shot a look at Elena, realized the medium was swaying on her feet. He went to her, was about to throw an arm around her, when Jessie gasped and said, "Here!"

Ben turned just in time to see Jessie yanking something down, a low-pitched scraping noise suddenly filling the chamber. As Ben watched, amazed, the wall before Jessie started to descend – a giant subterranean elevator, at least twenty feet across. He could see why they'd missed the lever. It was nearly flush with the earthen wall and looked just like another ridge of dirt.

"Get up here!" she shouted, and now Ben did drag Elena toward the gigantic elevator. Behind them the footfalls and sifting sounds had become a dull roar. He didn't know where the beast was, but he had no doubt it would be here soon. The elevator had lowered to chest level now, and through the light of Jessie's beam he discovered this was indeed the pit. If they could only beat the dead things behind them to the door above, they might yet live to make a run for the boat.

"Get up, get up!" Jessie urged. "I'll raise the lever before it gets all the way down."

Ben nodded, lifted Elena one-armed and practically hurled her onto the pit floor, which was level with Ben's waist now.

"Raise the lever!" Ben shouted. "I'll pull you through!"

Jessie did, though it cost her an effort. As Ben climbed onto the pit floor he realized he should have handed his baby to Elena and volunteered to push the lever himself, but there just wasn't time to think.

Ben was on his knees watching Jessie when the elevator began to rise again. The wall lever was only six feet away, but the elevator was grinding steadily higher now, at a level with Jessie's shoulders. She dashed over to where Ben knelt, his free arm extended, and had just taken hold of him when her eyes went wide with horror. The flashlight hit the elevator floor and flickered for an instant. But the beam stayed on, and in its weakening yellow glow Ben distinguished the numerous shadows converging on Jessie, the chortling, bloody face of the figure that had grabbed hold of her.

It was Troy Castillo.

Ben shielded Julia's ears as best he could, leaned forward, and placed the Ruger in Castillo's leering mouth. The dead man's eyes flicked to Ben, and in that instant Ben had no doubt there was recognition in them. Ben squeezed the trigger. Castillo's head snapped backward, a gout of ichor splashing the corpses behind him. Jessie leaped upward and threw her arms around Ben's neck. The pit floor continued its ascent, and for one horrible moment Ben was sure Jessie would be cut in half as the huge elevator passed above the ceiling of the chamber. But the toes of her sneakers slipped through the gap just before it closed. Two of the corpses – Nicky Irvin and Ray Rubio – that had clambered onto the lip of the elevator were sliced in half by the ascending pit floor. Nicky and Rubio bellowed with renewed anguish. By mutual consent, Ben, Jessie and Elena moved away from the flopping, twitching upper bodies of the dead gangsters. Ben decided that if any two men deserved to be killed twice, it was Nicky and Rubio.

The pit floor continued to rise. Ben had a moment's fear that the corpses would yank on the lever again and send them right back down to the chamber, but at last the pit floor jolted to a halt, and Ben made out a faint glimmer of light near the floor. It was the door to the basement, of course, and Ben remembered with a wicked stab of frustration that the door had been literally bent out of shape. He didn't think there was a lock on the door, which meant shooting out the knob would do little, if any, good. Jessie had already rushed over there and was now pushing on it, but as Ben suspected, it wouldn't budge.

"It's—" she began.

"I know," Ben said. He turned to Elena, ready to hand her his baby, but something in the woman's face stopped him. She was shivering, sweating, looking like whatever psychic attempts she'd made back there had indeed taxed her a great deal. He didn't trust her to hold Julia.

He moved quickly to Jessie. "Take Julia," he said, "and stand over there."

She carried Julia from him, the infant whimpering in protest. Jessie said, "If you couldn't get the door open before, why do you think—"

"That was pulling on it," he said, backing up. "Pushing is a lot different."

Ben halted about twenty feet from the door. Jessie clutched Julia in one arm and shone the flashlight with her other hand. Ben knew at any moment the pit floor could descend again. Or worse, the corpses might merely bleed through the concrete beneath them. He had no idea how that could be, nor did he understand how seemingly solid matter could move through earthen walls. All he knew was he wanted the hell out of this castle.

Ben broke for the door.

He took six hard strides, lowered his shoulder and launched himself like a missile at the center of the door. He connected – both his shoulder and the side of his head – with the thick wood, and miraculously, the thing crashed open. His deltoid felt as if it had been set aflame, and he was pretty sure he'd gashed his head wide open. But Jessie and Elena were beside him in the doorway, helping him to his feet. Jessie frowned in concern, asked him if he was all right.

In answer, he gathered Julia into his arms and nodded toward the stairs. "Let's get out of here. Before they follow us."

They had just set off up the steps when the low grinding noise began from the pit.

The corpses had found the lever.

Ben exchanged a glance with Jessie and they charged up the steps.

CHAPTER FOUR

They heard it even before they made it out of Castle Blackwood, the insectile *whump-whump* drone of a helicopter blade. Ben slammed the basement door behind them and barred the door for good measure. Ahead, Jessie was dragging Elena toward the front entrance. Something was seriously wrong with the little Russian woman, but Ben couldn't dwell on it now. If Gus and his helicopter really had arrived early – if their way off this hellish island really was right outside – they could soon find Elena all the medical and psychological care she required. If Gus was here, all their troubles might be over.

Jessie tore open the front door, glanced over her shoulder to make sure Ben and Julia were following, then moved onto the front porch trailing Elena after her. Jessie was clutching the medium by the arm, but when they descended the porch and made it onto the castle lawn, she let go and began running toward the sound of the helicopter.

At nearly the same moment, Ben caught his first glimpse of the whirling rotor. Then Gus's chopper was rising into view, the overcast day rendering the helicopter's form a bit ghostly but not obscuring it completely. Jessie turned and smiled at Ben. He saw with amazement that she was laughing, and even more astoundingly, he was laughing, too. They were going to survive this. They were going home. Ben glanced at Elena, who was staring off into the forest, and at first he attributed her troubled expression to whatever had been plaguing her since the tunnels.

Then two things happened at once.

One was the recurrence of a memory Ben had only relived in his worst nightmares. Yet now, in the gray light of the day, the memory unspooled in his mind with blazing, horrible clarity.

It was last summer, the night the second group had arrived on the Sorrows. Ben caught a quick glimpse of Joshua's face in the helicopter's side window. Claire, his future wife, was standing ahead of Ben on the castle lawn and smiling back at him and saying that Joshua looked just like him. Then the engine malfunction, the sick plummeting in his guts. The chopper yawing wildly, the runners nearly perpendicular to the castle lawn. The blade whumping like some giant's overtaxed heartbeat, the helicopter dipping deliriously toward the castle. The rotor thrashing the earth, ripping into the side of the castle, great spumes of dirt flying everywhere as the blades harrowed the wet ground. Then the crash and the smoke and the severed wires spitting evil blue sparks within the mangled hull. The shrieking. The certainty that Joshua was dead. The sight of his ex-wife's head torn almost completely from her body. The aftermath…

Ben remembered all of this in an instant. Every detail. He remembered the way the debris had injured Claire, the way it had gouged the flesh of her shoulder and had almost ripped her apart.

And Jessie was standing precisely where Claire had stood that night.

Then came the realization that Elena wasn't merely gazing into the woods like some upright vegetable. She was staring at something she'd noticed. And glancing that way, Ben noticed it too. It was something deep within the forest, something barreling along a ridge just below the level of the lawn, something racing in the direction of the approaching helicopter.

But Jessie, he realized with that same sick plummeting in his belly, had not spotted it. She was simply gazing up at the approaching chopper, her body tense with excitement and joy.

So when everything unfolded, she was the last to react.

Ben watched in paralyzed horror as the chopper swept over the evergreen trees, oblivious of the thing that tracked it from the ground. Ben could even see Gus waving at them as he began his descent toward the landing place on the castle lawn. Gus didn't glimpse the gigantic, bestial figure as it burst out of the forest behind the chopper, the muscular body moving with an obscene combination of panther-like lopes and human strides. The chopper was still twenty feet off the ground when the beast leapt, its great arms and legs still in terrible motion as it defied gravity and rose implacably toward the hovering runners. Ben had a moment's hope that the grasping talons would fall shy of the runners, that the beast would land before them and he and Jessie might have an opportunity to riddle it with bullets.

But the talons did not miss. They snagged the runners easily, the back end of the helicopter plunging with the sudden drag of the beast's immense weight, and though Gus had flown for many years, Ben couldn't blame him for forgetting himself at that moment, for turning in his seat to locate the source of the problem rather than taking some sort of action to unseat the beast from the bottom of the chopper. The tail of the helicopter swung toward the castle, the whirling rotor tilting drunkenly. The chopper described an almost graceful diagonal descent toward the lawn. Jessie turned to run just as Claire had run the year before. Ben wished he could help her, but there was Julia squirming against his chest, almost as though the infant could sense the disaster about to take place.

And then it did. The blade hit a moment before the tail, and as a result the helicopter furrowed the ground like a crazed rototiller for a full second before the back end plowed into the tall grass and sent the whole thing rising for an instant like a stone skipped on water. Then it slammed to the earth with merciless force. Dirt was catapulted several stories high, the groaning, whumping rotor finally giving way and launching shards of mangled steel spinning toward the castle façade, into the woods, toward where they lay huddled on the ground. Ben heard something directly to his left cleave the earth with a mechanical burring sound. He felt some large object slash the air just over his head, and careful not to crush Julia, who lay beneath him on the wet grass, Ben pushed them both lower. The clatter and clash of metal continued as the chopper broke up, now bouncing and writhing in its death throes. He smelled ozone, caught an acrid whiff of smoke, glimpsed a flash of bright light from within the cockpit. Then there came a quick suck of air and a whining explosion. A withering wave of heat burned over them, singeing the hair on Ben's forearms. Julia cried out, a sound scarcely audible beneath the maelstrom. Ben realized it had begun to rain more intensely, and with this observation came the knowledge that the chopper had finally ceased struggling. There was a sparking fire within the wrecked hull, a spreading fog of smoke. But the worst, he was sure, had passed.

He raised his head, saw to his surprise that Elena had survived. Despite her weird fugue state, she had still possessed the presence of mind to take cover before the crash. Ben swiveled his head with a sense of foreboding, positive Jessie had perished in the storm of debris.

He spotted her thirty feet away, far too near the accident to have survived. Yet she was climbing to her feet, seemingly unscathed. Ben laughed breathlessly, unable to believe it. He cradled Julia, began to rise. But at that moment a dark figure materialized within the curtain of smoke, its shoulders twice as wide as a powerful man's, its horns curled and tapered at the tips. It stalked toward them on immense, muscled legs, the haunches furry and a deep brown.

Its pupilless eyes glared at them in triumph.

"Jessie, look out!" Ben cried.

Behind Jessie, the beast reached down, scooped up something long and thin.

A fragment of helicopter blade at least six feet long.

Jessie just had time to turn as the beast reared back and whipped the blade at her, the twisted metal still lethally sharp. The blade spun once, twice, then tore into Jessie at the waistline. The blade sliced her in half, a brilliant spray of blood mushrooming out of her and then blending with the torrential rain, both halves of her body thumping down on the sodden grass, her eyes staring in sightless horror at Castle Blackwood.

Ben's eyes fixed on the beast.

The beast was grinning at him.

At that moment only one thing prevented Ben from charging at the beast and starting a battle that would likely end in his own death.

His daughter.

"Ben?" Elena whispered.

"Run," he said. He started toward her, saw the beast striding in their direction. Julia clutched tightly against his chest, Ben broke into a sprint. "Now!" he shouted.

Elena's trance broke. He caught up to her at the edge of the lawn and led her toward the path down which he and Teddy had run earlier, the path that would lead them to Marvin Irvin's boat. Even with Julia in his arms, he was faster than Elena. But she was doing her best to keep up, only falling behind a little bit. Running this fast he estimated it would be five minutes or so to the boat. They might make it.

Elena let out a strangled cry.

Ben turned and saw a dark shape closing the distance behind her.

The beast would catch her in moments.

Then it catches her! an ignoble voice in him cried. *The beast will be too occupied with her to stop you and Julia. You'll get away.*

But it wasn't right, and no amount of rationalizing could make it right. Yes, letting the beast have Elena might increase Julia's chances of surviving this hell, but it wouldn't guarantee her safety. And he'd be haunted for the rest of his life with the knowledge he'd let an innocent woman die to save his daughter and, far worse, to save himself.

But at least you'll both live.

Ben was still running, but he'd slackened enough for Elena to catch up. He bared his teeth in an agony of indecision. Against him, Julia moaned and squirmed, as if sensing the beast's proximity.

Decide, he told himself. *Decide now. It has to be now!*

"Elena," he said.

She stared up at him, the panic drawing her pretty features tight.

"Take Julia," he said.

"He's…he's coming," Elena panted.

"Take her," Ben growled and held out his daughter.

"And go where?" she asked, the words hardly intelligible through her labored breathing. But she took Julia into her arms, held her against her chest.

"When you get to the coast," Ben said, "go west until you reach the boat."

"Then what?"

"Then I'll meet you. Start the boat but don't leave without me. If…" He paused. "If it's just the beast that comes, drive away. Make sure Julia's safe. Give her water at least. She's dehydrated."

"Ben," she said, shaking her head. "What—"

"Don't argue!" he said, throwing a glance over his shoulder. The beast was not on the trail behind them. Had it cut through the forest? Surmised their plan and headed to the boat to disable their means of escape?

"No," Elena said. "That's not what I mean."

"Get moving," Ben demanded.

Elena looked around with frightened eyes. "What is this place?"

Ben glanced up and when he did, he understood her confusion. They'd taken the same path he and Teddy had followed earlier. Yet the path had now opened up into a large clearing, the same clearing for which he'd searched earlier. The clearing in which he'd battled the beast last summer.

"Ben?" she said, her voice scarcely a whisper. "This isn't the same. This can't be here."

She was right, he knew, but he didn't answer, only glanced around at the unfamiliar flora fringing the large glade. There were towering, ancient pine trees unlike the ones elsewhere on the island. Palm trees with deep green fronds. And what he thought might be olive trees. Yes, he'd seen them in California before, but he'd been all over this island, and what was more, he'd been in this clearing last summer. Then, there had only been redwoods reefing the shadowy glade. There were still redwoods here and there, but now everything was different… somehow foreign…

He realized he and Elena had stopped entirely, perhaps because no trail presented itself now. He scanned the clearing for another way out, and was just about to reach for his daughter again when he spotted the figure sitting at the base of one of the olive trees. Forty feet away, the dark figure lifted its horned head and stared at them with its huge alabaster eyes. It rose.

"*Give me my daughter,*" the beast rumbled.

★   ★   ★

Ben charged at the monster. The beast would not let them leave this island until it was ready to, and Ben knew waiting for that time was folly. Last summer they hadn't escaped the beast's clutches until Ben had finally lifted it into the air, shoved its hooves into the blur of the propeller, and cast its hemorrhaging body into the ocean. You either matched the monster's aggression, or it destroyed you.

The beast thundered toward Ben, a sadistic grin on its face. Its massive hooves pounded up gouts of muddy water, its brawny arms glistening in the rain.

Ben lowered his head, his gaze fixed on the monster.

The monster's grin widened.

Without breaking stride Ben reached into his pocket, tore out the Ruger.

The beast's grin vanished.

A moment before they crashed together, Ben swung the gun up and fired. The beast jerked its head aside, but the slug still tore off a large swatch of its left jaw. It tumbled into puddled soil and emitted a deep, booming shriek of pain. But with appalling quickness, it sprang to its feet and changed direction like no earthly creature could.

It lunged at Ben.

But Ben was ready for it. He skidded to a stop, pivoted and leveled the gun two-handed. As the creature knifed through the air toward him, its lethal talons raised, Ben pumped three more rounds into it, two of them punching it right under the sternum, the third puncturing one of its bulging black pectoral muscles. It slammed into Ben, but the impact was dramatically diminished by the gunshots. Ben staggered backward but did not go down. The beast hit the ground face first and began to rise, but its movements were sluggish.

Ben tracked it with the Ruger. He had four more shots and couldn't waste any. He wasn't foolhardy enough to believe he could end its life in this waterlogged clearing – if its legs could regenerate after being reduced to bloody vapor by a whirring helicopter blade, it could almost certainly recover from something as mundane as a gunshot wound – but if he could incapacitate the beast, put the merciless creature down for a little while, he might buy them enough time to escape the island.

He waited until it was nearly upon him – too late, he realized at the last second – and fired directly into its face. The first bullet took out its right eye. The second cleaved a trough down the center of its pate. But it crashed into Ben on the third shot, and though the slug shattered the curving top of one of its goat horns, Ben was driven backward into the earth with the beast's full weight on him. Its talons flashed out and clawed at Ben's ribs, which erupted in unbelievable starbursts of pain. The beast's hands dug and dug, stringing the meat of Ben's sides. In desperation he forced the gun into the beast's already disfigured jaw and unloaded his last slug.

The beast's head jerked with the impact, its talons immediately slumping on the ground at Ben's sides. It wasn't enough to kill the thing – Ben could hear it groaning its low bass growl, could feel its mangled face moving slowly from side to side as if to rouse itself back into full consciousness – but it proved enough to allow Ben to shove the beast off. His sides a screaming vortex of pain, Ben climbed slowly to his feet. For one wicked moment he was certain he would either pass out, or worse, find Elena and Julia somehow missing. But with an effort he stayed on his feet, and when his vision cleared he beheld Elena cradling his daughter at the rim of the clearing. He staggered toward them.

Elena's eyes were huge. "Is it dead?"

Ben shook his head, held out his arms. "Give her to me."

Wordlessly, Elena handed Julia over. But the medium's green eyes remained fixed on the fallen beast.

Without surprise Ben realized there was a trail leading out of the clearing now. Perhaps it had been there before, perhaps not. Regardless, he knew their time was short. The beast had godlike powers of recovery. It wouldn't be long before it hunted them again.

Ben knew he was losing too much blood, but they had to reach the boat. Once safely away from the island, he could make sure Julia had fluids in her body; he could mash up whatever food he found aboard the boat. Then maybe he could dress his wounds, or Elena could help him.

But getting off the island…that was the only thing that mattered now.

Though his sides throbbed horribly with each step, Ben forced his body into a run.

"How much farther?" Elena asked.

"Just keep going," he told her. "That thing won't stay down long."

Against his chest, Julia's feet moved weakly.

"Soon, darling," he whispered to her. "Hang on a little while longer. Daddy's going to get you home."

CHAPTER FIVE

When they reached Marvin's boat, Ben experienced a fleeting moment of dread that they'd find it in a similar condition to the state the *Blackie* had been in. But he saw as he splashed into the surf and prepared to climb over the side of the boat that the beast hadn't attacked this one, or if it had, the damage had been limited to the parts of the craft that weren't visible above the water.

But he didn't think the boat was damaged at all. If it were, the thing would already be sinking. As he threw one leg over the side and hauled himself in without jostling Julia too violently, this belief grew stronger. It appeared there was a cuddy cabin below deck. He reached down, grasped the door handle and drew it up. The opening revealed a decent-sized room below with a mattress in its center.

"Get the anchor," he told Elena as she climbed aboard.

Ben moved down the steps into the small sleeping quarters below deck, and after checking to make sure there were no nasty surprises down here waiting for them, he deposited Julia on the bare mattress. She cried weakly, her little face twisting, but he forced himself to ignore it. He glanced left and right, spotted a few scattered objects – a couple athletic bags, some lifejackets, some implements hung on the walls – but he didn't spot any food. He was growing desperate when his eyes happened on a small cooler in the corner. He moved over to it, holding his breath. On top of it he discerned a couple candy bars, a large knife, but no water. But when he opened it, there they were – half a dozen large water bottles. Moaning, he grabbed one, hustled over to Julia. Gingerly, he propped her up, brought the bottle to her lips and helped her drink. At once she began to slurp the water down, but he withheld it a moment, not wanting her to drink too much and make herself sick. When he was sure she'd be able to keep it down, he gave her more. He cursed himself for not bringing Claire's milk or some formula, but the water would at least rehydrate her. He held the bottle to her lips for several more seconds, then set the bottle aside. He kissed Julia on the forehead and raced up the steps. There, he saw Elena hoisting up the anchor. She seemed fully recovered from her weird trance. Ben's wounds were aching worse than ever, and waves of dizziness kept gusting through him. The rain had died down to a sprinkle, but Ben was still glad to have Julia out of the storm. He'd get her milk soon, medical attention. He'd make sure she had the best care possible.

But first they had to get away from Gabriel.

Ben plopped down in the captain's chair and winced at the pain in his sides. Forcing himself to concentrate, he extracted the keys from his shorts and managed to fit them into the ignition. He experienced a moment's anxiety about the boat not starting or being out of fuel, but the MerCruiser did start, the sound of its engine startlingly loud on the otherwise silent coast.

Ben hadn't driven a boat since he was a teenager, and then it had only been an old pontoon owned by his friend's family. But this gearshift seemed pretty basic, and being careful not to let his nervous energy take over, he eased the boat away from the shore for about twenty yards. Then, gaining speed as they emerged from the shoals, he turned the boat east and guided them away from the Sorrows.

Elena moved past him and descended below deck. That was good. Having someone with Julia might not help her in any practical way, but it was still reassuring. Elena had made sure Julia was safe in the clearing, and now she could watch over her again, perhaps give her a little more water.

They picked up speed.

Ben had a sudden fear of the beast climbing over the low wall of the craft and seizing him, but when he glanced over his shoulder, there was no sign of it. The shore was desolate, the path winding down to it barren. They were going to survive. They were going to return to Claire and Joshua, who would be just as happy as Ben was to be reunited. And Julia…thank God she'd never remember this nightmarish episode. He supposed they could tell her about it when she was older, but he doubted they ever would. Why traumatize her when the threat was over? They would move far inland, maybe even back to the Midwest. Ben had enjoyed growing up there, and they could still communicate with their movie contacts via the computer and their phones.

He flinched at a new stab of pain in his side. Man, the beast had really gotten him deep under his bottom rib. He considered inspecting the wound to determine just how severe it was, but even the thought of touching the ribboned flesh made him nauseated.

He leaned toward the steps that led below deck. "Hey, Elena," he called.

She didn't answer. That wasn't surprising. The motor of the MerCruiser was loud, and Ben's voice had sounded faint even to his own ears. But he needed her to come up here to take the wheel for a while, both so he could tend to Julia and because he needed to lie down for a few minutes.

"Elena!" he called, much louder this time.

Still no answer.

"Dammit," he muttered and lowered their speed to idle. It wouldn't matter – they were a good mile off the Sorrows now, and the beast was nowhere in sight. Ben pulled himself out of the chair, and with an effort made his way down the steps. He reached the small sleeping quarters and stopped, his eyes adjusting to the darkness.

Elena sat on her knees at the foot of the mattress, looming over Ben's daughter.

Something was in Elena's hand. It glinted in the light filtering down the stairs.

A knife.

Ben leapt forward as the knife descended. He hit Elena in the middle of the back and bulldozed her into the wall, acutely aware that in doing so both their bodies had dragged over his infant daughter. Elena smacked the wall face first, Ben's weight compacting them in the claustrophobic space. Elena squalled – an inhuman, bestial sound – but maintained her grip on the knife. Ben reached out to seize her wrist, but she was too fast for him. The moment Ben's weight shifted she spun toward him, whipping the knife in a whistling arc, and slit his chest from one nipple to the other. Ben gasped, pumped a fist into her stomach. She doubled over but did not relinquish her hold on the knife. She looked up, snarling at him, and Ben glimpsed the pupilless eyes, understood that Gabriel was controlling her. And though he didn't want to kill Elena, he had to stop her from hurting Julia.

Without warning she stabbed down with the knife, aiming its lethal tip at his daughter's face. Ben threw out a hand and bellowed in agony as the blade impaled his palm. Still belting out his hoarse cry, Ben pounded Elena's face with his left fist. They tumbled off the bed, but still Elena gripped the knife. They crashed to the floor, welded together by the knife embedded in Ben's hand. Elena endeavored to tug it free, but Ben grasped her wrist, drove with his legs until he was on top of her, his weight crushing the breath out of her.

Elena was a livewire of mad energy. She bucked beneath him and growled like a feral dog. He squeezed her wrist, felt the tendons within compressing, the bones reaching their snapping point. She released the knife. But her other hand assaulted him, raked at the side of his neck the same way the beast had harrowed his sides. Ben bore down harder on Elena with his left shoulder. She scratched at him, her teeth snapping at his throat. Ben raised up, slammed an elbow into her teeth. He heard a couple of them shatter, but still she fought, both hands digging at his side wounds now, the sharp claws attempting to cleave through the bloody meat to get at his internal organs. Ben reached down and with a furious cry tore the knife out of his palm.

"Elena," he tried to say, but he couldn't even hear himself above her doglike snarling. "Elena!" he shouted, but she only cored in harder, her claws tearing, shredding.

"Damn you!" he yelled, and brought the knife down. It punctured her chest, causing her whole body to go rigid. Her hands moved to her chest wound, her eyes now green again, her mouth a horrified O.

"*Elena*," he muttered, letting go of the knife and placing his hand atop hers. The blood spurted through her fingers, dousing both of them. Ben glanced over at Julia, realized she was writhing with more energy now. He didn't think she'd been injured in the fight. But Elena...he could hear the sucking wheeze issuing from her mouth, could see the panic in her enlarged eyes. She was fighting for breath, entreating him with her terrified face to help her, but Ben knew it was hopeless. The knife blade was huge, its wound gaping. He'd opened one of her lungs, and he was certain there was no immediate treatment for it. Still, he pushed to his feet, hunched over because of the low ceiling, and scanned the dim cabin for something to staunch her wound. He thought he'd seen a towel on one of the seats above, but he'd be damned if he was going to leave Julia for a second now. What if Elena turned back into the screeching, white-eyed horror again?

No. He couldn't move up the steps yet. But he had to do *something*. He backed up, straining his eyes to find something he could use. He stared down at his own tattered T-shirt. It wasn't good, but it would have to do. He peeled it off, folded it. Ben was standing in the spill of light at the foot of the stairs, ready to apply the shirt to Elena's wound, when the boat gave a sick lurch.

Ben went cold all over. Dimly, he could hear Elena's wheezy death throes growing weaker. But the sounds scarcely registered. Because something had hit the rear of the boat. Something had...

Ben moved up the steps, his eyes on the stern. For a moment, he stood there, the MerCruiser rising and falling with the gentle ocean waves.

Then a black, taloned hand slapped over the back wall of the boat.

★　　★　　★

Ben whirled and ducked down below deck, but just before he did he glimpsed the gigantic figure wriggling over the stern wall, the beast muscling its way effortlessly into the boat. Its face, though still bloody, had partially reformed, the flesh over its jaw already having begun to knit back together.

Ben spotted the knife and snatched it up, vaguely aware of Elena's sleepy gaze following him. The boat tremored as the beast's full weight landed on the deck above. The knife seemed a feeble defense against the beast. Ben placed the knife on the floor beside the athletic bag and with his good hand managed to unzip it. He found boxes of ammunition inside, which meant the weapons were either in the other bag, somewhere else on the boat, or back on the island. But it didn't matter now because the beast was descending the steps, the gray light blotted out by its monstrous frame. Ben bared his teeth. He couldn't allow the beast to reach Julia.

Ben retrieved the knife and spotted the beast's cloven hooves on the stairs. When a hoof landed on the bottom step, Ben jerked the knife sideways at the beast's calf. The blade plunged into the firm muscle all the way to the hilt. The beast roared. It reached down to clap a hand over the knife, but Ben launched himself straight up at the beast's face. The top of Ben's head crashed into the beast's nose, staggering it. It bellowed with rage. Ben grasped both sides of the narrow stairwell, leaned back and catapulted himself at the creature. Their bodies slammed together, but Ben continued driving up the steps with his legs. They crashed to the deck, the beast on its back, Ben on his stomach between the beast's legs. Ben bunched his good fist, jabbed at the creature's genitalia, but quicker than he would have imagined possible the creature's hand parried the blow, its other hand whacking Ben on the side of the head. Ben went tumbling between the captain's chair and the controls. He pawed at the little shelf beside the steering wheel for a new weapon but found only a silver lighter and a pack of chewing gum. The beast rose and groped toward him.

Ben reached up and yanked down on the throttle. The boat leaped forward, the beast thrown backward off its feet. There was a great thud as it collided with the stern wall, and for a moment Ben feared the boat would overturn. Its bow had risen with the sudden acceleration, but rather than smacking back down into the surf, it plowed forward that way, the bow tilted up, and gravity dragged Ben back against the captain's chair. If only the beast had been thrown out of the boat…

A harsh scrabbling sound as the beast recovered its balance. Ben peered around the side of the chair and saw it crawling toward him. Its great talons carved vicious grooves in the floor, the carpet tearing easily, the wood beneath splintering. Ben pushed up on the throttle but realized his mistake too late. The beast tumbled forward into the stairwell, its torso bumping down the steps.

Toward Julia.

No!

Ben grabbed the only thing at hand, a red fire extinguisher that was clipped to the wall. Snatching the extinguisher from its cradle, Ben leaped onto the beast's back, raised the canister and brought its hard base down on the back of the beast's head. The beast growled, pushed up on an elbow. Ben raised the canister again and delivered a bruising blow in the small of the back, and this time he did incur enough of its wrath to make it push up out of the stairwell after him.

Ben scuttled away toward the rear of the boat, the beast seeming to go on forever as it rose to its full height. But at least it was moving away from Julia.

The beast stalked closer. Black liquid pattered from its various wounds. The knife handle jutted absurdly out of its calf, but the beast behaved as though the wound was merely a matter of course, hatred and hunger the only emotions inscribed on its hideous caprine face. Ben pulled the pin on the red canister, got swayingly to his feet and aimed the nozzle at the creature's eyes. He'd just begun to squeeze the handle when a long, muscled arm looped toward him and smacked the canister aside. It struck the top of the low boat wall and tumbled into the sea. Ben had sprayed white foam in its face, but only enough to momentarily blind it. He glanced left and right and ripped open the first storage compartment he spotted. Within he found flotation devices, a gas can and behind that, a couple of oars.

Ben swallowed.

The gas was useless. If he set the beast on fire, the whole boat might go up in flames. The oars, though... If he could knock the beast out of the boat, perhaps he could simply motor them away.

He reached in, tossed out the red-and-white ring buoy so he could access the other items. He made to grab the gas can, but forgot how his palm had been skewered until he lifted the can halfway out. Hissing, he dropped the can on the deck, but thankfully, it didn't spill open. He glanced at the beast; it was wiping white foam out of its eyes and growling in irritation. Ben grabbed an oar, cocked it back and let loose with his hardest home-run swing. He caught the beast under the chin, its horned head snapping back. It bumped against the passenger's chair and rebounded at him, snarling. Ben swung again, but the beast caught the flat oar blade, ripped it out of his hands and slashed down at him with it. Ben dodged the oar, but before he could gain his balance, the beast kicked him in the belly with a huge hoof. Ben was propelled backward into the stern wall, the wind knocked out of him.

The beast gave him no time to recover. In an instant it had cast the oar aside and lunged for him. Ben rolled sideways but only partially avoided the beast's groping talons. It snagged his shorts and hauled him closer. One razor-sharp talon sheared through the side of his shorts and dug a deep gash in his thigh. The beast slashed at Ben's bare torso, tore three long stripes through the flesh of his stomach. Sucking in air, Ben sprang to his feet, and before the beast could react, he kicked it in the face. The beast's scimitar teeth clicked together and a look of surprise and pain showed in its features. Yet in the next instant, it had regained its poise and swung an enormous black fist at Ben's face. So sudden was its attack that the blow caught Ben in the mouth and sent him flailing backward against the side wall. His bottom lip had been pulverized, the flesh split so badly that his mouth immediately filled with blood. But this was a secondary consideration, for he had completely lost his equilibrium, was now tipping over the edge of the boat. He clutched the wooden rail mounted atop the side, but his body continued over. Then he was dangling one-armed along the side of the boat, his body trailing through the Pacific.

The beast stalked over, and Ben was fleetingly certain it would simply disengage his fingers and send him splashing into the ocean. But it seized him by the shoulders and hauled him back inside the boat. Then, without letting his feet touch the ground, it cinched its long fingers around his throat.

It lifted him, one-armed, into the air. Then Ben watched its jaws open wide and knew what it had planned.

A bloody feast before it took his daughter back to the island.

CHAPTER SIX

Ben seized the creature by the wrist, dug his fingers into its flesh, but its grip on his throat only tightened. He kicked madly at its groin, its stomach, but it scarcely jolted at all. Its maw yawned wider, wider, the teeth curved and tapered like scythe blades, the tongue resembling some deadly black viper eager to inflict its fatal bite.

It lowered Ben toward its open mouth, a dark gleam of delight in its pupilless eyes. Ben gave off squeezing the creature's wrist and set to battering its face, but it barely seemed to register the blows. As Ben drifted nearer and nearer to the creature's waiting mouth, he thought of Julia, who was likely close to succumbing to malnourishment. He thought of Joshua, who would grow up without a father after all, the boy so young he'd barely remember Ben after he was gone. And Claire, his wife of less than a year. She was a better woman than she realized, and now Ben would never have a chance to remind her of that again. Because the beast was throttling the life out of him, bringing his face ever closer to those dripping, lethal teeth.

Ben looked into Gabriel's eyes. He could see where he'd shot the beast earlier, the left eye that hadn't really mended from the bullet wound. He remembered something Joshua had said to him back at the airport, something that hadn't struck him as odd at the time:

Don't lose my claw.

The beast drew Ben nearer, its mouthful of discolored spears readying for a fatal bite. Its foul, pestilent breath – the odors of rancid meat and decaying vegetation – enveloped him. Ben yanked the eagle's talon from his pocket, clenched it between his fingers and plunged it into the beast's remaining eye.

The talon tore the beast's eye in half, a paroxysm of sclera and blood splattering over Ben's knuckles. Roaring with rage, the beast dropped him to the floor and tumbled backward into the controls. There was a brittle snapping sound, the boat's slow progress coming to a complete halt. Then the beast's immense body yawed toward the stairwell, and this time there was no preventing its fall. The boat jolted as it crashed to the cuddy cabin floor. Ben scrambled forward, dove into the stairwell and landed on top of the writhing beast. The creature's upper body lay at the foot of the mattress, but from where it was it could easily seize one of Julia's legs. Ben clambered over the beast, knowing he could not simply haul it back up the stairs. He lifted Julia from the mattress as gingerly as he could, then hurried past the roaring monster, whose hands were still clutching its hemorrhaging eye.

Ben scuttled up the stairs into the daylight, which had grown brighter, the rain dissipating. It mattered little, though. All that mattered now was finding a way to finish the beast. He had the lighter and the gas can, but he couldn't very well torch the bastard. It all came back to somehow getting the beast off the boat and driving away.

Ben placed Julia on the cushioned bench on the starboard side of the boat near the stern. The boat's gas tank, he saw at a glance, was almost half full. But the throttle, he realized with horror, was totally ruined. When the beast had fallen against it, it had snapped off most of the control, and what did still remain was twisted beyond functionality. Ben grasped the pitiful nub that had once been the throttle and attempted to move it up or down, but it was no use.

Oh Jesus, he thought. The boat was incapacitated. Which meant there was no means of escaping the beast even if he did manage to wrestle it off the boat. And that left them…

…where? There might be more weapons downstairs, but what good were they against the monster? Unless he could stuff a grenade in its mouth and blow the damned thing into a million pieces, it would simply keep coming. He'd pumped eight bullets into the beast back in that clearing, and a few minutes later it had pursued them into the ocean like some killer whale.

Ben took his hand off the busted throttle and closed his eyes. The only sounds were the bubbling hum of the MerCruiser's idling engine and the noises emanating from below. Only these noises were not bellows of rage and torment. They were…

Ben crouched in the stairwell and saw the beast huddled over Elena Pedachenko's corpse, its head bobbing as it feasted on her entrails.

Throat dry, Ben grabbed the gas can and returned to the stairwell.

He unscrewed the lid, straddled the far edge of the stairwell so he was directly over the beast's cloven hooves. Then, he upended the can, let the yellowish gasoline gurgle out. The wet chomping noises ceased immediately, a low-pitched, questioning sound echoing up from below. Then the beast looked straight up at Ben, one eye a mutilated hole, the other coated with a milky, mottled film. The rest of its face, Ben saw with revulsion, was sloppy with gore mined from Elena's abdomen. Something that looked like a purple sausage was impaled on the creature's teeth. Rivulets of blood spilled over its chin and throat.

It was climbing up the steps again, moving, Ben realized, by touch rather than sight. Ben reached over and grasped the lighter.

He hesitated. What if the whole boat went up with Julia still aboard? Worse, what if the beast simply flopped into the ocean to extinguish the fire and then climbed back aboard to resume its relentless onslaught? No, he had to send the monster back down the stairs and then seal it inside with the cuddy cabin door.

Ben stepped over the chair and seized an oar with the intention of forcing the beast back down the steps, but before he could act, the beast's forearm cleaved the air and cracked Ben on the bridge of the nose. Ben was thrown into the back corner of the boat opposite his daughter, his shattered nose pumping blood over his chest. Worse, the beast seemed not to be interested in finishing Ben now, but was instead groping around the other side of the boat.

Looking, Ben realized with a sick jolt, for Julia.

Ben toiled to gain his feet, but the world went gauzy. He had no idea how much blood he'd lost, but if he didn't end this immediately, he'd lose consciousness, and that would be the end of both Julia's life and his.

With a supreme effort Ben was able to partially focus his eyes. The beast was nearing where Ben lay, and at a glance Ben saw that Julia's tiny form was still bunched in the opposite corner of the stern.

The oar was only a couple feet away. Ben reached for it, hoping the beast's vision was too damaged to notice, but just before Ben's fingers grasped the wooden handle, a weak cry sounded from his daughter. Ben froze. The beast whipped its head toward Julia, a rabid leer stretching its blood-slicked mouth.

"NO!" Ben roared.

The beast's reflexes were evidently still sharp because the moment

Ben cried out, it was on him, its talons rending the flesh of his arms, which he'd thrown up to protect himself. Ben quit trying to stave off the attack and rolled sideways in an attempt to escape. But once on his stomach the beast pinned him down with a huge hand. With the other it set to work slashing at his back, scourging his flesh and filling his body with ghastly, sizzling agony. Ben knew in another moment it would be ended; if the beast reached his spine, it would tear through it like a celery stalk, and then Ben would only be able to watch, paralyzed, as it did what it pleased with Julia. Either it would devour her the way it had Elena, or it would spirit her back to the Sorrows. It all came to the same thing.

His eyes burning with the sting of tears, Ben reached back and grasped the only thing his fingers could reach – the creature's phallus. With all his might Ben squeezed it, and with a deep bellow of pain the beast pawed at Ben's wrist to disengage his grip.

But Ben was not going to let go. He twisted around as the beast rose, and now he clenched his gored right hand and aimed a brutal uppercut at the beast's stomach. The punch was true, the beast doubling over and knocking Ben's forehead a glancing blow with a wild elbow. Ben lost his hold, landed on the floor, but he found the oar immediately, and without pause he pivoted and let loose with another vicious swing. It caught the beast on the top of the head and consummated the damage Ben had done to its horn earlier. The whole thing shattered, the ancient brown fragments slapping the bench seat beyond. The beast glared up at Ben with a damaged eye, and Ben jabbed at it with the rounded handle of the oar. The squishing sound it made filled Ben with an insane species of joy. The creature reeled against the starboard wall. Ben could smell the gasoline wafting not only from below deck but also from the creature's soaked haunches, but he couldn't set it aflame. Not yet.

To keep it off balance, Ben raised the oar, chopped down at the side of its head. Ben raised the oar again, tore down at the beast, but its left arm shot up, caught the oar blade, then cast it into the ocean. Ben lunged for the lighter, which lay on the floor near the stern wall. He got hold of it, but before he could turn, a holocaust of pain exploded in his left bicep. The beast had bitten into his arm, its teeth sinking deep into his muscle, the pain indescribable. His arm still fixed in the beast's steely jaws, Ben opened the lighter with his bad right hand and flicked the wheel. A dim glow appeared. Ben forced the lighter toward the beast's gas-soaked haunch, but the fire went out. The beast's teeth sank deeper, deeper, the great razored teeth grinding against Ben's humerus. Moaning, Ben flicked the wheel again. The small flame appeared. Ben held it to the glistening fur.

Then a carpet of blue flame enveloped the creature's lower body, the beast releasing Ben's arm and staring down in mute dismay. Ben shoved it backward, and the creature blundered toward the stairwell. Ben was briefly hopeful it would tumble down the steps, but at the last instant, it caught itself. The flames continued to crawl up the creature's mountainous body. Ben reached down, gripped the gas can. The creature lunged for him.

Ben whipped the mostly full can at its face and smashed it in the nose. It staggered back. Ben swung the can again, but the creature caught his wrist, squeezed. The can tumbled into the darkness of the stairwell and overturned, the glugging sound just audible above the uselessly humming engine.

The beast was a seven-foot-tall torch. The flames shimmered the air around it, yet impossibly, it refused to relinquish its hold on Ben's wrist. Ben stepped toward the beast, hammered its chin with a head butt, and though he drove the beast back on its heels, it was still two feet away from the plunge into the stairwell and the spreading pool of gasoline. Then the arm not squeezing Ben's wrist snaked around Ben's back and drew him closer, like some hellish waltz, and Ben felt his chest and stomach blistering from the flames. The beast opened its horrid fanged maw for one more bite. Screaming with pain and fury, Ben drove his thumb into the creature's half-seeing eye and jerked down. The beast howled. The flames swarmed over Ben's hand, but the creature's hold was finally broken. Ben braced himself, and despite the way the flames scorched the flesh of his palms, he pushed on the beast's chest and drove it backward toward the stairwell. The beast plummeted, shrieking, into the darkness, and without pause Ben whirled and hooked the ring buoy with his useless right hand and scooped up Julia with his left. He bounded toward the stern and leapt as far as he could into the water. There was a low whump behind him as the gasoline pool in the cuddy cabin ignited. Ben hit the water, doing all he could to keep Julia from going under. She did so anyway, briefly, and then he was lifting her onto the ring buoy and kicking madly away with his sneakered feet. From the boat he heard the beast's tortured squalling. Ben felt slow, sluggish, but they moved steadily, the boat floating gradually in the other direction. On top of the ring buoy, Julia was coughing and spluttering, the sounds heartbreaking, but he dared not stop kicking for anything. They were perhaps thirty feet away when there came a high-pitched zipping noise. Knowing exactly what it was, Ben rose out of the water in an attempt to shield Julia. But when the explosion came, the blazing wind from the blast still propelled them forward, Ben's already bleeding back was singed by the gust of superheated air. He was aware of the hail of shrapnel assaulting the water around them. The ring buoy rocked wildly, but Ben kept Julia firmly perched atop it. To his vast relief, she was no longer spluttering or gasping for breath, but she was crying, and to Ben's ears this was for once the most amazing and welcome sound he'd ever heard.

"We're gonna make it, honey," he whispered. "Daddy's gonna keep you safe."

Julia wailed, a lusty, full-throated cry, and though Ben hated to see the pinched face and the gummy tears squeezing out of her eyes, he silently gave thanks that his baby was still alive. He peppered his little girl's reddened face with kisses. And moments later, when he spied the pieces of wreckage that had been catapulted in their direction, he was only a little surprised to find amongst the chunks of boat hull and splintered pieces of wood a half-melted lifejacket, the orange-and-white fabric looking like something that had been toasted over a campfire. Careful to keep Julia as safe and dry as possible, Ben worked the lifejacket over his shoulders, not yet bothering with the clasps. They were probably too melted to fasten anyway, and he was damned if he'd take both hands off Julia even for a moment.

They floated like that for a good while, and just when Ben started to grow paranoid that, like some low-budget rip-off of *Jaws*, the beast's one remaining horn would surface near them like a dorsal fin, he spotted something else floating in the water just a few feet away. Fighting down his revulsion, Ben reached out and inspected it.

It was a large scrap of the beast's hide, the entire thing charred from the blast. One side was crusted with the creature's black blood, though it was apparently caramelized by the explosion's heat. The other side revealed a blackened mat of scorched hair. From the looks of this scrap, the beast wouldn't be coming back any time soon.

Still…when he started to kick again, he did so with renewed vigor. He wanted the beast to be dead – he was nearly certain it *was* dead. But it wouldn't hurt to put as much distance between them as was humanly possible.

With Julia's little body slung over the red-and-white ring buoy and the lifejacket helping keep Ben afloat, he kicked them slowly eastward and prayed someone would find them before the sharks did.

Or the beast, if it still lived.

AFTER

Hours passed. Ben would kick for five minutes or so and then rest. His wounds seemed to have coagulated, but he knew his blood loss had been extreme. Several times he had to stop kicking just to focus on keeping hold of his daughter. Ben had, his entire life, battled with intrusive and terrible thoughts, and the image of Julia slipping off the buoy and sinking slowly to the ocean floor was nightmarish enough to keep him vigilant.

Night slowly fell, and for an hour or two the Pacific grew alarmingly restless. The waves that rolled toward them at dusk pushed them along in the right direction; however, they also threatened to splash over Julia's face. Ben developed a system of grasping her back with his mangled right hand and placing his other hand on the bottom of the ring buoy. Positioned on his back as he was, his face very near Julia's, he could see the waves coming before they reached her and was therefore able to lift her gently out of the water each time a particularly tall one lapped over them. Still, he did not think he'd be able to keep Julia safe much longer, especially if the waves intensified. There were no whitecaps yet, but Ben had spent enough time around the ocean to know how common they were, particularly during stormy weather.

But at around what he judged was eleven o'clock, the clouds moved away and left in their wake an unbroken dome of stars. Had Ben not been so exhausted, he would have basked in the sheer beauty of the night.

But he was exhausted. He hadn't slept for – he stumbled through a slow mental calculation – nearly sixty-five hours. God, had it been that long?

He stared up at the sky and chided himself for not pocketing at least one bottle of drinking water. Julia had imbibed a goodly amount before Elena had attacked, but that had been hours ago. Julia had been dehydrated then and was now likely in a state just as wretched as before – perhaps worse. And try though he might to keep them moving toward

California, they were still, what? Seventy miles away? More? What were the chances they would actually make it all the way to shore without dying of exposure or dehydration? And what if he was still bleeding? Couldn't sharks supposedly detect minute traces of blood from several miles away?

What if the beast had recovered?

This thought was the most haunting one of all. Ben had destroyed its eye in the clearing, yet it had healed somewhat by the time it climbed into the boat. How long would its entire body take to regenerate? Of course, that answer was dependent on how much damage had been inflicted on the beast in the fire and the subsequent explosion. Ben recalled the searing blast of heat, the incredible concussion of air. How bad would it have been at the explosion's source? Bad enough to destroy Gabriel once and for all? God, he hoped so. If ever a creature deserved to be permanently expunged from existence, it was the beast that roamed the Sorrows. The one that had killed Teddy and Jessie...

Ben was thinking of Jessie when he first became aware of a low buzzing sound from the east. He was thinking of how brave Jessie had been, how senseless it was that she had died. Even last summer, after the massive violence inflicted on the island, Ben was able to make sense of most of it in his mind. No, it wasn't fair that so many people had died, but the people who were truly innocent – particularly Joshua and Claire – had escaped with their lives.

But not this time. If anyone deserved to live – other than his daughter, who was still very much in danger – it was Jessie Gary. Ben caressed his daughter's back and saw the chopper flying low over the water.

To Ben the helicopter's speed seemed leisurely, but what did he know? He'd only ridden in one a few times, and on each of those occasions he'd been too distracted to pay attention to its speed. But as it drew closer, he discerned its spotlight, which was carving steady swaths through the darkness. Was it possible that the FBI had sent the helicopter out to search for signs of Gus's chopper? Ben supposed it was. Morton had no doubt placed a call before they'd departed yesterday informing his superiors where they were going and when they expected to return. The absence of three federal officers, Ben figured, represented more than enough cause to send out a search party.

The question was whether or not they'd find Ben and Julia.

The chopper drew nearer, and as it did, Ben reminded himself not to get his hopes up. It was a miracle the chopper had ventured close enough for him to see it; the chances that the spotlight would actually pick them out in the dark sea were small indeed.

But thinking this didn't make it any easier for Ben when the helicopter passed them by.

What appeared to be a trajectory that would bring the chopper directly over their position was actually a hundred or more yards away. Ben gesticulated wildly and shouted as much as his flagging energy would allow, but it did no good. Like a final vicious joke, the chopper moved steadily past, heedless of Ben's efforts.

It wasn't long after this that Julia's movements grew alarmingly sluggish. His daughter was awake, he was certain of that. Yet she'd grown so weak that even the act of breathing seemed too much for her. The rise and fall of her little torso was more frequent, but the amount of air she seemed to draw with each breath appeared to Ben very meager. As a newborn Joshua had gotten a bad cold – what the doctors labeled RSV – and as a result, he'd been hospitalized for more than a week with a breathing cannula in his nostrils and a feeding tube down his throat. That had been scary. But this…this was even worse. Because there were no doctors around, no one at all to help his little girl. And it wasn't fair, dammit, it wasn't fair that this should happen to her after everything else. She deserved to live, deserved to have her family back. Julia had done nothing wrong; she'd proved remarkably resilient. She'd endured untold horrors and now she deserved safety and warmth and her mother's milk and soothing touch. She deserved love and security and a body that wasn't failing.

Ben realized he was crying, but there was nothing he could do about it. He muttered to Julia how sorry he was, he kissed her damp temple over and over. She scarcely seemed to notice, only kept on descending into that tortured twilight state, her breathing now a pitiful series of gasps.

"Please," Ben murmured through his tears. "Please keep breathing."

He didn't know if he could do something to help her along, didn't know if administering some version of CPR would help her or exacerbate her condition. He stared helplessly at his daughter's little face.

"Please, Julia," he said to her, his voice a painful croak. "Please hold on for Daddy. Please…"

He was weeping silently, his head against hers, when his closed eyelids were suddenly assaulted with brilliant light. He swiveled his head and blinked up into the spotlight, and as though someone had just ripped a noise-blocking headset from his ears, the world filled with the buzzing roar of the helicopter's whirling propeller.

Ben would not let himself believe they were saved until the rope ladder had been lowered and first Julia and then he had been carried up to the chopper. He had a hard time believing they were safe even as the helicopter picked up speed and moved briskly eastward. And even after they had set down in Petaluma and Ben had allowed the nurses and paramedics to wheel Julia into the hospital, he believed they remained in imminent danger. A doctor told Ben he needed to trust them to care for Julia, told him his own wounds were worse. But Ben refused to let her out of his sight. He finally prevailed on them to treat him in the same room with his daughter, and even after they administered a heavy sedative, it was several minutes before Ben closed his eyes.

The last thing he saw before going under was his daughter's bare chest. She wasn't breathing normally, but the cannula they'd given her – nearly identical to the one used on Joshua years earlier – had restored her respiration to a rate far less frightening.

Reluctantly, Ben slipped into a troubled sleep.

★   ★   ★

And awakened a few hours later to find an attractive nurse standing over him with a look of concern. TRISHA, her name tag said. Ben sat up and peered through the semidarkness at his daughter. Dizziness and nausea crashed over him, but Ben forced his way through it. He kept his gaze fixed on Julia, who appeared to be breathing regularly now. She was facing the other direction.

"Is she asleep?" Ben whispered.

"She's been in and out," the nurse said.

"Will she be okay?"

"Yes," the nurse said at once. "We're more worried about you."

"You've fed her?"

"She's taken two bottles of formula. She wanted more, but we didn't want to overdo it."

Ben made to climb out of bed, but something tugged on his arm.

"Don't, Mr. Shadeland," the nurse said. Her hands were on his chest, forcing him back down. "You need blood."

Ben glanced down confusedly at the tube stuck in his forearm. It was attached to a red drip sack. Another wave of dizziness steamrolled through him.

"Rest, Mr. Shadeland. Your daughter will be fine. She was just exhausted and dehydrated."

Ben glanced up at the nurse and searched her eyes. "You're not just telling me that to calm me?"

She smiled. "I promise. I'll have the doctor stop in soon."

Ben nodded, but as the dizziness began to abate and his eyes adjusted to the dim room, he could see very well that what the nurse was telling him was probably true. Julia's breathing had clearly improved. The nurse went out shortly after, and when the door opened again Ben was greeted not by some distinguished-looking doctor, but rather by a tall, gaunt man around Ben's age. The federal agent introduced himself as Tim Horning. He had a receding hairline and a deeply furrowed forehead. Ben realized after a moment that Horning was nearly as sleep-deprived as Ben was.

The Coast Guard helicopter, Horning told him, had been dispatched a few hours after Gus Williams and his party failed to return to California. "It wouldn't have elicited such an immediate response," Horning explained, "if we hadn't already lost four other agents connected with this mess."

"Four?"

"Seven, counting Agents Morton, Gary and Castillo. You're certain they're dead?"

"Yes."

"How can you be sure?"

"I saw them die."

"How did you—"

"Who were the other four?"

"Moss and Early were the team sent to the Sorrows last fall. They disappeared entirely." Horning's expression went sour. "Then there was the team assigned to watch Marvin Irvin."

Ben opened his mouth to ask what happened to them, but Horning cut him off.

"They were butchered. I'd rather not talk about it now. What the hell happened on that island?"

Ben sighed. He looked at Tim Horning for a long moment. Though the agent seemed like a decent enough guy, Ben couldn't help but experience a sinking dread at the man's question. Ben was right back where he'd been last week – the authorities breathing down his neck for a story Ben couldn't possibly share.

He inhaled as deeply as he could, which wasn't deep at all due to his wretched state. He reached down, touched the bandages on his sides, but even that much motion shot white-hot arrows of pain through his body.

"Mr. Shadeland?" Horning prompted. "It's time for you to tell us the truth."

Ben looked up at Horning, considered telling him everything. What harm could there be? No sane person would believe such a tale, and perhaps if the FBI believed Ben had lost his mind, they just might leave him alone.

Ben opened his mouth to tell Horning everything, but before he could speak a freezing mental chill seized hold of him, made his jaws clench and his muscles tighten painfully.

"Mr. Shadeland?"

But the freezing terror would not relent. Ben's flesh had broken out in goosebumps, his hands trembling.

Horning stood. "Mr. Shadeland? What's the— nurse!" he called.

But Ben's terror only swelled. He was thinking of Teddy Brooks. Of Elena. Most of all, he was thinking of his wife and son.

Horning watched him uncertainly. "We'll have the doctor in here in a moment, Mr. Shadeland. I hope—"

"I need to speak to my wife," Ben said in a hoarse voice.

Horning shook his head. "The staff tried to call her shortly after you and your daughter were admitted, but no one answered."

"That's because they're not at the house," Ben said. "They're in Colorado with my in-laws."

But Horning was already nodding. "We told them that – remember, you told Agent Morton where your wife and son would be. Agent Morton made sure we knew as well."

"Then try her cell phone, dammit."

"We did. She didn't answer."

"What about her parents' landline?"

"No luck there either."

"Have them try again," Ben nearly shouted.

Horning seemed to hesitate. He made a pained face. "That might not work, Mr. Shadeland. There seemed to be…there seems to be a problem with the phone there. We keep getting a busy signal."

Ben swung his legs over the bed, the mental chill becoming a wild shuddering. The IV needle threatened to unmoor from his arm, but he scarcely felt it.

"Mr. Shadeland, you've got to sit back. They're—"

"They're in danger!" Ben yelled.

In her tiny clear plastic bed, Julia stirred.

"They're fine, Mr. Shadeland." Horning put a hand on his chest, attempted to ease him back down.

Ben smacked his hand away. "Don't tell me they're fine, dammit. If they were safe, you'd have talked to them by now."

"There was probably a downed phone line. It's been storming there since late afternoon."

Ben wanted to believe him, but he couldn't. He stared at his daughter, who was facing him now, her mouth twisting in what looked like the beginning stages of a hard cry.

"You need to lie down," Horning repeated.

"Get me a phone," Ben said. "*Now.*"

"Okay," Horning said, holding up a placating hand. He reached into his pocket and brought out a black cell phone. "You're more than welcome to use mine. Just take it easy, all right?"

Ben grabbed the phone and dialed Claire.

It rang five times before her voicemail came on. Grinding his teeth, Ben ended the call and tried again.

And as the phone continued to ring, unheeded, Ben's terror grew.

AFTER (TWO)

Several hours earlier, only a few minutes after Ben and his daughter were discovered by the Coast Guard helicopter, a floating object a few miles off the coast of the Sorrows gave a barely perceptible twitch. A languid wave overturned the object and revealed it to the clear dark night to be a severed head, one with a blackened layer of scorched flesh and a single curving horn, which had also been charred black. Numerous veins and arteries stringing out of the ragged stump of throat had already been gnawed on by curious marine life. But the animals that had tasted of the noxious black liquid oozing out of the dark tendrils died horribly, their convulsions and death spasms frightening away the other would-be diners.

And now the cracked and stiffened eyelids snapped awake and stared at the glowing hook of moon overhead. The eyes, though physically sightless, seemed to absorb the pallid rays drifting down through the cool night air. And the mouth, dreadfully burned as it was by the conflagration in the boat's cabin and the subsequent thunderblast that had blown the creature's body into a thousand different pieces, began to twitch itself into a look that might have been concentration.

Gabriel felt the moon's healing glow soothing his burnt flesh. Gabriel, who had lived for thousands of years and had been known by many names – most frequently the Great God Pan – closed his unseeing eyes and sent his thoughts eastward, toward the place called California. Then beyond that. And...

★   ★   ★

...in Boulder, Colorado, Dale Harden stood motionless in the sepulchral darkness of his bedroom. The look on his face was so unlike his normal one that even his wife wouldn't have recognized the man she'd been married to for twenty-nine years.

Had she seen his face at that moment, she would have fled screaming.

AFTER (THREE)

Claire awoke to the growl of thunder. Opening her eyes, she saw lightning silver the curtains of the guest bedroom, the storm preparing to kick up again. She reached out and felt for Joshua, whose little body lay at a diagonal to hers. He slept between her and Ben often, and though this cramped their sex life, she didn't mind it most of the time. She found Joshua's shoulder and let her hand linger there for a long moment. The boy was sleeping peacefully.

She gave him a gentle squeeze, propped up on her elbows and glanced at the luminous red numbers of the digital clock: 2:25 A.M.

It hit her like a club blow. It was already early morning and she still hadn't heard from Ben.

Stifling a sob, Claire reached for her cell phone. She frowned. It wasn't on the nightstand where she'd left it. She stared bewilderedly for a moment, then realized with a rush of anger what had happened. Her mother — whose good intentions were often accompanied by overbearing behavior — had insisted on Claire taking something to help her sleep. After a brief argument, Claire had agreed, but evidently, upon finding her daughter snoozing under the sedative's spell, her mom had removed Claire's cell phone from the room thinking to let her sleep even if Ben should call.

Claire exhaled frustrated breath. For all she knew, Ben had found Julia already, and both of them were safely home.

Lips a thin white line, Claire pushed out of bed and stalked over to the door. What an incredible relief it would be to be met with good news, to learn that Ben had found their daughter and that everything was just fine. Claire let herself out of the bedroom as quietly as possible and moved quickly down the hallway to the stairs.

There was a portable phone sitting atop a small table near the base of the stairs. Claire snatched the phone from its cradle and listened for a dial tone.

The phone was dead. She returned the useless phone to its cradle and peered down the hallway. She knew it wasn't her mom's fault the landline had been knocked out, but what if Ben had been trying to reach Claire? Had her mom left her cell phone on the nightstand, Claire would have known if Ben or anyone else had called her. Shaking her head, Claire proceeded down the dark hallway and hissed as her bare right foot came down on something. Wincing, she reached down and felt for the thing she'd stepped on. She picked it up, and even before the lightning strobed again and revealed the object for what it was, she knew it was her cell phone. But why it had been left lying in the middle of the hallway, she hadn't the slightest clue.

And why, she wondered, had her mother turned it completely off?

The trembling took hold of her. *Quit being stupid*, she told herself, but the shaking worsened. Why on earth was she so frightened? Nothing was wrong. For all she knew, Ben had left her a message already. She powered on the cell phone and was waiting for it to reveal its secrets when the lightning flashed and she caught a glimpse of something she hadn't noticed earlier.

The portable phone. The one she'd tried just a moment ago. The reason it wasn't working had nothing to do with a downed line.

Someone had unplugged it. The cord lay disconnected at the foot of the nightstand.

The light from her mobile phone suddenly illuminated the hallway. Heart hammering, Claire checked for messages. There were six of them.

Claire was about to push the playback button when the door to her parents' bedroom creaked open. Claire swiveled her head in that direction and saw a dark figure fill the doorway. Too large to be her mother's.

Dad then. But something about him was wrong. He seemed bigger, for one thing, but that was just the shadows, wasn't it? Pretty soon the lightning would flash again and show how the gathered darkness had stretched his shoulders, made his legs look broader and more powerful than they were.

She discovered another detail that made her heart perform a sick, breath-stealing lurch. It was ludicrous, of course, but for the briefest of moments it seemed to Claire that the figure in the doorway was not her father at all but one endowed with a pair of curling goat horns, one whose pupilless eyes raged at her with cruel white malice.

Lightning sizzled beyond the curtains and she realized it was only her dad after all. But this thought, rather than bringing on a surge of relief or a fit of cathartic laughter, carried with it a new species of dread. For her father wasn't moving at all, was merely gazing at her with unsettling hostility.

Now why should she think that? This was her dad, for goodness sakes, the man who'd read *Clifford the Big Red Dog* books when she was a kid and held her while she cried after botching a piano solo in the fourth grade. The man who'd wept when walking her down the aisle toward Ben because he was so happy for her, the man she hoped would come to be a father figure for Ben, who had always lacked one.

But why wasn't he moving? Or talking? Or doing anything at all for that matter? He was just…standing there. Staring at her. And when a gentler flurry of lightning tossed pale luminescence through the hall she noticed something that made her take a step backward, that made her forget all the wonderful things this man had done for her.

A butcher's knife dangled from his left hand.

No! a voice in her head cried. *You only think you saw a knife, but what you really saw was something else. It could be anything – a butcher's knife is the least likely.*

Then why isn't he moving?

Could he be sleepwalking? she wondered. Or in a state so close to sleep that the difference was negligible? Her dad was a heavy sleeper, so maybe he'd been partially awakened by the storm, and most of his mind was still in dreamland. That was plausible, wasn't it?

Brilliant quicksilver lit up the hall, and this time there could be no doubt. He was grasping a knife.

And there was something else. Beyond him, where the bed was situated, the shapes were arranged in an unorthodox way. Dad slept by the door because he was protective; also, her mom wanted to be near the master bathroom, which adjoined on the opposite side of the room. What Claire should have seen in that narrow gap between her father and the doorjamb was her father's rumpled side of the bed where the covers had been pushed back; beyond that would be the small mound of her mother's slumbering body.

Yet there appeared to be something dangling off the bed on her father's side, something that lay twisted like a broken mannequin.

"Mommy?" a voice above her called.

Claire gasped, clapped a hand over her mouth. She eyed her father's form, waiting for some sort of movement or gesture to show he recognized her.

"Claire?" Joshua called again, his voice tight with panic.

"Stay upstairs, honey," she answered, but her voice came out breathless and weak.

Her father took a step toward her. He moved with an unnatural mechanical hitch, like a movie zombie. Now she was sure her dad was asleep.

He took another drunken step toward her, and now he looked even less like her father.

"Where are you, Claire?" Joshua asked.

Her son's voice was different now, closer. He was out in the hallway searching for her.

Lightning again, and this time her father was in mid-step when it flashed. She was afforded a view of his face, which did nothing to calm her careening fears. But it finally compelled her to get moving, to take two backward steps so she could flip the light switch.

Yellow light washed the hallway. Claire's body went slack. Her dad was grinning at her, a sadistic, obscene grin that made his blood-speckled face look like something out of a carnival funhouse. Only this was no luridly painted clown meant to frighten patrons who'd dropped a few bucks for a harmless thrill; this was her loving, devoted father leering at her from ten feet away. His striped pajamas were drenched a ghastly wine color, his hair spiked up like he had just braved a windstorm.

The hallway light splashed into the bedroom just enough to reveal what she'd hoped was just some appalling trick played by the lightning. But it was no trick. And there was nothing funny or good about it. It was hideously real.

"What did you…" she whispered. But she couldn't finish. Couldn't speak or breathe or think. From above her Joshua called to her again. He was directly above her now, and soon he'd be down here, and she had to make sure he didn't see this. She needed to get him out of the house entirely, needed to get them both out of here and into town. She riffled through her memory to recall where she'd left her car keys. Then, as her father took another clumsy step toward her, the same grin plaguing his face, she remembered she had no car. They'd flown into Denver and her parents had picked them up and driven them to their house just outside Boulder, the one they'd built after her father retired just two years ago. The house nestled in the middle of ten acres, most of that forest, with her dad's woodworking shop adjoining the garage and her mother's art studio just off the kitchen. But her mom would not be painting any longer. Her mom's body was slumped over the edge of the bed, the eyes staring upside down at Claire. Her throat had been cut, and not just in a neat slender line either. No, torn open. As if the flesh there had been *sawn* by the blade rather than simply slit. The ragged mountain range of gore spanned her entire neck, but the horror didn't stop there. The gown she'd worn had been peeled open to allow her chest to be carved up, the breasts no longer breasts, just mounds of maroon gristle.

Claire was shaking her head, and at some point she'd leaned against the wall for support. But that wouldn't stop her legs from unbuckling. They were failing her now. And just when she thought she'd faint dead away, she heard her father's voice, the pleasant baritone she'd loved since childhood. In his truck, singing country music. In church and around the house. He was singing now, but it was just a melody without words, a song she couldn't place at first. She associated it with Ben, and for a confused instant thought it was one of Ben's pieces, something he'd written for a film.

Then she had it. The song.

She shook her head, finally beginning to cry now because her dad couldn't possibly know the song, or if he had heard it he'd never have the bad taste to hum it in her presence. But matters of taste had obviously been abandoned now, along with sanity and everything else she'd ever associated with Dale Harden.

He had murdered her mother, his wife of nearly three decades.

He was advancing on his daughter now, the butcher knife still dripping with blood.

He was humming "Forest of the Faun," the song she most associated with the monster of Castle Blackwood. With Gabriel and the Sorrows.

"Dad, please," she managed to whisper.

Five feet away, her dad raised the butcher knife.

Joshua's voice, from the stairs to her right, "What's Grandpa doing?"

"Go to the front door, honey," she said, her voice cracking.

"Mommy?" Joshua asked, his voice little more than a whimper.

"Run, baby. Please listen to your mommy. You have to—"

But she never finished because her dad suddenly strode toward her and swung the butcher knife. Claire tumbled back and threw out her arms to intercept the blow. The knife came whistling at her. Their forearms collided halfway down and the blade whooshed an inch from her shoulder. She'd moved sideways, and her dad, thrown off balance, hacked the wall and tumbled to the floor. But that placed him between her and Joshua, who'd reached the bottom of the stairs. Claire made an awkward lunge to step over her father. She cleared his body and had time to think she'd escaped him when he snarled at her. The whistling sound came again and the butcher knife sliced into her Achilles tendon.

Claire screamed and went down, the butcher knife buried in her ankle. Joshua was crouching over her, his hands wreathing her shoulders, and he was screaming at his Grandpa to stop hurting her, begging him to stop it, stop it. But Claire knew this was no longer her father. No, Gabriel had found them. Just as he had found and taken Julia. And now he wanted...he wanted...

"Go, Joshua," she said.

"Stop hurting her," Joshua was pleading. "Stop hurting my mom!"

The pain in her Achilles was sickening, and what was worse, Dale Harden was taking hold of the knife handle and attempting to wrench it loose.

Claire kicked at her dad, yelled, "Go now, Joshua! Run to the neighbors!"

But she didn't even know where the nearest neighbors were. Down the rutted gravel lane somewhere, she supposed. She'd seen mailboxes, breaks in the forest, but—

She yowled as her father ripped the butcher knife free. He straightened and raised the knife two-handed above his wild, thinning hair. The crazed murderous look never wavered from his face, the stretched lips and the bared teeth and the eyes that had rolled completely white.

Without taking her eyes off her dad, she pushed Joshua away. He stumbled and fell, but she didn't have time to think because the knife was cleaving the air. Claire jerked to the side just as the blade sliced down. It slammed into the hardwood floor and her father came with it, his hands slipping off the handle and smacking the floor. But not before his thumbs slid over the butcher blade. He howled and gaped in disbelief at his gushing thumbs. He'd slit both of them to the bone, and for a moment she caught a flicker of the man she knew beneath the blood-spattered berserker that had replaced him. Something tugged at the strap of her pajamas. The spaghetti strap jerked, stretched, and she realized it was Joshua who was yanking on her. Unthinkingly, she clambered to her feet and followed him, knowing even as she did she should have retrieved the knife from where it stuck in the floor. But she moved with Joshua instead past the phone her dad had unplugged and into the darkened living room. She'd only taken a few steps before the pain in her injured Achilles became unbearable. Joshua gripped her hand, attempted to drag her forward. But she fell anyway, breaking contact with her son as she did. With a backward glance she saw her dad had risen. Joshua hooked his hands under her armpits, was grunting with the effort of hauling her backward. She was weeping and struggling to rise, but the agony of her severed Achilles kept defeating her. On some level she marveled at her son's loyalty, at his courage. God, most people would've fled long ago, or else would've hidden.

"I told you to leave, baby," she said.

But Joshua remained grimly determined. Never before had he reminded her more of her husband. But never before had she so wished he'd act like a normal kid. Her dad was stalking into the living room now, the shadows swallowing him. The sight of her father's lurching gait finally galvanized her into rising. She forced herself to hobble with Joshua through the small entryway to the front door. Behind her came the same macabre humming she'd heard in the hallway, the voice nothing at all like her father's now, instead a deep rumble that sounded like boulders underground grinding together, a voice forged of hellfire and malevolent strength. It was Gabriel taunting them. Gabriel making sure they knew who was controlling her father and transforming him into a grinning butcher.

Claire and Joshua reached the door together, but her father was coming fast. His lurching movements were growing smoother, as if the intelligence inhabiting his mind were growing accustomed to its new host. Claire twisted the lock above the knob, made to open the door, then remembered the deadbolt.

Her father stepped around the corner.

Hands shaking wildly, the fear sweat thwarting her attempts at the deadbolt, Claire glanced down at her son. He was wrapped around her thigh, his small face upturned to hers, the eyes frightened but hopeful.

It steadied her enough to get the deadbolt open.

She ripped open the door, her father right behind her. She flung open the screen door – the wind so fearsome it whipped the door out of her hand and pinned it against the side of the house – and pushed Joshua through. Stumbling, he made it to the far edge of the covered porch, where the rain was slapping the concrete. Claire made to follow but a hand fell on the back of her neck, squeezed. Claire groaned, twisted away from her father's grip, but the fingers cored into her flesh, driving her to her knees. She moved with it, thinking to simply fall sideways onto the porch and then to somehow join Joshua in their flight from this place of horror. But the thing that was no longer her father was inexorable. It forced her to the concrete with its crushing grip. She was on her stomach then, her upper body tilted down on the porch, her legs and feet inside the doorway.

In that moment she saw herself through Joshua's eyes. Saw her own terrified face peering up from the porch, saw her hands splayed in futile resistance. She saw herself dragged back inside the house, her hips and her breasts abrading against the coarse stoop. She saw the grinning creature that scarcely resembled her father hauling her past the sweep of the door.

Then she was screaming as her dad strode past her prone body. She was bellowing for him to leave Joshua alone.

But he wasn't going back outside to get Joshua. Not yet.

He was seizing the door and flinging it shut hard enough to shatter the frame.

Then he turned and stared down at her.

Brandished the butcher knife.

His savage grin became triumphant.

He raised the knife.

"I'll have you all," he said.

And staring up at the knife, Claire screamed.

ACKNOWLEDGMENTS

Thank you to Tim and Tod, my pre-readers, for their continued feedback and suggestions. Thanks to Don D'Auria for his help. Thanks also to Brian Keene, Joe R. Lansdale, Kristopher Rufty, Mary SanGiovanni, Paul Tremblay, Mark Sieber, Jeff Strand, and the late Jack Ketchum for their friendship and support.

My wife and my kids are my support system and the best part of my life. They love me, inspire me, and help me to relax. Thank you for making me the happiest husband and father in the world.

FLAME TREE PRESS
FICTION WITHOUT FRONTIERS
Award-Winning Authors & Original Voices

Flame Tree Press is the trade fiction imprint of Flame Tree Publishing, focusing on excellent writing in horror and the supernatural, crime and mystery, science fiction and fantasy. Our aim is to explore beyond the boundaries of the everyday, with tales from both award-winning authors and original voices.

•

Other titles available by Jonathan Janz:
The Siren and the Specter
Wolf Land
The Sorrows
Savage Species
The Nightmare Girl
The Dark Game
House of Skin
Dust Devils

Other horror titles available include:
Thirteen Days by Sunset Beach by Ramsey Campbell
Think Yourself Lucky by Ramsey Campbell
The Hungry Moon by Ramsey Campbell
The Haunting of Henderson Close by Catherine Cavendish
The House by the Cemetery by John Everson
The Devil's Equinox by John Everson
The Toy Thief by D.W. Gillespie
Black Wings by Megan Hart
Stoker's Wilde by Steven Hopstaken & Melissa Prusi
The Playing Card Killer by Russell James
Will Haunt You by Brian Kirk
Creature by Hunter Shea
Ghost Mine by Hunter Shea
The Mouth of the Dark by Tim Waggonner
They Kill by Tim Waggonner

•

Join our mailing list for free short stories, new release details, news about our authors and special promotions:

flametreepress.com